W9-AHA-175

THE RETURN

BUZZ ALDRIN
& JOHN BARNES

TOR

A TOM DOHERTY ASSOCIATES BOOK
NEW YORK

This is a work of fiction. All of the characters, organizations, and events portrayed in this novel are either products of the author's imagination or are used fictitiously.

THE RETURN

Edited by Patrick Nielsen Hayden

A Tor Book
Published by Tom Doherty Associates
175 Fifth Avenue
New York, NY 10010

www.tor-forge.com

Tor® is a registered trademark of Macmillan Publishing Group, LLC.

ISBN 978-0-7653-9071-4

Our books may be purchased in bulk for promotional, educational, or business use. Please contact your local bookseller or the Macmillan Corporate and Premium Sales Department at 1-800-221-7945, extension 5442, or by e-mail at MacmillanSpecialMarkets@macmillan.com.

First Edition: May 2000
Second Mass Market Edition: December 2016

Printed in the United States of America

0 9 8 7 6 5 4 3 2 1

ACKNOWLEDGMENTS

Special thanks are due, this time, to:

Andrew Aldrin, for excellent technical notes on a wide variety of problems.

John Blaha, for insights into the actual operation of the shuttle, and answering many dumb questions with patience and good humor.

Dan Tam, for enthusiastic reading and more ideas than would fit in 100 books.

Hu Davis, for the engineer's perspective, and for many amazing and useful ideas and insights.

Maureen Gaetano, for her keen eye for what's corny.

Dr. Geoffrey Landis, for some very helpful back-of-the-envelope computations.

viii   AUTHORS' NOTE

AUTHORS' NOTE

The characters in this book really *are* fictional; there are plenty of people of their type in similar positions, but there is no way to match up an individual character to any existing person. And because institutions, finally, are the shadows of the people who staff them, the companies and agencies in this book are not always what they are in real life. So we have chosen to rename many of the key institutions in American and foreign space policy. NASA, of course, is real, but when they began privatizing most of their launch operations in the 1990s, the company they turned it over to was named USA (United Space Alliance), not ASU (American Space Universal), and USA is jointly owned by Boeing and Lockheed-Martin, not by our fictional Curtiss Aerospace and Republic Wright. In general, where we have created fictional companies, we have used names historically linked with the same field. Perhaps we should have carried this farther, so that Scott would drive a Nash and the federal agents in the book would work for the OSS, but in general we've adhered to this rule: where the fictional company is substantially different from its real counterpart, we have changed the name; where it's merely the brand name of something in the story, we have kept the name as it is in our real world. The one exception is our NASA, which is not really the present-day NASA; in that case, the name was too familiar not to use it.

CHAPTER ONE

SCOTT:

"So how are you planning to top this mission? Are you sending the Pope next time?"

All the reporters laughed. Of course the question wasn't serious, but it did give me a chance to work in a sound bite that my PR coach had suggested. "Eventually, we'll send everybody. But one step at a time, please."

Outside, it was seven in the morning on the kind of pleasant, clear Wednesday in October that makes you think of football, or a long drive someplace where the leaves are turning—the sort of day that whispers "too good to waste." Inside, the press conference room was just like its equivalent at any Washington hotel—plastic "crystalware," stiffbacked chairs, lots of room down front for cameras, a long table on folding platforms with all the legs concealed by fabric velcroed to the edges. I sat at one end of the long table, answering questions before the person the reporters wanted to talk to got here.

"Mr. Blackstone," the man from CBS asked, "we all know that you originally hoped to fly civilian tourist flights yourself, as pilot. Is there any chance that you'll be doing that any time in the next few Citizen Observer flights?"

"Of course I'd like to go," I said. "But it took some pretty generous offers to get ASU to let us put people into empty seats. My next spaceflight, pilot or passenger, is a few years away, I'm sure."

"Would you fly a shuttle again if ASU invited you to?" This reporter, for some reason, didn't seem to want to give the question up. "You've been very careful about keeping your qualification to fly a shuttle."

"I keep my pilot's license, too," I pointed out. "You really shouldn't read any more into it than that."

After that, the questions were less personal. I didn't mind the attention, particularly, but as CEO of ShareSpace, I'd rather it went to my company.

Then we went into the usual ritual questions—the reporters in the room already knew the answers, but their editors might need footage of someone saying those things.

"What kind of mission is this?"

"Like most of the ones *Columbia* flies nowadays. A general, mixed-bag deal—a little science, a little tech, a little business, a little promotion. You all know I can't talk about anything classified, but sometimes they do classified work, as well, for a defense or intelligence agency."

"Do you know what factors influenced Pegasus Corporation's decision about who to send?" It was the same guy from NBC who had needled me before.

"They wanted maximum publicity, I'd guess. Hard

to find a more famous person who would get more attention and be better identified with their shoes. Or maybe the Pope wasn't available." That got a laugh; I had just time to wonder if I'd crossed over one of those invisible boundaries that my PR people were always warning me about, before the next question. The reporter from the *Times* had me explain that the seats ShareSpace was selling were available because the International Space Station (ISS) was behind schedule, and so some shuttle flights had been released to other projects.

Then the tall woman from MSNBC walked me through a detailed review of who the first two Citizen Observers had been, in case somehow anyone watching the news now, in October, had managed to miss all the news in the previous May, or October a year ago. That seemed especially silly because "well, the first one is in the room," I said. "Why don't you tell us all about it, Fred?"

Fred Gernsback had been anchor for the Federal Broadcasting Network for almost two decades, and due to his enthusiasm for the space program, his voice had become more identified with spaceflight than that of any broadcaster since Walter Cronkite. He looked around the room, smiling broadly, and I wondered if anyone ever gets tired of being made the center of attention. "Well, it's not complicated and it's not all that interesting. The way it works is that ShareSpace is a private business, like a travel agency, except that Scott Blackstone only sells two or three tickets a year. ASU operates spacecraft, like an airline operates airplanes, because NASA got out of direct operation, for the most part, a few years ago. ASU bought *Columbia* from the government, and most of the time they lease the other three shuttles. So what happened was that

FBN bought my ticket from ShareSpace, which got me onto a flight on the *Columbia*, operated by ASU. No different from what happens when they buy me an airline ticket from Amex Travel Services to get me onto a 747 operated by United. Dull as dishwater."

Everyone groaned and laughed; Fred's irony was even more heavy-handed than usual. For ten days in October last year, millions of people had hurried home to catch Gernsback's evening broadcast from orbit. The American public's jaundiced perception of space travel—routine as airplanes and ancient as railroads—had been flipped right back over into wide-eyed wonder by Gernsback's babbling joy about everything connected with the mission.

Gernsback went on. "And so it's the same deal with this next Citizen Observer. Pegasus wanted publicity for their shoes, so they had to get publicity for their guy, so they went to Scott, Scott sold them a ticket, ASU is honoring the ticket, and tonight we're going to witness a new space record—the tallest man ever sent into orbit. Just an ordinary business deal."

"What does a company have to do to get someone on the shuttle, Mr. Blackstone?" a tall, slim black woman asked. "Officially for the record, and also because for all I know Pacific States Network might want to do that for me."

It took me a moment to realize who it was—Nikki Earl, radio correspondent for a little shoestring network that mostly ran very liberal commentary and covered social welfare issues. Normally they weren't big fans of the space program, so if she was here at all, it meant either they were gunning for us, or it was a slow news day. I answered, carefully, "I hope they can afford to send you, but for the moment it's pretty expensive. It starts with a corporation becoming one of ShareSpace's corporate partners, for one million dollars—or more, if you want to be near the top of the list.

"For your million you get a nice-looking plaque inside the shuttle, plus a turn at buying a ticket. When your turn comes up, we ask you for a five-million-dollar seat charge. Once you pay that, you can send anyone who can pass a medical exam and a security clearance. Your five million dollars does include meals and clothes for the trip." There were a few chuckles at that. "There's also a required commitment to devote at least eight million dollars to publicity—primarily about the sponsor itself, of course, but it also has to be clearly tied to ShareSpace and the orbital flight. So the real price of the cheapest ticket is about fourteen million, at the moment. We hope that within a decade we can be down under a million."

Nikki Earl nodded. "So why does any corporation buy a ticket? I can understand why it was worthwhile for Fred—someone else bought his ticket, and he had a good time, and I'd go, myself, in a *minute*, if PSN would pick up the tab—but how can that fourteen-million-dollar ticket be worthwhile for any of the corporate sponsors?"

Her tone was reasonable and friendly, so I thought chances were that she was just here because it was a slow news day, and not because PSN was out to do a hatchet job on ShareSpace. She had asked a question I'd have loved to devote a whole interview to, but she needed something a minute long at most.

I started off with the obvious. "Well, it *is* private money, and they have to answer to their stockholders, so mostly I can just assume they want it and let it go at that. After all, the baker doesn't care what you want his bread for, only that you'll buy it, and so far we've got eighteen buyers lined up, so we must be selling what they want.

"But if I were speculating . . . I guess the sponsors must figure that kids love space. Being associated with space is the best publicity there is for companies like Pegasus and Avery that are so strongly oriented toward the youth market. And just now things connected with space seem to be more popular than at any time since the late sixties, so the sponsors probably see being associated with space as a good investment in publicity, period, not just with kids. The best way to find out might be to ask them."

She nodded. "I have, and they said what you said. How about a follow-up?"

"Sure."

"As the parent of a ten-year-old, I can hardly miss that space is suddenly popular again. Why do you think that is?"

"Uh, I'm the parent of a ten-year-old boy myself, and I don't know that I understand it any better than you do. I can make some guesses: the millennium. The anniversaries of so many space events. The new private ventures. The new pictures from the new generation of telescopes. A couple of big realistic movies, where they got the special effects right, after all those years of pure fantasy movies. Take your pick. How does that sound?"

"Like a baker who doesn't know why he's selling more bread, but is real happy that he's selling it," Nikki Earl said, and grinned at me—*not* one of those media-fake smiles for the camera. Mentally I marked her down as a possible ally and someone to float a story to sometime soon. ShareSpace was riding high on a wave of good publicity right now, driven by our sending the third most recognizable name in America (after Jesus and Santa) on this mission. But I didn't want to neglect Nikki Earl—talking to her could be a chance to reach people we hadn't reached yet, and nobody in the public eye ever has enough friends or knows when they might need one more.

So far, ShareSpace had plenty of friends. We were riding the crest of a two-year wave of popularity. Fred Gernsback had just been the beginning for us; he had barely returned to Earth when we took our next step. Avery Filmworks, the dominating giant in family entertainment, had gotten their turn at a ShareSpace slot on a *Columbia* flight for the following May, and they'd come up with an ingenious way to use it: they had launched *Pyramid to Space*, a competitive quiz show on the Avery Channel. The show was in the form of a tournament of space knowledge (or space trivia—I wasn't sure how much an astronaut really needed to know how much the makers of Tang paid to have it included in the early space rations). During the winter holidays, fascination with the competition grew, for the winner—if physically fit enough—would be the next Citizen Observer.

In mid-January, *Pyramid to Space* was won by David Calderon, a garage mechanic from Brownsville, Texas. He had gone into orbit aboard *Columbia* last May, and if anything, he had done us even more good than Fred Gernsback had.

David could hardly have been better if Avery had created him from Central Casting—he was a good-looking twenty-five-year-old, muscular, slim, in perfect shape, a nonsmoker who drank rarely, and poised and confident as he revealed an encyclopedic knowledge of space and astronautics. When he won *Pyramid,* he was bombarded by congratulatory emails, phone calls, and letters, and not a few marriage proposals.

Between his victory, the MTV series that followed him through training, and his flight, he had been endlessly on camera for about six months, and during that whole time, he always enthusiastically boosted the launch, Avery Filmworks, *Pyramid to Space*, ShareSpace, the space program, and life in general. He had a knack for communicating, in ordinary language, his deep and broad knowledge of everything connected with space, astronomy, planetary science, and astronautics—a knowledge he had acquired from years of reading science magazines and watching space documentaries, sources available to anyone, so that even in that regard he seemed to have the common touch. He charmed Barbara Walters, and was so popular that Larry King brought him back on the show twice; for a few weeks he was on every talk show that could possibly book him.

He was especially a hit on radio and TV call-in programs, and all the calls for David Calderon were very much alike: people who just wanted to tell him that they too had applied to compete in *Pyramid to Space,* that family and friends had made fun of them, and now they felt vindicated. "You proved that ordinary people *will* go to space," they would say, or "This is what it's all about, that space is the future of the whole human race." Lots of people wished him luck and many suggested that if he had something else to do at the last minute, they'd be willing to take his place. He was good-humored and friendly through all of it, and every time David Calderon went on the air, we picked up more approval points, and another sponsor or two came banging on

ShareSpace's door, wanting to get in on the adventure.

On his flight, Dave was enthusiastic, happy, quotable, and still a brilliant commercial for the idea that space was going to be for everyone. We had put him on the payroll, and now he was out touring the country, visiting with corporate heads where we needed to sell a sponsorship, stopping off to talk to grade school classes and civic groups, speaking at high school commencements and Scout jamborees, and generally producing about as much good will as anyone possibly could.

But although Gernsback and Calderon had been wonderful, what was about to happen would trump every bit of past publicity ShareSpace had gotten, and make all our past triumphs mere prologue. Now that I had teased the room enough, "I think the time has come to meet the crew." I nodded toward the door, and Naomi, my secretary, nodded back and pushed it open.

Seven people came into the room and joined me on the dais, but for all practical purposes, there was only one person in the room—Michael James, or MJ, as pretty much the whole planet called him.

He was over seven feet tall, and graceful, which would have been impressive even if he had been just a random stranger. Knowing his accomplishments, you felt awe—he had presence enough for some ancient king or legendary hero.

Two years earlier, when MJ had retired after more than a dozen years as the top center in the NBA, every newsmagazine had put him on the cover, and *Time* had found an excuse to feature him twice.

After the success of the journalist in space, since we had the second Citizen Observer contract already nailed down, it was time to reach for something even bigger. I put all my effort into hustling a contact with MJ, and to persuade Pegasus—maker of the most famous athletic shoes in the world, which were the most famous largely thanks to the autograph "MJ Michael James" stamped on the side of every one—to sponsor him as the the third Citizen Observer.

He was perfect for more reasons than just his fame, or his immediate recognition. MJ was a widely admired role model for American kids, known for his polite good sportsmanship and his advocacy of excellence in all fields. He was bright, articulate, spontaneously funny, but also thoughtful and serious when the occasion called for it. Best of all he was a space enthusiast, and had been ever since he was small. (We had some wonderful footage of his mother, AnnaBeth James, reminiscing about when "Mikey" was ten, and unhappy because he was already too tall to be an astronaut by the NASA rules of the day.)

ShareSpace had announced MJ's selection nine days after David Calderon returned from orbit. Ever since, everything MJ had done had shown us that the idea was even more brilliant than we had thought. In the last four months, his appearances on kids' shows and news and talk shows had been the best of all possible publicity for everyone—himself, Pegasus, ShareSpace, ASU, NASA—and for that matter, me.

It was an extra hassle to fly the crew up from Canaveral the evening before, then back to Kennedy Space Center for an evening launch today, but that was another public relations maneuver that I felt was paying off pretty well. If you hold your big events at or near KSC, you get a mix of second-string reporters and older ones who want a quick trip to somewhere warm. But if you hold the same events in one of the cities where the media's first string is located, that's who covers you—and those cities, basically, are New York, Washington, or Los Angeles. Washington was the shortest flight to Florida, ShareSpace corporate headquarters was here, and best of all, Washington was the major media city with the most predictable schedule—in NY or LA you could be pushed right out of the evening news slot by any freak local story, but in DC only a war or a sex scandal could steal your coverage.

MJ made a few introductory remarks, and everyone relaxed and settled in as if the press conference had just become a group of friends sitting around the living room. "Let me introduce the rest of the crew," MJ said, spreading his arms as if to embrace all of them. "This man to my far right, next to Scott Blackstone, is Billy Kingston, the commander. During the mission, he's the guy who we all have to listen to. And if any kids are watching this—"

"They better be," said Samantha Carter, who headed the special team for Nickelodeon, and everyone laughed.

"—like I said, if there's any kids watching out there, something for you to pay attention to—Billy knows what he's doing and knows how the ship works and everything else, a hundred times more than I do. He has all the knowledge and experience. Just like your mom and dad and your teachers know more than you do. So when he says to do something, I do it, and I don't give him backtalk and I do it right away. When we're up in space, my ten thousand field goals are just ten thousand of nothing compared to his knowledge and skill and experience. Listening to him and respecting his authority is part of keeping me safe and out of trouble, because there's all kinds of trouble that can happen up there. Even M J has to do what people who know more tell him to do. It was the same way when I was little and Mama wanted me to do something."

In his deep Gulf Coast drawl, Kingston said, "In that case, your mission commander says to get the rest of the introductions done so we can get back to KSC."

"Yes, *sir!*—you see how I did that?—now, next to Major Kingston is Wes Packard, from West Virginia by way of West Point. He's the pilot, the one who actually flies *Columbia*, and the father of Kati and Mary Lou, who are watching this morning, I bet. This guy next to me is Josh Pritkin, mission specialist in electronics—" he gestured to the tall, thin man, who nodded to the cameras "—and he also plays pretty good ragtime piano, or at least he's good enough to fool a basketball player. Lorena Charette here—" he gestured to a short, stocky black woman on his left "—is from Baltimore, is a medical doctor, is an Air Force major, and has had a much more exciting and interesting life than any professional athlete ever did, and if you media folks had any sense you'd be interviewing her instead of me."

Actually, thanks to M J's quiet pressure, there had been a number of interviews with and features about Lorena, and she was on her way to becoming something of a celebrity in her own right.

"Now, the nervous-looking dude to Lorena's left, who is wondering what embarrassing personal facts I'm going to bring up, is Marc Clement, astronomy mission specialist and my roommate during training." M J winked and said, "But with a nice, good-looking guy like that, all I have to do is ask what his mother would have asked–'why is he still single?' " Clement blushed, everyone laughed, and MJ added, "I've done all I can, man, now it's up to you. And, finally, not at all least, all the way to the left, our military payload specialist and our poker wizard, Damian Agustino–" he nodded to the short, square-built man "–my fellow Texan on the flight, so you know with two Texans on board, ain't nothin' to worry about."

MJ was from Dallas, a fact that you couldn't help knowing within ten minutes of meeting him. There wasn't much about him you didn't know pretty quickly. We'd vetted him thoroughly. As far as we could tell his biggest personal vice was a liking for mystery novels and his biggest problem was the difficulty of meeting women who might think about him as a serious romantic possibility, rather than as a trophy. He really *was* as nice as he seemed on TV–it drove the detectives crazy.

The first question was from a short, balding man, way in the back. "I just wondered if you'd like to comment on the fact that while you're doing very well, and people will spend fourteen million dollars to send you to orbit, just this morning the House chopped twenty million out of the US Department of Education."

My heart stopped. Michael was a world-class nice guy, but he had a temper, and he wasn't used to being challenged about much of anything; I'd had a run-in or three with him over various things.

He stared at the man. "Well," MJ said, finally, "you know, I'm sure, that Pegasus will spend the money to send me to orbit, but they also give around a hundred million a year to schools around the country. They *have* to, in a country that's too damn cheap to take care of its own schoolchildren."

Great, I thought to myself, *we just lost ten more friends in the House.*

"And of course I'm going to go if I get the chance. Any human being with a soul would want to, you know. That's part of why questions like yours . . ." He looked down and shook his head. "Dude, where do you come up with something that dumb? You think I don't know that we need more and better education, and hospitals, and food for the hungry and shelter for the homeless? You think that's a surprise to your viewers? You think, maybe, you're going to make me ashamed of where I came from, or ashamed to be rich from my success? I'll tell you this. I know very well that I am a very lucky man. I know that I didn't 'deserve' my chances in life. But I also tell you this. I got those chances, I took them, I'm taking them, and that's the way it is. And more than that— because I do what people dream about, I give other people the power and the right to dream. And children—and grownups—all human beings need those dreams, the way they need oxygen and food and shelter. You tell me some people are poor? That's a damn shame and I'm sorry, but I gave more to charity last year than you make in ten. You tell me my country, the best place on Earth, is robbing its own children? I'll remember that when I vote. You tell me I ought to hang my head and feel bad about the greatest moment of my life? Chump, you can go to hell."

One part of me wanted to hug him, and another part wanted to run out and issue a denial that he'd ever been in the room. Balanced between the urges, I stood there for a second, before Naomi loudly said, "Hey, he isn't wearing a press badge!"

Hotel security closed in on the little man, who

rushed out the door and down the hallway. I never heard whether they caught him or not.

After that, the questioning was a lot more routine. M J deflected more than half of the questions directed at him to the rest of the crew, making sure that people understood that this was a team effort, and giving most of the credit to the regular astronauts. He kept the media focused on the nature of the mission and the vision of where it led in the great scheme of space exploration. "If we could afford him," I muttered to Naomi, who was handing up some papers to add to my swollen briefcase, "we'd put him on the payroll with Calderon. The two of them would get us a Mars mission set up and funded in no time."

"He might be willing to do that free, you know," she pointed out. "After he gets back, maybe you should ask."

"—and another person you should all be watching— the person who saw that there was a need for all kinds of people, and not just specialists, in space," M J said, "Scott Blackstone. I owe a lot to his company— metaphorically speaking. Pegasus owes the money."

I waved at the reporters. M J's re-introducing me was my cue to say that everyone needed to get back down to Florida. The seven of them posed for last-minute shots for the prescribed three minutes, and then I got them out the door while Naomi handed out thick press packets that insured that even the most un-awake reporter would have something accurate to start from.

"That's *sure* easier than the press conferences I used to have to do for the team," M J commented, as we settled into the bus that would take us to the charter plane at Washington Reagan. "You go to one of those conferences and they only let you say two things, over and over: you think the team's going to win and you're here to play basketball. And you have to find ways to keep saying that for an hour. Here, it was only twenty minutes, and there was something to talk about." He leaned back and said, "Damn, though, that first clown—the one that wasn't even a reporter— he pissed me off."

"I wasn't happy with him myself," I observed. "I'm sorry he got through security; we're going to have to check on that and find out how he did it."

"You do that. I'd like to see a report. Because if a rude little chump can get through that easy, how do you know the next guy won't have a gun? Makes me mad, and makes me scared, and this is one day when I didn't need to be upset."

Marc Clement was turned around, looking for a way to get a word in edgewise; the two of them had really bonded, which was good for the mission, and maybe better for M J. Now Clement said softly, "That's the problem with hotels."

"That's why you needed to hire your own," M J said, still talking to me. "And you didn't."

"No," I said, "we didn't bring our own security, and that was a mistake. I'm sorry."

M J blinked for a couple of moments, then extended his hand and shook mine. "It's okay, Scott. Really. I'm letting myself get more upset than it's worth. Sorry." He moved forward and sat down to talk with Marc Clement. That was Michael James for you; the terrible temper faded in seconds, as if it had never been there.

I stretched out in the back seat that I'd commandeered for myself, pulled out my cell phone, and made a call. It should be half an hour at least before

Amos was due to leave for school. On the second ring, I heard, "Hello?"

"Hello, Thalia, it's Scott. Does Amos have a minute to say hello?"

My ex hesitated a moment, which told me she'd been expecting my call and wasn't happy about it. "As long as it's just a minute. I have to drop him at school early this morning, so you can't talk to him long. But he didn't want to go without getting a call from you. You could have called earlier."

"Not really," I said.

"We'll have to go soon," she said. "I can't afford to be late today. I only have an hour to get things done before I have to get on a plane."

I felt like asking her how it felt to be always running for a plane, and maybe even quoting some of the things she'd said to me about not putting my family first, but fighting with Thalia would cause her to hang up, and I really wanted to talk to Amos this morning. So I just said, "I'm sorry. I didn't have much choice in the matter, but it was inconsiderate of me."

I heard her breath hiss over the mouthpiece and thought she was going to find one more way to get on my case, but then I heard Amos, in the background, saying, "Come on, Mom, let me talk to Dad, I've been waiting." The rustle and thud of the phone being handed over was followed by the *clat-clat* of her heels walking away from the phone, and then at last Amos said, "Dad?"

I swallowed hard and made my voice upbeat. "Hi, Amos! We're on our way out to the airport to get these guys into orbit, and I just wanted to squeeze in a second and say hello. How are things going?"

"School's fine, I'm going to do peewee wrestling

this winter, and I got that program I was playing with to work on the computer," he said, covering all the usual bases of conversation in one sentence. "Mom works too hard and isn't home enough, and I'm looking forward to seeing you the weekend after this."

"Hmmm," I said. "You're stealing all my lines."

"Well, we do have to go soon . . ." he said, sounding much too mature and responsible for a ten-year-old.

Maybe it was just that tone that made me feel like I had to offer something special to him. "Why don't we spend the weekend after next at the cabin?"

"In the *fall?*" He sounded like he thought I was crazy. "Is there anything to do? Won't it be too cold?"

"In the fall," I said, emphatically. "The cabin has a woodstove, remember? We can fire that up and be warm and comfortable. The only summer things we can't do are swim and buy cheap souvenirs. It will be sort of like camping out, but more comfortable. Probably it will be just you and me—nobody else on the beach. We can hang around and talk, you can beat me at chess, and we can build driftwood fires at night and tell ghost stories till we're both too scared to sleep. It's a nice time of year." Desperate to sell him on the idea, I pulled out a reference to one of his heroes, and to a time of life he was already fascinated with. "Back when we were in high school and college, your uncle Nick and I used to go down there in the fall a *lot*, just to hang out and do guy stuff."

That clinched the deal. "Sweet, Dad. Let's do it."

"Weekend after this. What're you up to this weekend?"

"Mom'll be getting back from California late on Friday, and then she says she's going to spend the whole weekend staring at the ceiling. I don't know, probably just play with my friends and catch a movie."

"Well, let her know that if she gets trapped in California, and Mrs. Talbert can't take you on short notice, you can come over to my place. I have some boring stuff I have to do, meetings and appearances and things, but I don't plan to be away this weekend."

"Okay, I'll tell her."

"I love you, Amos."

"I love you too, Dad." I was about to say "bye" when MJ plopped down beside me. "If your son's still there, let me talk to him."

"Amos?" I said. "Hey, Amos—"

"Dad?"

"Somebody here wants to talk to you." I handed the phone to MJ.

A few weeks before, MJ had come by my house late on a Friday to sign some papers. He arrived in a van, floating in a cloud of lawyers and assistants. The business had gotten concluded quickly, but just as MJ had been loading his entourage back into his van, Thalia had come by to drop off Amos for the weekend. While my ex and I had a nearly civil short conversation about clothing that was getting outgrown and persistent low grades in handwriting, the NBA's highest-paid player taught my son the basics of the layup and the jump shot. Afterwards, Amos was walking on air for days.

Now MJ was teasing him on the phone. "After all that work we did improving you in your b-ball, you gonna *wrestle?* . . . Oh, well, you just have to go and be the best wrestler you can, then, don't you? Listen, just make sure you do what your coach tells you, and you always do everything one hundred per cent, 'cause that's how you get somewhere. If your dad tells me you've been slacking off, I might have to come and dribble you around that driveway a few times before I slam you through that hoop, all right? . . . Yeah . . . now, you know, in every sport, there's fundamentals, and you make sure you know them and you're good at them. First two years in any sport, make sure you get the fundamentals, try to be the best at those. Never try to get fancy till you're perfect as you can be at the basics. . . . All right, you do that. . . . What? No, I'm not scared. Maybe a little bit. But not any more than your dad was when he flew into space. This is gonna be more fun than anything I ever did before. . . . Yeah! . . . All right, Amos, talk to you later."

He clicked off and handed my phone back to me. "That's a really nice son you have."

"Thank you," I said. "You just made his year."

MJ suddenly gave me the famous big toothy grin, full of mischief. "Hey, do you know anything about wrestling?"

"Not a thing," I admitted.

"Me neither. Couldn't think of a thing to tell him to work on! That's why I said that stuff about fundamentals."

I laughed. "You could've told him anything in the world and he'd be happy. Guess I have to bone up on wrestling, so I can at least have a faint idea what my son's talking about."

MJ smiled. "I'd call that a fundamental in parenting."

The van took one of the corporate entrances into Reagan. I shook hands with the whole crew and thanked them all again. They got on the charter jet.

Back at the van, I looked at my watch; it was only

nine A.M., and their liftoff was at 9:30 P.M. I had much to do in the next few hours, but I felt great. I sat back in the van and let the driver take me to the ShareSpace offices, up in Silver Spring.

It had been a long journey to this point in my life—the brink of total success—and I'd paid quite a toll for it. In a sense, my family had been paying it for decades before I was born. My great-grandfather, Peter Blackstone, the oldest of six brothers, had been a banker who loaned money to both the Wright brothers and the Curtiss family, and put some of his own money into stock with both fledgling companies. His kid brother, Henry, flew mail over the Appalachians in a Curtiss JNE, back when the best way to avoid too close a federal inspection was to be, literally, a fly-by-night operator; his three-airplane operation eventually ended up as the nucleus of the first airline on the same route.

Henry's oldest son Stephen escaped from Stanford and paid his own way to became a mechanical engineer, holding several patents on the earliest jet engines, and was a founding stockholder in Republic, which went on to buy out the Wrights and created the powerful Republic Wright aircraft company for which my older brother Nick would eventually work. His youngest brother, George, whom I remembered as Grandpa Blackstone, ran away from home before his parents could pressure him into going to Yale, thus depriving them of their other chance for a lawyer or politician in the family. Instead, George joined the Army Air Corps in the 1920s, worked as a liaison training the Nationalist Chinese Air Force in the 1930s, flew with the AVG (the Flying Tigers) during the Second World War, and finished his career as an Air Force colonel supervising training in the military test pilot program. Because that was where so many of the first generation of astronauts came from, Grandpa Blackstone used to brag that he had bawled out, insulted, and screamed at more future astronauts than any other living person.

When Dad, the older of Grandpa Blackstone's two sons, struck off on his own, he'd wanted nothing more than a quiet, settled life, one that didn't involve moving every couple of years, plane crashes, or shouting. He had found his place in the world building models for wind tunnels at Curtiss Aircraft, which was about to become Curtiss Aerospace. When I was four, his brother, my Uncle Ted, died in a T-38 crash, just after being selected for the astronaut corps.

Nick and I followed family tradition: one tycoon, one lunatic. Nick went off to engineering school, and then as fast as he could into management, and rapidly rose to corporate VP at Republic Wright. He used to enjoy telling Dad and me that he thought engineers and pilots were fine people, and he admired them so much that he wanted to own as many as he could.

I went from AFROTC to the Air Force to pilot training as fast as they'd let me, and from there into the astronaut corps. Along the way, I married Thalia Pendergast, whose family had been friendly with mine for decades. Thalia had finished her law degree during my first years in the Air Force, coping with moving every few months and getting most of her degree work completed on-line. She was four months pregnant with Amos on the day she got her invitation to serve as clerk to the Chief Justice of the Florida Supreme Court.

Life became more settled once I became an astronaut and we could buy a house in Orlando; from a family perspective, being an astronaut isn't so different from working for a company that requires lots of out-of-town trips. Thalia had a good position with the Florida Attorney General's Office, and though Amos spent most of his time at day care, he seemed pretty happy.

Common sense would have kept me in the astronaut corps for a long time, and might well have kept my family together, but that itchy need to be doing something different eventually won out. After I had flown three shuttle missions, I started to be bothered by a peculiar thought: we didn't really have a space *program* anymore.

Of course the United States had a presence in space, and we flew to Low Earth Orbit fairly often—I had been there three times myself. But no American—in fact, no human being—had gone farther than LEO since December 1972. We went to space for lots of things: commerce, navigation, communication, knowledge, military advantage. But a "program" would imply we were going somewhere, or had things to accomplish that we hadn't done yet, and I just felt that "going somewhere" was exactly what we weren't doing.

Any real space program would require getting many more people off the planet on a much more regular schedule than we had ever done before; the expression for it that emerged around 1985 was "airline-like operations." I decided I might as well learn what an airline operated like.

That entailed changing jobs and changing towns. At least Amos wasn't in school yet when we moved. Better still, since Global Airways, my new employer, was headquartered in DC, it was very little strain on Thalia—"You're moving me to lawyer heaven," she said, when I first brought the subject up.

I didn't plan to stay with Global, but it was a good place to get the knowledge and experience I needed. They were a charter airline that specialized in transporting high-income tourists to and from adventure experiences, and I was already fairly sure that high-cost adventure tourism would be the first major stepping-stone in the private-industry pathway to routine human space travel.

There was an obvious way for a highly experienced pilot to get some of the experience I needed, and that was what I applied for at Global. As a pilot, executive, and tour leader, I took planeloads of wealthy customers to Australia to snorkel the Great Barrier Reef, into and out of half the airports in East Africa and in the Cone of South America for safaris and climbing and fishing trips, and to South Pacific islands I could barely pronounce. I learned a great deal about pleasing tourists, even more about getting along with other companies (most flights were sponsored or paid for by some corporation), and far too much about international aviation law and coping with what we politely called "irregularities in the infrastructure."

You haven't really improvised until you're taking off from the boondocks of Bangladesh, you hit a water buffalo on the runway, and the plane veers into swampland and sinks to its belly—and you've got sixty Republic Wright execs, including your own hypercritical older brother, aboard, and they're all due home in forty-eight hours. I got them home, and stayed out of jail, and Global still made money—but it was a *very* long forty-eight hours.

Meanwhile I kept my shuttle rating. For four years I was a reserve Air Force officer, so that I could get in my monthly fifteen hours of jet time, and I got up early on many mornings so I could use the shuttle simulator at Langley AFB to do that part of maintaining qualification. As space gradually privatized throughout the nineties, and launch systems operations were moved out of NASA and turned over to the newly created private corporation ASU, Global had increasing hopes of being able to rent *Columbia* for a flight and have me take up a load of passengers.

On my fortieth birthday, I took stock of where I had been and what I was doing. By most people's standards, I had had four successful careers, as a military pilot, astronaut, airline pilot, and airline exec, but I felt I had just completed my training. I wanted to start doing something that actually got people into space, and I wanted to start right away.

Three days later the phone rang. The first-generation astronaut who had promoted Share-Space into being was ready to step down. He wanted someone with more of a day-to-day business-and-management perspective to take over, because with seats opening on the shuttle, the job would move from promotion to operations. "And when we started looking for a person to replace me," he said, "you seemed to have spent your life creating the perfect résumé for it."

I said I would take the job.

Four days later, I moved into my office. Three weeks after that, it was official—ShareSpace would be able to buy some seats from ASU, and plaque space on *Columbia.* We were in real business, we had things to sell, and we needed to start selling them now.

I'm not proud of how I handled that at home. Thalia had just launched the Coalition for Effective Justice, a group to push her ideas for how to make the criminal justice and prison systems work more effectively, and she didn't have much time. I can't claim I didn't know it would be a hard time for her—we had discussed it for more than a year before she made her move. But instead of supplying any stability, I suddenly grabbed a new job that was just as demanding as her new job, and dumped a load of new problems, issues, and crises into her lap and expected her to help out with them.

Probably a more sensitive man—or even one who thought about human relations at all—would have realized that it wasn't a good thing to do that without at least some discussion with my wife. Whatever the reason, I just presented all the big changes to her as a *fait accompli*, and expected that she would just adapt as she always had before.

With both of us launching new careers, the changes hit hard and fast. I had whole months living on yogurt, microwave burritos, and Big Macs, dashing out of the house early and getting home long after Amos was in bed, missing any appointment that wasn't business, skipping any chance of a normal social life. Once, for nine straight days, I got home past midnight and left the house again at six. I was living on a round of flights and phone calls, trying to make sure nothing derailed getting Fred Gernsback into orbit. Meanwhile, Thalia was struggling to get foundation funding for the Coalition, and to manage the house and be, at least, more of a mother than I was a father. I think she did better than I did at almost everything, but I truly didn't have the energy or attention to see it.

One reason why I was always so exhausted in those days was politics. I don't know anybody who genuinely does anything for a living, whether it's flying spacecraft or mopping floors, who has any use for politicians, and my first year at ShareSpace didn't make me like them any better. Probably a quarter of the Senate, and maybe as much as a third of the House, were avowedly hostile to what we were doing. I was over on Capitol Hill or at various agency headquarters almost every day, trying to make sure that all the deals stayed done. Over and over, Congressman Brian "Bingo" Rasmussen and his gang were getting on C-SPAN with speeches that rang with phrases like "completely irresponsible use of national resources," "putting civilians onto a barely controlled bomb," "wasting the taxpayer's dollar on toys for the rich," and so forth.

Like any set of lies, it was built around a core of truth. Space travel *is* dangerous. It takes big quantities of energy to get to LEO and that energy has to be released fairly fast, and it *can* get out of control, as it did on *Challenger*. Space has hazards—vacuum, radiation, orbital collision—that have no equivalent on Earth. If enough heat shielding tiles were to peel off during re-entry, the shuttle could go from a billion-dollar marvel of technology to a tumbling shattered meteor before the crew could do anything to save themselves. The shuttle slams down onto the runway at a steep angle, and hits the pavement rolling about as fast as the race cars at Indy, and it lands powerless, so it can't go around for another pass if something doesn't look right.

But millions of people run risks every year, as part of daily life or even purely for recreation, that are far greater than those run by the shuttle crews. Skydivers, skiers, stock car racers, surfers, rock climbers, even just people driving on the freeway—all run bigger risks, and do it more often. I wasn't kidnapping people onto the shuttle, nor were Citizen Observers taking seats away from any other, more important, purpose—those seats would have flown empty without ShareSpace.

The high price we charged for a seat, finally, was what won enough wavering congressmen and senators to our side, and made the Clinton/Gore administrators, who didn't much like or care for anything connected with space, grudgingly accept it. ASU would get a high-paying customer—ShareSpace—and that would allow it to charge its government customer, NASA, a little less. On the whole, it looked like the taxpayers would come out ahead, and that was what mattered in the waning years of the Clinton Administration.

One day, I came out of one meeting, on my way to another three meetings, and Thalia was waiting for me. I stared at her, unsure what she could be doing here, afraid that perhaps Amos had been hurt.

She handed me a thick stack of papers, and when I looked down, I saw that she was petitioning for divorce. I looked back up at her impassive face, and couldn't think of anything to say. I finally asked if she wanted to talk about anything, and she said she thought it would be better if we just let the lawyers handle everything.

I don't know if it was better, but since she didn't want to talk, that day or later, I didn't see too many other options. I told the lawyer from Gordon and Gordon, the Blackstone family firm, to be generous and quibble about nothing. In turn, Thalia wasn't asking for much except to get this too-busy stranger out of her house, so that her life could be less chaotic.

Of course I was miserable, but the same lack of time and space in my life that led to the divorce also gave me a way to get through the bad time. Share-

Space always needed something done, all the time. A growing company isn't as warm and supportive as a family, but like a family it can consume nearly unlimited energy and much more time than you have. They say that being a workaholic is a hard addiction to shake because it's the only addiction that improves your life, and that was certainly true in my case for many months. The only time I relaxed was during my visitation times with Amos, when I more or less forced myself to park the phone somewhere else and get away completely. At least it made me look forward to visitations.

After a while, Thalia and I started speaking to each other again, almost always about Amos, and usually not very kindly or happily. It was better than the terse, sullen way we'd communicated just after I moved out, but not much better.

As the van rolled into Silver Spring, and I yawned and stretched and wondered what it was like to go to bed without setting an alarm, I realized that no matter how things went, my workaholic days were going to be numbered, and that I was coming to the end of that grimly determined part of my life. In the business community, and particularly in aerospace, ShareSpace was no longer regarded as a goofy start-up project doomed to failure, but as a serious venture with a known path of expansion. We would be staffing up substantially over the next few months, and there were now routine procedures for things that, a year ago, we'd still been making up case-by-case.

Every single step was not going to require the CEO's intervention, and some time and regularity would come back into my life. I knew I wanted to spend more time with Amos, but beyond that I wasn't sure what to do with a more conventional life. Maybe

I should take a long vacation, or start a hobby, or try dating someone more seriously . . . perhaps I'd get some thinking done while I was down at the cabin with Amos, on the beach, ten days from now. Meanwhile, there was plenty to do. I picked up my cell phone, dialed my voice mail, and was rewarded with the phrase "Nineteen new messages. You last picked up messages at 10:50 P.M." With a sigh for the clear, crisp sunny fall day rolling past the van's windows, I got to work again.

CHAPTER TWO

SCOTT:

My third time through a ShareSpace Citizen Observer launch, I had the drill down cold. When I got to the office, I signed what had to be signed right then, looked at everything vital, and then sat down on the couch in the office, with the phone, and told Naomi I was in to all press and media calls. By the time I did that she had them stacked about ten deep, and after that I was on the phone, continually, with only brief breaks, for seven hours. I answered the same simple questions over and over, did my best to sound as if the question were a pleasant surprise each time, and kept firmly in mind that you never know when you're going out live from some big-transmitter station in the middle of the country, so you can't afford to sound like a jerk to anybody.

At 7:30, about two hours before launch time, I ducked into the small shower in the building, got clean and changed clothes, and went down to our press buffet, where we had set up a row of big-screen TVs and an array of food for the reporters who would be covering the event from our headquarters. I circulated around, shaking hands and talking to each of them.

A reporter is either eating from your hand, or eating you alive. For the moment, our diligent PR campaign and our cultivation of the press was paying off, and the media people were acting like I was doing them a favor, instead of vice versa.

The TV reporters were all sort of half-there, with one eye on the screen, lost in the audio feed from their earpieces; they mostly kept an eye on their own organization's coverage, so that, if they were suddenly called to speak to the viewing audience, they would know their context.

The screen that drew the newspaper reporters was tuned to the feed from inside the shuttle, which let you watch MJ lick his lips, squirm to get more comfortable, and occasionally answer a question, probably from someone running through a checklist. I was glad he was smiling frequently, and still looked more excited than bored or frustrated; I didn't need another display of that temper today. (Naomi had been monitoring the news coverage, and it looked like Michael's dressing down of the gatecrasher with the rude question had not made it onto any major network news by that evening—which meant it probably never would.) That last hour of countdown was never my favorite part—everything was either dull, or trouble.

We had a "capture" button for the press, so that they could record a still off the video whenever they liked. When MJ looked at the camera and grinned at the same moment, one reporter slapped the capture button. "Got it," he said. "Page one everywhere tomorrow, eh?"

"Right under the big slug headline, unless something big breaks between now and one A.M.," the woman beside him agreed. "Great smile, with lots of hardware in the background."

Nodding at the still shot still hanging there on the monitor, with MJ beaming like a kid at Christmas, Naomi said to me, "That's been missing from space for a long time—that feeling that this is something *great* to do."

"Maybe it's been missing from everything for a while," I said. "Just the idea of doing something because it's beautiful and fun and hard. How's the food holding up?"

"The reporters are nibbling and the crews are pounding it down, same as ever," Naomi said. "We'll be fine, Mr. Blackstone. The press reception is going just fine."

I kept circulating. Reporters kept soaking up free food and watching their own channels. The countdown crept downward. It was a publicity-perfect night launch, with a chance for some terrific photos.

Now all the screens showed *Columbia* in the harsh glare of the artificial lights, clouds of cold vapor rising around it. The gantry pulled back. The white glare burst from underneath the rocket as it began, slowly, to climb.

It never got old for me, and it never got completely comfortable, either. Having made three liftoffs myself, and seen more than I could easily remember, I stood there making sure I was grinning confidently, in case of any cameras pointed my way, but privately checking off each place where something could go wrong.

Nothing did. They stayed on trajectory. They

rolled over on time. The solid boosters separated
properly. All three SSME's, the main engines, kept
running at the appropriate 104 percent power, carrying them right through each abort point. Finally, as
they reached orbit, the SSME's shut down on the dot.
It was a perfect launch. I didn't have to fake the grin
anymore.

I became aware of a noise in the background—clap-
ping and cheering. I accepted handshakes and pats on
the back just as if I'd flown the shuttle myself, and
made sure that everyone got as much champagne as
they'd take.

The media had wanted to book every second of
MJ's time from liftoff to landing. ShareSpace and
Pegasus had often had to remind the more aggressive
ones that ASU and ShareSpace were private companies and therefore there was no "public right to
know" involved. If they wanted some of Mr. James's
time while he was in orbit, and he wanted to give it
to them or sell it to them, he could do so, but even
if we could compel him to provide them with endless
free footage, we wouldn't.

MJ declared that for his first orbit, he would not
talk to the media; he said he was going to spend as
much of that time as possible looking out the window.
In retrospect, I've always been glad he did. Billy Kingston said he'd never seen anyone more excited and
happy in all his life, or anyone who took to weightlessness more easily.

Meanwhile, down on Earth, I was keeping the
press amused with as jolly a party as the budget of a
small company allows. We had a teleconferencing
uplink arranged so that MJ could talk to all these
people at once, but that wasn't scheduled till 11:30
P.M., still almost two hours away—time enough for

him to have his first orbit, compose himself for the conference, and even get started on his official mission duty, taking photographs.

Our first two Citizen Observers had demonstrated that if a person shoots enough pictures, a few of them are bound to be interesting, and those few can then be sold as posters, rented to advertisers, distributed to the press, and so forth. A picture taken by Michael James, with his signature printed on the poster, should sell well, making us all some money, and a good set of slides could give him things to talk about, back on Earth, for decades of lectures.

You can't just shoot photographs through the window of the shuttle with a Wal-Mart disposable camera and expect to get much. The special glass is extremely thick, so that anything not directly in line with the camera lens appears distorted; glare is severe; contrasts between bright and dark are far greater than anything on Earth. Most of all, it's hard to know what you're seeing—one tall snow-peaked mountain, one blue winding river in a deep green plain, one shimmering white-brown desert streaked with shadows by the sunset, tends to look very much like another.

Thus we'd had to commission one piece of new technology, the only one so far that ShareSpace had had to develop for itself. The "CO camera" was a small miracle of self-correcting lens trains, adjusting polarizers, GPS and IR receivers, and gyrocompasses, plus a dedicated microprocessor that constantly knew the position of the camera in space, and the direction it was pointing, so that as the shutter clicked, the camera wrote a slugline at the bottom: time; altitude, latitude, and longitude of the shuttle; and latitude and longitude of the center of the picture. The camera always knew and recorded what you had photographed, from where, and when.

During the second orbit, before his conference with the reporters, MJ was supposed to use the CO camera to take two practice shots through the front window, so that the first shots on the roll would be dramatic. Then Marc Clement was supposed to take two pictures of MJ floating by each corporate plaque inside the shuttle, so that the sponsors got what they had paid for.

A modest complication was added while I was at the reception—Perry Lager, my customer-service guy, called me and said that he'd had a request from many of the sponsors for the very first picture on the roll to be a shot of MJ floating beside the wall of plaques, instead. At the rate they were paying, some of them were anxious to make sure that their logo got the full treatment, and it was no problem to do it.

I went into the bathroom, where I hoped no one would notice I had a phone contact going on with MJ, and called the patch-through number at Houston. In a minute, I had Michael on the line, and I relayed the request.

"No problem, man, no problem at all." His voice was full of pure glee; if there were a drug that could get you as high as he sounded, we'd all be addicts.

"Are you having a good time, Michael?"

"The best. The absolute best. I love it up here and I love all of you. Thanks for calling—we'll get you that shot."

"Thank you, MJ," I said, and we hung up.

As I came out of the stall, a short, balding dark-haired man in a blue suit emerged from the next stall. "I bet you came in here so that we wouldn't all jump at your phone and shout questions."

"That's right."

"Well, I didn't. But I *did* eavesdrop. Would you mind telling me what he said when you asked if he was having a good time?"

"He said he was bored stiff, he wanted to come home, and that kids everywhere in America should stop drinking milk, sass their parents, and take buckets of drugs."

The guy laughed out loud. "Serves me right." He stuck out his hand. "I'm Ken Elgin. *USReport.* I'll behave and save my questions for the press conference."

I thanked him. We went back out into the reception area and got sandwiches. He knew space issues well, so we ended up doing a little impromptu interview. Most of the other reporters were still busy eating, drinking, and watching the screens, but Nikki Earl came over and taped parts of what I said, too. I was just explaining how a "space hotel"—basically a one-launch space station that was set up to cater to tourists—could easily be a prototype for the living quarters of a ship that could go to Mars, when the room fell terribly silent.

Naomi ran forward and turned up the volume on FBN. Fred Gernsback was just saying, "We are guessing, from the last minute of radio traffic, that something has gone seriously wrong on the space shuttle *Columbia.*" For half an hour afterwards, except for Gernsback booming through the TV monitor, there was nothing but silence as the terrible news poured in.

SOMETIMES I STILL have nightmares about it. Probably I always will. I went over the evidence and the recordings more times than I can count. I knew what the cockpit and crew area of *Columbia* looked like. I knew all the crew well. It's hard for me to remember that I wasn't actually there myself—it feels like I was there and like I remember every moment.

The crew had gotten into coveralls and was settling into its normal work routine. The big payload bay doors were open, and the automated experiments in the bay were up and running. Billy Kingston called everyone to the mid deck, where they floated in a small group, hanging on to seats as needed. The commander read off the checklist of tasks.

Most astronauts, most of the time, are not only scientists and pilots, but also medical test animals. The environment of space is still new, and it's still customary to do a whole battery of medical tests on every member of every crew, building up a collection of data for space medicine. Usually one of the first jobs in orbit is to draw each other's blood samples and record vital signs.

Marc Clement and M J went first, drawing each other's blood and taking each other's temperatures and blood pressures. Josh Pritkin and Damian Agustino were scheduled to go next, and sat waiting their turn and teasing the other two. Meanwhile, Billy Kingston was slated to be a test subject for some experiments Lorena Charette was running in the LBNP—"lower body negative pressure"—device, a gadget disliked by many astronauts, that reduces air pressure on the lower part of your body and thus redistributes blood and other fluids for some experiments on the effects of weightlessness.

The only person concerned directly with shuttle operations was Wes Packard, who, as primary pilot for the mission, had the first watch in the pilot's chair. Normally, on a shuttle mission, that job is dull—while the shuttle is orbiting and not under power, there's very little "steering" or "flying" to do, and the pilot's seat can be left unattended for minutes at a time. Wes sipped at a bulb of coffee and watched the Earth roll by underneath.

"Well, according to all this, we're both still alive, so I guess we have to keep working," Marc Clement said, swimming back forward with MJ behind him. "Your turn, guys."

Pritkin and Agustino glanced at each other, shrugged, and began to take their own measurements.

MJ got the camera out of the locker, switched it on, and looked over the indicator lights. Everything was green. "Looks like we're ready for the pictures."

"Can you keep an eye on the pilot's chair while you're doing that, Marc?" Wes asked.

"Sure."

Wes unbuckled. "Then just a second, let me get past you. My coffee's coming through." Wes swam back to the head and closed the door.

"All clear," MJ said. "Okay, let me get in front of those plaques—or I guess more to the side, I'm probably not supposed to hide any of them—all right, show time."

He passed the camera in a gentle toss to Marc, who caught it easily.

Marc positioned himself, bumping with his hands to get the right angle, before pointing the camera. "Hang on a second . . . real good."

"Let me get stopped," MJ said. He was now slowly rotating. "I want this shot *perfect*."

He brought himself to a stop in the new position. Marc said, "Okay, your position is perfect and you're still. I've got all the plaques in the frame. Looking good. Give me your biggest smile."

"That'll be easy because—"

A *crack-boom!* reverberated through the ship. Billy Kingston and Lorena Charette both said it sounded more like a small cannon than a big rifle; in the tiny confined space of the shuttle, it was deafening.

The klaxon for pressure loss was going off. Kingston pushed out of the LBNP and scrambled forward, bellowing "What's going on?" Charette followed. They arrived in the forward area as Wes came out of the toilet and bounced to the pilot's seat.

Marc Clement was tumbling end over end, his head wobbling at a sickening angle; his face was crushed as if he had been rammed into a wall at great speed. M J floated against one wall, eyes and mouth wide open, blood drifting out of his mouth and a hole in his chest. His eyes were distended and bloodshot, sinking back to normal size even as they first saw him. Spheres of his blood bobbed around the cabin.

Kingston swam to him and felt his neck for a pulse; as he did, he saw there was a much larger hole between the big man's shoulder blades. Whatever had happened had killed him at once. Blood had splashed across the wall of plaques, and in the middle of the smear, sucking blood out into space, was a hole about a quarter inch in diameter. Kingston rammed his baseball cap into the hole, poking it in with a pen from his pocket until he could stuff it no further.

A moment later the klaxon turned off, and then the terrible silence was broken by Josh Pritkin saying, "Jesus, what happened?"

Lorena Charette snapped, "Over here, Josh, Damy. Marc's got a broken neck but he's alive. I'm trying to hold his spinal cord in line here. Josh, get me my kit. Damy, come here and help me support him."

Wes Packard said, "Pressure breach. We lost about three hundred pounds of air in less than two minutes, and we've still got a slow leak, with pressure dropping. We're yawing a little, no pitch or roll—basically we're in a slow flat spin."

"Wait till I have Marc stabilized before you correct," Lorena said.

"Roger."

"I've got at least one leak here," Kingston said, "with my hat stuffed into it. How's cabin pressure?"

"About a third of an atmosphere," Packard said.

Charette grunted with irritation. "We've got to get that higher, soon. The only reason we don't have anybody passed out is that we're all hyperventilating."

"Everyone who isn't helping with Marc, get into pressure suits, ASAP," Kingston said. "Trade off as soon as you're suited up." He climbed up on the mid deck to get his own from the rack. A moment later, Packard and Pritkin were suiting up beside him. "Is there anything we can do for Marc? M J is dead—no pulse and something went right through him."

"Just a sec," Charette said. A moment later, Charette and Agustino were suiting up. "We've got Marc secured into a bunk with his head tied down to keep his neck straight. He's in a bad way but it's hard to tell how bad. I'll do a trake on him, right now, because his breathing isn't good and I think there's a crushing injury to the neck. Damy, you be nurse."

"Tie M J down somewhere," Kingston said, quietly, to Pritkin, and then moved forward to the copilot's chair. "Okay, I'd better give them the bad news. Wes, get working on where we can do an emergency landing. No water ditch, and no rough country, even if we have to stay up a few extra minutes."

The shuttle doesn't float, and it lands too fast and hard to put down on water, or on any land that isn't a paved runway, without breaking up. Standard procedure for an emergency is for the crew to bail out once they are low and slow enough. With a crew member with a broken neck, they couldn't evacuate the shuttle; they would have to land it, somehow.

Packard pulled a laptop computer from its slot beside his chair, and began to work on the problem. Distantly, Kingston heard Lorena Charette saying, "Okay, here goes, get that suction in close." He took a deep breath, made sure he was on secure channel, and spoke into the radio. "Houston, we have an emergency situation here, hull breach, other unknown damage, one crew member dead, one severely injured. We're going for an emergency deorbit and a landing at the nearest emergency field—"

"Easter Island," Packard whispered. "Start burn in nine minutes."

"Nearest emergency field is Easter Island. Request all the emergency help you can get there, ASAP. Injured crew member has spinal cord injury. We're starting deorbit burn in—" he looked at the laptop Wes held up "—eight minutes ten seconds."

"Roger, *Columbia*, you are go. Be advised weather at Easter Island is clear. We're praying for you."

I HAD MORE chairs brought in. The caterer called out an emergency order of food and coffee. Our conference room had plenty of data links, and we allocated them to the reporters as evenly as we could. But after we made things as comfortable for the press and media as we could, we still could do nothing about what they needed most: some idea about what was going on.

Every news division had gone to live coverage at once. Since there was no information, they filled airtime by reviewing everything every couple of minutes, and called every possible field reporter over and over to confirm that nothing was happening in the field as well. Television reporters at ShareSpace's now suddenly somber press reception took turns standing in front of the ShareSpace corporate logo to recite, again, that no one here had any idea, sometimes adding that Scott Blackstone was right here and had promised to pass on information the moment he had it.

"HIS NECK IS broken, the front of his skull is crushed, and I don't see any way he can have missed spinal cord damage, but he's breathing on his own now that we have an oxygen tube going in through the tracheotomy," Lorena Charette said. "We have him immobilized as best we can, but even a perfect landing will probably kill him. You might as well start your maneuvers."

"Do it," Kingston said.

Without a word, or a glance at his crewmates, Wes Packard set his hands on the controls and applied the reaction control thrusters to stop the yaw and bring the shuttle into position for deorbit burn, with its tail pointed in the direction they were orbiting. "Burn starts in seven minutes. Get the payload doors closed and get strapped into those seats quick, people."

Everyone hurried to strap in. Pritkin and Agustino stopped going over the plaque wall, where they had been gathering up and bagging the blood droplets, stray bits of metal and flesh, and other shattered objects in the compartment, and started the automated sequence to shut down the experiments and close the big doors.

"What's our damage situation?" Kingston asked, over his shoulder.

"We were still working on it," Agustino said, "but it looks like damage was just that hole in the hull, the camera, and two crew members. It's lucky the hole is over the wing, not on the underside. We'd be in a real mess if we'd had a big hole in the tiles."

Kingston grunted. "I hate the idea of Easter Island but the next place after it would be most of an hour, and it's just an old bomber runway in western Siberia—we *know* that one hasn't been maintained, and there'd be nobody there to meet us or help Marc. At least people *say* they've maintained the strip on Easter Island."

An orbiting shuttle doesn't have much choice about where it goes. The enormous load of fuel that it takes off with is almost entirely burned in getting to orbit, and, for safety, what remains is jettisoned shortly after. Because the shuttle orbit is tipped at an angle to Earth's equator, in addition to going around the Earth it swings north and south of the equator by hundreds or thousands of miles. During the time it takes to make an orbit, the Earth turns through anywhere from 20 to 30 degrees of longitude, so that every orbit shifts to the west of the one that preceded it, drawing a kind of giant sine wave across the map of the Earth. A shuttle that passes over Chattanooga on this orbit will pass over Albuquerque on the next orbit, and won't pass over Chattanooga again for twenty-four hours. The Orbital Maneuvering System thrusters are small, and the Reaction Control System thrusters are even smaller. The shuttle can alter its trajectory only very slightly, and so it can land only on fields that are very close to its orbital path. Furthermore, since the shuttle lands as a glider, without thrust for a go-around, everything has to work right the first time.

There is a system of landing fields for the shuttle all around the world, in case of emergency, but not all are equally good. The main landing fields at Edwards Air Force Base in California and KSC in Florida are well-maintained and their crews are experienced. The field at Zaragosa, Spain, is nearly as good. But those were all out of reach.

Easter Island is something else again: a small dot on the map of the South Pacific, owned by Chile, one of the few Pacific islands on a regular flight path with room enough for a long, wide runway, but without much else. It was hardly the ideal place to come down with a damaged ship and a badly injured crewman.

"What do you think it was?" Damian asked. He was strapping into his seat; there were still seventy-five seconds left till time to begin the burn.

Packard shrugged. "Looks like the classic profile for a micrometeoroid, doesn't it? All the damage is in a straight line, and whatever it was hit with enough force to pass through the hull, right through MJ's chest, into the camera, and drive the last bits of the camera into Marc's head so hard it broke his neck. That looks like a very high velocity impact to me."

"Micrometeoroid or space junk," Pritkin added, as he rechecked his suit.

ASU Mission Control called then to ask for definitive information before making a press announcement, and Billy Kingston relayed their speculation about what had hit them, along with the news that Michael James was dead and Marc Clement very seriously injured.

WITHIN A COUPLE of minutes, an ASU executive was talking to the James family, and ASU had notified me privately. Ten minutes later, the whole planet knew, and world phone traffic set new records. I stood in front of the reporters and had to keep saying, "All I know is what Mission Control tells me, and what they are telling me is that Michael James was killed in an accident, Marc Clement was seriously injured and his survival remains in doubt, the shuttle was damaged, and they are going to try to land on the emergency field on Easter Island. That's all they've told me. ShareSpace is not in the chain of command for the mission, and this is all need-to-know information. I'll share everything they give me, but right now they are not giving me any more than that."

Nikki Earl waved a hand. "The crew is speculating that it may have been a micrometeoroid or a piece of space debris. For our listeners, could you just explain what those are and how they might be dangerous?"

It was a relief to have the chance to say something other than what I had been repeating for several minutes. "Micrometeoroids are meteors too small for radar to see—anywhere from the size of a pea down to the size of grain of sand. They're moving at very high velocities—twenty or more times the speed of a bullet—and so they hit with tremendous force. There aren't very many of them relative to all the empty space, and there's never been a known accident caused by one, but sooner or later something was bound to be hit.

"Space debris is stuff that got left up there from past space missions—bits and pieces of everything, broken-off bolts and screws and chips of paint, tools that escaped from building ISS, dead rocket upper stages, lots of other things. It's not usually moving as fast as a micrometeoroid, but it's still several times bullet speed, and most of it's bigger, and there's more of it. People have talked for decades about the need to clear that out, but no one's ever really done much more than think about the problem. Anyway, if the *Columbia* ran into either a micrometeoroid or a piece of debris, it probably went right through the skin of the ship—and anything else in its path—and that could certainly kill someone and damage the ship. Billy Kingston and his crew are there, and I'm not, and if their guess is that it's an impact accident, then that's probably the best guess that we're going to have for a while."

Nikki nodded and gestured to indicate that she had something coming in through her earpiece.

A couple of the cable networks kept asking me how I felt, and all I could do was keep telling them that like everyone else on Earth I felt overwhelming grief at the loss of Michael James, but having known him for several months as a friend, that it was hard to believe he was gone, and that I would miss him terribly. By making me repeat it, they got me more and more bothered, so that after a while I was blinking back tears. Perhaps that's what they really wanted, anyway.

The long minutes crawled by; finally it was time for the landing on Easter Island. Luckily for the American networks, a Chilean TV crew was there on another story, and they'd hurried to the emergency landing field and patched into satellite feed.

Easter Island is on Pacific Coast Time, minus a half hour, so it was about an hour after sunset when *Columbia* made her attempt. The runway was bright from the landing lights, the sky pitch black above it. The TV camera watched from near the end of the runway, where the shuttle would come to rest if the landing succeeded. We had managed to patch into their audio, but since I didn't speak Spanish, I had no idea what they were talking about.

For a moment it looked like the other shuttle night landings—a flash of white as the shuttle slid into the lights, a graceful suspended instant as it glided in and touched down. The ship leveled off and began to roll down the runway.

The nose wheel slammed into a pothole on top of a soft pocket, and the landing gear twisted sideways and collapsed. Still moving forward at a hundred miles an hour, the shuttle nosed down, the broken landing gear tipping it to one side. Then the nose bit into the crumbling pavement, and her tail bucked far up into the air as she slid down the runway, sparks flying and trailing tiles and bits of fuselage. The tail slammed back down, lifting the nose for a moment, and the shuttle skidded sideways out of control before the right-side landing gear buckled. *Columbia* slumped sideways, spinning another quarter turn before coming to a rest on the crumpled mess that had been the nose, with one wing broken against the ground, and one badly bent landing gear holding up the other side. Sirens wailed in the background as we watched the image of the shattered *Columbia* bounce around and grow larger; the Chilean camera crew, on the back of a pickup truck, was driving toward it.

The hatch on the side fell open. Slowly, painfully, the five survivors climbed out, pulling off their helmets. They just stood there, a few feet from the wreckage, staring at their smashed and battered spacecraft.

A minute later, medics rushed into the shuttle, and shortly afterwards they confirmed that Marc Clement had died during the re-entry or the crash.

The networks endlessly reran that crash, between reporters talking in front of an image of poor, broken *Columbia* lying in the glare of the sodium lights. I spent the next hour expressing my regrets and saying that the whole thing was terrible, so many times that I was afraid I would slur or rush it or sound like I didn't mean it. Finally the reporters left, and the caterer's staff were allowed to clean the place up. As we half-stumbled out, I noticed that Naomi's face was red from crying.

I had nowhere else to go, so I just drove back to the drab, lonely house that I had gotten after the divorce. All the art and the newer furniture had stayed at the house with Thalia and Amos. I had a scattered collection of used furniture between bare white walls. It had never looked more empty.

I poured a diet Coke, sat down on my couch, and pulled out a video called *M J! Grace Flies High!*—a collection of clips of his amazing ball handling and shooting. I watched him, the way he would laugh and smile when another one went in, the way he flowed through opposing players to get at the ball, "the most physically sublime athlete of our age," as Jorge Wimme had called him in a famous essay. Tears ran down my face. I didn't bother to brush them off.

At 2:30 or so I took a shower, as hot as it would go, and went to bed. I fell right asleep, but when the alarm went off and I sat up in the gray pre-dawn, I felt like I hadn't slept at all.

CHAPTER THREE

SCOTT:

I'd have to meet with the board, who would not be happy. In my head, on the drive over to the office, I outlined what I would have to say to them, so that I could dictate it that morning and be ready to deliver it that afternoon. We would have to tough this one out and spend more than we ever planned on PR, marketing, and advertising, and we'd have to manage much longer than we'd planned on without the big revenues of selling tickets into space. But the only way we were likely to lose everything would be to give up now. Those seemed to be the important points.

By the time I was turning the car into the Share-Space parking lot, I had worked out what I would say to reassure all the staff from the secretaries and custodians right on up through my three VP's. They were all good people, anyway, not prone to panic.

Probably by midmorning we could have everyone thoroughly on task for the difficult days ahead.

When I arrived at 7:30, half an hour earlier than usual, Naomi, who was crying and wouldn't look me in the eye, told me that the Board was already in the conference room holding a meeting.

I walked in on them. They seemed to be dripping with embarrassment. My first thought on seeing their wide stares and hasty turning away was that they had voted for something stupid and panicky, were already regretting it, and wanted me to talk them into reversing it.

A moment later, Norm Aquinas, my VP for finance—and now the CEO of ShareSpace—told me. There had been a unanimous vote to fire me and put Norm in my place.

Well, it was their circus, and they could fire any clown they wanted to. I had nothing to say, so I got out of there.

In my office, the security guards, being as nice about it as they could, were piling all the stuff from the desk into "personal" and "company." They also had a pile they wanted me to sort for them.

That took about half an hour. It's weird to sit in a chair and at a desk that aren't yours anymore, while a bunch of people who used to work for you make sure you don't steal any pieces of what used to be your life.

When I was finished, Gerry Richland, whom I'd hired personally and who had been with ShareSpace for three years, said, "They told me to check to make sure you're not taking any company documents. I ain't gonna do it. Damn, I'm sorry about all this, Mr. Blackstone."

"Me too. What time did they get in?"

"I guess there were three outside people they wanted to meet with, and those guys said they wanted to meet at six in the morning, so that's when the Board got here."

"Outside people?" I asked, not really curious.

"I don't know who they were, Mr. Blackstone, most guys in suits look alike to me—they look like trouble."

"Well, this time you were right," I said. They might have been PR consultants, or lawyers—almost anybody with some sense about publicity or law might have told them that getting rid of me would help save ShareSpace. Objectively speaking, they might be right.

Three boxes held four years of my life. Gerry, the other guard, and I each carried a box down to the parking lot. I put them in the trunk of the BMW, shook hands with the two guards and wished them well, got behind the wheel, and, having nothing else to do, went home, taking side streets and going slow. I wasn't eager to get back to the place where I slept and kept the television and fridge. Amos would be on his way to school by now, so I couldn't call him at Mrs. Talbert's. I could try my brother Nick, but he and I didn't talk much anymore. Besides, on any given day I didn't know whether to call him at his satellite office in DC, at the main Republic Wright Aircraft office in San Diego, or via the private line into RW's Advanced Projects Facility. Wherever he was, he'd probably be too busy to talk anyway.

I even thought about seeing if Thalia would talk to me; we often fought about petty things, but she was probably the person who understood me best, and maybe Thalia would be willing to listen, or say "I'm sorry," or suggest something or other that I could do.

But Thalia was in California, on Coalition business, and wouldn't be back till late this afternoon. We had each other's cell phone numbers, but those were strictly for emergencies involving Amos. Maybe I'd try calling her on Saturday or Sunday, at some convenient time—Amos had said she'd be home—if I still felt so raw and miserable.

Thinking of my son had made me think about that last phone conversation with MJ, and that had brought the whole terrible mess home to me again. I couldn't quite figure out what to do with myself just yet. Maybe I'd go to a movie or something. It looked like I was going to have time on my hands.

When I pulled into my driveway, I found a small mob of media types on my lawn. Ken Elgin and Nikki Earl were the only people I recognized. Even this early in the morning, the camera crews still had enough energy to run in and out of the flower beds and shrubs, trampling everything flat.

As I got out of the car, the NBC guy led off with "Congressman Rasmussen has issued a statement—if I may read you a brief part of it—and I thought you might care to comment. He says, 'It is not the job of civilians to get killed in space. Furthermore, since a civilian with very little training was given important responsibilities on this mission, it is clear that this accident could have been prevented.' Any comment, Mr. Blackstone?"

I cleared my throat. "I don't know, yet, what caused the accident," I said, "and neither does Congressman Rasmussen. But everything sounds like they ran into something, probably space debris, maybe a micrometeoroid. Neither the ground crews nor the shuttle crew themselves could have seen that coming. It would have happened no matter who was on board the shuttle or what they were doing."

Nikki Earl asked, "You said last night that at those speeds even a paint chip or a loose washer is dangerous?"

"*Very* dangerous," I said. "At orbital speeds, even a tiny object hits with many, many times the energy of a bullet from a gun. With an object the size of a pea in an orbit that's tens of thousands of miles long, traveling at several miles per second, you really can't keep track of it well enough to duck it every time. All you can do is hope you won't meet up with it, and that's all anyone has ever been able to do. Sooner or later our luck was bound to run out. It was absolutely unpreventable, and I think it's a disgrace that Congressman Rasmussen chooses to blame M J, or any of the regular crew, for the accident. It could have happened on any flight, to any crew, any time. It's terrible that it happened this time."

One advantage to losing my job, I realized, was that I could say what I was thinking, so after a pause, I added something. "It's especially appalling that Congressman Rasmussen, who has no facts about the case, and wouldn't be able to understand them if he did, has rushed to judgment and blamed the dead." I felt better for having said that.

"Can we quote you on that?" the CNN reporter asked, pushing her hair back from her face.

"I hope you put it on the six o'clock news, right after you run Bingo's statement," I said. "This was a terrible tragedy. Space is dangerous and will always be dangerous. That's why we make people sign so many waivers."

"What are the odds that anyone will ever be able to identify the object that did the damage?" Ken Elgin asked.

"Pretty poor," I said. "Parts of it will have vaporized, and the impact scattered a lot of other material around the cabin—bits of shuttle wall and of everything it went through." I realized I had just implied "bits of MJ" and hurried on, hoping no one would notice. "And the shuttle wrecked on landing, so very likely some gravel and small junk got loose in the cabin during that, making it harder to pick out which object is the one that did it. I assume right now that NASA's investigators are looking into all the possibilities, but we'll have to wait till there are more facts. Not being a congressman, I don't proceed further than the facts will take me."

The first questions had gone pretty well, I thought, but I still didn't like the look of this crowd—apprentices and B-teamers, very few business reporters, no science reporters—their surest road to advancement would be to really nail somebody, anybody—me.

Well, all the same, if you didn't tell the complete truth as you knew it, you were in ten times worse trouble. So, though what I really felt like doing was going inside, getting under the covers, and not coming out till Christmas, I looked around and said, "I'll be happy to answer questions after I get my personal stuff moved into my garage. For that matter you can talk to me while I carry these boxes in. It won't take long. Do you all know that I've been fired as CEO of ShareSpace?"

There was a startled silence, and then Nikki Earl stepped forward, holding out her recorder, and said, "Uh, no, Mr. Blackstone, I don't think any of us had any idea. Did they give a reason?"

"Good of the organization," I said, "the same reason anyone is given when they're fired. They didn't tell *me* anything other than to clear out my desk and go."

"Well, *that's* tacky," Ken Elgin muttered.

"Any other questions?" I asked.

They all looked at each other, and finally Nikki Earl shrugged and said, "I think if you already knew what we came here about, you'd have brought the subject up yourself, so I guess I'm elected to tell you this. Mr. Blackstone, the family of Michael James announced, this morning, that they will be suing you, ShareSpace, ASU, Curtiss Aerospace, Republic Wright, and NASA, for a just over a billion dollars. That's what they say he would have earned with his endorsements and appearances in the rest of his life."

My guts dropped a foot. I felt cold all over. All I could do was stare, for a long breath, before I finally I managed to say, "I know nothing about it as yet. You'll have to ask the James family what their intentions are. If I am being sued, I'll need to talk to an attorney before I say anything else."

"Then you haven't heard or seen AnnaBeth James's statement to the press this morning?"

"No, I haven't. I don't think I should talk till I do. That wouldn't do either me or the James family any good."

"Why are you worried about what will do you good? Why aren't you worried about what happened in the accident?" the man who shouted the question at me came up very close; he was making sure we'd both be in the video frame.

"I don't think the investigation will be helped if I start commenting on things I haven't seen or heard for myself. To my knowledge today, no one was even careless, let alone malicious. I'll tell you whatever I can whenever I learn it, but since I've been fired, my access to information is no better than yours."

"Sir! You were responsible for the completely un-precedented event of a global celebrity going on the space shuttle as a paying passenger, and that was fol-lowed immediately by an actual collision in orbit, the first one!" The aggressive way he delivered that made me wonder if he thought I had insulted him with my answer to his previous question.

"If you'll phrase that as a question," I said, walking back to my car, opening my trunk, and getting out the first box, "I'll answer it."

"Sir, it's a simple yes or no question."

"I don't know what yes or no would mean in re-sponse to the statement you just made," I persisted. I carried the box to the garage door, clicked the auto-matic opener, and carried it in to put it on a work-table.

I had closed my trunk; when I got back to the car several of them had cameras and faces pressed up against the car windows. One guy was working a screwdriver under my trunk lid. "Don't damage the paint, all right?" I said, coming up on him quickly so that he'd be visible in a couple of the TV camera views. Not that they would air it.

"Sir, are you going to answer the question?"

"When you phrase it as a question, so that I know what you're asking."

"Isn't it obvious that there *must* be a connection between the unprecedented decision to fly a major celebrity into space, and the unprecedented loss of a shuttle due to an accident in orbit?"

For an instant I wondered how Fred Gernsback or Senator Glenn would feel about being classed as "not major celebrities," but that didn't seem like a good response to the question. I unlocked the trunk, got out the second box, and slammed the trunk lid down quickly enough that a couple of people had to yank their heads and cameras back quickly. "Well, no, there doesn't have to be a connection. The only thing that Michael James going to orbit, and the orbital accident, had in common was that they were unprecedented events on the same flight, as far as anyone knows. More investigation is needed, but this has all the signs of just being a terrible accident, which would have happened no matter who was on board *Columbia*."

"Mr. Blackstone," Nikki Earl asked, "with one shuttle gone, are there going to be any more seats for space tourism?"

I carried the second box into the garage. "Probably not until some private passenger spacecraft enters the market."

"Do you think it was worth it?" someone shouted, from behind me.

"Having been there three times myself, I can say that I'd have run that risk to have that experience, myself. Ask Fred Gernsback or David Calderon, for that matter." I set the box down on the worktable and turned around to face the mob that had poured in behind me; I was certainly glad I'd never been the type to have pinups in the garage. The cameras kept running, pointed at two oil-change kits, a cluttered workbench, and a box of fishing gear I hadn't touched in ten years. I almost felt sorry for how hard they were working to get so little.

When they had backed through the door, I closed it and got the last box from the car.

"So you don't feel that there is any responsibility or blame for you in the death of a man who was loved by millions?" one woman demanded, holding the microphone up to my face as she walked backwards in front of me.

"I didn't say that. Like everyone else, I want to know how this happened. When we know that, we'll know who, if anyone, to blame."

"Will ShareSpace be issuing any statements?"

"I'm sure they'll have to, but I no longer work for them and they no longer tell me anything. Look," I said, "give me your business cards. I will either call you individually, or set up a press conference, as soon as I have any information or a public statement. You will be first in line for anything I have."

It was odd how few of them looked me in the eye as they handed me their cards. By the time I had rubber banded the stack of cards together and dropped it into my coat pocket, they were loading up vans and cars and leaving. Ken and Nikki, since he worked for a news magazine and she worked for a radio network, had no big crew to take with them, so they hung back until the others had gone, and then took a moment to express some sympathy. I smiled slightly and said, "I may be in more of a hurry to call either of you than the rest of the press."

"It's what we call developing a contact," Nikki said. "Lord, they trampled your yard. Hope your gardener likes a challenge."

Ken sighed. "Put a TV camera on anyone's shoulder and they immediately feel free to go anywhere and do anything."

After they left, I lay down on the couch and tried to nap. I couldn't, so I mostly just stared at the ceiling and tried to think of what, if anything, I could have done differently. After a while I wasn't thinking about Michael, but about Thalia, and Amos, and all the friends I'd lost track of. That didn't help my mood either.

The doorbell rang. I lurched off the couch, running a hand over my hair, and opened the door.

It was the papers for the James family's suit. I saw numbers that were even bigger than the billion dollars I had expected. Killing a celebrity, even by accident, is not cheap.

The James family had hired Jasper Haverford. I rarely follow crime stories or celebrity news, but *I* had heard of Jasper Haverford. I leaned back in the chair, sighed, tried to think of what to do. I'd have to get a lawyer.

Probably it could wait an hour. I turned on the television for distraction, but the first thing I clicked to was AnnaBeth James's press conference.

She looked just as terrible as I'd imagined. I doubted she had slept in the time between the accident and the press conference eighteen hours later. Michael's three sisters, beside her, looked no better, all of them crying.

AnnaBeth James read her statement from a typewritten page, stopping now and then to regain control of her feelings. "Our family always supported Michael in whatever he did. My husband Allen never missed a single game of Michael's, up to the day he died. His sisters and I have always stood behind whatever Michael wanted to do. And we knew how much space always meant to him. So when he told us he wanted to go into space for Pegasus, we were so happy for him. But we have learned that neither he nor we were properly informed of the dangers. There was negligence on the part of ShareSpace in selling the tickets, especially on the part of Scott Blackstone, the president and CEO of ShareSpace.

He, and ShareSpace, and every other organization named in our suit should have taken steps to make sure we were aware of the danger. Lack of information, and outright misinformation, directly affected Michael's decision to fly on the *Columbia*.

"These individuals and organizations created an atmosphere in which what was actually an extremely dangerous, high-risk activity was portrayed as reasonable and safe for anyone.

"Furthermore, the whole activity of sending civilians into space was portrayed to us individually and to the public in general as a positive, desirable project. We know now it was a commercial boondoggle whose only purpose was to enrich Scott Blackstone and the ShareSpace investors, to get favorable publicity for a government agency and the major aerospace contractors, and to provide the media with an exciting story.

"My son died in a deadly mix of shortsighted greed, reckless disregard for safety, media hype, and outright lying, amplified by private corporate deception and a government cover-up. I have no further comments at this time." She walked away; Jasper Haverford draped his coat around her shoulders, and the camera zoomed in to get a shot of his perfect staging of the grieving mother and of the strong man supporting her.

"Well," one of the commentators said, "that was heartbreaking. It clearly points up the terrible, terrible disaster this is, and how much the American people need to know, right away, that those responsible for this will pay."

My heart sank. I clicked the remote and shut off the TV. I looked down into my lap, at the papers I had been served a few minutes before. I wanted to

phone AnnaBeth James, but it was too late emotionally, and probably a bad idea legally.

I sat there for a long time, facing the blank television. It wasn't even noon yet.

At least I could try to find a lawyer. I left a message
on the family law firm's machine, made a sandwich,
and ate it without tasting it. The crunching sound
from my food seemed terribly loud in the very empty
house. I wished I'd either kept a couple of paintings,
or maybe bought some new ones.

About twenty minutes after I had left the message,
the phone rang. It was Harry Gordon, who mostly
handled things like deeds, property transfers, wills,
administering trust funds, and so forth for the Blackstone family. "To tell you the truth," he said, "I don't
think much of our trial lawyers here; mostly we write
documents to keep people out of court. We aren't the
right ones for your situation. And I'm not sure I know
who the right ones would be. I'll ask around and get
back to you."

"Thanks for doing that for me, Harry."

"It's what you pay a retainer for. I'll see what I can
turn up. How's Nick? Has he checked in with you?"

"Uh, not yet," I said. "We don't see much of each
other anymore."

"Ah, that's a shame," Harry said. "Times like this,
you need relatives and friends. And it seems really
strange to me that you're not in touch; remember
when I had the beach cabin not too far from your
dad's? You and Nick and Thalia and—what was that
other kid's name?"

"Eddie Killeret," I said, automatically. "Yeah, we
were all pretty close, back then. But it was a long
time ago, Harry," I said.

"Well, yeah. Funny how it's kids who make friends

so easily, and adults who need them so badly," Harry said. "Anyway, I will do my best to find the right guy to take your case, and I'll try to move fast on it. I'll at least give you a progress report by end of day today."

While I waited for Harry to call back, I leaned back in my chair and let myself just think. Me, Nick, Thalia, and Eddie. Inseparables, for a few summers as kids. Dad had referred to us as "the club," and we had called ourselves the Mars Four, but the Mars Four was not exactly a club. I don't think we ever even tried to figure out what it was. It had just been something we talked about, something we identified ourselves as. . . .

My mind drifted back, and if longing or wishing could make a thing so, I'd have stepped right onto that Virginia beach again, back when life was so much simpler and so much less complicated.

WHEN WE KIDS had formed the Mars Four, we had known each other as long as we could remember. Our parents' summer cabins on the Virginia beach were within a hundred yards of each other, and the families had started coming to the beach before I was born; Nick and Eddie, the oldest of the Mars Four, could each just barely remember that there had been a first summer and that they had met then. For Thalia and me, the summer cabins had always been there.

The Mars Four idea probably hit me harder than any of the others. We came up with it in the summer when I turned eleven, which was about as old as anyone can be and take something like Mars Four seriously.

It had been a complicated summer, emotionally.

Thalia had been thirteen and already mooning around about Wade Gordon, the sixteen-year-old down the block, son of Harry Gordon, and eventually a real-estate salesman in Vail.

Wade had never been one of our group, and I think his major ability, at sixteen and for that matter at fifty, was looking good in a bathing suit. For most of the summer, Thalia never managed to exchange two sentences with him, but he gave her something to talk about nearly constantly. Meanwhile, I had a hopeless crush on Thalia.

Nick and Eddie were fifteen, just coming into their strength, without an ounce of fat on their bodies or fatigue in their spirits, constantly running, swimming, building things, playing chess, arguing, reading things to have more ideas what to argue about, getting into trouble, lying their way out of trouble, and making Mom and Mrs. Killeret wonder what it was going to be every time the phone rang. Mom always said that if the phone rang and it was a lifeguard, telling her that Nick had been in a shark attack, she'd have asked if the shark was all right.

Nick and Eddie fascinated me, and I tagged along when I could. I was only sporadically welcome around them, but sporadically is better than nothing.

It was 1969—to me, a great time. Campus riots, Vietnam, ghetto riots, wars and repression around the world, and the first big news stories about pollution, were mostly the incomprehensible noise that came on at the beginning of the TV news and made my parents mutter and complain. I learned what had been going on much later, from history books. The country's troubles, to an eleven-year-old boy, were mere backdrop. I was right in the middle of the exciting couple of years when you're a big kid and can do things—swim, play sports, go places by yourself, and all the other things that are fun at the beach in the summer—while still being a kid, and therefore wanting to do them. I had a great time, most of the time, and many casual friends everywhere on the beach and in town.

Still, compared to previous summers, it was often lonely. Eddie Killeret and Nick were off in the world of their own intense competition, and Nick was really closer to Eddie than he was to me. Thally, my friend, mentor, and guide to getting out of trouble, whose sidekick I had been for several summers, was going through her own peculiar experiments in growing up, and though I saw more of her than I did of my brother and his friend, it wasn't a very satisfying experience. Every other day or so, Thally and I would sit on the beach and she'd talk endlessly about who she liked, who she didn't, what she wore, what she'd never wear, and so forth, always returning to the eternal fascination of Wade Gordon. I'd have sat next to her while she read the dictionary aloud, just to be there.

Usually, though, Thalia was off with girls her own age, hanging around the concession stands on the boardwalk and having fits of giggles about whatever it was they talked about.

Yet the excitement of finally being a big kid myself outweighed all that. I was everywhere, all the time, as if I were afraid that they might roll up the beach and take it away, so on the whole, 1969 would have been a grand year, just being on the beach with my energy and newfound big kid status, without anything else at all.

What made it perfect was that men were landing on the moon. All the kids were moon-mad by July

20, the landing date, but some of us had been crazy for years before. My brother had had space program fever first, because he had been seven years old, and able to follow what was going on, when Alan Shepard flew. He and Eddie had been enthusiasts for every flight after that; they could still name everyone, American and Russian, who had ever been to space. By the later Gemini flights, I was big enough to be as hooked as they were.

Even kids who had never been space-crazed before were space-crazed that July. All of us could find the Sea of Tranquility on the face of the moon, and knew all the major maneuvers and steps that would have to be accomplished to get to and from the moon. We knew all the abbreviations—LM and CM and EVA and so forth. Almost any afternoon you could see model rocket launches, the thin white streaks arcing up over the beach, and the occasional kid swimming out frantically to try to retrieve his rocket.

In the first week we had been at the cabin, Nick had built the big Estes flying model of the Saturn V, three feet tall with miles of glued-on plastic detail, which never flew very well but looked impressive taking off. Nick stopped flying it after its sixth flight, when it came down in the ocean. Eddie swam out and rescued it, but a dunking in seawater is not good for cardboard and balsa. Nick carefully sanded and repainted it, but if you knew where to look you could see it was slightly bent. Now it hung, like a trophy, from the rafters of the cabin's big attic room where Nick and I slept.

The Mars Four started as a conversation on the beach, just after Armstrong, Collins, and Aldrin had departed lunar orbit and started the long fall back to Earth. Space fever was fading in the kid community already. They all seemed to think it was over, even though three astronauts were still far from Earth.

Since the families had all gone to the movies and then to the seafood shack together, it had been natural for us to drift out the door, away from the adults playing cards in the Killeret cabin. We wandered along the beach for a short distance and sat down near the top on the sea side of a big dune, to look at the stars. Nick and Eddie sat close together, so that if one of them thought of something dirty they could whisper it to each other and giggle; Thalia and I sat in front of them. I felt awkward and strange sitting next to her, but very happy; she was wearing a pink dress, the sleeveless tube-shaped sort of thing that was popular then, and white sandals with slight, clunky heels. To me she looked practically adult.

The sea was calm, and it was just late enough so that there weren't many people out; a few older teenagers had a bonfire about half a mile south of us, and we could occasionally hear snatches of the Beatles or the Doors drifting up toward us, but mostly it was just us, the birds, and the soft crash of waves onto the shore. I watched waves roll in, and stole very discreet sideways glances at Thalia, and was happy just to be there with everyone. After a while Nick and Eddie began to discuss the one subject about which either of them could talk forever: what they wanted to do when they grew up.

"I can't believe you're both planning that far ahead," Thalia said, after the two of them had been going on for a while. "I mean, I don't even know what I'm going to do next week. Not literally, I mean we'll still be here at the cabin and all, but you know what I mean. It just doesn't seem real to me that you could already be planning what to study in college."

"If I don't plan," Nick said, "I might not take the right stuff in high school."

"It's pretty competitive, getting into the kind of programs we want to," Eddie said, "and we can't all rely on our natural brilliance and good looks."

Thalia stuck her tongue out at him.

I thought about Nick and that Saturn V rocket model. I remembered that before he took it out of its box to start assembling it, he had to make sure that he had every tool on the "required" list laid out on the workbench in perfect order, and all the glue and the Q-Tips to apply it with. Nick probably did have the rest of his life planned.

I'd been drifting away mentally, starting to fall asleep. Nick said, "You know what Dad said; we could probably have had a man in orbit in 1950 if we'd really had to do it, like if there'd been no atomic bomb and the war had gone on that long or something. He says the real miracle is that there was ever any people or money to go to space with at all. Even now, they aren't sure how many flights there will be after this one."

I had heard Dad saying that too, but I hadn't thought about it. People would just go to the moon once, then stop?

"Well, I'm going to find a way to keep it going," Eddie said, firmly.

"Me too. Did I say I wasn't?" Nick replied.

Thalia said, very seriously, "I don't know what I'm going to do about space, but I know why I'm going to do it."

"Explicate for us, oh Lady of Mysteries," Eddie said.

I wasn't sure what "explicate" meant but Eddie was always pulling out big words to intimidate us younger kids with, and I figured it probably meant "keep talking." Either Thalia knew what it meant, or she made the same guess I did.

"Well, I'm not good at the science stuff, but the whole space and moon thing just seems so beautiful to me. You know the way some pieces of art are so beautiful that you can't imagine how the world could have existed before they were there? Or some things, like a cathedral, you look at them and you say, a whole century went by, with people getting born and growing up and dying and everything, and all that human time was worth it because they made that one thing? Well, that's kind of what I feel about going to the moon. Do I sound really stupid?"

"Not to me," I said, loyally.

"It's so . . . *grand* that I just like being in a world where it happens." Then, maybe because it was all getting so serious, she said, "Of course, Scott just wants to fly, right?"

"Rocket Boy is ready to go any minute," Nick agreed. "If we had five hundred Estes engines, we could strap them on him and that poor idiot child would be ready to go this minute."

"There's nothing wrong with wanting to fly," Eddie Killeret said, instantly becoming my hero. "If we're going to go there, somebody's got to fly."

It got darker. Waves rumbled gently, slowly onto the beach. Maybe the conversation was over for the night.

Around the older kids, I tried not to call too much attention to myself. I didn't want to be treated as Nick's little brother.

Maybe everyone was going to just sit there for a while and then go home to bed. We had done that many evenings before. A cool breeze began to blow in off the sea, rustling the spots of long grass, and the waves picked up slightly, but it was still warm and still quiet. I felt my eyes drifting shut.

When Thalia spoke I almost jumped. "Wouldn't it be really, really cool," she said, "if fifty years from now—that would only be 2019—we could all come back to the beach?"

"I'll just be retiring," Nick said.

"Yeah, well, if we all came back to the cabin, and we were celebrating the first baby born on Mars?" Thalia persisted.

I was confused, and asked, "The first baby born on Mars?"

"I get it," Eddie said. "Thally's right. A baby on Mars would be the real sign that people had gotten serious about space. Because if a baby is born there, it's going to be because people have gone there to settle for good. By that time there'll probably be ten big cities on the moon."

"That's where I want to live," I said, immediately.

Nick made a funny noise, and said, "Jeez, this is hard to believe, but it's true. You probably *will* live on the moon someday, Scott. If you want to be a pilot you'll probably be flying a regular route between the moon and a space station in orbit around the Earth. Like in that movie, *2001*, you know? The PanAm Space Clipper. You can bring me back from a business trip up there, and then we'll both fly down to Earth to get to the reunion down here on the beach."

"It's still going to be a big job," Eddie said. "All the rest of our lives."

Nick's tone was surprisingly serious. "A big job is not the same thing as an impossible job."

"Wouldn't it be cool," Thalia said, "if we all promised, right now, that we were going to help it happen, and be a part of making the first settlement on Mars? Maybe even one of us would fly there, or live there, but not necessarily—just, like, help it any way we can. And in 2019 we'll have a big party here to celebrate however far we've gotten. You know, Scott won't even retire till 2023. None of us will even be seventy yet. Maybe we can all go on a trip just to see the settlement on Mars. We might even have *grandchildren* there."

When Thalia mentioned grandchildren, I was amazed to realize what a long time it would take.

"Tickets are going to be expensive," Nick said.

"Well, then, maybe we should start saving now," she said, teasing him. It was just like Nick to worry about something like that when we were talking about going to Mars fifty years in the future.

"All right, if we can afford a ticket, and they're selling them, we'll go," Nick said.

Eddie snorted. "Try and stop any of us from buying one, no matter what they cost."

"You have to promise to work to make it happen," Thalia said, "otherwise, it's just wishing."

" 'I promise to work to get people to Mars in the next fifty years'?" Nick asked. "Is that all we have to say?"

"That should do nicely," Thalia said. "I'll start off if you like. I promise to work to get people to Mars in the next fifty years. And I promise to come back here to celebrate in 2019. Your turn."

I repeated what she had said, then Eddie repeated it, and finally Nick did. We all sat quietly till it began to get chilly. I don't know what the others were doing, but I was trying to figure out if we had really done anything.

About the time I was starting to shiver, Mom called

for Nick and me. The group broke up in a quick little chorus of good-nights and see-you-tomorrows and so forth. Nick and I walked back up the beach, sand crunching under our feet, toward the bright yellow square of the cabin light, and I remember him resting a hand on my shoulder for just a second. Maybe he was just steadying himself from a bad step in the sand.

That evening, in the upstairs room, Nick fell asleep instantly, as he always did, but I lay awake a little while. The dust motes danced in the moonlight from the window, surrounding the Saturn model that hung on fishline from the ceiling. It glowed ghostly white, and in the dim light the glue spots, and the traces of re-sanding and repainting, vanished, and it seemed to hang there just as if, somehow, the whole big rocket were really in space. The dust motes seemed like distant twinkling stars, obscured and revealed by the Saturn and its shadow as it slowly turned. The nozzles (painted silver—in the dark you couldn't see that they were lumpy over the slightly charred parts) would swing into the brighter light, and back out; a while later, the escape tower, CM, and third stage, all painted stark white with black detailing, would swoop into the bright light for just a moment. I watched it turn around one more time, and then I was asleep, too.

WHEN I LOOKED at the clock, I realized I must have been daydreaming for an hour; that was probably the longest I'd spent just sitting in a chair, truly doing nothing, since my first year in the Air Force. I wondered how long it was going to take Harry Gordon to find me a lawyer, and if maybe I should start looking for one on my own. As involved in business as I was, and with a certain amount of time on the social circuit, I knew plenty of lawyers, and I had a nagging feeling that I knew someone who would be perfect.

It was a bitter joke when I realized it was Thalia. Beginning a year and a half before the divorce, she'd been running her small prisoner's-and-victim's-rights group (I had never quite understood how those two fit together). Much of it was lobbying and testifying in Congress and the state legislatures, but she also fought cases in court, helping victims sue the criminal and helping criminals sue the state. At least she had litigated plenty of civil cases, very much in the public eye, which was more than could be said for anyone Gordon was likely to find, and she might have a good idea who I should talk to. Though we weren't exactly friends since the divorce, my ex was a thoroughly honest person and I could trust whatever she recommended.

Just the same, I thought I'd wait a while to call her and ask; maybe if I didn't have anyone by end of day Monday, which seemed improbable. I didn't want to create unnecessary times in which to quarrel, and it bothered me to feel as if I were asking for free legal advice. I picked up the Yellow Pages.

What you can find there, unfortunately, is mostly "We'll make them pay" ads, or phone numbers with no information, but after spending the better part of an hour reading through the fine print, I found four names that I recognized, people I knew socially who seemed to be senior partners or proprietors of firms that might handle this kind of thing. I tried the first one, using my personal connection to get past the secretaries.

He talked with me for about ten minutes about a charity board we were both on. Then, before I could tell him my business, he told me that his firm couldn't take on any additional cases at this time. Strange that a business would turn away business, especially a big case with a lot of publicity value, but I didn't know much about law.

The next firm told me they had an unspecified conflict of interest. The guy I knew at the third firm, an old Air Force buddy, called me back after half an hour. "I hate to say this, Scott, but I just can't." He didn't give a reason and I didn't ask for one. The fourth and last one told me she couldn't afford to handle "such a sensitive case" at this time.

Sunlight was slanting east across the rug now, and the air conditioner had come on to cope with the late-afternoon heat of Indian summer. I wondered what to do next. As I was putting in a load of laundry, the phone rang.

It was Harry Gordon. He'd been calling around. Nobody wanted the case. I asked, but we hadn't called any of the same firms. Gordon would keep trying but wasn't hopeful.

"If we can't find anyone else, do you have somebody around in your firm who could handle it for me? Any lawyer is better than not having one."

Harry hemmed, hawed, and backpedaled pretty hard.

"Look," I said. "You obviously have some reason or other not to take the case. I bet it's the same reason why the other firms don't want it. And it might help me if I knew what that reason is. Why don't you just tell me? I've known you all my life; you're the family lawyer; you could at least tell me what the hell is going on."

Suddenly he had to take another call, and then his secretary called to say he'd get back to me.

It looked like I'd have to renew my quest for a lawyer in the morning. Tomorrow would be Friday, though, and I wondered how many lawyers would be around town to talk to me.

When you're up to your neck in bad publicity, you need to stay inside the news cycle, so I drafted a press release that expressed my admiration for Michael James and for Marc Clement, my sorrow at their deaths, my feeling of empathy for AnnaBeth James, and my belief that it would be shown that I was not at fault. All of that was true, so it wasn't that hard to organize it; coming up with words that couldn't possibly be misread as trite, dismissive, callous, or duplicitous took longer. I wrote it out carefully and then began calling my way through the deck of reporters' cards.

Since she'd been so helpful, I called Nikki Earl first. She recorded the statement in my voice, and then added, "I'll copy this and give one to Ken Elgin, so you don't have to call him. We're going to dinner tonight," she said. "I probably ought to thank you for that."

"Huh," I said, mildly surprised. "You work for the most liberal network, and he writes for the most conservative newsmagazine—"

"Yeah, but he's cute, for a Republican. And at least we understand each other's jobs, which is more than our exes did, and besides, he said the magic words that go right to any single mother's heart—'I'll pay for a sitter.'" Her voice got more serious. "Something Ken and I have both been noticing, Scott, that we thought maybe you should know about. PSN and *USReport* are both so small that we have just one reporter on the job, and you know we know you and we're sympathetic. The bigger outfits seem to be putting all their attack dogs on you. We don't know why, but it doesn't look good. You be careful."

"I will. And I know where I can go to get accurately quoted."

She chuckled. "I knew you'd see my point. Good luck. If I were you, I wouldn't watch television news for a while." We rang off. At least I had two friends in the media.

I left several messages on answering machines before Bryn Pogwell picked up the phone for CBS. She recorded my statement and then said, "I really appreciate your calling back with that statement." Then, after a long pause, she said, "I really don't like the editing they're doing. I think you were candid and fair with reporters this morning, and I don't think CBS is going to be fair with you."

"Should I watch CBS tonight?" I asked, my heart sinking.

"Evening news. Probably very early in the broadcast. I'm really sorry. I was overruled. I think you'll be pretty angry. I just wanted to say that it wasn't my idea, even if you don't believe me."

"I'll try to believe you," I said.

"Thanks." She hung up.

I got three more answering machines before I hit the reporter from NBC News, who was having dinner at his desk. After he realized that I was just calling with a follow-up statement, he seemed to relax and said, "Okay, I'll relay it to Brown. It's his story now."

"They've moved it to another desk already?" I asked.

"Yeah, I had a disagreement with management about how to use the material, and they took me off it and gave it to Brown. I'll see that he gets your statement. Of course he'll do whatever he wants with it. Thanks for calling." He hung up.

I set the phone down. The evening news was an hour and a half away; till then there must be something I could do. I thought about calling Nick, but we'd really drifted a long way apart. Nick was a big success at Republic Wright, their youngest corporate VP. People who are succeeding rarely have time for failures.

I tried to take a nap while I waited for the evening news. I still couldn't sleep.

Just before six, I set the phone to not ring, and the answering machine to pick up automatically, because I knew from bitter experience that if it was really a hatchet job, they'd be calling me while it was on the air, hoping to catch me while I was still mad and get an over-the-top reaction. I set the VCR to tape NBC while I watched CBS.

They didn't air any of my expressions of sympathy, or any of my definite statements. They did include every time I said that things weren't known yet, that I couldn't answer until I talked to a lawyer, and so forth. In between they interjected shouted questions that I was pretty sure I hadn't been asked at all. If I had been casually watching this on the evening news, I would be saying to myself, "This guy is a crook."

When I played the tape from NBC News, it was even worse.

I went to the answering machine, re-read my statement into the outgoing message, and left the ringer turned off on the phone. Maybe some local radio station would call up, get that message, tape it, and play it.

For an hour, as it got dark outside, I just drifted

around the house looking for any old thing to amuse me. My earlier attack of nostalgia led me to my copy of the family photo albums. If I had stared any harder I might have fallen forward through the photo onto the warm summer beach itself. Right then I'd have loved to.

THAT NIGHT, WHEN we made the promise on the beach, was the beginning of the Mars Four. I think maybe we got the idea for a name like that from the Chicago Seven trial that had just happened, or maybe from the Mercury Seven astronauts. I'm pretty sure we didn't dub ourselves the Mars Four that night; it must have been some time the following day, or even a few days later. But anyway, for the rest of the summer, it was both a joke we used on anyone who seemed to be too serious, and at the same time a unique, special thing that was just ours. Like most kids, we were pretty shy about the things that were most serious to us, and it was easiest to speak of them as a joke.

If somebody got an extra scoop of ice cream, we'd say "Shouldn't you be saving that money for your ticket to Mars?" Or if someone did something hazardous, we'd say "Don't get killed before we go to Mars." Late in the summer, Mrs. Pendergast caught Thalia kissing Wade Gordon behind the Pendergasts' cabin, and grounded her for three days. (Incidentally, she broke my heart into a thousand pieces.) After she "got out on parole," as Nick and Eddie called it, Nick said, "I'm afraid you are just not living up to the standards we expect of the Mars Four."

Gradually I came to think that I was the only person who still took it seriously, and that I'd been too young to realize that they were just kidding.

The Mars Four jokes stopped when we all got home and started school again. I don't remember any Mars Four jokes the next summer, though probably there were some. I kept quiet about it anyway, and made myself forget it as much as I could—though that was surprisingly hard. Young boys aren't the most rational people in the world about flying in space, or going to Mars, or keeping promises no matter what.

I WAS HUNGRY, and the photo album was only further depressing me. I could hear the answering machine clicking in the background, over and over, as it sent the outgoing message to who knew how many callers. I closed the album, got up, and got dinner: a diet Coke, some Doritos, and a thin ham sandwich, all I had the appetite for. The answering machine was still telling everyone in the universe that I was sorry for everyone's pain but confident that I would be completely exonerated. It must have fielded fifty calls in two hours.

I finished the meal, such as it was, thought about microwaving a breakfast burrito, and decided that I'd rather go to bed. The phone wasn't ringing quite so often anymore, so maybe they'd found someone else to bother, or maybe everyone who needed a copy of my message had one. I got up, stretched, put the dishes into the sink, and wondered whether I'd be able to get to sleep tonight.

The doorbell rang. Well, perhaps it would be Ken Elgin, or even Fred Gernsback—someone sympathetic, anyway.

I opened the door and found my brother Nick standing there with a pizza. "Is mushroom and roasted garlic still your favorite?" he asked, and

walked in past me, setting it down on my table.
"Have you eaten nothing at all, or just a sandwich
and a handful of chips?"

I closed the door. His pricey Italian suit was un-
wrinkled and perfectly in place, his shoes practically
glowed, and his neat mustache and close-cropped hair
looked fresh from the barber. He'd have looked like
that after swimming away from a shipwreck; Mom
had always sworn that he'd been born fully dressed
with his shoes shined. "You look good. When did
you become psychic?"

"About the time I decided to take a second job in
pizza delivery," he said. "If there are two clean glasses
and two clean plates in here, I'll be pleasantly surprised, and we can have a family dinner and I can
tell you about what's going on."

I grabbed the required stuff from the dishwasher,
and pulled out a big bottle of diet Coke from the
fridge. While I did, the phone answering machine ac-
tivated twice more.

Nick said, "By now that outgoing message of yours
must be on every channel except the Cartoon Network."

"I figured I couldn't improve matters by talking to
them," I said.

"Probably you're right, for tonight." He served the
pizza and I realized I was starving. With an amused
little smile, he watched me wolf two pieces while he
ate a few bites of his, carefully, with a knife and fork.
"I thought you'd probably need the food. When
you're upset, you don't eat. If you're ready to discuss
business, I do have some comforting news, but I'm
afraid it starts with some additional bad news."

I took a sip of the diet Coke and said, "You still
look as good as ever; how do you do it?"

"An outward mark of inner superiority," he said, smiling. It was an old joke between us. "How is Amos?"

"Pretty much a normal kid. He's doing peewee wrestling, so I'll have to learn something about wrestling. His sitter says he was heartbroken about MJ. He and I are going down to the cabin to spend some time next weekend."

Nick nodded. "This is the best time of year there, really, unless you insist on swimming. The tourists are gone and the beach is perfect for walking."

"Yeah," I said, putting down some more pizza. How had I ever thought I wasn't hungry?

For the next twenty minutes or so, between bites, I talked about Amos, mostly, and Thalia a little. Nick filled me in on what he was allowed to say about what was going in his life—which wasn't much. He had never married, he couldn't discuss much about work, and his life was nearly as busy as mine. Nick worked for Republic Wright, where he was the youngest vice-president at the company. He held the plum job there, the one he had probably wanted ever since he was ten years old—he ran their "black shop," the secret projects development facility. I'd gotten used to Nick not talking about work, and he barely had a personal life. As usual, he said he was busy, that there was some interesting new hardware that would go public within a few years, and that he spent ridiculous amounts of time commuting by corporate jet between DC, San Diego, and Scorpion Shack. "It's the only time I have to do any paperwork," he said cheerfully. "If they ever leave me in one city for an entire week, the administration of Scorpion Shack will collapse." He set aside the crust from his single piece of pizza—I

noted how perfect the arc he had cut with his knife
was. "Have I given you enough food and brotherly
support to prepare you to face the world again?"

I took another sip of the diet Coke, looked at the
remains of the pizza, and nodded. "Yes, thanks. I'll
nibble some more while you talk. Jeez. I needed somebody to take care of me just then."

"Well, we *are* family," he said, a little uncomfort-
ably. Nick doesn't like people to remember when he
does them favors; it makes him self-conscious. He's
always been that way.

He made a precise little tent with his fingers and
said, "This is a surprise, I expect, and not a pleasant
one. Curtiss Aerospace is selling you, and everybody
else, down the river, just as fast as they can. Furthermore, since they are the majority stockholder in ASU,
ASU will also be settling. All of that will prejudice
the case against the remaining defendants, which in-
cludes you, ShareSpace, and RW."

"Why?"

He shrugged. "They've got by far the deepest
pockets in the business. If there's a big financial settlement, Curtiss will be the one that pays the most.
So by settling early and making it easier for Haverford, they limit how much comes out of their pockets,
and they make it very likely that Republic Wright
will lose enough to go bankrupt or have to sell out.
Curtiss has aspired to be the one and only aerospace
company for a long time, and this might be their final
step.

"Then, too, every player in the aerospace industry
knows that space is privatizing sooner or later. The
communications companies need reliable space trans-
port for communications satellites, the shuttles are

getting old, and the federal government doesn't have much of a commitment to space anymore. But government, for the moment, is still the biggest single customer for launch services, and most of the government's business is currently going to Curtiss. That helps to keep us permanently in second place.

"Now, that would change if we had a more competitive launcher—and we're about to."

"I've heard about the Starcraft series," I said.

He nodded. "We try to keep that hushed up, of course, but a project that size can't be concealed. It's a miracle that *Aviation Week* hasn't already done a cover story about it. Yes, the first group of the Starcraft series is very close to flight test. Igor Jagavitz thinks this is what will make us a 'storefront space agency'—that's his expression for the kind of convenient, efficient service we could provide, with a reliable operations schedule and standardized pricing. My best guess is that Curtiss is a few years behind us in everything—they've maintained a commitment to their established products and services, because those were dominating the market. Therefore, in a year or two, Curtiss's launcher business can expect a serious, across-the-board market challenge from RW's Starcraft—unless something happens to RW in the interim. If something serious *enough* happens, Curtiss might own Republic Wright, six months from now, and reap the profits themselves. I'd imagine they're thinking that settling one large lawsuit is nothing compared to maintaining their dominance of the market. I don't need to tell you there are plenty of people in Washington who sympathize with Curtiss's view that there really ought to be just one big aerospace company—and just who it ought to be.

"So this is about RW's survival, which is why I'm going to spend a good part of tomorrow making sure that everyone else at the company sees it that way. We'll have to fight this with everything we have. But we do have plenty of resources, and we also have something the other side doesn't have—a real case in law and logic. And that's your good news. You're not alone. You're a long way from being alone. Now, no despair, no self-pity, and don't get sentimental and thank me, because that will embarrass us both. Besides, I have perfectly good business reasons for doing this for you, reasons that would be good even if I didn't know you from Adam. Is that all right?"

"Okay. Thanks, Nick." I felt my shoulders relaxing, my attention increasing, a calm awareness of everything; tennis had been my high school and college sport, and this was how it felt to be psyched before walking out onto the court. It was a million times better than the way I had been feeling an hour and a half ago.

After more small talk, mostly about things decades in the past, he left, and I tossed the empty pizza box and soda bottle into the wastebasket. Maybe due to his lingering influence, I got the clean dishes out of the dishwasher, and loaded the dirty ones in, while I listened to a music station on the radio; I even hummed along when an old Beatles song, "Get Back," came on. That had been all over the air during one of the best of those old summers. Not that there had been any bad ones . . .

I tried to remember if I ever *had* had any place, other than the dishwasher, for my coffee cups. Eventually I just picked a vacant stretch of cupboard shelf—there were plenty of those. This had been my house for more than two years, and I was finally moving in.

At one in the morning, tired but finally relaxed, knowing Nick would be on the job, I sank into my bed, and slept soundly.

CHAPTER FOUR

NICK:

Whenever I had been away for a few days, walking into my office in Washington always led directly into a series of unpleasant discoveries. My office at Scorpion Shack, down on the Texas Gulf Coast, was a workplace, a friendly, comfortable home base. Republic Wright maintained an office for me at corporate HQ in San Diego, but I was there so rarely that it held almost nothing of mine. The DC office was different—it was the place where problems came in, and where I decided what to do about them. In Washington, the inbox was always bursting with new crises, the outbox was always primed with notes to send accountants, engineers, and scientists scurrying in circles, and the phone rang all the time.

The first thing I did that morning was to give Roger Przeworski a call; he was an in-house Republic Wright lawyer, the legal consultant for the Starcraft project. In putting him on this case, I would have to be careful to use him only on issues that had a direct impact on Starcraft. If nothing else, I would get the benefit of his shrewd, impartial judgment.

I asked him to prepare an assessment of the impact of the James lawsuit on the space tourism business, and the effect of that on the eventual market for the StarBird I, which was far into its prototype stage. I further asked him to assess our probability of securing a favorable outcome (for us) from the James family case, depending on various strategies that ranged from outright surrender to fighting to the last ditch.

Roger said he could give me an oral report by end of day. I cleared him and his two assistants to get whatever information they needed from anywhere within Scorpion Shack, had my secretary send out the memo, and moved on.

Even for me, the last few months had been frenetic. Republic Wright needed nothing short of a miracle, but the Starcraft project *was* a miracle, very nearly ready to go. Now it was a race between my shop and disaster for my company. So far my shop was coming in ahead, but it was still a race; the best new technology in the world does you no good if it arrives a week after you're out of money and credit.

The case against Scott and the aerospace companies added one more ball to be juggled. I had to make sure that Starcraft survived as a viable commercial project. If the James family could sue space tourism out of existence, the market we needed for the middle phase of the Starcraft program would be lost. RW had a vital interest in winning this case, and it was certainly winnable. I had to make absolutely sure that that was clear to the rest of management, before I could put my full time and attention on Starcraft.

I should have known better. By midmorning I had a sinking feeling that this was spinning out of control. Few of my fellow executives could see how much of Republic Wright's future was tied up in this. I had found only one ally—Caitlin Delamartin, the VP for Market Development. Given what was expected of us, if Starcraft failed as a commercial project, the first heads to roll would be Caitlin's and mine, probably within a few months, but they would be far from the last and in a few years there would be nothing left of RW's current management.

Unfortunately, no one wanted to look more than a few months into the future. The finance people told us that settling would have a fixed price tag, and however much we might make eventually, by not settling, the gains were indefinite. Community Relations worried about appearing to be too tough on a grieving mother. Flight Ops was more worried about losing positions within ASU to Curtiss than they were about whether there would be anything to fly. Production profoundly didn't care; they just built whatever they were told to.

By the time I met Caitlin for lunch to plan strategy, we were both very discouraged. "I don't like to say this," she said, "but it seems to me that many of these people have already given up, or maybe they gave up a while ago, when we lost the last big bid on ISS or when Curtiss got the commitment from the Air Force for a bunch of Delta launches. A majority of our senior management seems to have decided that we're doomed to be another Curtiss brand name, like Douglas and Chance-Vought and Convair and all the others who were swallowed up before us. So they look at this situation and they say, 'Oh, let's just do whatever the Puget Sound big boys want to do, we don't want to have done anything they didn't like when we go under and they buy us out.' "

"I'm sure that's part of it," I said. "And besides, many of our people spent their whole lives in an environment where the federal government was our only customer, and we were one of a handful of suppliers. If all this ends with us as a branch of the Curtiss Aerospace Monopoly, many of our older executives will be much more comfortable than they would out in the world of real free enterprise, where Jagavitz is trying to lead us."

"But they won't *get* that security they're looking for," Caitlin said, sighing, and pouring herself more coffee from the pot on the table. "If Curtiss wins this, we're *all* doomed. Our production capacity is redundant to theirs; they'll just shut most of Republic Wright down, take over Starcraft, and cherry-pick our talent." She gulped her coffee. "We're in a grow-or-die situation; we have to get ourselves a growth path for new sales, and privatization is the only one that Curtiss isn't sitting square in the middle of already." She pushed her red hair back from her face and pulled out a small pad. "Let's see what we can figure out. I contacted all the people you asked me to talk to, and none of them is any better than neutral. How did you do?"

"The only person in the top leadership we haven't talked to so far is Jagavitz." Igor Jagavitz was CEO of Republic Wright, a crusty old engineer who'd come up through airframe design. Neither of us had any doubt that he'd be on our side, but a corporate CEO governs by consent. He could do little if the rest of management opposed him. "We have a meeting with him, and whichever other executives are also in Washington today, at one-thirty."

"Who else is in town?" she asked, scribbling a note.

"Barbara Quentin, who we should be able to persuade," I said, "and Riscaveau, unfortunately."

Caitlin made a face; that's what most people did when they heard Riscaveau's name, these days. Also like everyone else, she said, "Well, you can't argue with his results; he's caught more industrial spies and intercepted more stolen information than anyone else I've ever heard of. I suppose it's the way he insists on being thorough."

"I guess," I said. "He's certainly thorough about checking out everyone for *my* operation. And he's never vetted someone and then had to come back and tell me he screwed up and the guy shouldn't be working for me. I've never seen anyone manage *that* before—normally every system has a leak or two."

Caitlin nodded and turned back to her notes. "Well, we can't uninvite him, anyway, irritating as he is. Now, it happens I have a meeting on an unrelated matter with Jagavitz, at 12:45, before our meeting. I'll try to squeeze in a few minutes to brief him on what you and I are up to. I have a pretty good rapport with the guy. That's our first resource . . ." she made a note on the pad. ". . . Jagavitz will back us." She drew a line, dividing her notebook page into two columns, which she labeled RESOURCES/US and VULNERABILITIES/THEM.

"Now, resource two—we head up two of the more dynamic divisions of RW. So we have employees who we can count on to work late and do extra stuff for us during the campaign. I can't picture any of the bean counters in finance staying late to work on selling out the company and losing their jobs."

I nodded; it was a good point.

"Three, there's the prestige of your division; you're

still the king of the status heap around here, Nick, and you know it."

I could have tried to demur, but it would have rung hollow; what she said was the simple truth. Aerospace hasn't really lost the mystique of super-science that it picked up during the Second World War. Much of my power and influence within Republic Wright derives from my connection to our secret city of five thousand people in Kennedy County, Texas, with its five major labs—aerodynamics/supercomputing, metallurgy/materials science, fuels chemistry, avionics, and what we call "fundamental physics" to try not to give too much away of what we're doing. A world-of-tomorrow magic clings to our having the world's best design supercomputers, and our own machinists' shops, crucible-metals plant, and ceramics shop—not to mention three runways, each of which could handle a loaded B 52, and two launchpads—all where most maps show a big empty space on the Gulf Coast. Anybody who goes into aerospace has at least a touch of the romantic and a little feel for history, and therefore can't help being impressed by the kind of operation I head up.

Caitlin quickly enumerated the other places in the company where we had leverage, and the places where we didn't, and it looked to us as if we probably could secure a razor-thin agreement to fight the case out in the way we wanted.

BARBARA QUENTIN, THE head of Issues Management, smiled when I came into the meeting. She might or might not be on my side already, but I thought she would listen. Andrew Riscaveau, the security chief, didn't bother to look up from doodling on his pad. He would never be on my side; each of us had grudges against the other, dating back to well before we'd attained our present positions. It was unfortunate to have him here, but as head of a major section, he had his rights.

After Jagavitz arrived, Caitlin and I made our case that RW needed to fight the *Columbia* lawsuit, using the basic points we'd thrashed out at lunch. I was encouraged that Barbara Quentin nodded at most of the key points, and unsurprised that Riscaveau sat with his arms folded across his chest and a smug little smile.

When we finished and Jagavitz asked for comments, Riscaveau spoke at once. "The first thing I want to say is that we've got more or less carte blanche, from a security standpoint. I've done a lot of research and of course we're doing constant checkups. Lots of people know we have a project called Starcraft, and a few of them have heard of one or two components of the thing—the StarBooster, usually, and sometimes the StarBird—but not always very accurately. And we've kept most real information out of the trade press. So if we cancel it, no one will have any idea that we were close to success, and if we go ahead with it, our hand isn't tipped very much. Word would get out eventually, of course, but basically we can do whatever we want without any major reaction in the outside world. And even though he doesn't like all the hoops I make him jump through, a lot of the credit for the successful security goes to Nick Blackstone, who has been a big help." He nodded at me politely.

"Now," he went on, "the question is really whether we should fight this suit to keep our options open with regard to Starcraft. Nick says that if we win the suit—no matter what it costs us—we save Starcraft, and that way Starcraft can save the company. But let's seriously consider—is Starcraft a good idea? You're talking about killing expendable launchers, which have been a highly profitable bread and butter business for us for thirty years. Starcraft could easily trigger cutthroat competition that might completely destroy both our expendables business *and* Curtiss's.

"Besides, we've got access into the Chinese, Indian, Brazilian, and Korean markets by agreeing to subcontract so many of the systems on our expendables to facilities in their countries. We've moved thirty thousand jobs overseas in the last ten years, just to get market access. If we destroy the jobs that we gave them, you think the rising markets won't retaliate? They'll shut us out of their markets, *and* get serious about building a competing launch business."

Jagavitz raised his hand off the table, and nodded at both me and Riscaveau. "There is something that we have to think about here. First of all—bear with me on this, Nick—there's no magic about Starcraft—except that we've got it *now*. If we can make it work, so can someone in Beijing, or Rio, or probably anywhere eventually. So there will, will, will be a collapse in launch prices. We can either *make* that price collapse happen, and reap the profits—or we can keep hoping it won't, and jump into the pool with the other sharks once it does. I have to say, I'd rather drive than ride.

"In my gut, I feel, we've got to have Starcraft. We traded away first-rate American jobs for overseas markets, and as part of the trade we gave them a lot of our technology. Now, if Starcraft kills the expendables business . . . we'll have made everything we gave them *worthless*. We'll have those sharp-trading bastards over a barrel, and do what we want to them, and I have to admit I'd enjoy the hell out of *that*." He grinned in a way that always made me want to shudder; it was an expression that wouldn't have looked out of place on General Patton—or on Al Capone.

"*You'd* enjoy it?" Barbara Quentin said, grinning. Jagavitz started, but gestured for her to go ahead.

She leaned back in her chair and lightly ticked her points off with her fingers. "Do you realize what it would mean from an Issues Management standpoint? Just to begin with, the IAM and every other union would adore us. So would both political parties and the stock market. We'd be apple pie and mother to a hundred million Americans for five years afterwards. We'd have the kind of rep that AT&T got for operating communications during the Second World War—as golden as the glory days at Apple, Xerox, Ford, or General Dynamics. I know people here are always saying we mustn't make technical decisions based on PR considerations, but I can tell you, if you go this route, we'll be the most popular company in America inside three months."

Jagavitz nodded. "It's a consideration. All right, then, one more thing I'm thinking: yes, Starcraft kills our expendables business. But that just loses us a division that wasn't making money. Starcraft also kills *Curtiss*'s expendables business—if we're aggressive about getting StarCore II and StarBird flying, it also kills off their new expendable heavy lift, and cuts into their shuttle. And then we *clobber* them the way they did us. Payback time. It's a big play for all the marbles—and I didn't get into this business to be number two."

Riscaveau said, "May I raise just one more point? We have no idea how big, or how small, the market for launch services and general space transportation may really be. Maybe with the price cut we'll get it all back in volume—from tourism, from DBS media systems, from being able to do repairs in geosynchronous orbit for the first time, from government contracts to go up there and knock down all those old top stages that are hazards to astrogation. It could happen. I gotta admit that. But maybe the market for space transportation is actually only what it is now. Maybe the truth is that the few people who really, really have to go to space will pay whatever they have to pay, and nobody else will pay a dime. And in that case what we're doing is grabbing up all the business, sure, but we're also reducing what we can charge for it. We could wind up a hundred percent of a barely profitable market, instead of fifteen percent of a super-lucrative one, which is what we are now. I just wanted to point out that that's a problem."

Jagavitz nodded a couple of times and said, "This is a problem, possibly, something we should think about, eh? I see it is in our interests in the long term to continue Starcraft. But as Mr. Riscaveau and Barbara both made very clear before the meeting, the costs of fighting this lawsuit may run very high. So *for the moment*, we will play to win, big. We'll try to get a precedent in our favor. But if the bet starts to look worse, we'll reverse, quick. And along with the policy," he added, looking straight at me with a slight twinkle in his eye, "I would point out that one of us is heavily involved due to a family connection . . . and if that relative were to take a more aggressive stance . . . it might influence my decision in the future. Does one of us have the personal funds needed, eh?"

It was as much as an order to back Scott with my own money, but an order I was happy to receive. Jagavitz wasn't willing to declare for our side, yet, but he was practicing a very tilted neutrality.

"I think everything can be made to work out," I said.

From the way Riscaveau glared at me, and straightened his tie and vest, I knew we had done well.

Caitlin and I agreed, over a quick cup of coffee after the meeting, that Jagavitz had gone as far as he could go today; he wouldn't let RW settle out of court right away, but getting the Board to wade in and supply the deep pockets would be our problem. After shaking hands on our success, I went back to my office, thinking it would only take me a few minutes to find Scott a lawyer, given what I was prepared to pay.

By about three o'clock that afternoon, I had determined that obtaining any top-drawer lawyer who knew anything about space or aviation law was going to be more than tough. It had all the marks of the fix being in; the four firms at the top of my list all had been put on retainer by Curtiss, supposedly to supply "advice" to Jasper Haverford, probably just to make them unavailable. It was good that Republic Wright was going to play to win, because Curtiss certainly was.

The phone rang. "Mr. Blackstone, I have Edgar Killeret, from Curtiss Aerospace, on the line. He wouldn't say what it was about."

"Put him through," I said.

Eddie Killeret and I had been friends, rivals, comrades, opponents, or allies, in everything, since we could speak. The Blackstone summer cabin was two doors down and one across from the Killeret cabin, and our families both went so far back in the tight, intertwined world of aviation that Eddie's father had flown as a test pilot under my grandfather's skeptical eye. From the age of three we'd raced each other, competed at every game, spent hours together arguing and bickering, watched each other's backs against bullies. In college we'd played lacrosse for rival teams, dated some of the same girls, and sometimes called each other for hours at a time just to talk. But since we had become each other's counterparts at RW and Curtiss—he ran their black shop in southeast Utah, known as "Ghost Town"—we hadn't communicated much.

As always, Eddie cut right to business. "Nick, I'm calling because I imagine you will be involved in all the sound and fury about the *Columbia* accident."

"You're right. I'm up to my neck in it."

"Well, I thought you ought to know about something. You know that Curtiss is planning to settle with the James family out of court, and they'll probably vote their shares so that ASU does the same, leaving Scott, ShareSpace, RW, and whoever in the lurch?"

"I'd heard."

"The decision is *not* unanimous here at Curtiss. Some of us think it would be utterly stupid to destroy space tourism and the private market for a temporary advantage like this. Unfortunately, we've lost every vote so far."

"Do you mean there's a chance that decision might be reversed?"

I could see him, in my mind's eye, sitting at a desk in an office not unlike mine, looking out across the desert from his windows; just as he had when we were boys together, and he had to tell me something that he figured I wouldn't want to hear, he'd be looking up at the ceiling, lips pressed together. Sure enough, a moment later he gave his characteristic little sigh and said, "Well, no, I don't think the decision will be reversed." He sighed. "To tell you the truth, this is nearly a purely social call. I was worried about Scott, and I hated the idea of my company being on the wrong side of this thing, and of personally being on the losing side. I just wanted to tell somebody—and who else could I tell?"

"I really appreciate your calling—I'll relay the word to Scott."

Eddie said, "Thank you for listening. Nobody over here will. I wish I were calling with support. The accident is a bad thing all around for the business, but it will be a much worse thing if it sets back the future, the way *Challenger* did."

"I agree," I said, "and I'm sure Scott does, and I'll pass along your message."

"Have you—uh, been having trouble finding counsel?"

"Is there a reason to think that I will?"

"There's every stone wall Curtiss can put in your path," Killeret said. "It's disgraceful. My company is behaving as if we were the plaintiffs, and I don't understand it at all. No doubt you've run into our little 'retainer' program, to lock up most law firms with expertise in aerospace."

"I have," I admitted.

The pause stretched on, and I realized that Killeret probably didn't feel he could say anything any more critical about his own corporation, but he certainly wanted to. Finally, I said, "I'll pass your concern and sympathy along to Scott. He's feeling very alone."

"I bet. Did you catch CNN or any of the network coverage?"

"No."

"Well, from what I've seen, I think they're building up for a real hatchet job on Scott, on the evening news. It sounds like they will really play up Share-Space's having fired him. You know and I know that nothing Scott could have done would have changed the outcome, but I'm afraid the media has already found for the plaintiff."

"Well," I said, "I guess I'll have to watch some of the coverage. And on Scott's behalf, I really appreciate the support. It means a lot at the moment, and he'll be glad to hear from an old friend." I realized what a long time it had been, and asked, "Did you even know he and Thalia were divorced?"

"I think that's the last time I heard from either of them—just a short note from Thalia. I was really sorry to hear about it. Their son must be—what, five, now?"

"Ten."

He sighed. "Where does the time go? Anyway, I'm working on doing more for Scott than a friendly phone call, but I don't think I can say more about it until I know more. Meanwhile, does he have a private line I can call, just to offer support?"

I told him the number, and thanked him again. We spoke awkwardly for a few minutes about how little time we both had, how hard we both worked, and the general frustrations of fast-track career life; so much was confidential, or supposed to be, that it was hard to have anything like a normal conversation between old friends. Besides, both Eddie and I had always been rather reserved and formal, and neither of us was going to be the first to say "I miss you" or "Let's take a vacation and do something together," even though either of us would have been delighted if the other one had spoken first. So the conversation dwindled down to my thanking him for calling again, and promising to be in touch. Just before we said "goodbye," as I was thanking him for the third unnecessary time, he said, "Oh, don't mention it. Mars Four forever, you know?"

I laughed and said, "Mars Four. That's right." Then we hung up. I sat back in my chair, and though my eyes drifted to the window and the view across the brightly colored park—the leaves were just at their prime—I saw neither office nor park. Instead, it seemed I could hear Thalia's eleven-year-old voice saying, "Hey, couldn't you two *just* be friends, just once?," and the memory made me smile, and brought back several summers that, truth to tell, might have been the best in my life so far. In those days, I could probably have lived without oxygen more easily than without Eddie; now, we had a hard time even talking about making time to see each other.

IN THE SUMMER of 1969, I was caught between a hundred rocks and a thousand hard places. At my school, if you were fifteen, you had to have hair down to your shoulders and believe in peace and love and all that. If you knew the right songs and phrases you could usually pass, but it just wasn't cool to be enthusiastic about the moon landing—even though it made my heart want to jump out of my chest. I knew already, though, that you've got to maintain your network of peers, even if they're idiots—maybe *especially* if they're idiots. So I was supposed to either be very coldly cynical about the moon landing, or to deplore the waste of resources, or to see it as one big military stunt. I did my best to give the impression that those were my feelings.

It was so different with my beach friends. Eddie Killeret was the only other person my age who saw space the way I did. Thally and Scott at least didn't treat me like I was insane.

Dad's job should have been a source of comfort, but it was a mixed blessing. When I listened to my father, an engineer at Curtiss in the long-range development office, talking about projects and policy, I realized that it wasn't just my peers who were turning their backs on the new frontier. Politicians and businessmen needed the first landing to happen, but after that, now that we had beaten the Russians, most people with any power would be very happy if space just went away.

The space program, into which I wanted to pour my heart, soul, brains, and guts, looked like it was about to be over. Dad was already starting to look for some military project—he didn't even think they'd ever build the space shuttle that was then under discussion.

So when Thalia suggested that promise, in her very serious way, it felt like there were three more people in the world who understood, and I didn't feel so all alone. I'd have promised anything at all to my friends at the time, just because they were people who cared about what I cared about. As much as I tried to hide it under my teenage cynicism for the rest of the summer, there was no getting around it; a part of me had quite seriously made its commitment to the Mars Four. After a while I realized that Eddie was as serious as I was, and we got to be even closer buddies, if that was possible.

It was so strange that once we both began to work on real space projects, we had lost touch. We had expended more of our friendship, of our mutual words and love and attention, on that old, toy Saturn V that I had assembled and he had rescued from the sea, than we had on our real drives into space. It seemed terribly unfair.

When Eddie and I had been in second grade together, we'd read and re-read a picture book called *You Will Go to the Moon.* It had shown a very different way of getting there—winged rockets flying up to a donut-shaped space station, and specialized moon ships leaving the station to go to the lunar surface, and a permanent lunar base—all sorts of things that had never really happened. Yet one part of it had stuck with me . . . the realization that you don't ever go to space with just one thing, that besides the rocket itself, there's so much else that needs to be built.

And as I had come to be a businessman, I'd understood the real magic, the thing that made it all possible: paying as you went. If every gadget you needed began to pay for itself the moment you deployed it, then you had a chance. No one was going to build a dozen separate systems, none of which was profitable without the others, and try to set up everything all at once.

That was why Starcraft had appealed to me, from the moment that it had come to us from a team of older engineers and aerospace business people who—because they had no funding and nothing to lose—had asked a question that hadn't been asked in a long time: "What's the best way to *expand* American space operations? Not just to serve existing needs, or serving one additional new need in isolation, but to move from where we are to somewhere better?"

Unlike other such groups, they didn't disdain the successes of the shuttle and the expendable rockets; rather, they concentrated on how things could be done step-by-step, with each step paying for itself, and each step expanding our capabilities. No part of the Starcraft series was a "miracle machine," but collectively they could change everything.

First-generation Starcraft vehicles would close some of the holes into which money had been pouring for decades. The first stage of a big rocket is an immensely complicated piece of machinery, expensive to build and operate. In the expendable rockets that carried most satellites aloft, we used them for a few minutes during launch, and then just let them fall into the sea. For the shuttle, we reused them in a terribly expensive way—we let the solid rocket boosters parachute back into the ocean, pulled them out of the seawater with a ship, hauled them back to land, put them on railcars, and shipped them to Utah to be completely rebuilt. So the quickest way to cut costs, the Starcraft people told us, would be to bring boosters back for reuse.

StarBooster 200 was a cheap, pilotless airplane that enclosed an Atlas III first stage—the Starcraft people were so dedicated to doing things in small steps that they didn't even propose a new engine, or a new way to mount it. It was "StarBooster 200" because it carried about 200 tons of fuel; there were possible StarBooster 350s and 700s in the future, using other well-established engines, but the StarBooster 200 should be enough for several years.

Attach two Starbooster 200s to a cheap Athena II launcher—something our company already made, which was why the Starcraft group approached us first—and Athena went from launching small scientific packages to competing in the big communication satellite and defense markets. It was as if they'd turned a Volkswagen Minivan into a semi-truck.

When the StarBoosters separated from the Athena, they turned around, switched on an autopilot, and flew themselves back to a landing field near the launchpad. Crews could pull out the engines for overhaul and reconditioning, slap in new ones, and have the booster ready to use again within a matter of a day or two.

The StarBooster 200 was a graceful-looking ship, roughly the size of a 737, with an elongated lifting body, a short thick wing at the back, and a canard wing at the front. It didn't *fly* gracefully, but it didn't have to—just by bringing itself home for repair and re-use, it would allow us to beat the price of every expendable, except perhaps the French Ariane and the new heavy-lift Curtiss expendable rocket.

Logically, the next step in the process would be to replace the Athena with an upper stage big enough to surpass the Ariane. This was also nearly ready to go; StarCore I was just the first two stages of an Athena mated to the high-energy Centaur upper stage. With that, we'd have the lowest priced heavy-lift rocket on Earth.

StarBooster 200/StarCore I would put us on top of the industry for the next decade, but there were five more possible vehicles in the Starcraft series, and some of them were already in prototype; it might mean that RW would dominate spaceflight out to the 2040s or beyond. StarCore II, with a space shuttle main engine (SSME) inside a parachute-recovered pod, with two throwaway hydrogen fuel tanks, would be able to put heavier loads higher than anything else flying—giant communication satellites and modules for ISS, just to begin with; things nobody had ever thought of putting up there before.

Nor had we neglected crewed missions. We had a simple crew recovery vehicle, a lifting body that was roughly intermediate between a capsule and a glider, called StarRescue, which we hoped to sell to NASA as the ISS lifeboat. It had been designed to be

Starcraft-compatible, and if we used it with the propulsion system of a StarCore II, we had StarBird I— a spacecraft that could take ten people, but no cargo, to low Earth orbit, and compete with the shuttle for many missions.

Just on the drawing board and in the concept stage, there was a StarCore III/StarBooster 700 combination that might loft a whole space hotel into orbit at one shot, and a StarBird II that could take eighty to one hundred passengers per flight up to the hotel. The Starcraft family, if it all were built, would include every vehicle we would need, right out till we were routinely flying to Mars.

And yet each of the seven steps along the road was individually profitable; each craft would pay for itself, and create the conditions that would make its successor pay for itself.

It was all the wonders of *You Will Go to the Moon*, but with a timetable and a plan. It was the unbroken path from a cardboard Saturn V to being able to buy a ticket on the PanAm Space Clipper. It was the road to the stars we had dreamed of when we'd been the Mars Four, back on that Virginia beach so long ago.

In some ways I couldn't wait for Starcraft to go public. I wondered if Scott and Eddie and Thalia remembered, and if they would see the connection before I pointed it out to them. I wanted to tell someone, *See? Same old dream, just with real rockets and real money this time*, but a VP for black projects is not supposed to be that kind of a romantic; I thought my old friends might tolerate, or even welcome, my childishness a little better. I wanted them to know that, whatever had become of everyone else, for me, the dream of those summer nights had never ended.

I especially wanted to be able to tell Scott the whole

thing, and to tell him what it meant to me. It might give him a chance to laugh at his sentimental older brother, and I thought anything that could make him laugh would be good right now.

I SHRUGGED OFF the reverie and turned on the television. CNN Headline, and the teasers for the network nightly news, really, really didn't look good for our side. Killeret was absolutely right. Everything they were doing with the story looked like a setup before they jumped on Scott.

The intercom buzzed and the secretary let me know that Roger Przeworski, the Scorpion Shack house attorney that I'd put on the job of preparing an impact evaluation, was here to give his report.

Roger said hello, declined coffee, sat down, pulled out his notepad, folded his arms across his chest, looked at me intently, and went straight to the bad news. "Mr. Blackstone, it's always gambling when you get in front of a jury, but taking this case—and pouring Republic Wright money into it—would be a big gamble. No major firm will touch the defendant's case, the media's against you, Congress is in on the other side—not just from that clown Rasmussen. Name any big player and they're against us. And so far our side isn't even shooting back." He plainly had been chewing over many thoughts, none happy.

"Do you recommend we settle?"

"No. In our present position, Republic Wright would lose nearly everything. We *have* to play it out. But there's no point in playing if you don't play to win, and given the resources being poured into the other side, we need to start fighting, and we need to do it right away and with all the resources we can command. I'm not sure that the Board will stick their necks as far out as they would have to."

"The politicking is my problem," I pointed out. "I've made that Board see reason many times before. What's essential is that you do agree it's what we have to do."

He nodded once, emphatically. "It is. But the legal battle is going to be *big*. I think you're on the right track, Mr. Blackstone, but I can't really claim to be optimistic."

I thanked him for his candor and saw him to the door, then went back to sit, look out the window, and ransack my memory, running through all my personal contacts and friendships—there weren't many of those, Scorpion Shack and Republic Wright having been my life for a long time. I tried to think of any trial lawyer I knew, with any knowledge of civil procedure, in any connection at all, who might help.

The phone rang. I picked it up. The secretary said it was Andrew Riscaveau. I stared out the window for a moment while I tried to figure out a way to not have the conversation, but when you run a secret facility, you have to talk to security people. "Put him through." Probably he'd found out some trivial thing about a staff member and was going to present it to me triumphantly; he tended to see spies and conflicts of interest wherever he looked.

"Good afternoon, Mr. Blackstone. This is Andrew Riscaveau, Security." (He always began that way, as if I might not remember him from the last time.) "I've got two pieces of news for you, one good and one weird. The good news is that we vetted the three Chinese engineers you wanted—the one from Hong Kong and the two from Taiwan—and they're all clean as can be. Human Resources already has the clearance, so you can start them as soon as they can do the paperwork."

That was a fuels chemist and two metallurgists that I'd desperately wanted. "That news was more than good," I said, "that was wonderful. And a week early."

"Sometimes I get lucky. Now, on the other thing, I've got something kinda weird going on and you might be able to help me with it. Three of your employees from your Washington office, Meg Barlow, Roger Przeworski, and Percy MacKay, have requested extremely classified material in the last few hours."

"Yes," I said, wondering where the copy of my authorization had gotten lost to, "that was at my request. If you didn't get a copy of my authorization, I can have one forwarded to you; meanwhile, I'd appreciate it if you could just clear them to continue."

"But this isn't stuff they need to know," he said.

"They need to know it for the project I put them on," I said. Everything always had to be explained to Riscaveau more than once, though he was no fool. It must be his way of getting more than one version of the story, so he could compare the two and look for lies. "I did send out the authorization. I'll send it again if need be."

"I got the authorization. Why do you believe the company should be digging your brother out of his mess?"

"I don't believe that," I said. "I believe that the *Columbia* disaster is going to have major impacts on the space tourism business, and space tourism is the likely first market for StarBird. I authorized our attorneys for an impact study to figure out what the lawsuits arising from the accident will do to space tourism—and to suggest possible interventions to help things move in a direction favorable to us."

"Marketing and politics are not your territory and you shouldn't be messing in them. Plus you're authorizing people with no need to know to go prying into classified matters. And think about how it all looks. If Republic Wright gets seriously involved, it's going to call attention to you, because you're his brother, and there would be press accusations."

"Republic Wright already is involved—we're a defendant. And there are press accusations of every damned thing in the world," I said, trying to keep my temper.

"Well, exactly. There will be accusations, and that means attention will be called to you, and once attention is called to you, what happens to the secrecy around the Scorpion Shack? If you get involved in a highly publicized case, they'll make the connection, start looking into you, and before you know it, the cover's blown on Scorpion Shack."

"There's hardly any cover left," I pointed out. "We've been around for seventy-one years. You can find 'Scorpion Shack' in the index of almost any history of aviation. There are aviation buffs with binoculars out in boats in the Gulf for half our test flights. And I'm sure that every foreign embassy in the United States already knows who I am, and probably has my home phone number. The secrecy is more of a convenience for the company than anything else." I thought of Eddie, and it seemed to me sillier than ever that we had to pretend that Ghost Town and Scorpion Shack didn't exist, when we both knew almost everything about each other's operations. "And besides, I'll admit to being worried about my brother, but I'm not endangering Scorpion

Shack—or threatening your security concerns—in any way. The hypothetical security issues you're raising seem to be motivated by a dislike of the business policies I support. You've made no secret of your dislike for Starcraft, but decisions about it are not made at your level. I'm a vice-president; you're a section head. Are you so sure you're within your own bounds?"

After a long pause he said, "Should you mention that project on the phone?"

"Should you call the head of Scorpion Shack from a line whose security you don't trust?"

He slammed down the receiver. I let myself gloat for a moment before reminding myself that I had let my temper get the better of me and that as likely as not the whole affair would turn around and bite me. Riscaveau had a bad temper and once he lost it at someone he would find ways to cause trouble for months afterwards. I wouldn't be getting any more early, easy security clearances for a while—that was certain.

Perhaps I'd have to come up with something in the way of a peace offering, or maybe the time had finally come to crowd that annoying, petty man out of my company—I had the influence to do it, but I hadn't felt, until that moment, that it might be worthwhile.

I let my thoughts drift away from my clash with Riscaveau, and back to the problem of getting Scott a lawyer. Just before Riscaveau had called, I had had a thought on the tip of the brain, some idea that would work . . . I couldn't remember what that half-formed thought had been.

I jumped when the phone rang; it was the secretary letting me know that she was going home. I thanked her, wished her a good weekend, hung up, and realized I did know one Washington lawyer with a powerful reputation, who was good at difficult and desperate causes, and not afraid of anyone. Furthermore, she was an old friend.

A few minutes later I was driving north, toward Georgetown, in a much better frame of mind. No doubt this would be quite the sales job, but since she'd been seven years old and I'd been nine, I'd usually been able to get Thalia to see things my way. Even if she couldn't represent Scott, herself, she could find the right person.

Besides, no fight that Thalia got into was ever hopeless for her side. My ex-sister-in-law was probably the toughest and most tenacious person I knew.

I thought that I shouldn't just knock on her door after several months of not even saying hello, so I dialed her on the cell phone. In ten minutes I had persuaded her to let me stop by to explain things; Thalia and Scott didn't know it yet, but in a short time she was going to be his lawyer. I rang Scott, passed on Killeret's good wishes and the news that RW was moving toward getting serious about the legal fight, and told him I was very close to having a first-rate attorney for him.

"Is it going to be someone I've heard of?" he asked.

"I'm nearly certain you have." I hung up the cell phone and enjoyed the drive in the fine fall weather.

CHAPTER FIVE

THALIA:

I had been getting bits and pieces of the story of the shuttle crash every few hours as I went through my too-busy days. Just after checking into the hotel in Sacramento, I'd caught the launch on television. I was annoyed with myself; two years after the divorce, I still had the habit of seeing how my ex's business was doing. As far as I could tell, he'd made a clean break and only thought of me in connection with Amos; I still kept waking up in the night and wondering where he was and when he was coming home.

After turning off the television in annoyance, I'd gone out for a quick bite, and then to bed early. When I got up Thursday, an hour before dawn, the networks were fully into their macabre repetition of the footage of the crash on Easter Island.

Remembering how much M J had meant to Amos, I called Mrs. Talbert. She said Amos had already heard, and had seemed very sad, and that the teacher was doing a special session about M J's death. I didn't have any easy way to get hold of Amos at school, and besides it wasn't really the kind of emergency for which I could have him summoned to the phone.

While I ate room service breakfast, showered, made up, and dressed, I left the television on. I caught a glimpse of Scott surrounded by shouting reporters, just before I had to go testify. He really looked like hell, of course.

I was kept waiting all day (something that happens every time you go to Sacramento), until finally I got to give my testimony at 4:45 in the afternoon. By that time the cameras and microphones were all gone. Half the seats for the committee itself were empty. The only person in the audience was a guy waiting to testify after me, somebody from a parolees' organization that I wasn't familiar with.

Dutifully, I put in my hour of talking to bored legislators, explaining why the Coalition was concerned with prisoners, with victims, and with parolees, and why any policy that dealt with just one group without thinking about the other two was bound to fail. I testified that it was stupid to release dangerous people, and stupid to lock up people who were no danger to anyone, and perfectly possible to avoid doing either. Maybe it all did some good. Sometimes you testify just so that, later on, they can't pretend that they didn't know.

I had been able to get a red-eye flight to DC from San Francisco for the next morning, and I've gotten good at sleeping on planes. At Dulles, as I gulped some plastic-wrapped preservative-ridden pastry and stale burned coffee, I was able to hear twenty minutes or so of news from the snack bar TV. It really looked like they were out to get Scott. Most of it was sympathetic coverage of the James family's planned lawsuit.

I also saw Jasper Haverford, perfectly groomed and completely corrupt as always, at a press conference. I was worried about Scott, in the abstract, perhaps, but given the weakness of the case, any good lawyer should be able to chew Haverford up and spit him out.

I had to testify on Capitol Hill late that afternoon, but I was supposed to attend a parole hearing as an expert witness in Richmond at ten A.M., and with luck, in between those obligations, I'd be able to shower and change clothes. For now, I just washed my face and redid my makeup in the airport bathroom. I checked myself once more in the mirror before going. I looked tired. There wasn't much I could do about that.

The parole board kept me around for an hour, trying to decide whether they needed to hear from me that this prisoner was a bad candidate for parole because he had made a number of threats against victims who had testified against him, and violent offenders often do carry out such threats.

About the time I was thoroughly wilted and almost falling asleep in my chair, and my stomach was rumbling, the parole board noticed they didn't need to hear from me after all, since the prisoner had committed a violent crime while in prison, and therefore they couldn't grant parole anyway.

I drove back north and had time to dash into my house, pour bottled Italian dressing onto a bag of ready-to-go salad and devour that, heat and devour an entire frozen pizza (that and the salad had been most of what was left in the fridge, except for some bread, milk, and lunch meat), get a shower, redo my hair and makeup, put on clean clothes, and catch a twenty-minute catnap in my favorite armchair. I got out the door eleven minutes ahead of schedule, with my composure nearly intact. I even got to the hearing on the Hill early, and they were happy for the chance to start right on time.

As it turned out, the hearing was a show staged by three senators who had invited me so that they could be videotaped berating me, probably for campaign footage in their states. I didn't get to say much—the purpose of this hearing was to have me on camera, while the senators accused me of being soft on crime and of subverting the Constitution.

After forty minutes, I was allowed to read my testimony aloud, while the senators got up and walked around. There were no questions at the end. At last I was free.

I drove by Mrs. Talbert's and Amos was sitting in the chair nearest the door, his overnight bag, already packed, in his lap. He had most of his homework already done, except the math—if he'd had that already done, I'd have thought Mrs. Talbert must be giving me back the wrong child. Amos liked school, as much as any normal kid can, and did most of his homework without prodding, but making himself do math was not yet in his power.

Amos wasn't hungry and we both just wanted to get home. I talked with Amos about the trip, but I'm afraid it probably bored him; adult frustration and stress usually did.

When we got home, while I sorted out mail, email, voice mail, and all the other stuff that piles up any time I go out of town, and drafted some quick memos for Monday morning, Amos had some milk and cookies, and started his math homework—or rather, he drew airplanes and rockets all around the margins. I suggested that he ought to do a few problems. I wished this were Scott's weekend with him, because Scott seemed to have a knack for getting him to tolerate math.

For that matter, every so often, Scott, who was often lonely and bored, would take both of us out to dinner before departing with Amos. The idea of not having to do anything about dinner was very appealing right now, even though when Scott did that, as often as not, he and I ended up barely speaking before the meal was over, sniping at each other while Amos stared down at his plate and all of us wanted to be somewhere else.

I was disgusted with myself—wishing my ex would take care of me because I was tired. All the same, it would have been nice . . .

To banish the thought from my head, I reminded myself that Scott had gotten Amos into the idiotic idea of going to a beach cabin in the fall. I knew that the Blackstones frequently did that, but my side of the family had more sense. Just once, the year before we got married, Scott had talked me into doing that. It rained all weekend, we both got colds, and the power went out so that neither of us got anything that we were supposed to do done. The woodstove was too hard to light and neither of us was good at cooking on it, so we ate at Burger King, the nearest open restaurant. Scott spent half of Saturday afternoon splitting wood and ignoring me, took the first hot bath because his muscles were sore, and then wanted a back rub afterward, instead of letting me get *my* hot bath.

I couldn't quite believe I was letting myself get angry about a fight we'd had before even getting married, especially since Scott need not ever trouble my life again, but I hold grudges a long time, and this was one I'd probably hold till my dying day. Even today, with everything so different, just thinking about that cold, miserable weekend makes me furious.

And now he was trying to get Amos into it.

A therapist I had once, before I got too busy to make it to appointments, told me that when people are tired or have too much to do, they sometimes deliberately make themselves angry, just to get the adrenaline to attack the next problem. Maybe that's what I was doing, because after sitting there and stewing myself into a half-fury for a few minutes, I took a deep breath, sat down next to Amos, and made sure he was doing all the problems, especially the fractions and decimals he hated. I extorted a promise to work until he was done, stuck the kettle on the stove, and started getting things ready for my standard decompression routine.

When the kettle whistled five minutes later, Amos was still making his way through the worksheets. Usually that meant he had made a real commitment to getting his math done, and could be trusted to keep going. I poured the boiling water into the pot with the tea ball and carried the tray down to the bathroom. It was time to apply the process that usually humanized me: it started with putting on an Art Tatum CD, and pouring the first wonderful cup of Imperial Gunpowder. Then I took a long, extra-hot shower, to get the feel of airports and legislative chambers off. I dried with a couple of my favorite big, soft towels, and slipped into T-shirt, sweatpants, and fuzzy slippers, and sat down and read a chapter of one of Lawrence Block's "burglar" novels, sitting right there on the toilet, where I couldn't hear a ringing phone or be aware of anything other than the book in front of me, Art Tatum's swinging piano, and the perfect taste of the extra-strong tea.

Forty-five minutes after heading into the bathroom, I was most of the way back to human, though still tired. When I came out to the dining room, Amos had done his math, and was working on getting ahead for next week, reading an excruciatingly dull article about pioneers moving across the Appalachians. I settled onto the couch to drink the last cup from the pot and consider whether I should order a pizza, or Chinese, or just make up some sandwiches. I'd just eat and go to bed; Amos always thought it was funny that on the weekends we had the same bedtime. Tomorrow I had nothing in the morning, so I could look forward to a long night's sleep, until Amos would wake me up with his cartoons.

I finished the cup of tea, sighed with contentment, and set it down on the end table. "Kid, what would you like to eat tonight?"

"Anything except pizza, Chinese, or sandwiches."

"Got the homework about done?"

"Yeah. Mom, is the Cumberland Gap that place up in the mountains that we went to, that Saturday last month?"

"Yep."

"There's a thing in my social studies book about it. It says it was a vittle pass through the mountains."

"Vital."

"Whatever. Did we go there because it was vital?"

"Vital means life-and-death, Amos. Latin 'vita,' meaning life. Like vitamin and vitality. So they mean that the whole movement to go west and settle the frontier would have died out without it; if you didn't have the Cumberland Gap, you couldn't settle the West. But the Cumberland Gap isn't vital to you and me. *We* went there because it was close and cheap."

"Whatever." He flopped down on the couch next to me.

"Are you hungry?" I asked. "I'm not, yet."

"Naw. Mrs. Talbert gave me some soup and a sandwich and a piece of pie just before you picked me up, cause she said that you might not feel like getting dinner right away. We can have a late dinner tonight, as long as it's not pizza, Chinese, or sandwiches."

Clearly my son was not going to negotiate on that issue. "There's a Mexican place that delivers. I'll call them in a while," I offered.

"Excellent. Can we watch a video together tonight?"

For once I didn't have work to do at home, so of course I said yes. It was only 5:45 and I could still probably get to bed by nine, sleep right through till 7:00 the next morning, and still have the full day to spend with Amos.

Agreeing to watch a video was the easy part. Amos was ten years old, and his favorite movies were the ones that involved the maximum possible number of explosions. We finally agreed to some suspense movie in which there wouldn't be too much shooting—maybe an older mystery—and started to look through the shelves of videos (I'm a movie nut and I have a couple of hundred).

Naturally the phone rang. As I got it, out of the corner of my eye, I could see Amos shrug and turn the TV on, already sure the evening with his mother would vanish. I had disappointed him again. Worse yet, he was used to it.

"Thally, it's Nick." Nick is the only person who still calls me "Thally." "How are you?"

"I'm all right," I said. I couldn't remember when I had last spoken to my ex-brother-in-law—probably close to a year.

"Well, I imagine you've seen the news."

"Not in the last few hours. I know MJ was killed, the shuttle crashed on Easter Island, and the James family is going to sue Scott about it."

"Here's the additional news, then. Curtiss Aerospace is going to settle out of court in a way that leaves Republic Wright, ShareSpace—and Scott, as an individual—in a very bad position. Curtiss will walk away with minor damage and everyone else will be devastated."

"I see that this is terrible news for Scott, but is there something that you think I can do about it?"

Nick's voice broke up for a second and I had to ask him to repeat it.

"All right, can you hear me now?"

"Yes."

"Curtiss Aerospace, and Haverford, and maybe some other parties, are putting very heavy-handed pressure on the big firms not to take Scott's case. And for some reason I don't know, the pressure seems to be working. So I had hoped to get some advice about where we can find a good defense attorney who can take the pressure. I'll pay whatever I have to, but I want a Clarence Darrow or a Bill Kunstler or an F. Lee Bailey on this—someone that will fight to win, not find a nice friendly compromise to take a big share of."

"Well, I know plenty of people with the personal-

ity, but most of them are more acquainted with criminal law than civil, and more up to date on
breaking-and-entering than on space law. This is a
terrible break for Scott, to be caught in the middle of
something like this. Does the other side have any gen-
uine grounds for the suit?"

"Well, it's my opinion that the poor idiot child
didn't do anything wrong, but that is just my opinion."

Nick is only four years older than Scott, but I suppose that when Scott is 80, and Nick is 84, he'll still
be calling his younger brother "the poor idiot child."

Amos had come creeping in to see what was up; I
mouthed "Uncle Nick" at him. His eyes got wide, and
he went back to the room with the TV. Scott was
Amos's hero, of course, but his Uncle Nick was sort
of a mythic demigod, partly because Amos had seen
him so rarely in the last few years.

"Anyway," Nick said, "it happens that business is
taking me through your part of the city, and I've got
a while before I've got to go to a late dinner. I was
wondering if I could come by and just get some of
your thoughts. This isn't something I should discuss
over the phone, especially not over an unsecured cell
phone. It has some delicate points about it. And
there's some complexity."

" 'Some complexity,' " I said, laughing. "You almost had me fooled into the whole deal for a second
there, Nick." I wasn't angry at all. It was all too familiar. Ever since I'd been six years old, and Nick
and Eddie had been my eight-year-old heroes at the
beach, I knew that when Nick said "there's some
complexity" what he meant was "I've got several angles of my own that I don't intend to tell you about"
or "Please don't ask me about the way I'm shading

the truth"—usually both. Whether the question involved a chilled watermelon stolen from a neighbor's
porch, or a kite that happened to be blown apart with
illegal fireworks within sight of the township consta-
ble, or the question of how Scott had happened to be
dyed that funny color all over with cranberries, one
of the first things out of Nick's mouth was always
"Well, there's some complexity."

Nick laughed too. "Okay, you caught me. But it so
happens that getting Scott out of this mess would do
me good, and that's turning out to be much harder
than I'd ever have guessed. And I do need a far better
defense lawyer than I seem to be able to find on my
own. That much is absolute truth." He paused. "May
I come by, to talk? It wouldn't take more than half
an hour."

"Aw, Nick, I flew back from California real early,
and it's been a real long day. I look like hell, I'm
incredibly tired, and Amos and I were going to watch
a video and go to bed. My calendar's pretty open
tomorrow; couldn't it keep till sometime tomorrow
morning?" I couldn't imagine letting my super-neat
ex-brother-in-law see how I lived.

Nick said, "Oh, well, I had hoped to get something
put together so I could tell Scott about it. I'd rather
he didn't go through another night of worrying."

I had caught him, but that hadn't made Nick stop
working angles. He knew that though living with
each other had proved to be impossible, Scott and I
were still friends, deep down, going back too far to
remember. And Nick was right. Scott would worry
and brood until some kind of help arrived.

I decided. "You win. Come over, and we'll talk.
Call Scott and tell him I'll try to find him a tough
lawyer that can get him out of this."

"Will do. I'll see you in a few minutes. And thanks, Thally."

"Hey, the Mars Four stick together," I said.

"Amen." He chuckled and hung up; I was smiling myself. Funny how memories of our childhood club came back, even now.

WHEN MY MIND ranged back to the summer of 1969, I remembered the way I kept veering all summer between dressing up, putting on makeup, and going out to do girl stuff, or hanging around with Scott, Nick, and Eddie and still being one of the guys. It wasn't an easy decision to make. I suppose such things never are.

Favoring "stay one of the guys for another year," there was adventure, creativity, and peers I could punch in the nose when they deserved it. Favoring "get girlish," if I managed to have a summer romance I'd be the envy of the rest of the girls in eighth grade, next fall.

The idea of the Mars promise had come to me because I'd gone through a phase, the year before, of reading the kind of bad biographies of great achievers that are written for schoolkids. Usually there was a scene where the great-man-to-be (there were just starting to be a few books about great women in 1969) vows to do the thing for which he will become famous. I more or less borrowed the whole idea from those books.

I guess I needed to feel like I had a *real* future. Even then I knew that the silly girlish period of adolescence wouldn't last forever. In me, it didn't even make it all the way through eighth grade. After a short period of trying to live for boys, clothes, and makeup, I found out that it was just easier to stop hiding my brains and behave like a person.

Somehow, having made the Mars promise helped that happen sooner and faster. Back there on that sand dune in July 1969, I realized it was a world where people could go to the moon if they decided to, and four kids promising each other might start a journey that ended on Mars. I needed to feel that the world really was that big and open.

Many years later, I thought that a human voyage to Mars would probably never happen. I knew politics and law and public policy, and I knew how difficult it would be to put it together; I had spent years trying to put some rationality into a basic government function like criminal justice, with almost no success.

For a while, I had thought I might contribute indirectly to the human future in space, by keeping Scott functional, but I came to see that that had to be Scott's job.

Maybe, when I had extracted that promise by the Atlantic, more than thirty years before, I had pledged us all to a cause that we were all doomed to give up on. Yet, back then, it had done wonders for me, inside. The feeling that I *could* contribute, or be somebody apart from what I wore and who sat next to me on the bus, stayed with me. Just having said *I am a person who can decide to go to Mars*—no matter how impossible it had turned out by the time I was forty—made being thirteen and fourteen slightly less miserable.

AMOS HAD TUNED to CNN and was solemnly watching the who-knew-how-many-times rerun of the crash, which kept intercutting with pictures of his father answering questions. He had it muted, but I didn't like the look of the visual—when they start showing big dramatic scary moments, and follow them up with pictures of a guy talking calmly, it's usually a way to make the guy who is talking calmly look like either a fool or a liar.

When the commercials came on, Amos killed the screen, still without ever having turned up the volume, and asked me, "Is Dad going to go to jail? They don't think he murdered MJ, do they? They were *friends*."

"It's not a murder case—it's a wrongful-death suit. He's not at risk of jail, but life is going to be pretty tough on your father for a while." I tried to explain the difference between civil and criminal negligence, but he was more interested in the question of what the shuttle had run into. A hole in a spaceship is an easier concept for a ten-year-old than "liability" or "tort."

"So what did Uncle Nick want?"

"He's trying to help your dad out by finding a good lawyer, and it's not going very well, so he's asking me to help him. He'll be coming over here tonight to talk about who he can try to get to represent your father."

Amos's eyes widened. "Wow."

"Wow?"

"You're a lawyer. You could defend Dad in court."

"Most good lawyers keep things out of court, Amos, if they can. But yes, if I had to, I could do it. Right now Nick and I are just going to try to figure out what would be best for Scott. If we're lucky that won't even involve going to court."

"Why, if you're lucky?"

"Because, kid, as you have heard me say so many times before, you never know what a judge or a jury will do. Better to settle it where everyone can make a deal together than to have a bunch of strangers decide what's fair."

"But you still could defend him in court. I mean if you wanted to, and he wanted you to, you could defend Dad. Like lawyers on TV."

"Yes, I might."

"Wow."

I could have tried to clarify things, but this was really the first time I'd ever impressed my son. If he wanted to imagine me in the style of the television trial lawyers, maybe I could let him.

CNN showed a replay of AnnaBeth James making her speech. It was even worse, for Scott's case, than the footage of the wreck.

"Mom? Why did MJ die?"

Amos's eyes were serious, but also trusting; he was about as old as you can be and still think your parents might have all the answers.

"Well," I said, "everybody dies, Amos. Someday I will, someday you will. People who do dangerous things—even if they're very, very careful, like your dad—sometimes they have to depend on luck, and sometimes the luck just isn't with them. But even people who never take any chances die sooner or later. So I guess there's not really a why about it."

"It doesn't seem fair."

"No, it doesn't."

"He was really cool. He taught me all that basketball stuff, and he remembered my name. He even talked to me on the phone, that morning when he flew."

"Yes," I said, not sure where Amos was going with it, and just letting him find his own way.

"And now nobody's ever going to believe me."

"Your dad and I will."

"I meant my friends."

"But you know it's true."

"Yeah."

He was quiet for a while, so I slipped my arm around his bony shoulders. He cuddled against me, in a way he hadn't in some years. I could see tears running quietly down his face. "He was really cool," Amos repeated.

I stroked his hair, gently, and handed him a tissue when he snuffled, but my eye was quickly drawn back to the TV screen. The more I saw of AnnaBeth James and the presentations that Jasper Haverford was having her make, the more I thought—I could beat this. I could win this case for Scott.

It was an interesting set of problems, not so much in law as in PR. You'd have to handle the whole case so carefully—a mother wanting justice for her dead son, the reality that it had just happened and it hadn't been anyone's fault, the need to isolate her from too much jury sympathy while always respecting her grief—entirely apart from my concern for my old friend and the father of my child, this was one *interesting* case.

Normally any good trial lawyer could have won this one hands down, but with so much money and expertise on the other side, plus their huge PR advantage, the very simplicity of the case would work against you. You'd have to keep the idea simple and clear while a huge PR blitz and dozens of high-paid lawyers tried to make it complex enough to argue for liability.

It was a great case; high stakes and high challenge. What Nick needed to find was somebody sharp but new, out to make a reputation, with the right kind of

passion. I knew a few attorneys, going hungry on too
much pro bono work, who might enjoy a challenge
like this, and would love the money.

Just as CNN went to sports news, the doorbell
rang. I opened it, and there was Nick, carrying a small
briefcase as always. If I hadn't known him as a kid,
I'd have thought he'd been born in a dark suit.

He said hi to Amos, accepted the offer of instant
coffee, and sat down on my couch. I went out to brew
up two cups.

Through the kitchen door, I could hear Amos talking and Nick answering questions. I knew that the
blank pad of drawing paper had come out of Nick's
briefcase, and he was sketching things about orbits
and physics. I wished we saw more of him—though
no longer exactly family to me, he was an old close
friend, after all, and still Amos's uncle.

I stuck the cups of water and coffee powder into
the microwave, and drifted mentally back to the Mars
Four and all the things that had happened since those
happy days.

The microwave dinged and I got out the coffee,
stirred it a couple of times, and carried it out to the
living room. "Okay," I said, "now tell me what could
be so important that you'd risk the sight of me in my
fuzzy slippers to tell me about it."

Nick chuckled. "If you had put it that way, perhaps
I *would* have waited for tomorrow. Er, Amos, your
mother and I will have to do that unpleasant adult
thing of sending you to some other part of the house."

"This is to help Dad, right?"

"You bet."

"Okay." He went off to his room. Because he was
so often a latchkey kid I'd broken down and let him
have a TV and VCR in there; in a few moments I

heard blaring music followed by multiple explosions.

"Well," Nick said, as we sat down at my dinette table, and he carefully squared up his pad to align with the edge of the table, "the facts *are* pretty much what you hear on the news. The accident looks like a collision with a micrometeoroid or orbiting debris.

"Now, here's why I'm so involved, aside from my interest in Scott. There is a big project that this impacts, at the Scorpion Shack, because the project will depend on space tourism to become profitable. Right now it's in that gray area where we haven't actually rolled it out in public yet, but it's very much an open secret in the industry. I think Curtiss may be hoping to strangle our project, and preserve their position, by throwing this suit—at our expense, and NASA's, and Scott's. It's the only explanation that makes any sense of their behavior. Furthermore, there seems to be a fix in, dedicated to keeping us from getting any decent legal representation."

Nick told me about all of it in some detail, and ran far over the half hour we had agreed on, but by now I was fascinated—there was something so clearly wrong here.

Normally plenty of firms would have taken Scott's case just for the connections and the publicity. That's how a law firm accumulates clout. Scott's phone should have been ringing off the hook with offers of representation. Surely the James family wasn't frightening them away, and though Curtiss might buy up some of the available talent, there was no way in which they could buy all of it.

"There has to be another player in the game," I said. "One that neither you, nor RW's legal staff, nor Scott, know anything about. That's who's putting in most of the fix, though they're obviously getting help from Curtiss."

He stared at me. "You really think so?"

"Curtiss wouldn't spend so much money, or use so much influence, just to *lose* a lawsuit. Sure, they don't much care if they don't win. Sure, they benefit from *you* losing. Nevertheless, they're still parties to the suit, and could still lose a lot. And the James family doesn't have the money—they're rich but not *that* kind of rich—or the influence. So Curtiss wouldn't, the Jameses can't, and yet it's clearly being done. Therefore there's at least one more adversary than you know about."

"Who could it possibly be?" Nick asked.

"I have no idea. I was hoping you'd snap your fingers and tell me who you thought it must be. But I can tell you this—sponsoring a suit without acknowledging it in public is *not* the behavior of honest people with honest gains in mind. Depending on what they're doing and how far they're going, it could even be highly illegal. So they're risking millions in something covert. . . . I think you're up against a very big, tough opponent, and whoever you hire as a lawyer will have his or her hands full."

"It seems to me that some lawyers *like* a good, difficult fight," Nick said. "Is there anyone who'd be attracted to a case like this?"

I sighed and admitted the truth. "If Scott will have me, I'm beginning to think of taking this case myself. If I were in private practice, and didn't know Scott, I'd take it in heartbeat. It doesn't belong in court in the first place. There's no way that it's reasonable to hold him liable. That's something their lawyer must have pointed out to them. I would bet that's why they brought in Jasper Haverford, as a hired gun, because their own lawyer, who was probably more prudent, wouldn't touch it. There's nothing about Scott's case that any smart law student couldn't win, hands down, as long as the case is on the up and up—so I don't think it is. And whoever the forces behind it are, they act as if they are very afraid of exposure. That tells me everything I need to know—there's some bastard out there that I can beat, and I'd like to beat." By that time I had the pad out and had been scrawling notes to myself for a while. I don't know whether I have a good memory or not, because I've been a note taker since the minute I could write. I do know that I never feel like I'll remember anything unless I write it down.

I scanned over the notes. "I *could* get a leave of absence and handle the case myself if I wanted to, and I'm beginning to want to." I hadn't tackled anything as interesting as Scott's case in a long time. If the politics around it were really as bad as they looked . . . well, Scott wouldn't get a better lawyer, my life had gotten dull, and the thought of doing anything other than Coalition work for a while had some charm.

Besides, I was intrigued by the question of who was really behind this and what they were after. Not to mention that I had really liked the expression on Amos's face when he realized I might be the one to defend Scott. "If you can provide the funding, I'll take the case. If we're lucky they'll file in New York State—that's the place where it's easiest to win a claim for damages—and it so happens I'm still admitted to the New York bar. If we have to cope with California law, I'll need to find someone to serve as my partner out there."

"I'll get you whatever you need. Money won't be

a problem," Nick said. "Well, now that we've solved Scott's problems, how do we let him know they're solved? I would bet that he's at home, but he has his ringer turned off and his automatic answerer on."

"He only lives fifteen minutes from here," I pointed out. "Let's go knock on his door. Just let me tell Amos what's up."

I leaned into the room, where Amos was watching actors run away from an exploding building, and said, "Nick and I are going over to Dad's house for a few minutes. We'll get him and then come back here. Is there anything you need?"

"We need supper, sooner or later, Mom," he said. "You haven't had any either."

"Well, neither have I," Nick said behind me. "We'll get something on the way back and all eat together."

"Sweet," Amos said.

"He wants something sweet?" Nick asked.

I shook my head. "It means what you or I would mean if we said 'cool.' " I nodded at Amos and said, "Don't open the door for people who aren't us."

As we got into Nick's car, I suddenly thought of something. "Didn't you have a dinner engagement? Can you afford to cancel it?"

"Uh, I kind of figured we'd end up doing this," Nick explained. "So I just figured my dinner was already scheduled, for later at night, so I said—"

"Not exactly the truth, was it?"

"There was some complexity." He backed quickly out of my driveway, as if afraid I might get out of the car and tell him to go find another lawyer.

CHAPTER SIX

SCOTT:

The doorbell rang. Maybe it would be somebody friendly, like Nikki Earl or Ken Elgin, or even Fred Gernsback. It might be Nick.

Nick and Thalia were standing there. "Here's your attorney," Nick said, "I happen to know she's very good. And I seriously doubt the other side can buy her off."

"But—the Coalition—"

Thalia shrugged and gave me that great smile of hers that I hadn't seen in so many years. "I needed a break from it, anyway. And the more I heard from Nick, the more I realized that you were in real trouble. Besides, Amos thinks I'm going to come to your rescue, personally catch the bad guys, and generally fix the whole world, like a movie lawyer. How often do *I* get to be the hero in the family?"

I had a funny tight feeling in my chest. "That's . . . How are you getting paid?"

"I'm paying her," Nick said. "At least until I get my employer to do the right thing."

"Thank you. Thank you a lot. All right, I have a lawyer. Now what?"

"Come on, you're coming to dinner at my house," Thalia added. "And then we're going to talk about getting you out of this mess you're in."

My eyes were swimming with tears. I hugged Nick, which startled the hell out of my poor old stiff plank of a brother, and Thalia, who hugged back. "Hey, you're welcome," Thalia said. "Let's go. This dump is no place to be when you're depressed."

Once I was out of the empty, echoing house, I felt much better. Inexplicably, a few blocks later, we stopped at a grocery store. Nick jumped out, said we'd just slow him down if we tried to come along, and went in. Thalia and I sat in the car. I think we were both afraid to talk. I was worried that we might start to fight and that I'd lose my lawyer.

In less than fifteen minutes, Nick came back, pushing a cart with three big sacks of groceries. "We're going to be up late tonight," he said, "and we haven't been together as a family since three Christmases ago."

"Well, we're not exactly a family anymore—" Thalia pointed out.

"Nonsense. You're the mother of my nephew and of Scott's son. We've got ten more years of being family ahead of us, whether we like it or not. So, we're going to have a meal together. I'm doing the cooking, and Scott's cleaning the kitchen, and Thalia is supplying the place."

"This is what's called a take-charge leadership

style, right?" Thalia asked, winking at me.

"If you're his employer," I responded. "His little brother always called it something else."

"Absolutely," Nick said. "Somebody has to take charge. If there are no further questions, let's get going."

We drove back to Thalia's place and I helped Nick carry the groceries in. It would be hard to explain how much better I was already feeling; part of it, I'm sure, is that at least I wasn't feeling nearly so *alone* anymore, and part of it was sheer familiarity. Nick and Thalia had rescued me from so many situations when I was younger . . .

After the groceries were in, I spent a few minutes talking to Amos, and going over his math homework with him—he had covered the margins with airplanes and rockets, but he'd solved most of the problems. He was still having some trouble with decimals.

Meanwhile, Nick made all sorts of noise and clatter in the kitchen, punctuated by Thalia's answers to questions about where things were. They were laughing a lot. I heard Thalia say, "No kidding, you're really going to do that, aren't you?"

Amos and I exchanged glances. We went to the kitchen together, to see what was going on.

Nick was laying out an array of food on the kitchen table. I saw it at once. "Friday nights!"

"Well, it *is* Friday night," Nick said, with a twinkle in his eye.

"What's Friday night?" Amos demanded, looking at the kitchen table that had probably never held anything like that before.

"Baked beans, tomato and lettuce salad with French dressing, tater tots, and sloppy joes," I said. "I bet there's vanilla ice cream for dessert."

"But of course," Nick said.

Amos gave me the dirty look you get from a kid who isn't being let in on a joke.

Thalia grinned and put her arm around him. "Well, back when all the families had cabins near each other, down at the beach, we had a shared cooking system. Saturday nights, when the fathers were all down from the city, all the families went out to dinner, usually to the big seafood shack, which was still open then—you know, that burned-out building we go by on our way to the beach. The other nights, we'd feed all three families at one cabin, because making a big meal every third night is much easier than making a middle-sized one every night, and besides that way we all got to spend the time together and help each other with cleanup.

"So Mom—your Grandma Pendergast, Amos, she died before you were born—had Tuesdays and Fridays, Grandma Blackstone had Wednesdays and Sundays, and Mrs. Killeret had Mondays and Thursdays, you see? Now you might remember how we used to go to Grandma Blackstone's for Thanksgiving, before she died, when you were really little, and if you do you probably remember that your Grandma Blackstone was a pretty good cook. Eddie Killeret's mother was even better, nearly a genius in the kitchen. But then there was my mom. She was a great mother but not much of a cook. She had two very simple meals she made, one for Tuesday and one for Friday, every week, every summer, for I don't know how many years. So tonight, evil Uncle Nick is teasing your dad and me by making the Friday night meal—which, I'd have to say, it looks like he's done much better than Mom ever did."

"They kept right on doing it even after the kids

were grown, and not coming to the beach anymore," I said, remembering. "Those three women just really liked each other's company, and it was an excuse to enjoy it all summer long. How many years *do* you think they did that?"

Nick looked up at the ceiling. "I think Mrs. Pendergast and Mrs. Killeret were trading off meals for a couple of years before our folks bought our cabin, Scott. And I think they had Mom in the rotation . . . oh, probably within a month of the first summer we were there, because I remember it pretty well. So it would have been—hmm. 1958. The summer Mom was pregnant with you."

"Right," Thalia said, "and the last time they really did the rotation was the summer before my mother died—I was home for the summer, as a sophomore from college, and at the cabin for several weeks. All three of them were still doing it. 1976, remember all the Bicentennial traffic? Anyway, it was around twenty summers of the same thing every Tuesday and Friday, and what Uncle Nick has laid out here is an absolutely perfect copy of the Friday night meal."

"We only got down to the cabin two times last summer," Amos said sadly.

Nick said, "It *is* kind of a shame that we don't get the use out of it we once did."

Amos looked sideways at me, obviously asking a question, and I said, "Well, Amos and I are going to go down there next weekend. Matter of fact, it's a surer thing than it was before, Amos, because at the moment I don't have a job or anywhere else I have to be."

"Fall's great down there," Nick said, and a faraway look came into his eyes.

"If you like cold and rain," Thalia added.

I decided not to have the old fight with her. "Well, let's eat," I said.

Carrying dinner out to the dining room table was almost a ceremony. Nick had copied Friday night dinner so well that my mind kept wandering off into all those summers in the past, and the dreams and hopes we'd held, and the way that the future had seemed to open in front of us like a vast, untouched country, bursting with adventure and achievement for the taking.

I felt sad, as you do about a good thing that's past, but it would have been hard to feel depressed. I felt like I was really home and really where I belonged.

NICK:

I manage people for a living, and management mostly is a matter of getting people to work together when it doesn't come naturally to them. I had thought we'd better get back together emotionally before we tried to take action together. Something as intimate and "family" as a meal had seemed like a good bet.

Oddly, as I was mixing the sloppy joes, it really touched *me*. Almost, I could hear the waves and taste the salt in the air; almost, I could feel the night chill and the cold damp breeze blowing off the ocean, the comfort of curling up by the fire with a magazine on a day with nasty weather. I hadn't made enough time for these people I cared about, in much too long a time. As feelings and senses poured back to me, I realized that whether or not I had made *them* feel like a team, I had made myself feel that way.

While everyone ate, and later over coffee, we all

got into telling Amos stories about life on the beach. It occurred to me that this was something of a dirty trick on Thalia, because he would lobby all the harder for the summer cabin for the next year. I might very well like to spend some time there myself— maybe I could spell Thalia and Scott with Amos, so that neither of them would have to try to get the whole summer off? At least if I was down there, Amos would get a decent meal now and then. He looked thin to me.

Amos seemed to like the tales of life at the cabin, anyway, though really they were no more than everyday funny occurrences, and things we'd done like building and flying model rockets, or reading our way through all of the *Mutiny on the Bounty* books in one long week, or that kind of thing.

The meal was a hit, and even the coffee afterwards came in for some praise. (I had discreetly cleaned the coffeemaker, since neither my ex-sister-in-law nor my brother ever does, and I'm not partial to the flavor you get from months of coffee tar.) I'd forgotten how much more fun it is to cook for more people than just me.

After a while, Amos seemed to be tired, and happy enough to go back quietly to his room. Thalia made a pot of fresh coffee, and pulled out one of her notepads. "This will take a while," she said, "but I don't think any of us was going to do anything else tonight, were we? All right, what does everyone know? Let's start with Scott."

He told his story for about half an hour, and her pad got fuller and fuller. Finally, she said, "Do you guys realize that you are playing for the soul of the space program here? Not just its future, but its soul?"

She looked at both of us and shrugged. "Serious question. Do you realize how much is at stake?"

THALIA:

I'd enjoyed wallowing in the nostalgia, but at the same time the power of the memories alarmed me. What I remembered more than anything else about summers at the cabin was the way we'd all been bursting with life; every day we got up knowing that something interesting was bound to happen today.

Even as I took notes on what Scott told me, part of my mind wandered off into questions about what the deep issues were here, what kinds of values and ideas were at stake. I had that habit from working on reforming the criminal code—because it's not just about one criminal or one victim, but about getting the system to pay attention to what is just, effective, merciful, and compassionate for *all* the cases, *all* the people that might become criminals, *all* the victims that there might be in the future.

Thus when Scott finished his account, I was struck by the depth of the issues at stake.

"Thally, I still don't see it," Nick said, after a considerable pause. "Without space tourism it's going to be a much slower road to the stars, to be sure, and we won't travel nearly as far down that road in our lifetimes. I understand that. But what do you mean, 'the soul'?"

"I mean this is the case that settles whether space exploration finally becomes what we all hoped it would be when we were kids. The dream was always that people would fly in space—real people, ordinary people, people with kids and mortgages and jobs.

Sure, it would be a very small elite that would blaze the trail. Everyone understood that the first people to go up would be highly trained military test pilots, natural athletes with PhDs in science, and other unusual, dedicated people. But the frontier was *supposed* to be opening up to all of us. We hoped that in our lifetimes we would get past one guy in a cramped cockpit who was mainly concerned with getting the spacecraft to fly, and move forward to a whole crew with places to go and things to accomplish, and from there, maybe, to thousands of settlers at a time, spreading out from Earth across the solar system, and maybe even eventually on to the stars, as dreams could reach . . . and *everybody* being part of it."

I looked at the two brothers and couldn't read their expressions. "Remember, guys? We were going to grow up and *live in the space age*. Not just in a period when trained specialists would go above the atmosphere, but the age when the frontier of space would open out in front of us. The final frontier, you know?

"Well, so far, space is settling into being just another industry, no more special than telephones or steel or electricity—everybody knows you need it, and it keeps on going, but there's no spark, no excitement any more.

"And that was the moment when you did something that was just beautiful, Scott. Fred Gernsback's mission reminded people what space used to be about. It showed us the open door to the frontier. Then David Calderon showed that an ordinary person from Anywhere, USA, can go out there and make a contribution. Before the accident you were so *close*. The dream was alive again and growing and spreading.

"Millions of people watching on television were

rooting and cheering—remember David Calderon on the Larry King show? How many people sounded like they wanted to go? Don't you both see it? People who had barely looked at the sky in ten years were alive and awake to the possibilities—and they still are.

"If we lose the lawsuit, in the eyes of everyone who shapes opinion, it proves that the whole dream was foolish, and space is for professionals the way that coal mines and operating rooms are for professionals, too dangerous to send people who don't absolutely have to go, just another industry with a not-great safety record.

"*But if we win*—people can start to think about living in the space age, again, about a time when you don't even have to be lucky or rich . . ."

My ex and his brother were staring at me intently.

"Okay, have I run off at the mouth here? Do you think I've had too much coffee or something?"

Scott shook his head. "Thalia, I just wish you'd been writing ad copy for me a year ago."

My god, I had impressed my ex. When was the last time that had happened? To cover my confused feelings, I got back to work. "Okay, now I need whatever you can give me, Nick."

"Let me see," he said. "Officially I'm breaching all kinds of corporate and national security. Since I'm paying you, would what I say be covered by attorney-client privilege?"

"Yep," I said. "And what Scott says to me is also covered. On the other hand, what Scott hears from you isn't covered."

Nick shrugged, nodded, and told us the whole story of Starcraft. He explained why anything that killed space tourism would kill StarBird, and dead-end the Starcraft program, and might well bankrupt Republic Wright itself.

I looked at my notes again and said, "Well, this clinches it. The stakes are more than big enough. There's a fix in, all right, and it can't be anybody that we know about. Mrs. James is a sweet old lady—but all she is, is the mother of a dead athlete. And Curtiss isn't going to come out of this badly, win or lose—so they couldn't possibly have the level of commitment that would be required to go out there and twist so many arms so hard. We're up against someone with incredibly deep pockets and more drive than I think any American corporation has, and we don't know who they are. Finding out is going to be one of my first priorities. Can you guys give me fifteen minutes to just think while I look at my notes?" I like to do that before I tell a client anything. I had already arrived at a conclusion, but I wanted to check my own thinking.

The two of them went out on the couch to talk aerospace industry gossip.

I sat down and checked over my notes. I had no doubt. Not only was there a big, powerful silent partner on the other side, but for some reason they were specifically trying to scapegoat Scott and ShareSpace. It didn't look like personal revenge—hardly anyone taking revenge can resist telling their victim what is going on. Scott had no business competitors, so the most likely objective was to make Starcraft fail.

I called them in, summed up, and said, "Therefore, our first job is to find out who we're really fighting, so that we know what the stakes are, what the other side might do, and most of all what we have to offer them in the way of compromises or threats."

"I can't believe you're convinced there's a conspir-

acy agsint me in this. That just sounds so paranoid
to me," Scott complained.

"There's an old saying among lawyers that even
paranoids have enemies," I said. "And don't knock
paranoia—in moderation, it's a survival trait. The interesting question is, *who*? Bingo Rasmussen hates
your guts, because besides being a shortsighted hick
who plays to his most ignorant constituents' preju-
dices, he's also petty and vengeful. But he wouldn't
have the pull to do all this, and though I'm sure he
hopes you lose the suit, he also wouldn't have the
imagination to see it as anything more than a way of
harassing one space business, one time, into bank-
ruptcy. This is more like a subtle way of redirecting
American space policy, and guys like Rasmussen
aren't subtle. There must be far more money or
power at stake than I can see here."

"What about Curtiss?" Nick asked. "Is there a way
they could get money out of losing the suit, or having
it all land on Scott?"

"I don't see how. They've already got more than
fifty percent of shuttle operations and they're the
prime contractor for the space station. An expanding
private market might inconvenience some old execs
there who are set in their ways, but I can't believe
the company as a whole could resist the reward of
having their market expand enormously."

"That sounds right to me," Nick said. "So do you
want me to ask around, try to find out who this could
be?" He sat back, straightened his tie—I just realized
that he had cooked all of dinner in his three-piece suit
and hadn't gotten a spot on him, which was perfectly
Nick. For that matter, so was being in a coat and tie,
visiting family at eleven at night.

"That might be helpful," I said. "But I can't imagine that there's much in the US aerospace industry you haven't already heard about. So it must be somebody who's not even part of the US aerospace industry, and that makes no sense at all." I yawned and stretched. "I'm probably about ready to pull this together into a plan, after which we can all get some sleep. Would you guys like to switch over to beer?"

Scott and Nick both shook their heads; those two brothers had always been kind of straight-arrow. "Diet Coke?" I asked, and they nodded.

I got a beer for me and diet Coke for them, opened them all up, and carried them back from the kitchen on a tray. As I served them out, I held up my can of beer and said, "Spirit of the Mars Four. I kind of wish Eddie was here."

Nick chuckled—I had been sure he'd remember and probably think it was sort of childish, which I guess it had been. Scott, on the other hand, gaped at me as if I'd really startled him. We clinked our cans together, smiling at each other.

I explained. "The only way we will get anywhere is to fight it out, head-on, and force our real opponents to disclose themselves. Until we do know who's behind this, we play this out like any ridiculous lawsuit by someone going after the deep pockets for an accident that wasn't anybody's fault. The grounds for that are overwhelming, anyway. So if we push hard, sooner or later, whoever they are, they're going to have to show themselves."

The phone rang. I picked it up. "Hello?"

"Thalia Blackstone?"

"Yes?"

"We know what you're talking about with the Blackstone brothers, and we want you to stop. If we see any evidence at all that you are continuing with this, you'll be sorry." There was a click and a dial tone.

I hung up the phone and told the guys, "See, there they are now."

After I told Nick and Scott about it, they were both determined to stay there and protect me and Amos. That was really silly, and I said so. "Do you know how many calls I get every month from people who think that what the Coalition does is wrong? And how many of those threaten me? This is routine for anybody in any kind of political activism. The world is full of people who can't be bothered to have a coherent opinion or try to solve a problem, but who have unlimited time to make anonymous threats. It's part of the cost of accomplishing anything. You *know* that, Scott. We got harassing phone calls a couple of times a week after I set up the Coalition; you used to get furious about them."

"Well, I'm still furious about them. And it used to be just people calling up and being rude. This was a direct threat."

"Oh, I get those too, nowadays," I pointed out. "You can't let them run your life, really."

"How often do people act on those threats?" Scott asked.

I shrugged. "Depends on what you mean by 'act on the threats.' Now, come on, we all have a lot to do tomorrow."

Nick said, "Not so fast. You're avoiding the question."

"You could at least call me when something like that happens," Scott added.

"How often do you stand next to machinery that could kill you? And how often do *you* call *me* about that?"

"You're evading again, Thally," Nick said.

"Right. I'm a lawyer. I can evade all night if I have to. But I want to get to bed, and I don't want you guys camping on my floor tonight. This one didn't sound nearly as serious as some of the others I've had. If there are more threats, I'll hire a bodyguard. Why don't you both go home and get some sleep, so that tomorrow we are not all exhausted, with frayed nerves?"

I had to repeat that argument, pretty much exactly the same way, three times before they left. Finally they did, making me promise to call them if anything even slightly out of the ordinary happened. I did check the locks, but otherwise I just went to bed.

CHAPTER SEVEN

THALIA:

The next morning, Saturday, I phoned all the board members of the Coalition and told them I would be taking a few months off to handle a private case. They weren't happy, but they were all well aware that the Coalition had been my creation from the start and that I had more than trained the staff to keep it running. By the time I was finished with Scott's case, either the Board would be eager to have me come back again, or more likely they would find out that the people I had trained were as good as they needed to be, and I would have to go start another job for myself elsewhere. There are always enough things wrong for a reform-minded lawyer to be able to create some work.

After that, I made sure Amos had the rest of his homework done, and spent most of the day running necessary errands and setting up an office, plus deliveries and appointments. Amos went out and played with his friends; it was probably the first "weekend off" he'd had since the divorce, and he came in tired out and happy.

On Sunday, Scott took Amos to the Air and Space Museum, while I made up an extensive set of "to do" lists.

On Monday morning, I was finally able to get to work on my side of the problem, and I was up early to do it, eager to get started, which told me, more than anything else, that electing to defend Scott had been the right choice. I hadn't had a big, high-publicity case in a long time, and I'd forgotten how much you "get up" for them.

I was officially out of the office at the Coalition by noon, leaving things in the hands of Maggie and Craig, my two assistants, who had been practically running everything for the last couple of years anyway. That afternoon I looked at four offices, picked one, signed a by-the-month agreement on it, and made some more calls. Late in the afternoon, I recorded a couple hours of an interview with Scott, and talked to Nick on the phone, to make sure I had absolutely anything that they knew or could think of in connection with the case.

Scott ran through everything once again: He had been interested in getting space tourism going as a profit-making venture for a long time. He had sold tickets on the single most reliable method of getting human beings into orbit ever invented. He had been scrupulous in every aspect of his dealings. There was no reason apart from sheer bad luck for him to be in the dock.

Nick supplied a few more details of background: Republic Wright had to win this or be bought out, and there seemed to be some people within the company who thought that getting bought out would be a good thing.

Despite all my re-emphasizing that they were to tell me everything, no matter how trivial or how unimportant it might seem, neither of them could remember anything very different from what they had come up with on Friday night. I hadn't really expected them to, but you always have to try.

Tuesday morning went into setting up some rented furniture in the by-the-month office—I refuse to work out of my home, since I'm convinced it's the shortest road to utter madness for anyone who has to be both a lawyer and a mother. I called Jasper Haverford's office, along with ShareSpace, Curtiss, Republic Wright, and the NASA investigators, to let them know that I was Scott's attorney and where I was accepting mail.

During the afternoon I had a temp agency send over a bunch of people and interviewed them. By dinnertime I had a staff of one secretary, a researcher, and a paralegal, and a good private detective whom I'd worked with a couple of times before. I called Nick and told him how expensive it would be. He laughed and said he'd thought about spending more than that on a private jet last year.

Early Wednesday morning, the FedEx guy brought in a book-sized red and blue cardboard box, stuffed with all the documents Haverford had filed with the court and all the responses he had received so far. Haverford was corrupt, hyper-aggressive, and as near a crook as he could legally be, but he was a pro (or at least one of his junior attorneys was) and it was exactly what he was required to give me.

The first page contained the best news, as far as I

was concerned—we would be in the New York courts, which meant a jury that was friendly to the plaintiff, but smart. Since the alternatives were Florida (friendly to the plaintiff and maybe not so smart) or California (friendly to every flaky argument in the world and, worse yet, creative) I was pleased. "In a New York court, even if we get no more breaks," I told Scott on the phone, "we stand a good chance of getting the jury to see the law and the evidence the way we do, and if we do, we win. When you have a strong team, you want a good ref."

The first part of winning a celebrity lawsuit is pure PR, because just as it's possible to have a client convicted in the media, it's also possible to have a client acquitted there. It's hard to say how much influence public opinion has on the verdict, but there is no question at all that it affects the size of settlements and what kind of life your client will have once the case fades from the headlines.

I set up interviews with reporters who I knew would be sympathetic to Scott, like Nikki Earl and Fred Gernsback, and worked on getting placement in syndicated columns and feature stories. I lined up as many appearances, press conferences, and public communications of all kinds as I could, which is what you do when your guy is not only innocent, but obviously and sympathetically innocent. I declined anything that would put Scott on the same stage with any member of the James family—when you're doing a public appearance, you just can't win if you're bluntly telling an obviously suffering victim that they aren't entitled to a settlement. If you want people to think your client is the "real victim in all of this," you'd better not have them sitting too near to anyone who looks like a better candidate.

I got two of the lower-rung cable channels interested in doing stories about the dangers of space with a promise of getting Scott, plus a bunch of people that Nick would set up for me, for their interviews. Within a few weeks, they'd be doing something tied to Michael James and space travel anyway, and if our side didn't have input, then the other side would go unanswered. This way we could probably steer coverage toward the challenge and adventure—and the general feeling that tourist space flights were a positive thing with relatively little risk—and make it sound as if the big question were "Are we going to let one grief-maddened family, having fallen under the sway of a sleazeball lawyer, shut every American out of space just to gratify their feelings of remorse?"

On the other hand, if I let those same producers run along on their own, without providing them with anything from our side, no doubt the issue would have been presented as something like "Are we going to let greedy businessmen steal spacecraft that the taxpayer paid for, specifically to use to kill the celebrities who are most loved by children?"

Neither question really had much to do with the merits of the case, in fact or law, but whichever one of them was in the public mind by the day the verdict came back would determine the course of our whole next generation in space. It was a silly way to run anything, but, at least in the near future, my job was to win the case, not fix the system.

I had told Scott early on that even if there had not been an issue of truth, it made little sense to try to claim that space *wasn't* dangerous; manifestly some people had died in space, getting to space, and coming back from space, and any points made about the relative odds compared with other destinations and transportation would be perceived as technically picky, word games, or beside the point. It made more sense to claim that the dangers had nothing to do with having a civilian travel in space, and that the accident had resulted from bad luck, not negligence and certainly not malice. If we could get that claim out in dozens of different print and media channels, then pretty soon people would be repeating it as if they had thought of it themselves, and our spin on the subject would become part of the "climate of opinion" or the "conventional wisdom." In a highly public case, that means that if the client loses, the public reaction is "Don't those people have any commmon sense?" and if the client wins, it's "Well, of course, what else could the jury do?"

Sooner or later there would be some real evidence, of course, and I'd be able to get to work on the case to be presented in court—but for right now, understandably enough, NASA was keeping all the evidence under wraps while they performed their own investigation, and so I kept right on working on the public-relations/issues-management side of the problem. Time enough to do other things, when there were other things to do.

The most unpleasant part of the whole business was that to win in the court of public opinion, we would have to isolate AnnaBeth James from much of the sympathy and support she had been receiving, and get people to begin saying out loud that, sorry as they felt for MJ's mother, her emotional need for "closure" was far outweighed by the greater social need for progress and opportunity. We would have to encourage people to see her as unreasonable, obsessive, even a little crazy.

It was a cruel sort of face to paint on a woman

who had lost a son like Michael James. I couldn't imagine the pain that she and MJ's sisters must have been feeling. All the same, I was out to win our case, not the James family's, and their lawsuit, however emotionally cathartic it might be, had little equity or justice about it. I couldn't let it prevail in the public mind. Ultimately the goal had to be not just to win, and not just to have people believe we deserved to win, but to have people think that suing us had been a ridiculous thing to do; that was what would free Scott and ShareSpace, and the whole community of space activists and entrepreneurs, to push ahead in the years to come.

During those first few weeks, at least every other day, the lawyers for ShareSpace, Curtiss, and ASU would call. They always urged me to settle out of court, even before the NASA report gave us any facts to go on. They kept edging closer and closer to offering to pay any judgment against Scott, which was nice of them, but not the issue that interested us.

Every time they would call with another offer, I'd get on the phone and try to reinstall the spines in the attorneys working for Republic Wright, and then call up Nick's house lawyer, Roger Przeworski, and have him call them too. The RW attorneys were Boucher, Baker & Chandler, a huge New York firm, and it seemed that when I called them, I never spoke to the same person twice. Przeworski was having much the same experience, and we were both becoming convinced that this was one of those law firms that was used to handling things "professionally," meaning that they never did anything that could be construed as a failure to act correctly, but they were much more interested in being correct—and racking up fees—than in winning.

My problem, and Przeworski's, was to try to get them to make some kind of commitment to doing what it took to win the case; from their viewpoint, that was much more risky than just jumping through all the right hoops, having RW pay an out-of-court settlement, and sending in a bill. They kept calling me about ways that perhaps we could get Curtiss, ASU, and ShareSpace to pay more of the settlement deal, even though we'd emphatically said we had no desire to settle at all.

After the third such call from Boucher, Baker & Chandler within a week, Nick suggested that I have a talk with Eddie Killeret, and gave me his home number. "Just like the rest of us," he said, "Eddie's been too busy for family, and so he's divorced and mainly living out of his company apartment at Ghost Town."

"What became of his wife?" I asked.

"No idea. She came and went while I was out of touch with Eddie. You never knew her either, did you?"

"No. I think he invited Scott and me to the wedding, and I think we scribbled him a note to say we couldn't make it, and that was probably the last contact we had. Other than that, it's been what? . . . wow, probably fifteen years since I saw him or spoke to him," I said. "It's strange how time and people slip away."

Since Nick said that Ghost Town was on Mountain Time, I waited till about nine that evening to phone Eddie, figuring I'd give him time to get home from a late meeting and get some dinner. When I did call, I was amazed at how glad I was to hear him speak, and at the obvious pleasure in his voice. "Thally! Nick said you were going to call."

"And he was right. It sounds like you two are talking much more these days; doesn't that make your companies nervous?"

"It makes my director of security nervous, and it makes the guy at Nick's shop, a jerk named Andrew Riscaveau, completely screaming over-the-top-and-down-again paranoid. But, you know, if you work in a development facility of any kind, security guys are never going to be your friends; guys like Nick and me want our engineers to talk to each other—and security wants them to talk to nobody. Yeah, it's been nice to talk to Nick again; there aren't too many people in the world, besides us, who understand us. And now I get to talk to you again; I guess some good came of this whole mess. You ought to have Scott call me, too, for that matter. Don't forget, it's less than twenty years till the Mars Four have our reunion." It was more words than I'd ever heard Eddie utter at once before; he must really be lonely.

"Not looking so good for getting to Mars, though, is it?" I said.

"You never know. Things happen. But, yes, objectively speaking, I'd have to agree with you." He sighed. "The thing Nick wanted me to tell you about is that the politics of this case are looking worse and worse within Curtiss. I'm about out of allies here. These idiots are still cozying up to the James family instead of trying to win the case. I'm not at all sure what's up. At first I thought they were just out to strangle the tourist business, hoping to bankrupt RW, but it's looking much more like the whole company is changing direction. I'm alarmed at how many of our more talented guys are leaving, and the way that our no-vision bottom-liners seem to be finding all the allies and support in Congress.

"Used to be you couldn't get Bingo Rasmussen out to any of our facilities on a bet; he and a bunch of his cronies have been to corporate headquarters a couple of times this month. There's a big change of policy going on, and I don't think I'm going to like it. So the bad news is that you can expect even more pressure to settle. And I don't think you're going to see any turnaround or get any help from Curtiss."

"Well, it's not *unexpected* bad news," I pointed out.

"I wish I could be more definite about this, but there's something else going on as well," Killeret added. "It's like there's another hand at work in the company, or a force that I can't quite put my finger on. People I've known for years seem uncomfortable and unwilling to talk to me—and there's been quite a turnover in middle and upper management; every couple of days an old face disappears and a new one comes in. It just seems as if this isn't the Curtiss I used to work for. I've been through some corporate transitions before, but this is by far the biggest, accompanied by the least information. That's just . . . well, it's weird. I don't know that it proves anything, but it is certainly weird, and I don't quite know what to make of it."

"Any idea who these new people coming in are?"

"Many of them are out of think tanks and they seem to be much more political than the people they are replacing—they're either strongly Democrats or strongly Republicans, and they come from places that have 'Public Policy' in the name, or out of government agencies, especially the finance and budget ones. But they don't all seem to be from the same place—it doesn't exactly feel like the kind of corporate mafia you see after some takeovers. And on the other hand, it might just be my paranoia. Most of upper management is still in place; there just seems to be something new going on, underneath and around them."

I asked a few more questions, but Eddie had told me about as much as he knew; the thing he was most worried about was painfully vague. Then we got to talking about all the intervening years, and what we'd done with our lives, and by the end of that conversation, it was half-past midnight my time, and Eddie was apologizing, and I was thanking him for spending so long talking, and we'd agreed that we'd have to be in touch again, even after this case was settled.

THE WEEKS WENT by while I waited for NASA to get around to releasing its report, and our case stayed somewhere near the top of the hour on the television news while November came, and the calendar crawled down toward Thanksgiving; I was beginning to really hope for a major scandal to erupt, because in a few weeks the national government would virtually shut down for the holidays, and if nothing took public attention away from our case, we'd be stuck as the lead story for another six weeks.

Besides coping with all of the PR aspects, and responding to a huge volume of correspondence and then adding to it myself (every civil case begins with lawyers demanding information from each others' clients), and a certain amount of legal strategizing and intelligence gathering, there was also the task of getting my team to function together as a team, to understand what we were about to do, and how we were going to do it.

Still, if the case was moving slowly, at least my home life was better than it had been in a few years. I almost always got home on time for dinner, and if I didn't, Scott, having little to do, was happy to pick up Amos from school and take him somewhere to eat, often stopping on the way to pick me up as well. Amos and I saw more than I'd ever planned to of Chuck E. Cheese's and Red Robin, and much more of Scott; it was good for Amos to see so much of his father, and I really didn't mind, since we were getting along better. I hadn't quite realized how lonely I had been after the divorce, and now that he wasn't nursing a fledgling company through a series of crises, and had time to relax and think and be with his son, Scott was surprisingly good company.

Nick checked in daily, occasionally by having lunch with me when he was in Washington, more often calling from Scorpion Shack, and though he wasn't happy with how slowly Republic Wright was moving towards supporting us, he seemed to think they might eventually. At least RW would not throw themselves all the way over to the other side, as Curtiss had done. About once a week Eddie Killeret would call, and though his news was usually that the change in personnel and the anti-new-development policy at Curtiss were continuing, at least things there didn't seem to be much worse.

By the second week of November, we were getting some traction. Several television news stories and newspaper pieces had pushed our point of view. Spot polls showed that we were reaching the public with our message, and we were also pulling ahead in the support of those who said that they were getting tired of the Michael James case. As the OJ case had demonstrated and the Monica Lewinsky affair had confirmed, some of the best support you could get was from people who said, loudly, "Oh not that again" and "Isn't that over *yet?*" every time the story ran on the evening news.

On the Wednesday two weeks before Thanksgiving, I was going over a report from my researcher on the number of occasions, and their exact times, when MJ or a member of his family had been briefed on the dangers of the flight. There was perhaps a ten percent chance that we would need to use it in court, but just in case, I had to know everything about it. Still, it was absolutely dull. I was drifting off every few minutes as I prepared some notes for my secretary.

The phone rang—a woman from the NASA investigation who wanted to know if I could be in Houston the next morning for a private presentation of the commission's findings, prior to the public presentation later in the afternoon. I said of course and got a time and a location. They wanted only attorneys present, so I wouldn't be able to bring Scott or Nick along. I thanked her, hung up the phone, and got busy, getting a plane ticket, making sure that Scott would be able to take Amos for the day, and letting Nick know what was going on.

"Cross your fingers," I told him. "Three things could happen here. The least probable, I think, is that they're going to turn up some crew error, or some mechanical problem, on the shuttle, that contributed to MJ's death. If they do that, we're screwed, especially if it's anything Scott could have known about—nowadays juries tend to say if you could have, you should have. Most likely of all it will turn out to be just what Billy Kingston and the crew thought in the first place, and it won't affect a thing. But I suppose there's just a chance—because there always is—that they'll have turned up something that kicks a big hole in Haverford's case. If that happens, it might be all over before the holidays. So cross those fingers *hard*."

"I'll do that," Nick said. "By any chance, would you like to take Roger Przeworski along? One more lawyer on the side of the angels?"

"Sure."

It took just a minute to arrange to meet Przeworski for breakfast in Houston—we were both going to be staying at the Airport Sheraton—and that was that. I'd fly out tonight, be back late afternoon tomorrow, and at least get a breath of warm air and sunshine before returning to cold, rainy DC.

THE NEXT MORNING, in the hotel room in Houston, came too early. I hadn't been able to get to bed until past midnight. Just the same, I was up and ready, showered, made up, and dressed, with the briefcase in perfect order, half an hour before I was due to meet Przeworski. I decided to go down to the café; I could have coffee until he got there, and I was too nervous, pacing around the room all by myself. I tossed the key into the return box, put the overnight bag into my rental car, and went into the café, still twenty minutes early.

Roger Przeworski, hair and suit in perfect order, was sitting there having coffee and looking nervous. We realized we'd had the same kind of morning—too excited to wait—and rather than fight it any longer, we just ordered breakfast and started to speculate about what we were going to hear. "It's strange how long it's taken," Przeworski pointed out. "You'd think if they were hit by a meteorite, all they'd have to do is confirm that, and then decide whether Kingston did a good job of landing it or not."

"But if it was anything other than what we think, it doesn't seem like they'd have had time to establish what else it was. So maybe the time was awfully short." I buttered a roll and glanced down; Przewor-ski wore a wedding ring. Well, he was kind of tall for my tastes, anyway.

"So it seems like it was either too long or too short . . ." Przeworski said, letting it trail off. "Well, I guess those are all the alternatives there could be, aren't they? This is really theorizing in the absence of data. And I suppose another possibility, while we're at it, is that they're just announcing one espe-cially interesting partial result. Maybe they found out that MJ died of some cause other than the obvious, or that somebody should have identified the piece of space junk that got them, and the rest of the investi-gation will continue."

"As you say, it's all theory in the absence of data," I pointed out. "We'll know at nine-thirty, for sure. How long till then?"

"An hour. Plenty of time for some more irrespon-sible speculation."

"Let me get another cup of coffee first."

Finally it was time to get over to Johnson Space Center and get however much of the truth there was supposed to be. The drive was uneventful, and the room could have been any room for a press confer-ence or a public announcment anywhere; so much of the business of government happens in places that are completely anonymous.

The team from BB&C, the Republic Wright law-yers, came over and sat with us, and we made the usual small talk, mostly establishing that we all knew someone in common. In the opposite front corner, the Curtiss and the ShareSpace lawyers huddled to-gether and whispered, obviously locked in some kind of strategy conference. I wondered if they had gotten an early tipoff, and if they had, how I could get in on it. Just before the meeting began, Jasper Haverford swept in, flanked by two junior lawyers, said hello to everyone by name, and shook all our hands, just as if he had called the meeting himself.

He was a handsome man, but handsome in a way that obviously required plenty of expensive maintenance. He had silver hair, fine-boned features, a deep tan, and dark eyes, teeth that were straighter and whiter than occurred in nature, and a way of grinning that looked absolutely sincere; this was a man who could look you right in the eye and ask for your trust while rifling through your purse. The fact that he was looking so cheerful this morning was a mixed sign; either he was working hard to keep up appearances, or he had an inside line. From what I knew of Jasper Haverford, it could be either.

The NASA investigating committee came in and did the usual round of introductions. As was traditional, there were two astronauts on the team, since it was assumed that they knew something more about space operations than most people. Colonel Pete Slendwick, the senior of the two astronauts, who had commanded two missions, was the chair of the inquiry; Victor Carlson, a four-time shuttle pilot, was the other active astronaut. There were also two senior engineers, one each from Curtiss and Republic Wright; a couple of experienced coroners, one of whom had been the doctor on a shuttle flight ten years before; and a nearly expressionless FBI agent.

Aside from the actual investigators, it was necessary to have some celebrities, because Americans wouldn't trust a report from a commission that didn't include people they knew, so they had gotten Sally Ride to sit on this commission, as she had on the *Challenger* investigation. They had also gotten one of the old Apollo astronauts, to supply prestige and experience, and the physicist who had hosted the popular *Beyond Micro* series on PBS. *At least none of them seems likely to do any harm,* I thought.

The official report was delivered by Colonel Slendwick, who looked nervous. He had a habit of sucking on his lower lip between sentences, as if wondering which sentence would cause the room to go up in an uproar. "Thank you for coming," he said. "We felt that this information was so directly important to you, as the involved attorneys, and had so much bearing on the case, that you should know it before we release it to the media later this afternoon." He paused and looked around the room. "I emphasize that although this is a preliminary report, our conclusions are firm. Our full report will come after the first of the year, but only two parts are unfinished at this date—the minute-by-minute chronology of what happened from the moment of the explosion, and the review of the security breaches believed to have occurred."

Heads whipped around as we all looked at each other—the mentions of "explosion" and "security breach" had been enough to change everything. Whatever had happened up there, the commission didn't think it was a micrometeoroid impact.

Slendwick seemed to give us all a moment to absorb all that and get ready for what he was going to say. "Here's what we have determined. After careful investigation, including reconstruction of the surface through which the object exited, and of the camera, and studies of the injuries to Michael Tyree James and Marc Akira Clement, we have found that the event is absolutely inconsistent with any scenario involving an impact with an external object, either orbiting the Earth or from interplanetary space. We have found instead—"

"I have an injunction here," Jasper Haverford said, "which prohibits your going on with this, as prejudicial to an ongoing court case."

Colonel Slendwick looked stunned. Haverford rose and triumphantly handed out copies of the injunction; in a room full of lawyers, that immediately created a storm of shouting. I was part of that storm myself.

Haverford's injunction was written in such a way that it might very well allow Haverford to suppress *any* report that didn't support his client's case, until the trial was over. It was also from a New York State court, which meant that they didn't have jurisdiction here anyway.

Naturally the NASA bureaucrats in the room wanted to hold the report back and make sure everything was all right before going on. The engineers, scientists, and astronauts on the commission wanted to just bull ahead with the report. Przeworski, BB&C, and I thought the injunction was invalid. To no one's surprise, the lawyers from Curtiss, ASU, and ShareSpace lined up with Haverford. Presumably that was what they'd been whispering about before the meeting.

Luckily for the good guys, Przeworski was a better improviser than the rest of us. He whispered what he was up to in my ear and said "Just make sure nobody leaves for an hour or so." While I argued, objected, and leaned on the NASA people, Przeworski sat down, hand-scribbled a plea, slipped out the side door, walked across the road to a Kinko's, and faxed it to a federal district judge who was an old buddy of his from law school. Forty minutes after Haverford's rolling his bombshell onto the carpet, while everyone was still quarreling, and after Jasper Haverford had called me a number of names that I was more accustomed to hear from people doing life without parole, and threatened to call the police to have the meeting broken up, Roger Przeworski walked in with a fax of a federal order, voiding the injunction.

There was a stunned silence once Przeworski had managed to make it clear what he had. After a long moment, Haverford said, "All right, I'm forced to concede that you win this one. And I admit I'm curious."

Slendwick looked about as irritated as I've ever seen anyone look. Everyone sat down again. After a pause, Slendwick resumed. "The results are consistent with an explosive device which was inside a very exact replica of the CO camera. The device appears to have been made up of about half a pound of Semtex sealed inside a ten-centimeter length of tapering steel pipe, designed to fire a tungsten projectile about a centimeter in diameter by three centimeters long.

"The projectile had a hole in its base to cause it to seal against the walls of the tube, exactly like a bullet in a conventional rifle, and a hollow nose and series of grooves around the outside to cause it to break up when it hit the forward window—where it was supposed to be pointed for the first photograph. The steel tube, out of which the projectile was fired, was tapered to produce greater compression and a much higher muzzle velocity, very much like the barrel of a modern anti-armor cannon. Probably by design, the explosion fragmented the camera case and destroyed most of the device. The device appears to have been rigged to be fired by the first pull of the shutter."

Slendwick looked around the room once and said, "We believe that we can reconstruct the intentions of whoever planted this device, because plans were changed at the last minute, as the testimony of Mr. Scott Blackstone and of Mr. Perry Lager clearly shows, and which is corroborated from several other sources. The original plan would have had Mr. James attempting to take the initial photograph through the forward cabin window.

"Our reconstruction of the projectile indicates that it was intended to hit at very high velocity and deform on impact. If it had hit its intended target, the projectile would have shattered most of the forward window, resulting in explosive decompression of the crew cabin and the almost instant deaths of the entire crew. We would have had no idea what had happened; *Columbia* would simply have been slowly tumbling along in orbit, apparently dead, with telemetry indicating that cabin pressure was zero. Given the extra care we would have had to take in preparing a mission to investigate, and the difficulty of a rendezvous with *Columbia*, and the fact that the most incriminating objects might well have gone out the shattered window to be lost forever, it would have been months, perhaps years, before we had any idea that this was a deliberate attack. It is quite probable that we would have concluded what the crew first thought, that the loss of *Columbia* was caused by a micrometeoroid impact. Had things gone according to plan, this could have been a nearly perfect crime, and one that would have grounded the American shuttle fleet for months or years."

He looked around the room. "We were lucky enough to learn the truth. The death of Michael James almost certainly saved the lives of most of his crewmates, because the projectile lost a great deal of force as it broke through his sternum, chest cavity, and spinal column. The collision with the bone caused the projectile to break up prematurely, leaving several pieces embedded in his chest cavity. Only a part of it continued on, at much reduced speed, to make a half-centimeter-wide hole in the hull.

"The broken neck that killed Marc Clement was caused by the explosion, directly in front of his face, of a block of Semtex, fracturing the front of his skull as well as whipping his head back hard enough to break his neck. Given that the skull damage would have been consistent with a massive cerebral hemmorhage, Dr. Clement could not have been expected to survive in any case. He probably died during the strong, varying accelerations he experienced during re-entry, but in any case could not have survived more than a few hours, even if he had been on the ground and state-of-the-art care had been available immediately.

"Two members of the packing crew left the United States within less than an hour of *Columbia*'s liftoff, and one of them was in fact responsible for the CO camera. The FBI believes that they are now either underground with a terrorist organization, or concealed in some hostile foreign nation.

"Those are the essentials of our results; you'll find much more detail in the report. As I stated before, after the first of the year, we'll release some additional supporting documentation, but our conclusion stands."

"Is there any indication at all as to who planted the camera-bomb?" I asked. "Not the packing crew members, but the people who paid them to plant it?"

"That investigation is continuing," the FBI agent said, quietly. "We have not narrowed it down to any particular outside terrorist organization or hostile foreign power. Naturally we do find some nations and groups more suspicious than others, but we have no reason to point the finger at any one of them just yet."

There was as much uproar as a dozen lawyers can make. NASA had been wise enough to have full packets of photocopies, covering all the major reports about the evidence, for each of us, and that helped us formulate questions, but within a few minutes, Przeworski and I were nodding vigorously, and in a mood to celebrate. The evidence was as strong we could have hoped for—ballistics, autopsy, chemical traces, reconstruction of the explosive device, even a decent match between the chunk missing from the tungsten slug and the hole in the hull. "If this were evidence *against* my client, I'd settle," Roger said cheerfully.

"Me too."

The beauty of this, from our standpoint, was that if this were an international terrorist incident or an attack by a hostile foreign power, legally it would be an act of war, and you can't sue the US government for enemy actions. Doubtless that explained why so much of the yelling and objecting was coming from Haverford and his staff. They held that this whole report had to be suppressed, that the facts were impinging on Mrs. James's rights to win a judgment, and that there could be no public disclosure of this report since it was clearly prejudicial. The committee, as an administrative body and a purely fact-finding one, included no lawyers and did not make any decisions by itself on what to release and when, so Haverford couldn't have any real effect on them, but either it was taking some time for him to understand that, or he hoped to intimidate them with sheer presence, or he was trying to build up evidence that they had not taken his client's rights into account. Whatever it was, he was making himself annoying.

When we were sure it was over—when you're dealing with characters like Haverford, you don't let them be the last to leave a meeting—Roger Przeworski and I went to a quick lunch, agreed that this might well mean the whole case would be dropped within a few days, and called Nick and Scott to let them know the good news.

Scott seemed pleased but distracted, as if he had something else on his mind. I finally asked him why, almost having to shout over the noise of the dining room behind me.

"Uh, it's your car," he said. "Someone set it on fire at the airport parking garage. The airport cops left a message on your answering machine. When I talked to them, they said it looked like someone just stuck a Molotov cocktail under the front end, lit it, and walked away. I'm afraid, from what they tell me, it's totaled."

"That's what I buy insurance for," I said, relieved to realize nothing of any importance had been in the car. "I guess I'll need a ride at the airport."

"You don't seem to be taking this seriously."

"We've just about already won the case," I pointed out. "Really, we couldn't lose it now if we wanted to. So if this is someone trying to threaten us, they probably didn't know that they'd already lost at the time that they torched my car. Most likely they'll dry up and blow away once they do know. Or, you know, it always could be just some bored kid vandalizing a pricey car for thrills."

He wasn't pleased with my attitude, but I managed to get him to focus his attention on picking me up at the airport, and on the good news that the other side's case had just gone to pieces.

After I hung up, said goodbye to Roger Przeworski, drove to the airport, turned in the rental car, and got on the plane, I leaned back in my seat, stared out the window, and allowed myself to be quietly scared out of my mind. This was by far the closest anyone had ever come to carrying out a threat, and I was worried sick. You just can't allow the client to see that kind of thing, and I'd need to have my game face back on by the time I saw Scott.

CHAPTER EIGHT

THALIA:

When I checked my voice mail at the office, some-body had used a computer-speech program to call my office number and leave the phrase "Drop this case now" repeating for five minutes. My guess was that even if a phone trace had been available, it would turn out to lead only to some pay phone.

I did *not* win the argument with Scott that night; he stayed on the couch in the house. I though it must be pretty weird and depressing to be back in his old house, but not in the bedroom, but he actually seemed to cheer up. The next morning I awoke to the smell of breakfast cooking and came out to find Amos getting through his second helping of French toast. "Hey, remember, I don't have a job anymore," Scott said, apologetically. "I guess I could see if NASA or Global would take me back—I've kept up my train-ing flight time and my time on the simulator—but for the moment my best prospect is to find some nice woman to support me, so I'm practicing my domestic skills. I'll even clean up after myself, really. It won't take you a bit of extra effort to have me here."

"The apron is what makes the image," I assured him.

"Are you going to go to the police about your car getting bombed?" Scott asked.

"I already did. And I reported that first threatening phone call, back when that happened, too. For one thing, if the cops have a record of incidents, and if there's anything that looks like an escalation, they would take that very seriously. Besides, I haven't done anything criminal and keeping the cops informed keeps them from getting suspicious. And to judge by what I got from them over the phone last night, they seem to be doing a good job. The airport cops are working very much by the book for an arson case, and I know from two past cases that the Arlington arson investigator knows his stuff. But if the people who did it are professionals, there won't be anything they can trace. The airport detective guessed it would turn out to be a plastic bottle of flammable liquid put under the car, inside a metal bowl to make it flash upwards, set off with a long strip of oil-soaked rags. Nothing traceable to any source, and chances are they didn't leave prints."

"So what are you going to do about it?"

I was getting irritated with Scott for discussing it in front of Amos, who was studiously keeping his face down in his plate and shoveling in more breakfast. "I'm not expecting this case to go much longer," I said. "So I'll spend some of Nick's money and hire a bodyguard service; I've had to do that a few times for the Coalition's lawyers."

"Is that going to be enough?"

"It always has been for the Coalition," I said, with a tone that I hoped would close the argument.

After we dropped Amos off at school, Scott gave me a ride to the office, and on the way he fretted some more. We started to get into a fight about his having brought the matter up in front of Amos, and that seemed like a bad thing if he was going to be sleeping on my couch for a while, so I did my best to ignore my annoyance and put things in perspective for him.

In dealing with a take-charge guy like Scott, you're generally better off telling them the truth, so I explained it to him as well as I could. "Look," I said, "yes, having my car burned is weird and scary. I won't pretend it's not. And I don't know how much of my past experience is relevant. With the Coalition, usually anybody who is making threats is a relative of the victim or the prisoner, someone who's really emotionally worked up, and they do some crude, stupid things. As soon as they see the bodyguards, they usually lose their nerve.

"What bothers me is that I can't imagine who's doing this. Curtiss Aerospace isn't the kind of operation that you expect to hire goons. As far as I know, the federal government is on our side, even the secret agencies that sometimes do illegal action. And I've never heard a breath of organized crime being involved. So that leaves Jasper Haverford—and no slick lawyer would ever need to resort to violence, and trust me, he's *really* slick—or just maybe the James family, but they're a bunch of straight arrows if ever there were any. Considering that they all grew up in the projects and none of them ever carried a pocket knife or stole a stick of gum, and that AnnaBeth and her daughters spend most of their spare time in church, I'm finding it hard to picture them sending a hit man after me."

"So what you're saying is that it is frightening, and you don't know who it is. I'm sorry I talked about it in front of Amos, but it is very serious, Thalia, you can't deny that." Scott drove another block in silence. The fall drizzle had settled in, and all the red brick houses looked washed out, as if I were seeing them through a shower curtain. "What about this 'mystery force' that Eddie Killeret keeps talking about? The one that he thinks is taking over Curtiss?"

"By definition, we don't know who they are or what they're doing," I pointed out. "I suppose it's possible that it's a mob family or something—but the Mafia's gotten burned lots of times, trying to take over legitimate companies, even when it was just garbage hauling, laundry, or supermarkets. Are they really going to try to make a big move on a company that's a vital national security asset, and be as blatant as this? It seems like they'd be asking for so much trouble."

We talked more but didn't come to any resolution. After, Scott walked me upstairs to the office, and made sure that there were a couple of people already there.

"Will you need a ride?" he asked.

"I'll get a cab it's pretty unpredictable when I'll be done," I said. "Don't worry, now that I'm here, I'm fine."

"If you don't mind, I'll spend the day at your house," Scott said, oddly formal and shy about it. "You've got a lot of winterizing that needs doing, and besides, if I'm there, nobody will try breaking in, or planting anything."

"If you like," I said. I handed him the spare house key. I still thought he was overreacting, but surely it wouldn't hurt to have him there, anyway. Besides, whatever "winterizing" was, it was probably something that should be done, anyway.

I watched through the rain-streaked window as he drove away; I stood there for a few seconds, thinking of nothing in particular, before getting on with the day's work. I didn't think about much else until the bodyguards showed, up right on time, at eleven.

Two real surprises hit that day, which was busier than most lawyers' Fridays. The first was word from Haverford; he had filed dozens of petitions and motions in the New York court, demanding that the NASA report be suppressed and trying in various ways to claim that the actual cause of the accident should be completely irrelevant as to whether or not anyone could be sued about it. This did not look like a man who knew he was beaten and was giving up.

With a sigh, I phoned the New York court, and after a variety of delays and back-and-forthing, determined that hearings on all these motions would be next Tuesday. They all seemed so open-and-shut that I might be able to deal with them in a single day, but it seemed like a better idea to reserve rooms for a couple of days.

Late in the afternoon, I was typing out a rough draft of the outline of my case to deny all of Haverford's motions. My basic strategy was to argue that since all of Haverford's arguments rested on the same premises and had the same intent, that if the judge dismissed any of them, he ought to dismiss all of them; that would keep Haverford from dribbling them out, an item at a time, delaying and delaying.

That was when the second surprise—one the whole

world shared—began, for me, with the phone ringing. When I picked it up, it was Nick, calling from the air-cellular on the RW company plane—something he never used for personal business, so this was strange. Usually the tracking satellite uplink in the plane could deliver every call crystal-clear, but this time the call had the scratchy, fading-in-and-out quality that I remembered from long-distance calls when I had first gone off to college. "Thalia, if you've got a TV in your office, you'd better turn it on to CNN. I think Scott's case is off the front page for a while, and things are about to get completely crazy in the aerospace industry. Figured you'd better know about it if you didn't already. I have to run . . . love to Amos and Scott. Maybe we can all have dinner tonight? I'll call back when I'm on the ground, in a couple hours."

"Come by my place about seven, we can all decide what to do," I said. "Call my cellular if you have to change plans."

"If it's working," he said. "Will do."

Why would he think that my cell phone might not be working? "Thanks, Nick, I'll take a look."

He hung up without saying goodbye.

When you're handling a highly publicized case, you always have a TV in the office. I grabbed the remote from the coffee sideboard and turned on CNN. As the picture emerged, I saw many worried faces, and maps with arrows and lines on them—I recognized Kashmir. The broadcast was surprisingly fuzzy, and every so often you got one of those jerky slow-motion movements that happen when there's not quite enough bandwidth for a signal. I turned up the volume and was surprised to hear some occasional hisses and crackles, and fuzziness in the tone.

Pakistan and India were at war again. Pakistani

troops had crossed the line. Fighting was flaring all over Kashmir and along much of the frontier between the two nations. Pakistan had begun its attack by firing a secret weapon which had worked far better than it was supposed to, which the news commentators had already dubbed the "proton bomb."

The idea had been talked about for decades. You don't need to get up to orbital speed to go to space; you only need orbital speed to *stay* in space. The old V-2s during World War II had gone most of the way outside the atmosphere; they just hadn't reached speeds that would allow them to stay in orbit. All the way back in 1949 an Army two-stage rocket experiment had gone up three hundred miles, twice as high as the altitude at which the first satellites orbited. Although it takes a big rocket to put a satellite into orbit, the same rocket can put a much bigger payload into space, up above the atmosphere, for a short period of time, if all it has to do is be there briefly.

In this case, the payload had been a curious object. Superficially, it looked like an old, crude hydrogen bomb. The body was an elongated steel egg, sixty feet long by some forty feet at the widest point. Internally it was an ellipsoid—a shape that has two internal foci, such that anything released at one focus will be reflected into the other focus. In one focus rested a half-megaton nuclear bomb—a much better bomb than the Pakistanis could make, but we didn't yet know that. In the other focus was a 22-foot-diameter sphere, filled with twelve tons of liquid hydrogen. The rest of the ellipsoidal had been pumped down to a very thin vacuum.

They launched it straight up; it wasn't going nearly fast enough to reach orbit, but it was going more than high enough. One hundred and thirty miles above

Kashmir, just as the steel egg reached its peak altitude and began to fall back to earth, they detonated the bomb.

The first effect out of an atomic bomb is a burst of very intense X-rays, and this bomb had been built to enhance that effect. X-rays reflect off steel like light off a mirror; the ellipsoidal focused all of them on the tank of liquid hydrogen. The dense X-ray flux instantly compressed the tank enough to raise its temperature to many tens of millions of kelvins—hotter than the cores of most stars.

Other kinds of light and radiation followed the same pathway, from the focus with the atom bomb into the focus at the center of that tank of hydrogen, but only for microseconds. Then the nuclear bomb's heat and pressure ate the steel egg and every other solid object around it.

The twelve-ton blob of hydrogen, at a temperature of just over 45 million degrees Fahrenheit, began to expand.

Hydrogen is the simplest and lightest atom: just a proton with an electron going around it. At a mere few thousand degrees, the electron and proton will separate, forming plasma. (A gas in which many electrons are separated from their nuclei is a plasma—flames, the Northern Lights, and the glowing gas inside fluorescent lights, are ordinary plasmas.)

This was no ordinary plasma. In the vacuum of space, the soup of protons and electrons expanded at hundreds of miles per second.

If the electrons and protons had been electrically neutral, they would have continued right on out of the Earth's magnetic field, and out of the solar system, with no further ado. But a proton, by itself, carries a charge of $+1$, and an electron a charge of -1,

and the Earth's magnetic field acts on charged particles. The protons and electrons spreading out above
Kashmir were grabbed by the magnetic field of the
Earth itself, and whipped to higher and higher speeds.
When they came out of the proton bomb, they had
only a few hundred electron-volts of energy each—not
enough to penetrate a sheet of tissue paper. But the
magnetic field grabbed the protons and electrons,
and pulled them along, accelerating them every instant; they accelerated at the equivalent of 5,000 g.
Five minutes after the bomb had exploded, the uni-
maginably thin cloud of hydrogen plasma—a swirl of
protons and electrons so thin that there were only
about 1.5 million of them in a cubic foot—had been
flung around by the Earth's magnetic field with such
force that most of the particles were at relativistic velocities, and instead of a few thousand electron-volts,
each particle now packed millions or tens of millions
of electron-volts.

The invisible cloud swirled out to embrace the
Earth; less than ten minutes after the initial explosion,
so great was the velocity of the protons and electrons
it had scattered, the charged particles were slamming
into every object between the top of the atmosphere
and 40,000 kilometers up. At such high speeds and
low density, the hydrogen was no longer recognizable
as hydrogen. It had become pure hard radiation, what
the physicists call "ionizing radiation": charged particles moving so fast that when they crash into solid
matter, they knock or pull electrons off atoms, as well
as producing a nasty, dangerous spray of X-rays or
gamma rays.

Traveling through hundreds or thousands of miles
in the vacuum of space, whipping around the planet
several times per second, accelerated all the way by

the Earth's magnetic field, by the time the protons and electrons struck satellites, they had enough energy to produce a burst of hard radiation that could cut the microscopic conductors, pierce the dielectric films, burn through the transistors, chemically alter the semiconductors, send huge charges racing through ciruits never designed to carry them, and, in a hundred other ways, fry the microelectronics, on which every satellite depends, into uselessness.

The Pakistani government was loudly proclaiming that they had intended only to destroy satellites in the immediate vicinity of the detonation and to create a cloud that would wipe out satellites passing through low Earth orbit above that part of the world for a few hours. They wanted to disable India's intelligence and communication satellites, and they were willing to smash up the satellites of some other nations to do it.

If that had been their intention, somewhere they had gotten their numbers wrong. They hadn't realized how rapidly the high-energy protons and electrons would accelerate in the Earth's magnetic field, or how long they would remain trapped in the field. As the plasma cloud flew apart, picking up energy as it followed the magnetic field lines out away from the Earth, a very small fraction of it plunged down to the magnetic poles, blasting into the ionosphere high above Canada's Melville Island and Antarctica's Wilkes Land, but most of the particles were swept outward by the Earth's magnetic field, forming a denser, stronger, more powerful—and far more extensive—set of Van Allen radiation belts than the Earth had had within recorded time. That radiation would remain there for weeks, extending from 80 to 30,000 miles from the Earth's surface. While it lasted, all of the near Earth orbits would be bathed in enough radiation to destroy the electronics on satellites within an hour or two.

The hot zone reached out far enough to include geosynchronous orbit, where the communication satellites were—usually the furthest orbits in commercial use—destroying nearly all the electronic circuitry in space, making almost all of the world's satellites useless.

It had been a long time since college physics, and I had to watch the news stories several times before I understood even the basics. Meanwhile, the nations of the world were trying to get some idea of the scope of the catastrophe. The Canadians had sent up sounding rockets, and measurements taken by those showed that the protons were mostly still up there, gaining speed and energy until they either smashed into the Earth's atmosphere above the magnetic poles, or collided with some satellite and added to the radiation damage. So far the electrons were barely coming down at all, and based on the Starfish experiments, done decades ago, it was feared that they might linger in the radiation belts for decades.

It had taken the world about half a century to construct a vast network of communication, navigation, intelligence, weather, environmental, and scientific satellites overhead—and now, in less than four hours, all of them were damaged, dying, or dead. Billions of dollars of high-tech property on which the planet depended was swiftly turning to junk.

That was why telephone and television service was degrading rapidly; the satellites were dying, their microcircuitry burning out and becoming unreliable under the impact of the radiation, their radio receivers jammed by the tremendous electronic noise that drowned out the ground signals that were necessary for keeping their antennas pointed correctly and for telling them when to do correcting maneuvers, the electronic controls on their station-keeping rocket motors failing to work and leaving them to tumble helplessly under the influence of the micro-tides from the Earth and moon, as they lost the ability to correct their positions.

Fiber-optic landlines and microwave towers couldn't carry the load, especially not for trans-ocean transmission; the world's communications were snarling in one vast traffic jam.

NASA was issuing no word on what had happened to the crew of ISS; there was a "storm cellar" on the station for solar flares and other high-radiation events, but no word on whether it was adequate for the very high levels of radiation now bathing the station. There was a lifeboat Soyuz capsule docked at the station as well, but no announcement that the crew had bailed out, either. Commentators—who knew nothing yet, but had to say something—kept saying that we had to hope for the best for that crew.

The Pakistani and Indian armies had been ordered by the UN Security Council to get back out of the border areas, sit down, and not move; it appeared that the major powers were all backing the Security Council's decision. Probably the war would stop here. For all their effort at what the generals thought would be a brilliant coup, Pakistan had only managed to make an international pariah of itself, and to forfeit any support among other nations. Stories were leaking out of the Pakistani government, blaming Chinese technical advisors for having steered them wrong, but no one knew yet whether this was the truth or just a desperate attempt to shift the blame.

I sat back and stared at the screen, almost not

thinking, as the information poured in through the flickering images and crackling, staticky audio. I watched a dozen experts of all kinds argue with each other. Abstractedly, I thought, this is one of those days that I'll always remember, always be able to recall where I was when I heard about it, like when Nixon resigned, *Challenger* exploded, or the Berlin Wall came down. The total achievements of the whole world's space industry had been swept away in an hour.

Well, Nick was right. At least this was going to get Scott off the front page for a while. And now I knew why Nick had thought that my cell phone might not work.

I picked up the phone, called my house, listened through my message, and said, several times, loudly, "Scott, pick up the phone."

Finally he did. "Hi, Thalia, what's up? I was just getting storm windows up; did you even do that last fall?" It was a local call, so his voice was perfectly clear.

"No," I admitted, "it was easier to just pay for more heat. That's not what I called about. Turn on CNN. I don't think it's connected with our case, but something very big just happened. You're off the front page. I also think that sometime fairly soon, they're going to need every qualified shuttle pilot, no matter what they have to pay them, so I think you're also assured of work."

After a while I knew that I wasn't going to do any more work before Monday morning, that I was just sitting there in my darkening office as a grim gray wet November afternoon wound down outside the window, matching my mood. I was just looking out the window, not really paying attention to the television anymore, half-hypnotized by the endless repetitions of the few things anyone knew about the disaster, reported by people who were all either in shock (those who understood what was happening) or confusion (those who interviewed the people who understood). I told Clara, the temp secretary, to call me a cab, and then to go home, herself.

TWO HOURS LATER, sitting at home, watching the news as the very last surviving satellites were fading out, the only reason we could get CNN reliably in Washington was because there was a fiber-optic landline to Atlanta. The CNN main desk in Atlanta was reporting whatever could reach them by surface methods, mainly voice telephone and email. AM radio was a roar of white noise, as the storm of charged particles began to pour into the upper ionosphere; FM radio would remain all right. The President had declared a set of national priorities, so that newscasts and government messages would go out first, and the remaining landline bandwidth would be rotated among the many competing purposes; those with satellite dishes instead of cable, of course, were out of luck.

When Nick dropped by at seven, he was in an oddly cheerful mood, insisting that we had to do "something fun, right away. This is going to be my last weekend off for at least a year," Nick said. "There is absolutely nothing anyone can do about this for a few weeks, until the Earth's magnetic field has its way and the protons have either come down, moved out, or gotten trapped in the Van Allen belts. Background radiation near the Earth will be measurably higher for twenty years, but should be down to tolerable levels for spaceflight in a month or two. Once the radiation is at levels we can cope with, we'll be building and launching as fast as we can for the next two or three years, and they may very well blow the dust off some of our Scorpion Shack proposals and let us start building some new rockets."

We all stopped talking for a minute to hear a statement from the Pakistani ambassador to the UN. Pakistan claimed that what they had intended had been a bomb set off at no more than sixty miles height, with the liquid hydrogen only providing a radiation burst directly overhead to kill satellites, and most of the effect concentrated into an EMP on the ground. They said the Chinese technical crew that was helping them had launched a bigger bomb, higher, with much more hydrogen, in contradiction to all the orders given. Some commentators believed them, some believed the Chinese denials, and in any case it hardly mattered, now, what the intention had been.

After the announcement, Nick shrugged. "If I thought this really was a case of somebody tricking the Pakistanis, I'd think it had to be us or Curtiss—between losing a shuttle for more than a year, and now losing all the orbital assets, there must be five hundred billion dollars' worth of new satellite construction and launching to do, right away. It's better than being a general contractor the day after a hurricane. Which brings me back to why I need to get away for this weekend, while there's still nothing to be done. If I should be stupid enough to go into the office, or to be anywhere where they can find me easily, I will be forced to spend all weekend reassuring people about all sorts of things that they either already know anyway, or don't understand well enough to grasp the reassurances."

"I have an idea," Scott said. He looked over to

where Amos was quietly finishing his homework. "Hey, Amos, how was the trip to the cabin three weeks ago?"

"You know it was great, Dad," Amos said. "It's cold down by the ocean, but there's all sorts of things to do out on the beach, and the cabin stays warm with the woodstove."

"And your father stays warm cutting wood," Scott added.

"I wanted to try."

"I've still got to get used to seeing you swing an ax, kid, but we could give you some more practice tomorrow morning. Why don't all four of us go to the cabin? If Nick takes his cell phone, he'll be *almost* being responsible about it—even though they won't be able to reach him—and he gets two days of goofing off—"

"And cooking," Nick said, grinning. "True."

I thought about it. Nothing would be happening with the case until Monday, I could get my notes together as well down there as up here, and even if a world war were about to break out, we'd be better off at the cabin than in DC. We could be packed by seven, stop and get groceries on the way . . . "I just need to call Mrs. Banks to make sure the power and water will be on when we get there," I said. Since I was beginning to smile, just thinking about it, it might even be a good idea. "Let's do it."

THREE HOURS LATER, having done everything faster than I'd have thought possible, Amos, Scott, Nick, and I were each carrying a bag of groceries into the surprisingly clean kitchen of the cabin. For once, Scott had tidied up after himself, or maybe Amos had nagged him into it; he was becoming almost domesticated. The place was freezing cold, but Scott had left some pre-cut wood, and he got busy lighting a fire in the woodstove.

There was a note from Mrs. Banks on the kitchen table to let us know that a couple of light bulbs were burned out but the power and water were on; the refrigerator was humming, on its way to being cold, and didn't smell particularly musty.

"I haven't been back here in at least ten years," Nick said. "Is the Saturn V model still hanging in the attic? It was the last time . . ."

Amos looked embarrassed. "I have it hanging in my room at home, Uncle Nick," he said. "No one was using it here and I was afraid some summer tenant would throw it away."

Nick clapped him on the shoulder. "Perfect place for it. I'm honored."

"Friday night," I said, "is sloppy joes. Can you do those on a woodstove, Nick?"

"Can Amos stay up till midnight to eat one? It'll take Scott a while to get the fire really going, and then it takes a woodstove a while to heat up. But, yeah, sure, can do."

"Or you can use my cheater kit," Scott said, from where he was just touching off the newspaper under the kindling.

"Cheater kit?" I asked.

Scott shrugged. "Nick can cook on a woodstove, but I'm not the cook he is. I like a burner. So you'll find three electric hot plates, and a toaster oven, in the lower right cupboard next to the fridge."

"Perfect," Nick said, and reached down to pull out the hot plates. "Why don't you guys see if the television is working, and then see if there's any word yet on what's going on with the space station?"

"Amos, you're official television set operator," I said, "and I'm electing myself as cook's assistant and trainee. I still don't make them like Mom did, but your Uncle Nick does, and I'm going to learn how."

From the living room I heard Scott and Amos discovering that the cable TV was working but there were only four stations available. "Just like pioneer days," Scott was teasing Amos. "You know, when Lewis and Clark crossed the country, television was steam-powered, and only Mike Wallace was there to cover it when they reached the Pacific."

"Aw, Dad."

I had just gotten the celery and onions chopped, proudly noting I still hadn't cut myself, when Amos stuck his head in the kitchen and said, "Mom, Uncle Nick, you gotta see this," so we went out to join Scott and Amos. There were plenty of places to sit down, but once we heard the news coming from the TV screen, we stood to listen to all of it, unable to think of anything else.

SCOTT:

Much later, I was on the inquiry commission to look into exactly what happened on ISS that day. Just hearing about it was terrifying enough for me; I wouldn't ever want to be in a spot like that. But still, it was a relief to have heard the whole story. Machines failed, in extraordinary and unanticipated circumstances, but people didn't.

Alarms on ISS sound if radiation levels become unacceptable. Radiation is imperceptible to human senses; an area that is deadly looks, sounds, smells, and feels exactly like one that is perfectly safe. Injury from radiation is cumulative—the longer the exposure, the more damage. Thus it is always vital to know whether you're being irradiated, because sources of radiation are ubiquitous in space, and situations can change in a heartbeat. Solar flares, the huge gas eruptions from the sun that dump swarms of protons into the Earth's magnetic field, arrive within hours of the solar observer satellites and ground-based astronomers seeing the vast explosions tear through the solar atmosphere.

The proton bomb released far more protons than Earth receives from any solar flare. The first warning the crew got was when it set off the Geiger counters, which detect ionizing radiation. Sprays of secondary electromagnetic radiation from every piece of exposed metal set off the X-ray and gamma detectors. As successive protons had been accelerated for longer and longer before striking ISS, the energy and amount of radiation rose swiftly.

Sheer luck allowed the crew to survive. If anyone had been doing an EVA, that person might well have taken a fatal dose of radiation before being able to get back inside. But as it happened, the three "construction crew" astronauts on board were in about the best places they could be in the situation. Doris McIntyre, the medical/biological mission specialist, was asleep in her bunk, and when the alarms went off, she simply rolled out of bed and swam into the "storm cellar"—the command/control area, about the size of a motel bathroom, that was specially hardened against radiation. A moment later, as she was rubbing the sleep from her eyes with the heels of her hands, she was joined by Stephen Tebworthy, a tall thin Briton who was there as a specialist in microgravity welding. The storm cellar monitors had already come up automatically; he leaned forward, read the counts and intensities, and said, "Jesus, those numbers are unbelievable, way out of range—they can't possibly be right. It looks like the sun blew up."

Carl Tanaka, the commander and the third member of the team, swam in and closed the hatch. "What are radiation levels like here?" he asked. "Every monitor lit up like a Christmas tree."

Doris checked the internal monitors. "Shit. We're all taking a dose that could kill us in an hour or two."

"Then let's get out of here. We can figure out what it was once we're on the ground," Tanaka said. He turned to head for the hatch.

"Wait a minute, chief—right now we're in a safe spot, but it's *really* hot between us and the Soyuz," Tebworthy pointed out. "We'd better power the Soyuz up by remote, so that all we have to do is dive into it, close the door, strap down, and go."

Doris pulled herself to the storm shelter's workstation, pounded at the keyboard, and said, "Okay, it's better to go no matter where we come down, but I think it'll be the North Atlantic or maybe Europe, and there's no storms—power-up sequence is under way and—shit! shit! shit! Can you believe a system crash right now?" She pounded the keys again, hard, in frustration, making mistakes, scrambling to correct them. "Reboot and I'll have it in a minute—"

"*Maybe* you'll have it, Doris." Carl Tanaka did his best to sound calm, but the other two crew members could hear him making the effort. "There are incredible amounts of static on every radio channel. We're in the worst radiation anyone's ever seen up here. Electronics aren't going to last long, especially not if they're outside the storm cellar."

Doris had kept working with the computer while

she listened to the commander. "Damn. Well, it did come up . . . okay. It should be powered up by the time we get to it."

"Good." Carl Tanaka headed through the hatch. "Let's go."

The lifeboat for the station was a Curtiss Soyuz, built from the basic Russian capsule design but with American materials and more precise engineering tolerances. Normally it sat in the dock, hatch closed and powered down, but it could be readied in less than two minutes, either by crew inside it or remotely.

The three astronauts squirmed down the long passageway that led to where the Soyuz was docked. When they were halfway there, with a sound like thunder, the station shook. The walls lurched sickeningly around them, and everything drifted toward the walls as though they had suddenly become magnetized.

Without a word, Carl Tanaka lunged down the corridor to the Soyuz hatch. Doris and Tebworthy followed, not knowing what was going on. Carl threw the Soyuz hatch open, and plunged headfirst into the capsule. The other two followed him, squeezing into their seats beside his pilot's chair.

The board was a wild profusion of green and red lights, and the LCD displays flickered and wavered in a way they had never done in training.

Tanaka had already grabbed at the controls and was fighting with them, pounding the board in front of him in frustration. The thunder was now very loud, and the interior of the little capsule whirled like a carnival ride. He fought the controls again and again, pushed at buttons with no apparent effect, and then shouted over the roar. "Get back to the storm cellar. I'll come in and tell you what's going on in just a minute." As Tebworthy and Doris climbed back up the corridor that had suddenly become a vertical shaft, he hollered after them, "And get out the dosimeters, the film badges, and the Geiger counter."

They were halfway back to the storm cellar when the thunder stopped, as abruptly as it had begun; in the sudden silence, they could hear Tanaka swearing with fury.

As they reached the storm cellar, Tanaka came up behind them and crawled in after them. Once they were all there, he sat down, and said, "I'd say we have almost a tenth of a g in here. Nuisance, having to climb instead of swim, isn't it?"

They stared at him. He shrugged and spread his hands. "People, we're in trouble. When the Soyuz powered up, some of the attitude thrusters failed on, instead of failing safe. That's what the noise was, and that's what has started us into a slow spin. I couldn't get them to turn off. They've drained the tank. Even if we could get the Soyuz clear of the station, now, we couldn't maneuver—and that means we can't make a try at re-entry. Even if we had a spare tank of fuel for the attitude thruster—which we fucking don't, and isn't *that* stupid!" For a moment the commander looked down at his hands, clenching and unclenching them in a near rage. "Yeah, it's stupid. Well, even if we had the fuel to gas it back up, and we knew that the attitude jets wouldn't do that again, with radiation levels what they are outside the storm cellar, you couldn't get the refueling done without running some major risks. And the attitude thrusters are only what we know about. As damaged as the electronics are, the controls in the Soyuz are all dubious anyway. Who knows if we could even fly it? I'd say our lifeboat is dead; I don't think we even have a decent way to jettison it from our dock.

"The reason we have this little bit of gravity is that the thruster firing started us tumbling. I just had a look at the main thrusters for the station itself, and there's nothing working. We can't stabilize the place, so we're going to continue to tumble, and to precess, which will keep us in this fractional g for the foreseeable future and would also complicate the hell out of getting off the station, even if we still had a Soyuz."

After he let the situation sink in, he asked, "What are radiation levels like in here?"

Doris sighed. "Well, at the present level, here in the shelter, we're about five days from radiation sickness, and maybe ten from being walking dead. But the level peaked two minutes ago, and it's drifting down now. Here's what I think we ought to do. There's tons of material we can move around inside the station, and if we can pile it all up against the outside of the storm cellar—especially dense stuff like water tanks, and food, and batteries, and construction materials—then we can increase the effect of our shielding. If the radiation keeps falling off at the rate it's doing, we might be able to last for days or weeks."

"And then?" Tebworthy said, quietly.

"And then we have time to hope, and to get in touch with Houston and let them know we're alive and how bad our situation is," Doris said. "I don't know whether they'll have any way to come and get us, but they might—maybe there's an Ariane almost ready to go that could bring us a new Soyuz. Maybe they'll be able to diagnose our broken Soyuz remotely and use a Progress to bring us up a basket of spare parts to fix it, and fuel for the thrusters. Maybe radiation is going to fall to zero three hours from now, or maybe the little green men in the saucers will overhear and come rescue us. I don't care. All we have to hope for is good luck. But we can't have any good luck if we just sit here and let the radiation kill us, now can we?"

After a quick dry ration and a drink of water, they clipped on their dosimeters—which already showed alarmingly high cumulative readings—and their film badges, and set to gutting the station from the inside and strapping the pieces around their storm cellar, with "artificial gravity" from the spinning station that was just enough to make the work hard and not enough to consistently keep things where they were put.

When they finished, they crept in through the bent tunnel, formed of crates, water containers, and aluminum sheets, along with not-yet-assembled crew bunks still in the boxes, that formed the entrance to their little habitat in the center of the junk pile. By that time, most of the lighting circuits were out, and they were working by flashlight. Air recirculation could be done manually, but someone would have to crawl out and do it now and then, changing tank connections and turning hand pumps. There was food and water, and a "honey bucket," in the shelter.

Grimly, having established that none of the radios they had brought to the shelter from storage worked anymore, they sat down and began assembling components cannibalized from all of them, hoping to get a set of parts at random that were all functional. It was slow, difficult work in the dark by flashlight, and not really anyone's area of expertise, but they kept at it until they had a set they thought might work. Stephen Tebworthy drew the short straw, and climbed out into the rest of the station, briefly, to determine a rough position and trajectory from ground land-

marks that swung terrifyingly by the viewports now
and then. They made a best guess of when they
would be line of sight to Houston, and then, attaching
the antenna wire to the wall, hoping that the station
would act as a giant antenna, they broadcast their
appeal for help. They repeated their simple two-
minute message, verbatim, for thirty minutes, hoping
that someone on the ground could put it together
through all the radio noise.

When, three minutes after they stopped, they received a garbled, crackling, only half-understandable
message—just enough to tell them that their message
had come through—and it began to repeat, they celebrated silently, afraid to miss a single word, listening
over and over as they sipped their water and sat in
the dark chamber that tumbled end over end, falling
forever.

THALIA:

The news from the International Space Station was
that the crew was alive but the station was dying.
Microelectronics were slowly being blasted out of existence by the invisible proton-electron bombardment
that poured against every metal surface, scattering X-
rays and gamma rays. They could live some time
yet—the guess was several weeks—in the dark and the
slowly intensifying cold, hoarding power from batteries and fuel cells, fixing a thing here and a subsystem
there (at the expense of taking more radiation in their
damaged bodies). But, although no one wanted to say
it outright, they probably couldn't live long enough
for anyone to be able to rescue them.

"A couple of years from now, there would have

been a possibility of a quick response," Nick said, gloomily. "Right now, we'd have to have a shuttle or the Russians would have to have a Soyuz ready to go, and we'd have to work like mad all the same, and it still might not make it. Anyway, with it tumbling like that, you can't dock. Even if they're alive, they aren't going to be for much longer." He stood up. "Well, the situation won't improve if dinner is burned or late. Thally, I can take it from here—it's just mixing it together and heating it up and serving it. Dinner in ten minutes." Nick headed out for the kitchen; I thought he probably wanted to do something to relax.

I knew, from having grown up around my father and my aunt, both aerospace engineers, that there's no stress quite as miserable as the stress on a ground-based engineer who is waiting for word about whether the hardware has failed and lives have been lost or are in peril. I figured a few minutes of doing something soothing was the best thing for Nick; this wasn't being much of a "day off." From the kitchen, I heard the pots and pans thumping and clanging gently, and the soft scrape of a wooden spoon in a pan, as he got the last of it ready.

"Dad, is Uncle Nick right? If they live through the radiation, after it settles down, couldn't they go get them on one of the shuttles?" Amos asked.

Scott made a balancing gesture with his hand. "They're saying a month till you can fly a crewed mission up there—and with the station tumbling and everyone weak and sick, you've got to send a person or two across to the station to go and get the crew, by the time you can go at all. I don't think any of them will be in any shape for an EVA on their own.

"Even to be ready in a month, they are going to have to rush the daylights out of getting *Atlantis* ready, and who knows how much time the survivors on ISS might have. Normally it takes several months to get one ready—and even if they accelerate it, then there's the problem of having to spacewalk between the shuttle and the tumbling station, take off anybody who's injured . . . it would be what we technically call a real bastard."

"Mom doesn't let me call things that."

"Mom is right," Scott said, glancing apologetically at me. "But there are some situations that call for adult language, and this is one of them. Anyway, it would be so difficult, and so risky, that odds are really against anything working. On the other hand, we've never left someone up there to die, and I hope we never will. It's an unwritten part of the deal they make with you when you sign up—if you'll risk your neck for any mission they ask you to, they'll risk more necks to get you back. So I'm sure if anyone can rescue them, or might just possibly try to rescue them, they'll make the attempt. But that's as much hope as there is, and I don't know of anyone who could do such a rescue."

It was just past eleven before we finally ate, but neither my ex nor my son complained about the delay. Something about the sea air or the tension had us all eating like wolves; even I had two sloppy joes. ISS was undoubtedly still on Nick's mind, but he didn't seem sad as much as quiet. Probably he was thinking about the possibilities for rescue.

After everyone had finished eating, and we were just sitting, not speaking, enjoying the sense of being warm and well fed, Nick said, "Hmm. I think I do need to get down here more often. We have the beach to ourselves, and as you all know, after September thirtieth, this little town doesn't even leave its streetlights on. So my guess is that right now we're going to have the best aurora borealis of our lifetimes. Would anyone like to go for a short night walk on the beach?"

"Absolutely," Scott said. "Just let me get the dishes into the tub to soak." He grabbed the plates, pots, and pans and scraped them into the garbage, then set them in a big iron tub on the woodstove and used a hose from the kitchen sink to fill it, adding a bit of soap. "Those should be ready to wash by the time we get back," he said.

In a few minutes, all bundled in coats and sweaters, we stepped out onto the back porch. The beach was lit in flickering red, green, and blue, bright as a barn burning half a mile away. In the northern sky, halfway to the zenith, great dancing curtains, sheets, and curving lines of color constantly changed. Vast cold films of green and blue light, laced with red streaks, appeared, curled, twisted, and disappeared like ghosts. The aurora covered the northern sky, swirling to a bright vortex just to the right of the handle of the Little Dipper, which showed faintly through the wild sprays of light.

Scott explained to Amos. "The normal aurora is caused by charged particles from the solar wind getting swept down into the upper atmosphere by the Earth's magnetic field; when the charged particles hit the upper atmosphere they hit the molecules so hard that the molecules give off light. The proton bomb created many times more charged particles than the solar wind normally ever supplies, and that's what happens when so many charged particles get into the magnetosphere. It's a big problem for the world, but it certainly is beautiful."

We stood and watched it much later than we

meant to; it was just too glorious to look away from, despite all the loss and destruction it signified. When we finally went in, we were all hushed, as if we'd been to a very special church service in the world's grandest cathedral.

Scott had the dishes still to wash, and I had some things I wanted to set up for breakfast the next morning, so we spent a while in the kitchen, just quietly working next to each other, the way we used to when we came up to the Blackstone family cabin in the years before Amos was born and life got frantic.

"It feels good to be here," I ventured, after a while.

Scott set a plate in the rack to dry and said, "Yes, it does. I hadn't thought we'd ever do it again. Especially not in the fall."

"Well," I admitted, "so far this is more pleasant than the last time. Not being sick and not having rain makes a difference."

He scrubbed a pot while I pre-sliced some tomatoes and onions for tomorrow's lunch. After a while, he said, "I always thought you were a pretty good sport about that."

"I tried to be. It was important to the relationship and all that."

"Yeah."

The long silence stretched on until finally we banked the fire to get ready for bed. By then it was about 12:30. Neither of us had paid any attention to what Nick and Amos were doing. When we checked, we discovered they were asleep in the twin bunks in the attic bedroom. Amos was in the top one, sound asleep with a beautiful smile. Nick was really too tall a man for the lower bunk, but he was folded up into it anyway, snoring loudly.

"Do you think they're really asleep, or is this a

routine to convince us they're asleep?" Scott asked.

"It's a convincing routine, if it's a routine," I said. "Amos hardly ever sleeps that well at home."

"Not when he's over at my place, either," Scott said. "Trouble is, this leaves us the queen-sized bed, or the couch. I suspect some manipulation here."

"Duh. You think? And Nick is worse than Amos about it. Well, the choices are that one of us gets on the couch, or I count on your being the gentleman you always have been. I've got pajamas," I said.

"Me too. I vote for sharing a bed and behaving ourselves," my ex replied. "It'll be warmer."

The next morning, when we awoke, it was a beautiful sunny morning, with light pouring in through the white curtains, and we had snuggled up during the night so that we were holding each other. Fortunately neither Nick nor Amos saw us, so we weren't raising any false hopes, and by the time they stumbled down, drawn by the smell of bacon, eggs, and coffee, we had made up the bed, dressed, and in short destroyed the evidence. Both Scott and I were kind of embarrassed by the whole situation, but it was also sort of funny, and we ended up laughing about it, as a private joke, for the rest of the day.

Just after lunch on Saturday, we all took a break to turn the television on and see what was happening with ISS. There were some brief recordings of the crew's voices, as they made a few banal comments and dished out some bland assurances. An expert told us that as radiation decreased in LEO, transmissions from the space station became clearer. Other experts assured us that the whole situation was being dealt with by ground engineers telling the astronauts how to fix everything, "Just like Apollo 13."

Scott snorted at that. "Astronauts are good at fol-

lowing directions. They have to be or they don't survive. But you can't fix a microchip; you can only
build a new one. And right now there's no way for
a capsule to dock to bring them up any spare parts,
and if there were, they don't have the electronics to
guide it in, and it's still way, way too hot to go EVA.
I'm sure they're getting some stuff fixed, but I'm just
as sure it's not much, yet, and they're still screwed."

I sighed. "Some NASA PR officer, or the Issues
Management consultant if they were smart enough to
hire him, is earning his keep today. They're making
so much out of the parallel to Apollo 13 because they
want this story off the front page for a while. So they
make it sound as if it's routine—you know, Gene
Kranz got them back by just telling them what to do
with a roll of duct tape, and that's all we have to do
whenever something goes wrong. Bullshit, but very
salable bullshit."

"My parents are giving me a heck of a vocabulary,"
Amos said.

"I follow the same rule as your father. It's okay
when the situation calls for it. And adults are the
judge of when a situation calls for it."

"Amos, perhaps, as your uncle and positive role
model, I should get you away from these crude, un-
civilized people," Nick said. "Would you like to go
throw a football around on the beach? I'll pretend I
can throw if you'll pretend you can catch."

"Sweet."

The two of them took off in a burst of noise, laughing and teasing each other.

"Nick should have been a dad," I said, making conversation.

Scott shrugged. "He's better as an uncle. Busy guys

just can't do what kids need them to do, which is mostly be around."

"Voice of experience?" I asked.

"Could be. Busy women probably have the same problem, hunh?"

"Yeah." We had skirted around the edge of a fight, and I, for one, didn't want to get any closer to it than we already had. For another indefinite silence, we watched the man and the boy run and throw the ball around, and the big waves roll onto the bright cold beach, and the white fluffy clouds march slowly out to sea, headed over the horizon.

"You know," Scott said, "most really dedicated engineering managers either get married right after college or right after they retire. So Nick's missed one chance and it will be a long time before the next time. Maybe *we* should start conspiring to get *Nick* married off. It would serve him right, eh?"

"It would." I leaned back against the railing of the deck, and watched Nick throw a wild pass that Amos very nearly caught. "So you think the ISS crew is going to die?"

"We all do sometime. Astronauts often die early." He sighed. "I just don't want them to die without someone having tried, down here. Like I said, it's part of the deal. And I don't have any great amount of faith in an Apollo 13 solution. I was at a reception for Jim Lovell once, and I heard him point out how much luck was involved, and how easily it could have gone some other way. I want to see us get them back down here, safely, from some combination of brains and skill and courage and pure willpower." He stared off toward the sea; I noticed how cold it was for so fine a day. "Of course I'd be damn happy to get them back, alive, by any old stroke of luck at all, right now.

Want to grab some nice big mugs of coffee and walk up the beach? It's getting cold just standing here."

"Sure."

We didn't say much on the walk but the company was nice.

The rest of the weekend passed in a pleasant blur of "camp life," long walks, another spectacular aurora, and a long talk looking into the red glow of the stove. It was very much like what Scott had told me our first fall weekend here, so many years ago, would be like.

Nick spent the rest of the afternoon with Amos, doing what they called boy stuff—throwing rocks into the water, racing each other up and down the beach, and Nick explaining rockets and orbits in simplified terms. By dinner time, Amos was pestering me about letting him build model rockets, and I figured that either Scott or I would have to get him an Estes starter kit for Christmas. "Looks like genetics is winning out," I said to Scott, as we ended up curled up together in the bed for the second night.

Scott shrugged, and carefully put his arm around me in a way that was affectionate without being too familiar. The man always had been a gentleman. "It's in the Blackstone blood, I guess. Wonder if he's going to be a pilot or a robber baron?"

I had some clever reply in mind, but Scott fell asleep, and a moment later I did too, with the November ocean rumbling in the distance, and the walls still lighted by the flashes of that weird aurora.

CHAPTER NINE

NICK:

On that first Monday after the proton bomb, it seemed that the crew on ISS was far from the biggest problem the space program was facing. Estimates were that the crew up there might last four weeks without lasting health consequences. *Atlantis* could be ready to go, ASU thought, in nineteen days, with some kind of improvised radiation shielding in the crew compartment. The situation was tight, but not at all hopeless.

Email from Ned Robertson, my chief of engineering on the Starcraft project, said that some of his engineers had "an idea that might be relevant to the ISS problem." That probably meant an interesting hour sometime soon—I had enjoyed every conversation I had ever had with Robertson, and every presentation he had made. Perhaps, since I was planning to be at Scorpion Shack all day tomorrow, I could squeeze that one in, early; it would at least assure me that there would be one pleasant hour in a day otherwise filled with meetings. I sent Angie, my secretary at Scorpion Shack, an email to see if she could put together a breakfast meeting with Robertson's team for tomorrow.

I had arrived at the office in DC at 7 A.M., and there was a pile of paper the size of a small city phone book waiting for me, accompanied by a couple of meg of email. Republic Wright had some interest in about eighty communication satellites—we had built them, or built a major subsystem, or operated their station-keeping. We also had weather satellites, military intelligence, and some of GPS. In addition to the satellites themselves, all now dead and in need of replacement, we were flooded with emergency orders for replacement launches.

For every satellite, launch request, subsystem, or other Republic Wright involvement, there was a memo, about three pages long, which could be summarized as "Republic Wright must fix it for us right away." I printed them all out, sorted them into the really urgent and the merely urgent, dealt them out in piles to my assistants' inboxes, left scrawled instructions on top of each pile, and phoned for the cab.

I swallowed a big, strong coffee while I waited, and was getting into the cab to Washington Reagan by 8:30, starting on a trip that would take me about 5,500 miles before the day was out.

On the plane I pulled up the email copies on my laptop computer and read through the memos I had flagged. I would need a clear mental picture of the total situation later this afternoon, when the upper management of RW would meet in San Diego to formulate a rough strategy.

The only silver lining in that whole dark cloud of complaints and demands was the possibility that this might get me the funds, people, and resources to accelerate the Starcraft project, since the world was going to need anything at all that could deliver a satellite to orbit. Potentially a fleet of six StarBoosters, mated with StarCores, could carry satellites up faster than the manufacturers could build them. That was a potential that everyone needed to be aware of.

I had arranged to stop off at Scorpion Shack in Texas, not to hear where matters stood on the different projects—I always kept current and I already knew—but to hold a kind of halftime talk to get my engineers and scientists thinking hard about spelling out the full range of what we might be able to do, how well and how soon.

As the jet's wheels touched the Scorpion Shack runway and we rumbled toward the limo, I had just one hour to get ready for my meeting with my technical people. Angie, my secretary, was waiting in the limo with a prioritized stack of paper and a schedule. Peering at me over her harlequin glasses and pushing her unconvincing blonde wig to the side, with the kind of accent you get from living your entire life in Armstrong, Texas, she looked like she had escaped from a Gary Larson cartoon, but she'd been with me five years and there was no more efficient human being anywhere. "Twenty-one routine signatures," she said, "for stuff you already approved. You can sign while you listen."

I did.

"Breakfast meeting with Robertson tomorrow, big conference room off the cafeteria, seven-fifteen. About thirty people. And he's ordered a PowerPoint projector. Whatever it is, you're getting quite a show. Phil

Tenn wants to talk to you about space junk and that thing he calls the Starbaggie, and he's penciled in for ten. A whole new flock of email arrived in the last three hours, which you'll want to see for your meeting in San Diego. Here's a copy." She handed me a floppy that I tucked into my coat pocket as I finished the last signing.

"At the rate it's coming in," she added, "I'll be giving you another floppy when you go, so make sure you get it from me. I'll run some interference to make sure that you get off the ground here in time. Now, this last thing here is a chart that I pulled off the current delivery and report schedules, the list of responsibilities, and some stuff from the organizational handbook, sort of cross-collated. I thought you might want to know what you're being held accountable for, officially, and when, while you talk to those people."

"Perfect," I said. I hadn't thought of it myself but it was exactly what I needed.

"I also took the liberty of setting up a cold buffet in your office. I checked your closet there and you have a spare suit and clothes. What you have on can go to the cleaners while you're in San Diego, and it'll be back in your apartment tonight. So we'll keep you presentable, too. Just make sure you eat in what you have on, then change.

"Oh, and there's some personal stuff too. I called your brother's lawyer to make sure, if it got too busy, there wouldn't be any delays if you don't have time to sign checks. She said everything was fine, financially, at the moment, and sounded pretty confident.

"And your nephew emailed you a thank-you note that sounds like your brother wrote it."

I laughed. Angie allowed herself half a smile before

she added, "Hope you enjoyed your time off. Until time for your meeting, I'm planning to hold all calls and give you some decompression and thinking time. I've also warned all staff that if they try to catch you between the limo and the office, they may consider themselves dead."

Just as Angie had planned, I was comfortably fed, showered, changed, alert, and ready for the meeting. The table was ringed by some of the most energized technical people I'd ever seen. It warmed my heart, but there wasn't much time to enjoy it—I had seventy-five minutes until Angie would hurl me into the back of another limo and I'd be off to San Diego like a high-priority mailbag.

"Well," I said, "I wanted to talk about how this whole facility, and everyone in it, ought to respond to this extraordinary opportunity. You all know the old factoid that the Chinese ideogram for 'crisis' is a combination of the ideograms for 'danger' and 'opportunity.' What we've got to do, completely, is focus on the opportunity side.

"Here's how I see it. The world is just finding out how much they've come to depend on satellites and space travel. They will be willing to pay whatever it takes to get the space systems back up, as soon as possible. If we do it *right* this time, we can do it as a planned systematic development, instead of piecemeal across forty years. That way, when we're done re building, we'll be in a much better position to expand. So no matter how busy we all get, I want you always thinking about one issue: how can we re-expand into space in a better, more systematic, more open-ended way?"

Ned Robertson, senior engineer on my staff, and also the driving force behind Starcraft, asked, "Any word on how we're getting the crew down from ISS?"

"As of the memos I had this morning, NASA is still assessing, but it looks like if they go to round-the-clock shifts, they can get *Atlantis* up there the minute the radiation people say they can go—probably with extra shielding, so they can go sooner. I think they can make it, based on the tentative stuff I saw."

Ned leaned back, surveyed the room, and said, "I don't know if you want to hear this question, just now, Nick, but is there a backup plan? The shuttle gets routine delays all the time. It wouldn't be improbable that they'd be delayed a month, even on a super-hurry-up schedule. And that could be a month more than the ISS crew have."

I thought for a moment; I had business to cover, and time was short, but I had learned that when Ned looked at me that particular way—head cocked to the side, fixing me with his right eye, lips pressed tight and curling into a little sardonic smile—there was something he thought was important, that I might not want to hear, and he was signaling me that he wanted to be asked about it.

Every time I had seen that expression, it had eventually turned out to be something I absolutely did need to know about. That's one of the effects of hiring talented people, I suppose.

"You have an idea in mind for that backup," I said. "Tell me."

"Well, suppose we skip a few steps in the current development plan. The StarBooster has been tested with Athena, and we have a StarCore I sitting there almost built, and two more coming along, right? So we just combine all the tests into one shot . . . put dual StarBoosters on the StarCore and let 'er rip. If it all flies, then we tear down the StarBoosters, get them ready to go as quick as we can . . . and put StarRescue on top of the next StarCore, and go get the ISS crew."

"So your suggestion is that—" I tried to keep my voice neutral "—we ought to . . . fly *one* test of a major component, then fly it with a completely untested component, *plus* people?"

"Well, I didn't say it was the best way," Ned said, primly. "And StarRescue has had some drop tests. It's at least a partially tested component."

"Ned, the 'partially tested component' is a whole spacecraft. I'll be happy to hear all the ideas—even that one—tomorrow," I said. "You might convince me, but it will take a great deal of convincing."

Robertson nodded, obviously happy for the moment. He didn't need to hear "yes" all the time, or even most of the time, but my listening seemed to be important to him.

"All right," I said. "Now, even if we don't use it for anything as dramatic as the ISS rescue, the whole Starcraft series is vital. I think we'll be building more StarBooster 200s than anyone ever envisioned, and flying every configuration of Athenas and StarCores we've ever thought of with them. The question is, what *else* can we do? I know we have other rocket motors and packages in development—lots of them—and what I want us to do is *quickly* identify all the ones that could be made compatible with Starcraft systems, to add even more capability."

Phil Tenn cleared his throat. "Except for some very low altitude stuff, all the dead satellites are now long-duration space junk. We'd been messing around with an air-launched version of Starbaggie for wartime, but we could probably send ten or twelve of them up at a time on a StarBooster/Athena—or slip them in, space-a, on every payload going up. There's tons of trash now taking up valuable space in the commercially important orbits."

"Starbaggie" was a nickname; it had originally been a DARPA project intended to be used, in time of war, to knock down surveillance or communication satellites. It was supposed to be carried aloft on a rocket launched from an airplane, much like the commercial Pegasus system, for a near-rendezvous with the target satellite, at which point it would deploy a Kevlar net about a mile across, swallow the satellite by reeling in the net, and then deploy either a small rocket motor or a long, dragging tether to de-orbit it.

Angie signaled me from the door, and I looked around the room. Probably there were six other teams with ideas, but just at the moment I didn't have time to hear all of them. I held up a hand and said, "All right, people, I know I can depend on all of you for ideas, creativity, and problem-solving. Phil, if I get a chance, I'll raise the space junk issue at the big meeting this afternoon—that could be very lucrative for us, if we can get somebody to pay a bonus on clearing junk out of orbits.

"Ned, I'm looking forward to your presentation tomorrow, but keep it as conservative as you can. For the moment, I won't say anything about that idea in San Diego.

"Everybody, I need all of your enthusiasm and support. Give your people a heads-up: we might be changing everything we're doing tomorrow, so stay creative and flexible. We're adjourned."

Nearly everyone had to shake my hand and say a few words. Angie truly had to scramble to get me off the ground in time to make the big meeting in San Diego.

On the plane, I read through the disks of email she had given me. Every other member of upper management at Republic Wright was jockeying for position, too. A quick scan revealed three groups—the ones who saw the situation as an opportunity (whom I dubbed "aggressives"), the ones who saw it as a menace (whom I dubbed "fearfuls"), and many who didn't see it at all—people who said the company should just keep doing what it was doing. (I dubbed those "oblivious.")

It was discouraging. The oblivious were the largest single group. Somehow or other the fearful and the aggressive would have to find their way into an alliance.

When we landed at the company field outside San Diego, I was sure I'd be late. I was already mentally writing a memo to the pilot's supervisor, saying that I'd given the pilot a late start and he'd gotten some pretty bad headwinds. As it was, I wrote a note congratulating the limo driver, though I don't ever want to go through that much southern California freeway quite that quickly again. I arrived at the meeting with plenty of extra adrenaline, which might be to my advantage.

A minute after I had settled in, unfolded my laptop, and taken the first welcome sip of hot coffee, Jagavitz walked in, sat down, and said, "All right, gentlemen and ladies, I've read all your memos and notes. I can boil it down to a choice. We can do one of three things. We jump in and fight like a tiger for all the market we can get. We hunker down like a turtle and try not to lose anything we already have. Or we freeze like a goddam deer in the headlights and wait for Curtiss to take us over." As usual, when he got emotional, his slight Central European accent got stronger. "That is what I will say to the Board. Surely you all know that I will recommend the tiger, not the turtle or the deer. The Board will either agree with me, or they will fire me. If I am not fired, then all of you must either see things my way, or take a walk." He looked around the room, and from his expression, I concluded that most of my anxiety and worry about this meeting had been, blessedly, wasted. I had won before I had arrived.

Jagavitz went on. "Our policy with regard to Curtiss is that we must surpass them and win a long-run advantage. Whatever the situation was a week ago, today it is—what's the expression? in football?—today fate has punted. Loose ball, anyone's to grab. We will grab that ball, and if we have to break some noses to do it, that adds to the fun." He now had that famous expression that *Business Week* always described as "sharklike" and *Forbes* called "fearsome." "So," he continued. "So. Now we make money. Now we pioneer. Now we show everyone how it is done. Don't tell me what they told you at Harvard MBA school, unless it tells me how to do what I want. These next few years, *we* write the book, and all the experts can study *us*."

His bald, liver-spotted head shone like a skull, but the crinkles around his eyes were warm and filled with pleasure. "I want every space launch product that can fly to be flying, as soon as it safely can. I want our sales force to be drowning in orders for all of them.

"That's what the program is, if the Board keeps me. If you think I'm going to still be the CEO after tomorrow morning—and I plan to be—then you had better get ready to work harder, faster, and better than you ever have before."

My first thought was that I hoped that I'd be allowed to hand out a tape or a transcript of that speech at Scorpion Shack.

"Comments?" Jagavitz said.

A hand went up down at the end of the table—Andrew Riscaveau. He wasn't senior management, but because so much of our work was classified, he attended our meetings as a consultant. He didn't have a vote, and normally he only spoke if security issues were involved.

"I just wanted to point out that that strategy could have very serious security repercussions. First of all, moving so much high tech out of the lab and into production, so quickly, is going to enormously increase the opportunities for espionage and sabotage, domestic or foreign. Second, and more important, the government security authorities have to be concerned about having a stable and productive aerospace industry, and that kind of market-grabbing is going to be disruptive at a time when the country really needs a smooth-functioning system. I don't think they'll let us get away with it, if they're doing their job."

Jagavitz stared as if he'd just seen a dead rat in Riscaveau's mouth. "We will be increasing launch capacity, and that is what the country needs; 'stability' is a polite expression for 'the comfort of people who are already on top.' Since, at the moment, we are not the ones on top, we have no interest in their comfort. As for Curtiss's markets, let them keep them and serve them—if they can. If not, we will.

"As for the first part, it is your responsibility, is it not, to prevent espionage and sabotage on the company grounds? And didn't you just hear me say that everyone will have to work harder? Well, work harder. Make sure it doesn't happen."

Riscaveau was nearly pouting. Instead of sensibly shutting up, he rambled for a full minute, stressing how he was just trying to help, no one understood the need for a real security perspective, and in a high-tech company that was involved in national security, every issue was a security issue.

While Riscaveau rambled, I watched him. My managers and engineers at Scorpion Shack detested him. At any meeting to which he had to be invited—no one ever invited him if it was optional—he always took great pains to assure us that he was a good security man, who could have had his choice of jobs in security. He took *pleasure* in asserting that guarding anything is always the same job, and he was the best judge of how to guard anything. He loved to remind engineers and managers that no matter what astonishing work they might do, no matter how far into the new frontier they might push humanity, Riscaveau would always be there to check their front door pass.

Riscaveau finally ran down, unable to wriggle out of Jagavitz's glare. Not hiding his impatience, Jagavitz asked for more comments and questions.

He got a few minor issues, mostly from people too junior to realize that Jagavitz wasn't a detail person, and the CFO gave him some notes about how long the company could afford to run at a loss until the new revenue streams came in. Then, at Jagavitz's request, I got up and talked in a general way about the enormous potential increase in launch capability from Starcraft. Finally, Jagavitz adjourned the meeting, and I caught a flight back to Scorpion Shack, where I arrived at about eleven P.M. local time. When the limo picked me up at the airport, for the first time that day, I could tell a driver to take his time. It had been a nineteen-hour day, and I more or less fell into bed.

CHAPTER TEN

NICK:

Breakfast with engineers is not relaxing; very few people are as nervous as an engineer compelled to socialize with management, and it is always an atmosphere of forced laughter and awkward silences. Everyone gulps the food as if someone might take it all back.

The nine people from the StarBooster, StarCore I and II, and StarBird projects suddenly developed a consuming interest in the muffins and scrambled eggs. Ned Robertson and I, who knew each other well, exchanged platitudes and pleasantries over our breakfasts, while everyone else ate in tense silence. When, after about twenty minutes, the trays had been cleared, table wiped, and notebooks brought out, and everyone was sipping coffee or tea, I said, "So, tell me your ideas."

Robertson nodded. "I should warn you, Mr. Blackstone, we stayed up till one o'clock last night getting this all together, and most of us are a little wired on caffeine. So if you ask for hard evidence for any point, plenty of it will come at you very fast and with great passion, before I can get it under control." A low chuckle ran through his engineers. He had probably been urging them to stay out of technical thickets.

"I understand. If I ask you to prove anything, what happens will serve me right."

They all smiled at me, brightly enough for people who must have been exhausted.

Robertson began. "Well, Mr. Blackstone, here's the gist: if you authorize unlimited overtime, and allow us to go straight to a full dual-StarBooster/StarCore I launch, then we would have a pretty good heavy-lift launcher. And if we put StarRescue on top of it, we could go get the crew off ISS. We might even be ready before *Atlantis*." He popped a critical path chart onto the screen and started indicating points with his laser pointer. "The two piloted drop tests of Star-Rescue alone, with Andre Johnston flying it down, worked perfectly. And StarCore I's working parts are almost entirely well-established, off-the-shelf technology. So, even though dual-StarBooster/StarCore I/ StarRescue would be a new system, in the sense of not having flown together before, it would in fact be much more proven-out than most things we fly. Give us the word for the dual-StarBooster/StarCore I test, and we can fly it just four days from now.

"If that first test works, then in a pinch we can do the ISS rescue on about a week's notice. Even if we *don't* end up doing the ISS rescue, a successful flight will mean we've got a ready-to-go, cheap, fast satellite launcher, with heavy lift capability, right in the mid-

dle of the biggest demand for launch services there's
ever been.

"If that first test fails—well, we go back to the regular test sequence, and little harm done.

"So the deal is: run this StarBooster/StarCore test.
If it succeeds, we're a full year ahead, *and* in position
to do the ISS rescue if anything goes wrong with *Atlantis*. If it fails, we're only a month behind."

I was impressed despite myself. "All right, you've
made a case for an early StarCore test. But how do
you get from that to the idea that we should then go
on and fly StarRescue, *manned?*"

"Well, all right, that one is a stretch," Robertson said
cheerfully. "But the only part of the flight that would
be completely unprecedented would be the return
from orbit, and even that's using a well-proven
method, because it comes down exactly the same way
the shuttle does—we even modeled the controls off the
shuttle, so that an experienced shuttle pilot needs almost no time to get up on StarRescue or StarBird.

"Now, I'm not saying that we *should* do this. I *am* saying that if the shuttle craps out, and the ISS crew is
dying up there, we could be ready to go with the dual-
StarBooster/StarCore I/StarRescue configuration. And
if we've got people dying up there, we *have* to try to get
them home, even at very great risks."

Robertson sat back down and clicked off the
PowerPoint projector; when the hum of its fan went
out, the room was amazingly quiet. "That's what we
all think, Mr. Blackstone. There's going to be a couple hundred pages of justification on your desk for it,
soon, but you know we wouldn't try to fool you
about a thing like this. We think we can do it. If we
have to, we can make the trip to ISS the test flight.

A StarRescue mounted on a StarCore I with two StarBooster 200s could do it."

I looked around the room. "All right," I said. "Who among you has the biggest doubts?" Finally, Caroline Ralston spoke up and said, "Red Cheney has some."

Cheney shrugged. "I think it's ninety-nine percent likely that the flight would make it and everything would be fine," he said.

"That likely?" I asked. "I don't place bets on the shuttle and it's been flying for twenty years."

"Yeah, I know. I've been over the test data on StarBooster, StarCore I, and StarRescue, though, with a fine-tooth comb, and there is just not one component, apart from the StarRescue airframe, that hasn't already been tested under stresses that are bigger than the ones for this mission.

"So apart from bad luck and human error, the only thing to worry about is a negative synergy—two things that work fine in isolation interacting in an unanticipated, undesirable way. I have somewhat more doubt than the others that our computer simulations would spot them. But the potential gain is huge, and for unproven hardware, the risks can't get much lower."

I went around the room twice, but Red Cheney really was the biggest doubter; the rest were convinced that they could have Robertson's proposed configuration fully flyable in three weeks.

Finally Robertson summed up. "You know, something people forget is that though of course they did test those early space capsules, the early astronauts all went up in unique, hand-built machines, and got back."

"They also had nearly unlimited quantities of

money and public good will," I pointed out, "which makes running risks a lot easier." Still, you back your team if at all possible. I would have an extremely unhappy team if I told them to give up on the idea. "Well, there's nothing wrong with getting ahead on our test program. I'll give you the go for StarBooster/ StarCore. As for StarRescue, I pray that won't be necessary, but I suppose I'd hate to have thrown the possibility away, if everything else goes to pieces. So get me your proposal and schedules, in detail, and if you manage to convince me, then I'll take it to Jagavitz. But no rosy projections, no excess optimism, no stacking the deck. Just tell the truth about how far we would have to go, and how fast, to make the plan work."

They stared at me until Ned started to clap. Then they all joined in. I'd never received a round of applause from my engineers before, and wasn't sure I liked it.

Robertson walked along with me, back to my office, to fill me in on some other points. When we got there, Angie had just received word that Jagavitz had won his battle with the Board, hands down. Robertson, Angie, and I celebrated with soft drinks from the machine, for about five minutes, then got back to work.

IN THE NEXT few days, Scorpion Shack was transformed. The break rooms and hallways were full of the kind of excited babble that only our oldest employees, who had worked, decades ago, on Apollo, Skylab, Stealth, or the SSME, could remember. I spent as much time around my excited, creative engineers and scientists as possible, but I was needed more urgently to keep well-meaning management elsewhere in the company from taking up the talent's time with paperwork, reports, evaluations, and assessments.

For half of Wednesday morning I was on the phone to Barbara Quentin, the corporate VP for Issues Management. Usually she was a sensible person, but now she insisted that we promise the public that new satellites would be invulnerable against proton bursts. Eventually I successfully explained (I think) that every pound of shielding that you sent to orbit was a pound of payload that didn't go, and that to do what she was asking, you would need several pounds of shielding for every pound of payload.

Anyway, nothing could protect the Earth's satellites against anyone who really wanted to harm them. Orbital velocities are around thirty times that of a rifle bullet, the damage done by an impact depends on the square of the velocity, and thus a satellite running into a projectile gets about nine hundred times the devastating blow it would if it were hit by that same object fired out of a gun. A ton of concrete, lofted into the pathway of a satellite, would destroy it even if you had armored it like a battleship. "In the long run, the only real way to protect space-based assets is to not have wars," I explained to Barbara.

That call had been aggravating, but it was nothing compared to the next one, from Andrew Riscaveau. "We have an interesting situation."

"Oh?" I asked.

Riscaveau said, "I have a call coming in to your private line that I need to talk to you about, before you take the call."

"You should not be intercepting my calls."

"You're the head of Scorpion Shack. We intercept

everything in or out. It's just we don't usually talk with you about it."

It was an old argument that I didn't want to have again. "Is the person still on the line?"

"I told him he'd have to wait for me to talk to you. He knows it might take a while. Here's the thing. It's Killeret, from Curtiss."

"Do you know what it's about?"

"I didn't ask him."

"Is there a reason why I shouldn't talk to him?"

"Not really."

"Then why are you delaying both of us? Why don't you just record the conversation like you do all the others, and stay out of the way?"

"Look, we have good reason to believe that Mr. Killeret is about to propose something that he thinks is going to be good for Curtiss," Riscaveau said, "and it's our belief that it may be in the interests of Republic Wright as well."

I *had* been working on controlling my temper. "*Our* belief? Was there a meeting? Who was there and what's their mission?"

"Well, there's a company policy that—"

"Now, wait a minute. I *make* policy, along with other upper management. We hold meetings to do it. If this is really policy, then I should have been at the meeting where you set it."

"Well, it's not policy in the sense of a set policy or anything like that, Mr. Blackstone, but it's in the general interests of the company—"

"And there is some reason why you know the general interests of the company better than I do?"

"Well, when there's a conflict of interest—"

"Are you aware that that's a serious accusation, not just a buzzword to sling around in the way you're accustomed to?" I hadn't blown up that way in a long time, but leave it to Riscaveau to bring it out in me.

He said stiffly, "Go ahead with your call."

When Killeret came on the line, I began with, "First of all, I've got to apologize on behalf of all of Republic Wright for the extremely embarrassing and unprofessional behavior of our security chief, who is meddling in all sorts of things he has no business meddling in." I enjoyed the thought that Riscaveau would be recording that.

Killeret laughed. "Ever the diplomat, Nick. Here's the story, and my security guy is going to wet himself about my telling you, too, but I need you to know this for the sake of both our companies. Over at Ghost Town we've been developing a new, big expendable rocket, and we've also been working, mostly on our own, on an advanced CRV, a follow-on to Soyuz. Crew of four, smaller than your StarRescue, but still a perfectly fine vehicle for all kinds of other functions. For example, an unmanned version would be a perfect cargo ship for sending supplies to ISS."

"So what's the good news for us?"

"The good news is that if our CRV does end up flying as a spacecraft, Curtiss will be a market for StarBooster, and we'll be ordering some of them whenever you'll sell them to us. The bad news is that we might not get to do it. Yesterday there was a big meeting, corporate level, and I didn't recognize half the faces there. We've had a real turnover of upper management and various key departments, and the new people seem to be coming in from everywhere except aerospace, science, or engineering. I'd had no idea it had gone so far. And the new crew here seem to be determined to drag their feet. The company policy is that with space in such grave doubt in the public mind, we can't afford to have anything go wrong at all under any circumstances, and therefore we need to slow down, plan months of extra tests, and evaluate the 'risks' of adding a new technology to the mix. They want a yearlong slowdown on the advanced CRV."

"*New* technology?" I said. "Individual pieces might be new, but a capsule on top of an expendable rocket is the same basic technology that got Yuri Gagarin into orbit."

"Well, yeah." Killeret sighed. "So here's the favor I'm asking. The good guys don't seem to be winning the argument over here. I think that the go-slow policy is going to be made official. What I'm thinking is, maybe if you could go public with StarBooster a little sooner—or even reveal that you're planning to get competitive in expendables again—"

"We've got a test coming up very soon for something that'll knock all of your expendables out of the race for a good long while," I said. "And you're going to end up wanting to buy StarBoosters by the dozen once that happens, to get back into the race. In two weeks we'll be talking about something completely different. But thanks for the heads-up; it's good to know in advance about the potential market."

"Well, Nick, you know, Mars Four forever."

I laughed. "We were just down at the cabin this past weekend. We should have called and invited you."

"Do it, next time. How are you doing at throwing Scott and Thally back together?" He knew about that because I had told him about it during one of the long calls last week; once we started talking to each other, after years of barely communicating, we had suddenly had all sorts of things to say.

"Some progress," I said, "but I'm dealing with two stubborn people who know most of my negotiating and management tricks. I'll have to proceed carefully."

"I have faith in you," he said. "And thanks for talking to me. I read a report about Jagavitz's speech at your meeting. It must be fun to be at an aerospace company that's interested in flying."

"You can send me a résumé any time," I said. "Take care. Mars Four forever."

"You bet. Talk to you soon."

We rang off and I sat back and scribbled out the points I wanted to make to Jagavitz at our meeting the next day. The CEO's style of conversation, one-on-one with a subordinate, was often more like interrogation, and it helped to have all your ideas clear in mind before talking to him. I had just finished numbering the points when the phone rang.

Without preamble, Riscaveau said, "Now, you're really just doing things to make a mess, and I don't see any way I can do anything except report this."

I was startled. "You said you thought I should *take* the deal that Killeret was going to offer. As it turned out, he made no offer, per se, but he did discuss an area where cooperation would do us tremendous good, and so I'm cooperating. I'd have to be crazy not to. If his faction wins out at Curtiss, it could *double* the market for StarBooster. You were absolutely right. What's the matter now?"

"That wasn't what I thought the call was going to be about, and it shouldn't have been what you thought the call was going to be about, either." There was a weird tension to his voice, as if a simple misunderstanding were a matter of life and death. "I thought he would be calling to urge you to take Curtiss's new offer for your brother's case; they wanted to offer a firm contract to pay any judgment against him, so that he'd be able to just take the deal, settle the case, and get on with his life."

"Why would Killeret be the one to bring that offer to me, and why me, instead of just talking directly to Scott or his attorney? And why should Scott settle now when all the new evidence is that it's not anything the James family can sue about?"

"You and Killeret are old friends, and your first loyalty is not to your companies. You are financing your brother's court expenses totally against the interests of Republic Wright, regardless of what Jagavitz says. And yes, if you have to, you can tell him I said that. I've said it to his face. I can't believe that he's persisting in this whole crazy—"

"The Board upheld him yesterday. By a big majority," I pointed out. "And you didn't answer my question. You're also far outside your territory. How is security involved in this, at all?"

Riscaveau's voice had the kind of infuriating self-satisfaction that your kindergarten teacher had when she was insisting it was time for a nap whether you were sleepy or not. "Because you're having an irregular contact with a secure facility at our major competitor. Because accelerating the StarBooster runs a greater risk of an accident and the accident could cost the company time and money, and because if StarBooster is delivered early it's going to completely disrupt the space-launch market at a time when things are already in chaos, so it is in the interests of stability and ordered development to keep it right on schedule, not speed it up. And most of all because when you come right down to it, Republic Wright is a company that makes the basic hardware for national security, and that means everything the company does is a security affair."

I forgot all about keeping my temper. "Everything the company does is *not* a security affair. Only *some* of our interests involve security. And *when* they don't, which is *most* of the time—*particularly* at Scorpion Shack—*keep your ratty little nose out.* You are meddling outside your charter. StarBooster is not a security matter. There is no theft, treason, arson, or whatever going on. So get out of it and stay out." I hung up.

One of the advantages of being at a high level in the company is the opportunity it gives you to calm down when you need to. If I'd still been a project leader of an engineering team, right then, I'd have been so angry that I might have done something foolish in front of other people. As it was, I just had Angie hold my calls, then paced angrily around the office thinking of all the nasty things I should have said to Riscaveau. After a few minutes, I went into my private washroom and rinsed my face, went to the office refrigerator for an orange, a pear, and a big bottle of spring water, and had a calming snack while I played Pachelbel's Canon on the stereo, over and over.

Half an hour later I was a perfectly reasonable person again. With a sigh—it was nice and peaceful in here and I was about to invite trouble back in—I picked up the phone and told the secretary that I officially existed again.

Angie said, "I had two calls from Andrew Riscaveau, asking you not to return a call from Clifford Welch. Mr. Riscaveau sounded very upset. Mr. Welch did call, and left his number."

"Who is Clifford Welch?"

"Deep Blue. He said he needed to talk to you before the StarBird presentation this afternoon. And he also said he'd be at the presentation and if it's not convenient to return the call, he can come early and meet you beforehand."

"I'll return his call," I said. "Call him back. If he can't come to the phone right now, I can wait."

Much of our work at Scorpion Shack in recent years had probably been for Deep Blue, but even I didn't know exactly what or exactly how much. Everything connected with Deep Blue was "SCI"—Sensitive Compartmented Information—which is a whole set of classifications, all of which are considerably more restricted than the old "top secret" category that is still in use for more routine information. Most of the people at Scorpion Shack had a clearance for Secret, and a large minority were cleared for Top Secret, but I only had about thirty people with SCI clearances—and every SCI clearance is different, a permit to see only what is needed for the job at hand and nothing more.

Even the table of organization itself was secret; probably Deep Blue was part of the National Reconnaissance Office. The NRO itself was a completely SCI agency, the government office for spy satellites, and although it was established by President Kennedy, it was only in the last weeks of the Bush Administration that it was publicly admitted that it existed.

Deep Blue was quieter than *that*. Like many of the most secret projects since World War II, its name gave nothing away at all. My occasional interactions with them usually involved a covert space launch from Scorpion Shack's pad or by one of our experimental air-launched missiles. Deep Blue missions often were connected to some of our experimental work with spaceborne, stealth-piercing radar to track various objects that didn't "officially" exist in space; several times we had launched a small package, delivered just hours before launch, into an orbit that intercepted one of those ghosts.

I thought Deep Blue was probably the counterintelligence branch of the NRO. Perhaps what we were doing was shooting down some other nation's unacknowledged spy satellites, since those radar objects tended to disappear shortly after the covert launches. But for all I knew, Deep Blue could just as easily have been a branch of the NSA or CIA, or a freestanding body reporting to the President. And the packages might not have been interceptors; they might have been couriers, going up to stealthed American satellites to pick up material too secret to send by any other method, or tugboats repositioning the satellites, or even tiny robots to repair them. The stuff that the super-secret agencies use has always been twenty to fifty years ahead of its time; they're the only organizations on Earth that make Scorpion Shack and Ghost Town look backward.

Given what must have happened to Deep Blue's orbital assets, along with everyone else's, I figured that they probably needed one or more emergency launches, ASAP, or perhaps they had an armored probe ready to go up and take some measurements on just how intense the radiation was in orbit, something it would be good for them to know before anyone else did. As I waited for Angie to put me through to Welch, I thought of everything we had that could reach orbit. Maybe we could use the StarBooster/StarCore test to fly it . . . that way there'd be no budget line for a payload (although, as usually happened with a Deep Blue launch, there would probably be a mysterious increase in one of my budget accounts within a couple of weeks).

The only thing I was really supposed to know was that standing orders were "Deep Blue gets whatever they want and none of it ever appears in the budget; be nice to Deep Blue no matter what the cost, and more than the cost will always turn up for Republic Wright somehow," as Jagavitz had told me when I first took over Scorpion Shack.

The phone rang and Angie said, "I have Mr. Welch on the line. Go ahead."

"Mr. Welch?"

"Mr. Blackstone. We know a few people in common but we've never met. I'm part of Deep Blue, but I'm not a part you've ever had to deal with before. As for my official status in the secret agencies, I can at least say that the head of Deep Blue is a deputy director and I answer directly to him."

"Good enough," I said. That put Welch three down from the President of the United States. I was suitably impressed.

"Here's what I need from you. I'll be one of the insignificant suits in the big delegation of congress-people and bureaucrats that's coming by to look at StarBird this afternoon. If you were planning to dep-utize the job of showing them around, I strongly sug-gest that you de-deputize it and meet the delegation."

Inwardly I sighed; I *had* planned to delegate it to a subordinate, and thus create an uninterrupted hour to catch up on business and administrivia.

"Now," he went on, "I also have one other agent in the delegation, and one in the StarBird hangar. I'm doing all this because we think that you've been pen-etrated by what's very possibly a violent organization with foreign sponsorship. We have reason to think they are opposed to the development of the Starcraft series in general. We'll be keeping an eye on things. There's some information I need from you, and some things it would be helpful to have you do, that might be very important, so that's why I called today."

"So you just want me to act normally?"

"At least for the moment. But we thought it might be a good idea to let you in on the overall situation. If something strange starts to happen, at least you'll be prepared for it, and maybe that will help. And at the least I want you to think about any additional security measures you can take."

A thought occurred to me. "That's very strange. We have a very gung-ho security chief, but he specifically urged me not to return your call. If what you're asking for is more security, our guy should have been delighted."

"Really? That's *extremely* interesting. Well, if he should ask if you *did* talk to me—he will—tell him no, and that you have no idea who I am."

"Got it."

"Don't call Andrew Riscaveau's attention to anything connected with Deep Blue, at all. I know that you normally wouldn't refer to SCI material anyway, and this whole conversation, and the fact that it happened, is all SCI.

"Anyway, if things go all right at the StarBird presentation, I'll be coming around to your office about forty minutes afterward, for a much more detailed conversation that will probably clear up a large number of things that must have been very confusing for you. Thank you for your cooperation." He hung up, not waiting for me to say I'd cooperate; it didn't seem to me that I had very many choices, anyway.

I checked with Angie to make sure I hadn't already delegated the job of doing the presentation. I hadn't, so all I need do was proceed according to schedule. Then I forgot about Welch, Riscaveau, and everything complicated or annoying, and got on with the paper-shuffle that has to be done, day in and day out, whether or not the whole world is going to pieces. I thought I might begin to like the monthly overtime report; it had the soothing qualities of requiring attention, not mattering much, and containing no real surprises.

To make sure the tour would go smoothly, I called Robertson. "We need to show them a good time," I said. "And if they like what they see and hear, everything will be easier. So we need a good show, and I want your staff to spend the next couple hours getting ready for one. No exceptions, no matter how high a priority. Is that clear?"

"It is. You know engineers, but I'll make 'em see reason."

"Thanks, Ned—I really appreciate that. Work areas need to look busy but don't let any of them be sloppy. If somebody just must have some huge project spread all over a table, move the table somewhere out of sight—you can move it back once the delegation's gone. Don't let the ship be seen with its guts hanging out—close up everything, hatches, access doors, the works. Now, most important of all, make sure we have a completely safe pathway for them to walk along. Nothing spoils a tour like killing a Deputy Undersecretary, and the average bureaucrat has no idea how dangerous a place like the Shack is."

"I'll be right on top of it, then, Mr. Blackstone. Clean, neat, safe, and our bird gets the best plumage we can manage. Everybody helps whether they want to or not. Anything else?"

"If you can do all that in a couple of hours, that will be plenty."

"No kidding. But we'll have it done. When do you arrive?"

"About fifteen minutes till showtime, but I might be late."

"We'll be ready at twenty till."

After I hung up, and got back to working my way through various small documents that, if not filled out, would cost precious time later, I kept thinking that the stereotype of the engineer is one of the more misleading ones. Supposedly they lack people skills, and some do, of course, but you'd be surprised how many managers and counselors are even worse than the average engineer. I was pleasantly sure that not only would everything be set up for my arrival, but Robertson would find a way to have his team in a good mood about it, though nobody hates interruptions more than an engineer on a tight schedule.

The phone rang.

Riscaveau didn't bother to say hello, and he didn't ask; he made a flat statement sound like an accusation of murder. "Your secure line was busy but our computer log doesn't show any record of a call, and we couldn't access the voice line to hear what was going on."

So Deep Blue could get an untraceable phone call into one of the most secure facilities on the planet, and scramble it so that our own security people couldn't eavesdrop. I was even more impressed than I had been before.

"Something is wrong with either your computer log

or with the phone system itself," I said. "Which call are you talking about?"

"Which call? You were on the phone for half an hour."

"I'm sure I wasn't talking to Ned Robertson for that long," I said.

"Not the one to Robertson! The one before!"

"Well, there were a bunch of calls before," I said, stalling. I was not sure how good an actor I might be, and he was probably looking at voice stress meters to see if I was lying, so I decided to be blatant. "I had three or four business calls in the last two hours, but none of them was more than two minutes. Which ones are you talking about?"

"I told you, there's no record in the computer log and your line was busy—"

"Or the phone system was reporting it busy. Maybe after the call from my brother I set it down wrong in the cradle, and then I bumped it later and it came back on."

"You didn't get a call from your brother!"

"You mean, the computer log doesn't show it."

"Oh, fuck you." He hung up. At least he hadn't asked me whether I had talked to Clifford Welch.

I would have to remember to report that conversation to Welch after the presentation, when I'd meet with him.

I signed off on the overtime report and opened up the weekly budget report.

The phone rang again. I picked it up, and my secretary said, "It's your brother."

"Put him through."

"Nick?"

"Yes, Scott?"

He sounded as if he were enraged. "I just got a call

from an obnoxious little troll who said he was your security person, and he seemed to think I shouldn't call you, or else he wanted me to say I'm not going to call you, or that I never call you, or something. I told the son of a bitch I'd call you when I damned well pleased, this afternoon or any afternoon, and if you didn't want the call you could just hang up on me." I was stifling laughter; when Scott and I were teenagers, he used to play "irate man," in which he'd call up some hapless business with an irrational complaint and keep building it up until they acquired the courage to hang up. What I was hearing now was the "irate man" voice, and I had no doubt it was adding to Riscaveau's confusion as he listened in. "I hope I didn't cause you any problems."

"Only problems that I enjoy having," I said. "Thanks for letting me know about that. I'll make sure there's a note about this erratic behavior in that man's personnel file. Mars Four forever."

"Mars Four forever to you too. Hope you get some time off so we can see you soon, Nick."

"I hope so too, but it isn't going to happen."

After we hung up, I leaned back in the chair and laughed myself half sick. My kid brother had never, never in his life been a snitch. When some authority demanded that he contradict something I'd said, he would look them straight in the eye and absolutely confirm it, *especially* if he had any reason to think it wasn't true. Well, he'd done it again.

Angie's alert guarding secured me an hour and a half during which I rerouted tons of trivia away from the productive people, and knocked down a pile of administrative barriers; there's an almost sadistic glee in destroying all the little traps and barriers that some managerial voles put up against progress, and letting the stream of ideas and creativity pour through, sweeping all before it. When I looked up from my monitor, I had used up most of my time, but I was roaring with energy, concentrated like a laser, and feeling like I could work forever.

I made myself take a few minutes to maintain myself. I stretched, got a cold orange juice, and splashed water on my face from the sideboard sink. Life was definitely all right with me, I thought, as I looked at the empty inbox and the bulging outbox.

It was getting to be time for the presentation, and November is a nice month in the southern Panhandle. I decided to walk over to the StarBird hangar. I let Angie know where I was going and that I wouldn't be available for at least two hours after getting back—I figured I should leave a generous allowance for the meeting with Clifford Welch.

I didn't know why I was feeling so cheerful. It might have been that I'd spared a few moments, mentally, for the ISS situation, and had realized that, bad as the global catastrophe was, it could hardly be better PR for space. The rescue would wipe the whole MJ affair out of the news and create a brand new positive spin.

Or it might have been that I was glad I had decided to do the presentation myself. There's a bit of ham in every development project manager, and one of our guilty pleasures is to pull a great new project out in front of an appreciative audience. This presentation was one of the first steps in preparing to go fully public. The bureaucrats, congressmen, and staffers in the group would leak all sorts of things—favorable things, we hoped—and with luck we might generate some favorable rumors to smooth the way. In short order, we'd be welcoming reporters in, and getting the campaign going seriously. I love that stage of a project.

Or I might only have been happy because I was getting to take a walk in perfect weather. It was about seventy degrees, there wasn't a cloud in the deep blue sky, and everything seemed to leap out of the background in extra color. The fifteen-minute walk from my office to StarBird was the most private time I'd had all day, spoiled only by the occasional golf cart full of engineers that would swoop in to ask if I needed a ride. I waved them all off, enjoyed the walk, and arrived five minutes early, fully refreshed.

And then again, perhaps the good feeling was mostly anticipation of the pleasure I always felt when I stepped into the hangar.

I stepped through the door. My breath caught. I suppose there's an overgrown child in me somewhere. Whenever I look at one of Scorpion Shack's planes or spacecraft, there's always a touch of magic about it. It might be just knowing that there isn't anything else like it in the world yet, that it's the first one, some of the future sitting in our hangars, like a newborn eagle. Maybe it's just that the most aerodynamic shapes for extreme environments—which is what we build—often look like something out of a comic book. Whatever the reason, when I walked into the hangar where StarBird I sat, in the center of a sprawl of data and power cables, I felt a touch of awe.

"The display lights?" Ned Robertson stood at my elbow.

"Definitely the display lights," I said.

Robertson gestured at someone over his shoulder. Hangars are big, and even when there are lots of bright lights, they have plenty of dark corners; a moment later, the big floods were off and the dimmer ceiling lights left the room shadowy, almost dark.

All around the StarBird, dozens of small floodlights came on, shaping a cool, white light around its smooth curves. It was a beautiful craft, no question about it—a long, slim lifting body with short wings at the back; from the front, small canard stabilizers sprouted, the wings of StarRescue if that should need to separate. It seemed like the offspring of the shuttle and the Concorde, but more graceful than either. We had painted it bright white with a black stripe down the side. The single-piece "keel" of heat-resistant composite was steel blue, its natural color, since we'd found no paint that we could trust to stick to it.

On the side the words REPUBLIC WRIGHT STAR-BIRD 001 implied that we hoped to build more than a hundred of them; I remembered that Robertson had told me he wished we had made that "0001," to leave room for thousands. Above that there was the logo we had settled on—a stylized eagle forming out of a spiral emerging from a star.

At the moment it was still mostly a fake, or a promise of things to come, but parts of it were almost finished. The passenger compartment that formed StarBird's nose was real enough, and had had three flights already. It was the StarRescue that we had used to flight test the StarBooster. In that test we had replaced the nose on a StarBooster prototype with the StarRescue and dropped the whole thing from a 747; Andre Johnston had flown it down to our runway, thus proving out the airframe for both StarBooster and StarBird and cutting years off our development time. Johnston had also flown two drop tests from a B-52 with the StarRescue alone. So the front one-fifth of StarBird—the StarRescue—was as real as it gets; theoretically if it were fueled up and put into orbit, it would be ready to fly down to Earth today.

The composite plate on the bottom, the advanced descendant of space shuttle tiles, was real too. And two days before, we'd slipped an old SSME and its oxygen tank into her tail, and bolted that into place. (In a sense, that superannuated SSME was the most-proven part of the whole device, for it had been to space many times, after many flights on the shuttle. We would replace it with a new one, of course, when and if StarBird 001 went to space—but for the present tests, it was the right shape and weight, and cheap.)

A few more days would see enough control electronics go into StarBird 001 to allow for a taxi test—just taking it out to rumble slowly up and down the runway to see what might fall off, and checking the throttling and landing gear, simple things that could wreck an experimental craft during takeoff and landing.

It had been beautiful to me, just sitting in the hangar, but with the display lights—I hoped—*everyone* should be able to see, right away, how beautiful it really was.

That was probably a forlorn hope. Delegations from Washington always give you a mixed response—a few like kids at a *Star Wars* movie, some determined to show you how blasé they can be, and a small percentage are actually trying to learn something.

"If it flies as well as it looks," Robertson said beside me, "then this might be the biggest publicity hit that RW—or the space program—has had in a real long time."

A staffer jogged up to ask if we were ready. We said yes, and she turned and ran for the door. Less than a minute later, the delegation filed in.

There were about forty of them, mostly men in conservative suits and women in dark dresses with matching jackets. As they came in, I could hear some of them exclaiming—little cries of "oh!," whistles, and soft "oh, wow" 's. It looked like the preliminary report was good, anyway. When they'd all come in, and had a chance to let the first impression settle, I said to Robertson, "Okay, we need regular lights for the presentation." He spoke into his phone, and a moment later the bright hangar lights came on, pushing back the darkness into the further corners, and leaving the crowd blinking.

I stepped forward and launched into the standard spiel—our line of progression from StarBooster to StarCore to StarBird, the incremental approach, how we'd developed the first total system architecture for spaceflight, and so forth. When I finished, ten minutes later, I cued a tech standing by to lower the big projection screen and bring the first slide up. Robertson came forward, and, as drawings, charts, and photos went clicking by at the three-per-minute pace that works best for keeping people interested, he gave a surprisingly un-technical account of why StarBird would be a much better ship than the shuttle, while relying almost entirely on proven technology.

A hand rose in the crowd, and Robertson said "Yes?"

My stomach turned over when I saw that it was Bingo Rasmussen stepping out of the group. He must have been a last-minute addition—I couldn't have missed his name on the roster.

In that sarcastic Midwest drawl, that, thanks to C-SPAN, made everyone in the space industry automatically wince, Rasmussen demanded, "So this thing outperforms the shuttle but uses no new technology?"

"*Minimal* new technology," Robertson said. "Sometimes the cheapest thing you can do is find a better material or concept than anything you have. For example, instead of using the heat-shielding tiles that you may recall were a problem back when the shuttle started flying, we are able to go to a new single-sheet composite, which is much stronger, much more effective, and doesn't require anything like the same amount of time or the number of skilled workers to maintain. It would have been silly to stay with the old way with such an effective new way right at hand. But for the most part, we stuck with things we understand well."

"Well, then, my question to you, sir, is why you didn't just build the shuttle right in the first place." He didn't say it like a question—it was a quotable remark that would float around Capitol Hill for the next few months, helping to poison the well for every space project. I drew in a breath, not sure what I would say but knowing that I had to say something.

Robertson got there first. "Because the reason we understand the materials, and high-Mach aerodynamics, and all the other mechanics of reusable spacecraft, as well as we do, is that we've had about twenty years of experience operating STS—which was designed in the Nixon Administration. Back then most every element of the design was a best guess. Now we have decades of real-world experience with flying the shuttle, and we know what worked, what didn't, and what could work better. So we're designing from a vastly better base of knowledge. And of course in the last thirty years we've also had a tremendous increase in the ability to do computer-aided design, supercomputer simulations, and all sorts of other tricks that depend on having lots and lots of cheap, fast computing time. And materials science has advanced very far and fast, too, so that there are better materials to make it out of. So we take much more knowledge, process it with much better tools, and build the ship out of better stuff—and you *bet* we can beat the daylights out of what a slide-rule-and-drafting-board engineer could do back when you were in grade school."

I relaxed at once. Robertson had made Rasmussen look ignorant, rather than like he was the voice of common sense. I made a strong mental note to get Robertson in front of key audiences more often. A fine engineer who can think on his feet and speak well is a resource that should be exploited.

Rasmussen, recognizing that the tide had turned, nodded and stepped back into the crowd.

I gave a quick overview, pointing out that if Republic Wright were allowed to build and operate these in a for-profit environment, depending on the government as an anchor tenant rather than as the source of funding and control, a fleet of six Star-Boosters, going up two at a time with StarCore I's, could launch replacements for every important orbital asset faster than they could be built, and that the whole human infrastrure in space could be back up in less than three years. Moreover, if we went to ten StarBoosters, and added two StarBirds, we would roughly double the number of people we could send to and from ISS in any given time. "That's because of the short turnaround," I explained. "Much of the time StarBird would probably fly with fewer people than the shuttle, but unlike the shuttle it doesn't have to spend weeks or months being reconditioned on the ground—we just land it, pull the engine, shove another one in, check it out, and go again."

"Does that at least mean we could ground the shuttle fleet and stop paying for that?" Rasmussen asked.

"I doubt it. The shuttle can take up a big crew and twenty tons of cargo. StarBird carries no more cargo than hand luggage; if you want to put cargo up there with the crew, you have to rendezvous with something sent up on an unmanned StarCore. Anytime you need both a big cargo and a big crew, in the same place at the same time, there's just nothing else like the shuttle, and we've grown to depend on that ability. But for things like routine crew rotations from ISS, StarBird is highly competitive, and there can be more StarBird flights in a year, so it would tend to make station operations more convenient and practical," I said. "And StarBooster/StarCore can handle any cargo that doesn't have to have people with it. That's more than enough for any one system to accomplish."

"Why don't you just take this StarBird up there and get the ISS crew down?" a young woman asked. The older man beside her—probably her boss—looked painfully embarrassed.

"Well, because several major systems aren't in it yet," I said. "Right at the moment, it's pretty much a hollow shell. The StarRescue—the crew compartment, which can fly back by itself in the event of trouble—is nearly done but needs a lot of testing. The body, as you can see, is done. We just put the heat shielding on, and the engine went in two days ago. There's too many things we can't do with it yet—such as steer."

"I can see where that might be important," she said, smiling. Her boss, whoever he was, looked relieved.

Robertson handed me a hard hat and put one on

himself. He picked up a small cableless video camera, switched it on, and pointed it at me.

On a big overhead screen, my image was projected twenty feet high; it's an unsettling way to see yourself, and even after a few rehearsals, I hadn't really gotten used to it. "Testing," I said, to make sure the mike in the hard hat was picking up. It came through fine, followed by a slight ping of feedback. Robertson and I walked back toward the StarBird, and after we were behind the screen's speakers, I said, as naturally as I could manage, "The interior of StarBird I is still under construction, and it's a hard-hat area, so it wouldn't be practical to take you back here physically, even if there were room for all of you. So if you'll watch the big screen, we'll give you a quick virtual tour."

Robertson and I would trade off on camera and narration duties as we went through; the script called for taking a quick tour around the airframe, starting from the newly installed engine and oxygen tank, and then spending most of our time in the crew compartment, where there would be more things that might be relevant to the audience. "Millions of pounds of thrust" sounds impressive, but "here's where the crew will heat their meals" means more to the layman.

We stood behind StarBird, looking into the immense nozzle of the SSME. StarBird as a whole was the size of a middling airliner, a fact that was not immediately apparent until we got close enough to it for people to get a sense of scale. I turned to face the camera that Ned was holding and said, "We're going to look at the SSME propulsion module—SSME stands for 'space shuttle main engine,' which is the proven technology at the heart of StarBird, and, after all these years, still one of the most impressive rocket engines you'll ever see. Then we'll take a walk around the outside before going into StarRescue.

"But first of all, let's take a look at what's probably the most innovative single feature on the StarBird, the single-piece composite keel that serves as the heat shield."

With Ned backing away in front of me, keeping the camera on me, I walked forward until Ned passed under the tail. From there he walked carefully and slowly backwards, keeping the camera level. I followed him in, feeling the same awe as always, as the tail of the big craft blocked my view of the hangar roof far above; it seemed amazing that anything so big could leap right off the earth. "Now, here's what we've done," I said, as Ned turned on the camera light and pointed it up at the shiny blue surface over our heads.

Something cracked like a deer rifle fired inside a garbage can. Metal groaned and shrieked somewhere nearby. I had an instant to look up and try to make sense of what I was seeing—the undersurface of StarBird tilting down in front of me. Then it hit me, and I found myself smashed against the pavement, struggling to get out from under the huge weight, unable even to free my arm to push with. In a few seconds, which seemed like hours, it got dark and quiet.

CHAPTER ELEVEN

THALIA:

We three were just back from an early movie when the phone rang. It was Angie, Nick's secretary, with the news that Nick had been hurt. Naturally I was worried about him—I could hear the tears and tension in Angie's voice—but she quickly explained that Nick was okay. He'd been knocked out and bruised all over, but there was no concussion, no internal bleeding, probably not even a broken bone.

Once I knew that, and relayed it to Scott and Amos, I stopped worrying about Nick and started worrying about Scott. He was pacing around my living room like a watchdog that heard something weird two hours ago and doesn't want to miss it if it happens again.

An hour after the first call, when the Scorpion Shack hospital called officially, they said Nick was resting comfortably, had regained consciousness quickly, and was already complaining about their plans to confine him to bed for a few days of observation. They let Scott talk to him on the phone for just a minute, and that helped.

Scott had landed a space shuttle three times and had flown 747's off remote Third World runways, but he seemed barely able to hold together at the prospect of his big brother being injured. He had leaped to the conclusion that it had something to do with the threatening phone calls and the arson of my car, and it was all his fault.

When they realized that Scott had a security clearance adequate for the Scorpion Shack hospital, they immediately invited him to come down to Texas and keep Nick company. That made Scott feel much better, and reading between the lines when I talked to them, I thought that probably what they really wanted was something to distract Nick, who was already feeling much too well to tolerate a hospital bed placidly. Mrs. Blackstone had always said she was glad she'd had two boys, because, like kittens, only they could be active enough to amuse each other.

The doctor seemed to be pretty sure that Nick had just been pinned in a way that didn't let him breathe for about a minute, until someone got a jack under whatever landed on his chest.

After we hung up, I pointed out to Scott that Nick would be cranky and trying to escape from the hospital by the time Scott got there. He laughed and agreed.

An hour later we were pulling into the private RW area at Reagan; Scott would be riding in one of the corporate jets that Nick was forever catching. "Nick cranky might be harder to deal with than Nick hurt," Scott said, "and if I'm not any help to him, at least I can be a help to his nurses and doctors. Tell Amos I'll be back soon and not to worry about Nick," he said. "I'll call when I know the day and time I'm coming back."

He kissed me goodbye, grabbed his bag, and was gone. Dropping him off at airports had been such a routine experience for me that it seemed comfortingly familiar, as if it had filled in a missing spot in my life, and I was driving out of the airport before I realized that we didn't do that anymore.

I turned and headed for the train station; my own bags were in the trunk, and I would be catching a train right away and heading up to New York City for the hearings tomorrow. Amos was at Mrs. Talbert's, staying in her guest room, as he did whenever Scott and I had to be out of town at the same time.

A light turned yellow in front of me and I reminded myself to not try to beat it; the bodyguard car, behind me, needed to be able to stay with me safely. Anyway, it was drizzling yet again, and I was probably better off not trying to run lights. The wipers slapped out a dull rhythm, and my mind drifted off to my slightly irregular family again. I could think of nothing I hadn't thought a hundred times before.

THE TUESDAY ARGUMENTS went all right in New York, though they had to be extended into Wednesday; after hours of back-and-forth, the BB&C attorneys and I managed to get the judge to agree that the cause of the *Columbia* disaster could not be excluded from a case about who was responsible. I began to hope, again, that we might have Scott entirely out of the woods by the Christmas recess.

In the court of public opinion, we were holding our own, as well. The news coverage on Wednesday night was extremely sympathetic, and the only clip they showed of AnnaBeth James was one where she had lost her cool on a talk show and shouted at a caller. The next day, the *Times* carried an editorial saying that the case should be dropped, basing it on the act-of-war principle. Radio call-in was running seven to four in our favor, and we had clearly pulled ahead in the polls.

As I was packing in the hotel room that evening for an early-morning train back to DC, I was tired, mildly annoyed by the institutionalized stupidity of civil law, but still feeling pretty good, since we'd gotten in there and won. Scott had called and said that Nick was being discharged and allowed to return to his full-time duties, so that problem was under control. It was nice, too, to be going home tomorrow morning—I'd thought about catching a train that night but I'd have gotten home so late that Amos might as well just spend the night at Mrs. Talbert's anyway.

The phone rang again, and it was Nick. I'd spoken to him briefly three or four times since the accident, but there hadn't been much to talk about. We went over the usual pleasantries—Nick could be reached at his apartment at Scorpion Shack now, instead of at the hospital, and was feeling fine, "or no worse than mildly beat up." I filled him in about our victories of the day, and said, "I'm beginning to think that Jasper Haverford is impossible to get off a case by any means except beating him in court. He gave no sign this afternoon that he was even thinking of dropping the suit, even though he must know it's doomed. Of course, the James family may still be pushing him hard to keep it going, but he should be advising them not to, and looking for some kind of face-saving deal."

"Maybe he still has a card up his sleeve?"

"I don't see how there can be. The bomb in the camera makes it an act of war, and you can't sue any of the current defendants about that. If they find out who planted the bomb, they can sue them, but that's all they can do."

"Well, you've always thought he had a hidden backer somewhere, besides the Jameses, that wants the case to go on. I suppose if you find the hidden backer, you'll find the motivation." He paused and then said, "I was supposed to call you up and tell you to expect a call from Clifford Welch."

"Who's he?"

"He's legit, he's heavily connected with national security, and he'd better be the one to tell you whatever it is that you ought to know. There's a national security aspect of the case that you should know about, and he's going to be arriving at LaGuardia within an hour; he has a tendency to just phone people or turn up, so I wanted to make sure you didn't go to bed early."

"Good idea. I was thinking about it. Can you tell me anything?"

"Just that you can believe what he tells you. And he'll probably suggest that you want to stay in New York one more day—he'll be talking to the judge in Scott's case, so he'll want all the lawyers there. You might want to arrange to keep the room. For what it's worth, it's good news for us, I can tell you that much."

"Okay, I'm sure I can get the room. Damn, though, Amos is going to be disappointed."

"Let me give you to Scott to talk about that."

A moment later, my ex came on the line and said, "Hi, Thalia, just wanted to let you know, I'll be getting back home tomorrow afternoon, early, so I can pick up Amos and take him over to my place. Is there anything that he needs from your place?"

"Clean clothes if he doesn't have any at yours."

"Got him covered there. And I've already talked to him and Mrs. Talbert about picking him up, so it's all set."

"Great," I said, meaning it. One less thing to worry about and Amos would be glad to see him.

"Uh, listen, I'm sorry about the kiss. Flashback or something. You know, we used to say goodbye at the airport pretty often."

"Yeah, I figured. It's okay," I babbled. "It wasn't a traumatic experience or anything. I mean, not that I would expect it to be. But if you were worried."

"Uh, I was. I didn't mean anything. Uh, not that I kiss everybody, or anything, but it was . . . you know, old habit." He sounded like he was desperately trying to get away from the phone, which wasn't far from what I was feeling.

"Exactly."

"Right. Well, I'm glad you understand that."

"Oh, yeah. I'm glad you brought it up."

We talked about Amos and his homework for another long, awkward minute, and then finally we hung up. I've never been so happy in my life to get out of a phone conversation.

I always travel with two days' spare business clothes—you never know when you may get stuck with an out-of-town court proceeding going extra time—so that wouldn't be a problem, and if I stayed the extra day I could send a couple things out to be dry-cleaned and have them come back tomorrow afternoon. I phoned the front desk, got the room for another day, had a bellhop come up to take two suits and some other stuff down for cleaning, and re-unpacked into the hotel closet and drawers. I turned on the television and caught part of a silly sci-fi movie, something about a businessman trying to get control of an alien library that had been left on Mars, and had just flipped over to watch the Weather Channel instead when the phone rang.

"Ms. Thalia Blackstone? My name is Clifford Welch. Did Nick tell you I would call?"

"He did."

"I'm at my club, which is a few blocks from your hotel. I'll send a cab around for you, if that's all right, and you can come over here and we can have a talk. If you haven't had dinner, you can be my guest for that, as well."

I was about to say that I wasn't hungry when I realized my stomach was rumbling. "Sure, I'd be happy to."

"The cab should be at your hotel door in about fifteen minutes, if that's convenient. Dress for the club is absolutely whatever you care to wear—this place is intended as a retreat, not as a place to show off. The food is excellent, confidentiality is guaranteed, and I believe you'll find what I have to tell you interesting. So come as you are, enjoy dinner, and perhaps I can clear up a whole array of mysteries for you."

"It's a deal. I'll be down at the entrance in fifteen. Thank you."

"Thank you, Ms. Blackstone."

I checked myself in the mirror; I was in decent pants and blouse, so I threw on a dark jacket that matched and a pair of loafers, fussed for a moment with my hair, and decided that I was at least a notch above "absolutely whatever." I called the bodyguard in the next room, told him what was up, and had him come down and watch me until the cab came. He wasn't entirely pleased; when you get paid to keep someone safe, you don't like to let them out of your sight, and I had to promise that I'd call before I got in the cab to come back, so that he could be waiting in the lobby for me.

The cab pulled up at the front door, seemingly correct to the second, and the driver got out and called, "Ms. Blackstone?"

"That's me," I said.

I sprinted through the cold misty rain and got in the cab; he closed the door after me and then dashed around to get inside the cab himself; it wasn't raining hard, but New York's version of November rain is cold and miserable. I was glad the heater was roaring in the cab.

"Skitta-lee Club, right?" he asked.

"As far as I know. Mr. Welch didn't tell me the name of the place."

"Yeah, if it's for Mr. Welch, that's right."

Three blocks later, as we cruised down Fifth, he made a hard right into what seemed barely an alley, somewhere just south of Thirtieth Street. He drove a block into a cul-de-sac that faced the locked iron gate of a little park, then right into a long semicircular drive, around a couple of small office buildings, and finally up under an orange awning that read, in white letters, SKYTALE CLUB. Below the name there was an odd pictograph—an open eye with a dagger behind it, enclosed by a square-root sign. "This is the place," he said. "I dunno why, but Mr. Welch always asks to have me drive his guests."

"Maybe he thinks you always do a good job."

"He tips good," the driver agreed, pulling to a stop. He got out, trotted around, and had the door open

before the doorman could quite get there. As I got
out, the doorman was handing the driver an enve-
lope, and the driver got back into the cab, gave me
a friendly wave, and took off within a few seconds.

"You're Mr. Welch's guest, Ms. Blackstone, I pre-
sume?" the doorman said. He was a muscular type
who looked like a bodybuilder and carried himself in
a way that said "career military" to me.

"Yes."

"This way." He guided me in, and turned me over
to "Miss Marx," a small black woman, quite young,
who walked and moved like an athlete and had the
kind of poise you see in good boxers and fencers; I
followed her down a long hallway, through a large
common room filled with armchairs, through another
long hallway, and up a flight of stairs. On the way I
noted that unlike many of the more secretive New
York clubs, this one seemed to be racially integrated
and open to women—the people in the armchairs
were of all colors and both genders, dressed in everything from evening clothes to jeans.

Something about the way the employees all moved
told me that they were either from some combat
branch of the military, or maybe ex-cops.

It clicked for me then. The driver had pronounced
it "skitta-lee." This wasn't an aviator's club, as I might
have guessed, where people told tales of the sky; this
was a club named after the skytale, an ancient Greek
device used for sending secret messages—probably the
first "code machine" ever invented—and most of the
people here must have some connection to intelligence.

Well, at least my bodyguard had been worrying in
vain. I probably couldn't be in a safer, or more private, place.

Welch was waiting in a small, comfortable room with a table set for two in the center, a map table along one wall, and bookcases full of old encyclopedias. The wood paneling was so dark that it was almost black, and the flocked deep red wallpaper above it was scarcely brighter. There was a small fire in the gas fireplace. It was cozy, snug, dark, and absolutely a place for discussing secrets.

A voice behind me said, "Ms. Blackstone. I recognize you from television. It doesn't do you justice."

I smiled at him and said, "Television interferes with justice; sometimes I think that's what it's for."

"A good point." He was handsome enough, and yet a curiously nondescript man; if you met him at a big party you'd never be able to recall his appearance the next day. His hair was iron-gray, his horn-rimmed glasses made him look like Clark Kent's undistinguished brother, and he was of average height and medium build. The most notable thing about him was his voice; he spoke with great precision. "I've ordered a light red wine, a platter of mixed hot meats, the pumpkin soup—make sure you try that, it's excellent—breads, cheeses, and the vegetable platter. We can enjoy some conversation and get to know each other first; you will want to form an impression of me before you decide how much you want to believe the things I have to tell you, I'm sure."

Everything about Welch was quiet and dignified, and spoke of intense intelligence. He insisted on no business until we had finished dinner, and so we made small talk and discussed a wide range of public issues. He was unfailingly gracious and polite, and seemed to me to be very shrewd in his judgments. His interest extended to a wide range of things, and he surprised me by revealing quite a bit of knowledge about prison reform. When I complimented him on that, he smiled warmly and said, "I did some research on you during my flight here. Your positions are extremely well thought out; if prisons and victims were part of my territory, I'd be very likely to rely on you for advice."

Dinner wound down into coffee, and finally he said, "Well, time for business, then. I think you've done a remarkable job with this case, Ms. Blackstone. In all seriousness, you are good at this game, and I wish we had more talents like yours working in space policy."

"Thank you."

"I will begin with just one thought for you. If the camera bomb was the action of a foreign power—and you may trust me that it was—cui bono?"

That phrase is lawyer's Latin for "good to whom?," and it's the basic question in establishing motive—*who is better off because of this?* "I really don't know," I admitted. "I guess we all thought it must be some international terror organization, probably backed by a rogue state, like the North Koreans or Iran."

He nodded. "I think it was *intended* that nearly everyone would think that. Or that it was the work of some disgruntled NASA employee, or something similar. But terrorism *very* rarely aims at these kinds of targets. You don't need to kill Michael James in space to get publicity, when it's fifty times easier to kill a whole airliner full of passengers. Especially you don't do it and then keep quiet; the first thing a terrorist outfit does after an action is phone the networks to claim the credit, if that's the word for it. Besides, the terrorists' audience has usually been people in the Third World, who have no reason to like America.

That's why they target anonymous, insignificant civilians; they're easier targets, and since no one in the
Third World has heard of them, it allows the Third
World types to say 'Aha, they got those Americans
thoroughly this time. Good for them.'

"But Michael James was a hero all over the world,
not to mention a particular hero in most of black
Africa because of the good-will tours he did there and
some of his charity work. So MJ was absolutely the
public figure they'd never kill; it would win no new
friends and make many new enemies. So the whole
incident just doesn't make sense as a terrorist act.

"And the chances of it being a disgruntled RW
employee—I'd say none. If anything it's less probable
than an international terrorist. Any engineer/machin-
ist good enough to make that weapon was too good
to be disgruntled—he'd be making a quarter million a
year someplace, and have a house and mortgage,
steady job and family, and all the things that make a
man love peace. The people who decide to suddenly
slaughter a crowd of other people are always losers—
crazy people like the Unabomber, morons like Tim
McVeigh, crazy morons usually. They build simple
gadgets and the simple gadgets don't work very well.
But that bomb-in-the-camera was a brilliant design for
an armor-piercing mine, hidden inside a real camera
body, which is not an easy thing to do.

"Now, that would take a lot of good engineering
to make it work, including firing off some test shots
somewhere. I won't say a hobbyist *couldn't* build one
in his basement, but I will say it would have to be an
awfully skilled hobbyist and a really well-equipped
basement—how many home workshops can machine
tungsten to fine tolerances? And even if he had the
equipment, unless he had a proving area to test it out,

he'd still need the very best of luck for it to work at all, the first few times. Yet it worked perfectly—seemingly the first time.

"So nothing is consistent with the common hypotheses. The unknown enemy's choice of target leads me to conclude that it wasn't the usual suspects out of the rogues' gallery of international terrorism. And the unknown enemy's method leads me to conclude that it probably wasn't a disgruntled RW or NASA employee. So, then, somebody must have gained something out of it; the question is, who gained what?"

I thought about it for a moment. "Well, the shuttle fleet is reduced by one quarter."

"Right," he said, pouring another cup of coffee. "And this happens just before there's a supposed accident that wipes out everything in space, so that we have to spend a year rebuilding one shuttle—and if things had gone even slightly differently, we would have lost it completely—reducing our launch capacity just weeks before the world suddenly needs more launchers than it has ever needed at any time before.

"Who benefits? Any country that has good ready-to-go space launch. *Especially* if it's new, improved stuff, because you can charge way above nominal cost on the first few launches, get your development money back right away, and make the customer bear the whole burden of developing your new systems. We have good space launch, but I can't imagine an American company blowing up the shuttle to expand their market. Arianespace has some good engineers, but they have to work tight and small. The Japanese NSDA is even tighter and smaller. And though the Russians have some of the best hardware around, they got it by being master incrementalists, making stuff a few steps better each generation. It's worked, so far, but you can still see Korolev's dead hand in everything they fly, and you can see that they don't *have* another Korolev to take them into the new century.

"Everybody is flying stuff that's decades behind what's possible, at costs that are far more than they need to be, to accomplish much less than they could, but the existing space powers have had such a long head start that they were able to just sit on that huge potential market, collecting plenty of money without doing much innovation."

"Why didn't we?" I asked. "I mean, do some innovation? Space is a big, big business. Wouldn't a better launcher have paid for itself pretty fast?"

"In a world where there was plenty of competition, that might have happened, but Curtiss and Republic Wright are essentially the whole American aerospace industry, and their only real competitors are state monopolies. They don't face much incentive. The 1950s, 60s, and 70s vintage expendable rockets are still getting stuff up to where it's supposed to go. People will pay the price for using them, plus a hefty premium that becomes your profit. If you can mark up about thirty percent over the cost of operations, why drop your cost by three-quarters, even if you can? There might not *be* that many more markets for satellites. You might trigger a price war where the other side will bring in something even cheaper. You're sitting on top of a very comfortable division of the global market—why risk it all by reaching further?

"So back to the question that started this. There's a spacefaring nation I haven't mentioned that the old comfortable launch market really *didn't* suit. A minor player that got into the game late, but has plenty of a pretty good launcher, and, if our intelligence studies can be believed, maybe even a superior one ready to go."

"You have to mean China."

"I do. Consider what's emerging about their role in the Pakistani proton burst—it looks like a team of Chinese advisors cooked the numbers and ran the launch, and the Pakistanis had no idea at all of what was about to happen. Even without the *Columbia* crash, the proton burst would have put anyone with a really good, cheap, reliable space launch system in a terrific position. If you have a good horse, but every other horse got a head start, the best thing that can happen would be for something to restart the race from the starting line.

"Add the Pakistani proton burst to the *Columbia* crash, and a variety of other things in the last six months, and the Chinese space program is in great shape. Not only that. The thing that really makes us most suspicious is they seem to have known they were about to be in great shape. I've got reports that show that they started rolling out Long March launchers a few months ago as fast as they could, but they haven't announced what they're planning to do with them. Now if we consider a few tests down at Hainan that look like a Long March II is mostly ready to go, and their sudden interest in getting a rocket section going at the Curtiss China plant in Sanxian, and I think they're making a move that they planned a while ago.

"There might even be a revenge element. The Long March launches used to be a very lucrative source of foreign exchange—and Communist countries are always short of that, because they have to buy so much of their higher tech and they produce so little that's exportable. They were launching for all kinds of Western companies and organizations, before some people in my office finally managed to convince the Clinton people that this wasn't a good thing. When we stopped buying Long March launches, the Chinese were *extremely* unhappy."

He stared into space; I had a sense that he was remembering whole volumes of clues, hints, puzzle pieces, and little, half-known things. "Now, finally, here is what I wanted to ask for your thoughts and observations on. The MJ lawsuit is a whole different kind of a kick in the kneecaps to the American space effort. It could result in any amount of loss of political suport, of stupid regulations drawn up in haste, maybe even things like grounding the shuttles for political reasons. It's bound to tie up vast amounts of time and energy that could go to something better, with engineers and scientists that we critically need to do creative work being squandered as expert witnesses and so forth. So if the Chinese are really operating against our commercial space programs, that's a pie where I'd expect to see their fingerprints, which are usually big clumsy ones.

"And yet, from the look of the actual operation—if there even *is* an operation—it feels all wrong for them to be doing this. They're good at espionage, and they can pull off a pretty good special-ops kind of raid. Just ask any soldier in Taiwan or Vietnam about those. But they've got no subtlcty in their special ops—everything is the sledgehammer approach. They've always been lousy at any kind of systematic covert operations—heavy-handed, impatient, and usually with a poor sense of what's going to lead to what. I still don't see how they can be doing as much as they appear to be, to impede investigations and hamstring the space industry in court; that looks more like something a sharp, unscrupulous American firm that was really playing hardball could do, not like something within the capacity of a nation with a couple of hundred mostly identified agents of influence."

I said, "Well, what if someone with Chinese contacts were muscling into Curtiss? Maybe somebody way up in management, or maybe whoever chairs the search committee?" I told him everything I could remember of what Killeret had told me, and as I told him, he leaned forward and nodded vigorously.

"Now, hmmm. *That* is interesting. You wouldn't even need to put in overt Chinese agents, just timid managers, go-slow types, stuffed shirts, and keep feeding their fears. The aerospace companies already have a case of hardening of the arteries, all the Chinese would have to do would be to clog things up more. It's still more subtle than I'd expect from their regular operations . . . but then I have reason to think that this isn't the people I'm used to working against, either."

He grasped his chin with his thumb and middle finger, slowly stroking his cheek with his index finger, eyes far away. It reminded me very much of the way that Professor Dunbar had looked just before springing nightmare questions in Constitutional Law. Finally he said, "Well, we've always known that having so much of our high-tech development in private hands is a vulnerability as much as a strength. It means that no bureaucrat can just squash or bottle up a good idea permanently, but it also means control of the enterprise can change hands without anyone asking about its implications for policy.

"Curtiss has plenty of contacts in China, starting with that huge plant they built at Sanxian. To sell all those airliners to the Chinese, they had to agree to transfer all kinds of technology and build all kinds of factories over there. That isn't supposed to include high-tech or military-application stuff—but the Clinton people were pretty desperate for trade agreements, and we're still finding out what they traded away. So, for example, if Curtiss had a joint advanced launcher project going with China, or even maybe if the Long March II is partly a Curtiss development—with all the advantages of being able to use Chinese facilities outside the US, without our health and safety regulations . . . and had some major part of their planned future over there . . . well. That would explain three things at least—one, how the Chinese were able to move so fast, and two, why there seems to be such a desperate need to cover up, and three, most of all, why Curtiss is acting like they're trying to freeze the head of their advanced projects facility out of the loop."

He poured coffee for both of us, but didn't touch his; instead, he got up and walked slowly around the room, as if the answer were in one of the nineteenth-century German and French encyclopedias that lined the walls. At last he stopped by the fire; the flickering orange glow underlit his face and made his grim expression darker, grimmer, almost a gargoyle. There was nothing nondescript about him now.

Finally he said, "If this is really the last piece of the puzzle—the new people coming into Curtiss from places unknown—and it turns out to fit, well, my god, my god, my god. We might be talking about the biggest security breach since Jonathan Pollard or Aldrich Ames—maybe the biggest since Klaus Fuchs. I'm certainly glad I talked to you."

"That wasn't what you asked me here for, though, was it?"

"No," Welch said, smiling. "It wasn't. But I've

found that I get some of the best mix of information about everything under the sun just by sharing all the information I'm allowed to. We had reason to think Curtiss was the deep pockets behind the MJ suit, but couldn't see any reason why a company would be covertly paying to sue itself. The answer to that is probably that the people doing it are working very directly at the behest of the Chinese. That makes all kinds of sense. And your observations helped me focus on that idea.

"Of course maybe I'm just frightening myself; for thirty years I've been in a business where paranoia is a gift. I don't know that any of what I've just outlined is going on. It's merely a line of speculation that happens to fit all the facts. But I think that I shall just breathe it in the ear of the Attorney General, and the NASA Administrator, and the CIA, NSA, and FBI, and see if I can stir up some trouble for the Chinese, with maybe a heavy reference to what might be happening to Curtiss Aerospace.

"Even if they *haven't* messed around there and the actual explanation for Curtiss's behavior is just stupidity, the Chinese have certainly done plenty of other things that I don't much like, lately, and they need a strong reminder that playing rough has a cost. Besides, at least in aerospace and other high-tech stuff, trouble for them tends to be good for us."

He sat back down. "All right, now we must get down to what I called you about. I hope you'll pardon the long digression. After forming an impression of you, I decided we could talk about more high-level matters as well, and I do trust that, if I should ever need your discreet help on some matter of national security—I am free to ask?"

I nodded.

"Good. At times I feel like the Godfather, but the accumulated mass of people willing to help *is* my most potent weapon.

"Now, here's the script for your case. Tomorrow morning, at about ten A.M., you'll get a call from the judge, and you and everyone else will gather at one P.M. At that time I'll present selected documents that will make it clear that the entire case of the *Columbia* crash is impacted by various material that, for national security reasons, must remain secret. After letting Mr. Haverford pose and shout, to keep his clients happy—this is already arranged—the judge will dismiss the case. You may then expect a storm of public criticism and uproar, but the excellent PR you've done in the last few weeks should eventually stand you in good stead, after the initial outcry. In a few months, you should have space tourism back in the public's good graces."

"Why are you intervening in this case at all?" I asked. "We were pretty sure of winning it, and any attorney other than Haverford would have thrown in the towel weeks ago. Why not just let us win in the next few weeks? There'll be less outcry if it doesn't look like a coverup."

He smiled. "Normally you'd be right, but we happen to know that there is much more evidence than has been revealed publicly to tie the bomb in the CO camera to China, and some of that evidence is out where anyone can find it, so that in the course of winning your case, you might create an international situation that ties the President's hands. We can cope with this problem rather better behind the scenes, and quietly, than the Justice Department could do overtly through the courts, and if things come out in court, Justice will have to be involved. And since trials by definition, in this country, are public—thank God—this case must never come to trial."

"Anyone that wants to make most of my problems go away in an evening is welcome to do it," I said, "and you're right, we'll be able to handle the outcry."

He got up, and I stood; clearly the interview was over. He looked at me with critical scrutiny, as if wondering if he should say anything, and then seemed to make up his mind to say it. "If what we've hit on as the possible situation should actually be the case, it needs to be looked into, and the people responsible need to be caught and stopped, but the first effect of this will be to turn up the heat on them, pressure them, corner them. And if I'm guessing right—well, people who are in over their heads are apt to do stupid things. I could be putting you and your friends into considerable danger."

I hadn't thought of that, but I wasn't going to back down now. "We'll look after ourselves," I said. "You just get to the bottom of all this. Something really has to be done."

Welch called in Miss Marx to see me out. As she guided me through the big common room, I saw an odd decoration hanging over the door that led to the front hallway—odd because everything else in the place was quiet, understated, and well kept up. This was a steel sign, painted bold yellow, scarred by rust and bent by having been broken off a wall or fence; a rusty bolt, its nut still on, dangled from a twisted hole at the lower right corner. In black gothic letters, the sign read

WHAT YOU SEE HERE
WHAT YOU HEAR HERE

WHEN YOU LEAVE HERE
LET IT STAY HERE

"That's the original," Miss Marx explained to me, as if it were a Picasso.

"The original from—"

"From the Manhattan Project. It used to hang over the gates at Los Alamos. It's sort of the unofficial motto of the Skytale Club. It's part of why our members can feel relaxed here."

"I imagine so," I said, because I couldn't think of much else to say. She led me out, shook my hand, and said, "Pleasure to have you here, Ms. Blackstone." As she turned to go inside, the same cab I had come in was already pulling up.

"Most boring people in the world," the cabdriver said, as he pulled away. "The money's really good but hardly anybody interesting ever goes in or comes out. Since the fares hardly ever talk, I can get caught up on the news on the radio. But other than that, they could put you to sleep. Dullest club in New York."

"The food's good," I said.

"Yeah, I bet. No point in being rich if you don't eat good, eh?" He took the turn to head uptown and said, "So, if you been in there, you ain't heard about the thing that blew up at the Cape?"

My stomach dropped like a ball of lead. "No, I didn't hear about it. Is anyone hurt?"

"They don't think so. It was some rocket that they had, like, in storage or being worked on, and they had some kind of explosion with it, or maybe they thought it was going to explode. The radio in this cab, you don't always hear too clearly."

When he dropped me off, I gave him a decent tip

and ran to the elevator inside the building, barreling through a tour group on my way. Somewhere in my trajectory, the bodyguard got in behind me and ran also, pacing me step for step. As the elevator doors closed, he said, "Where are they?" He was reaching into his jacket.

The elevator door closed, and he seemed to relax slightly. It took me an instant to realize. "Oh," I said. "I'm sorry. Nobody was chasing me or anything. I just got a very garbled story of something from Cape Canaveral—"

"The solid rocket booster story," he said. "Yeah, that's pretty awful."

"What is it?"

"Oh. Well, they had a small batch of solid propellant blow up, out in Utah, where they make those rockets. And somebody anonymous called in and said he'd doped it to make it blow up, and that he'd been doping some batches of solid fuel off and on for weeks or months. That means they don't know whether the solid rocket boosters they've got now can go or not. They're still testing out in Utah. A guy on TV was saying there's nothing you could put in the solid fuel that wouldn't be detected, and somebody else said yeah, but you have to look for it, and they've got a whole bunch of suits arguing with each other."

Well, it was clearer than what the cabdriver had said, and at least there hadn't been an explosion at KSC. The elevator door opened and I thanked the bodyguard for his alertness.

I went into my room and turned the TV on to CNN. It was pretty much as I'd heard it; chemical analysis was under way to confirm that the batch that had blown up had been doped, but they had found the contaminant in two other batches, and the fuels chemists thought that whatever the contaminant was, putting it into solid rocket booster fuel would make it very explosion-prone. And, as the engineers were explaining, there was no way to know whether it was inside any of the already-loaded solid rocket boosters; if it were deep inside, it couldn't be detected until it blew up and caused a *Challenger*-type accident.

"He may or may not have managed to get the stuff into a batch that was then loaded into a rocket," one of them was explaining. "But a solid rocket isn't like liquid. We can't just drain out the fuel, replace the tank, put in clean fuel, and be good to go. You're looking at what's basically a several-stories-high stack of solid plastic, which is supposed to burn very fast. The trouble is, if it burns *faster*—and while I can't tell you what was added, I can say it's a known catalyst that *would* accelerate the burning—well, then you get an explosion.

"Every rocket engine, to do what it does, has to operate somewhere near the edge of being a bomb. It doesn't take much to tip it over into suddenly becoming a bomb. So, yes, the threat is credible, and since we don't have any way to tear the engine down to check, without destroying it, it means basically that we have no SRB's for the shuttle."

"And without SRB's—"

"It can't make orbit. I don't know how we will get the ISS crew down, or how we'll try to, but I can tell you it won't be using *Atlantis*."

THE NEXT DAY'S charade went pretty much as Welch had said it would; the relevant papers, photos, and documents were shown, and affidavits were brought out, demonstrating that in the opinion of national security officials, both the accident itself and the James

272 Buzz Aldrin & John Barnes

family's case were probably "sponsored and promoted by forces inimical to American national security." Everything else followed the script as well. The judge said he was going to throw out the case, Jasper Haverford raised a bunch of objections, AnnaBeth James had a good cry—I don't think that was in the script—and finally the judge threw it out. Everyone else pretended they'd never seen or heard of Clifford Welch before, so I did too.

In the hall, afterward, Haverford quietly said, "Just so you know, I was telling Mrs. James we were going to lose, ever since the NASA report. Sometimes you get a stubborn client, you know."

"I've certainly seen those," I said.

"Also, and you can believe this or not, after what was just presented, I wasn't about to take any more of that money, once I knew where it was coming from. I like to believe I'm a good lawyer, but I guess most people would say I'm a crooked lawyer. Well, one thing I'm *not* is a treasonous lawyer. See you in some other court; you're pretty good at this stuff."

He shook my hand and turned away, going back down the hall to his clients. I felt two things: flattered, and an urge to wash my hand.

CHAPTER TWELVE

SCOTT:

I was glad to hear that the case was dismissed, and it was good to see Thalia flushed with victory. Amos volunteered to go to Mrs. Talbert's for the evening, so that Thalia and I could celebrate. "Pretty transparent move, kid," I said, as I dropped him off.

"It was Uncle Nick's idea," he said, cheerfully, grabbing his bag and running inside.

It's hard not to be irritated with your big brother when he decides to run your life, especially when you've got a life and kids of your own. I turned into the driveway of her house—which had been our house. She came out in a dark dress that I'd always liked, wearing a necklace I'd given her.

As I drove to the restaurant, a favorite place of ours that was worth driving to Baltimore for, Thalia leaned forward and turned on the radio, scanning around to find an all-news station. "Basically, to give the James family enough time to get somewhere where they can have some privacy," she said, "and because of something or other, I don't know what, that Clifford Welch whispered in his ear, the judge was delaying the official announcement till 7:30."

"We still have fifteen minutes," I said. "I always set the clock in the car ten minutes fast."

"If you do that," she said, "doesn't that mean that you already know that, and just subtract ten minutes all the time?"

"Logically it would, but this works for me."

We listened till 7:40 or so, but the solid rocket booster sabotage, and the terrible likelihood that the ISS crew would remain stranded until they died of radiation sickness, seemed to be all the news there was. It was good from our PR standpoint but I could have been happier.

After a while I turned the radio off and said, "Welch is really a strange character. I met him twice out at Scorpion Shack, and I gather he had some business with Nick. He seems to have a really strange web of connections."

"He does," Thalia agreed, and told me about her visit to the Skytale Club. "I think at the end of my evening there," she said, "I half expected to be given a false passport, a wig, and a cyanide pill. Part of what makes that place so scary is that it's all so low key."

We talked for another few minutes, and finally I said, "You know, there's something I've been thinking about—not all the time or anything. I've really enjoyed seeing so much of you these past few weeks. It's the only good thing to come out of this whole terrible mess. So . . . uh, maybe . . . well, what I'm trying to say is that I'm sort of sad to have the case coming to an end, because I'm going to miss seeing so much of you."

She chuckled and said, "Scott, that's so sweet. Also so naive. The case is dismissed but it's not over. We've got weeks or months of work to do, if you're ever going to be able to get a decent job in aerospace again. You and I both know what's going on, but so far the media don't and this dismissal is going to *reek* of coverup, and I have no doubt at all that talk radio, and the Internet, and everything else will light up with accusations. What we have to do is to find out how much of the truth we're allowed to reveal, and let it leak out in some highly credible way, until eventually you look like just what you are—an innocent man that people have ganged up on for their own reasons." She sighed. "And sometimes, buddy, you're a *very* innocent man. Not that I mind. Your faith in justice is really touching, even to an experienced lawyer."

"And you're going to stick with me through that part of things?"

"Well, I don't usually leave a fight halfway through. Or leave the father of my kid in the lurch." She hesitated, and then finally added, "Uh, on the other hand . . . well, I like seeing you, too, and it's nice that we're getting along better, but I've been noticing that my life does go better without a man in it right now. There's nobody else, but I don't think I want to think about anything romantic for quite some time yet. I guess I like my independence."

I felt a sad twinge, but I had to admit that life with me had probably not been as rewarding or interesting as life without me. "Well, friends forever, then," I said. "It's good not to be angry all the time, anyway."

"Yeah," she said. "And it's good for Amos. I'm

sorry that I just don't feel like getting into anything deeper."

"Hey, there's nothing deeper than the spirit of the Mars Four," I said.

"It's a little scary that you might be right."

We both laughed at that, and the silence afterwards was comfortable again. The radio still had no news at eight o'clock. Thalia thought maybe the judge had delayed announcing the verdict even longer.

We turned in at the restaurant, and the talk turned much less serious; mostly it was about Amos, and old times, and what it had been like to try to keep my big brother in a hospital bed until the doctors said it was okay for him to get out of it. "His engineers didn't help," I said. "They were in there all the time. There was a test flight that they wanted to delay until he could see it—till he told them to 'just get me a monitor in here, so I can watch the test, and that'll be good enough, dammit! Everybody involved in a test is watching it on monitor anyway!' "

"Couldn't they have used the test flight to deliver a package to ISS?" she asked.

"Uh . . ." I dropped my voice and told her. "They're pretty sick up there. They aren't going to run out of air, food, or water, because, if we don't get them help, they won't be alive long enough to run out. And nobody there is in any shape to spacewalk even in normal conditions. With the station tumbling like it is, they wouldn't be able to retrieve a package, and even if they could, we couldn't send them anything that would help. Even if we'd had a Soyuz to put on it, the rocket they were testing is too fragile in the upper stage to mount it on. And they'd have been in no shape to spacewalk over to it and fly it down.

Somehow, somebody's got to send a crew up to them."

"You don't sound like you think anyone will."

"I don't. But I don't know everything. Maybe somebody's got a secret project somewhere and the President is talking to them. Maybe they're building something backstage at Scorpion Shack or Ghost Town. Maybe there really is something that they can do with a robot, that I haven't thought of."

"What about . . . uh, the thing that fell on Nick."

"StarBird I. Nowhere near ready to go, unfortunately. It's got an engine pod, and an airframe, and a lot of electronics. No hydrogen drop tanks yet, and some of the control systems aren't there, and . . . well—it looks great, but right now we don't even know how it would do just rolling to the end of a runway. Not to mention that it was damaged pretty badly." I shrugged; I'd seen the crushed metal. "Whoever did it—yeah, it was sabotage—set off the explosive bolts to separate StarRescue from the rest of StarBird. StarRescue just slumped forward on its nose, and all that they have to do is replace a couple of panels—it's a tough little ship, really well-designed, and if it flies like its simulator, about as much fun as anything coming down from orbit can be. But Starbird I is pretty much a loss. When that dropped onto Nick, the SSME broke loose and smashed up everything around it, and the bottom heat shield got a meter-long crack. Even if it had been ready—and it wasn't—it would be useless now. Hey, you should have heard what he said to the doctor who wanted to CT scan his head again, just in case—" I did my best to turn the conversation to lighter topics, because despite what she'd said before about the case not being really over, I wasn't completely sure that we'd be seeing as much of each other, and I felt like I needed to make this evening as pleasant for her as I possibly could.

It helped that she cooperated. We smiled and laughed often, completely forgot to check the radio on the way home, and we were an hour late to pick up Amos. It was a good thing that Mrs. Talbert was tolerant.

I had been crashing out on Thalia's couch often in the last few weeks, due to the threats and the burned car, generally with a ball bat that I borrowed from Amos lying under the coffee table beside me, in case of trouble. Amos went cheerfully off to bed, since he knew that I would be staying that night, and Thalia and I stayed up to catch the news. I was still hoping that the dismissal would be a minor story with no reactions, but it was the lead story on CNN Headline.

A few minutes into it, she was shaking her head and saying, "Well, you've certainly made an impression."

The announcement that the case was being dropped had been greeted by exactly the kind of uproar that the media love to report—or to make, depending on what you think it is they actually do. M J had been a world-class nice guy, and a world-class celebrity—not a very common combination, in my experience—and the result was that a very large number of famous people were sad and angry that he had died. Thus it took almost nothing for a reporter to get an actor, politician, athlete, singer, activist, or whatever to declare loudly that something must be wrong.

"This stinks of coverup and I don't know if we'll ever get justice for Michael," one rapper said.

"I was starting to think this was just an accident,

just one of those terrible things that sometimes happen, but now that this case is just dismissed out of nowhere, it looks like a coverup to me," an "actress/novelist" (that's what it said on the screen under her image) said on *Politically Incorrect*.

The judge had said only that there were elements of national security involved but that the files would be unsealed at the earliest possible date. That gave Jay Leno some great material, as he explained that next year the number of games the Rams lost was going to be top secret, as were "all batting averages in the Eastern Division of the National League. God knows what could happen if that fell into the wrong hands." The news that the James family had accepted the situation, and the reference to national security, gave Howard Stern room for some tasteless jokes about what M J's secret mission had been as well; I was grateful, because he drew some of the fire off of me, ShareSpace, and all the other defendants.

The next morning, when I phoned in to check by remote, there were seventy-four new messages: sixty-one from news media, ten angry threats, and three from financial services salespeople who wondered if I'd like to refinance my house. I put a stock message on my answering machine again, and Nick came up with some more cash so I could have two bodyguards in my house all the time, because every so often the picket line out there got frisky. I stayed at Thalia's house; landing a spacecraft is one thing, but when it comes to angry mobs, I'm no braver than the next guy.

Watching the picket line on the MSNBC broadcast, late that afternoon, it looked to me like a strange mixture. Such leadership as they had was coming from a few political activists who thought a black family was being denied justice. But most of the followers weren't exactly following the "leaders." Much of the crowd consisted of sports fans who thought they were doing something for their hero, plus an equal or maybe greater number of people who just liked the excitement of the crowd.

"You'd be better off with just the activists," Thalia said. "Most of them are pros at what they do. They know enough to stay off your property, they don't usually violate the noise ordinances, and they don't want to look like louts on television. Plus there's only maybe two dozen of them at any one time. You'd be able to go out, give them some hot coffee for the cold weather, have a talk with them if you wanted to. Even though they'd keep picketing, you could feel pretty safe. It's the same old principle as anything else: if you want something done right, go to people with experience. Unfortunately, most of the crowd has never done anything like this before, and they have no idea how to behave. Which is why they're acting like a damned bunch of amateurs and the police are having to work a lot harder." She slid two sandwiches onto my plate. "I hope you're staying the night again. The bodyguards get paid to deal with the hassle, and you don't. And for some reason they're targeting the evil businessman instead of his evil lawyer, so it's been quiet over here."

I looked up at the television screen, which was doing a quick recap of the days' events at my house. There was a brief statement, reasonably coherent though (I thought) unfair, from an older woman holding a sign that read "Justice *IS* National Security." She thought that "they" were getting away with something, and "we have to stop them." Thalia had a point—she did look like somebody I could at least try to talk to.

Then the camera cut to twenty fraternity guys in a row, each with one letter painted in red on his bare chest. They were standing out in the cold November evening, waving their arms over their heads and shrieking as if they were at a basketball game. The letters spelled out JUSTICE FOR M…J WE LOVE M…J. They must have seen their image appear on television, because they began to jump up and down and whoop a few seconds after the network cut to them, making it harder to read the message. When the microphone got close to one, he jumped forward and yelled, "We are totally here to support M J!" and they all started whooping again, loud enough so that the reporter never did get to ask the question, whatever it might have been. As the on-the-scene reporter was signing off, the crowd went into a long, rolling chant of "M J! M J! M J!"

"I'm glad he can't see *this*," I said. "He'd be so embarrassed."

"Oh, yeah," Thalia said, and was just reaching to turn off the television when something made her stop. The commentator was adding, "No comment yet from the White House or the State Department about the now rapidly developing rumor that the FBI and American intelligence sources have definitely traced the cause of the *Columbia* accident to deliberate sabotage by the Chinese, or about the comment by General Hofstadter of the Air Force Space Command, speaking at a retired officers' dinner earlier this evening, that the disaster that killed Michael James and wrecked a space shuttle formed 'a key move in a coherent strategy,' linking it to the proton bomb that destroyed all orbiting satellites last month." He looked straight out of the screen, and said in the sort of firm voice that they usually reserve for advertising, "We understand that this is a matter of great concern to all Americans, based on the mail we're receiving at our Web site and the volume of phone calls we're getting, but unfortunately we just don't have any more facts than what we have just told you. The only person in authority who has said anything is General Hofstadter, and he has not been available for comment since making that statement. We will keep you informed as developments happen." He turned to his left and forced a big smile. "And on a happier note, Betty, I understand that the big Christmas toy for this season is going to be pink and fuzzy!"

"That's right, Jack, and we'll have all the—"

Thalia clicked it off. "Hmm. Your public relations luck might be holding. Though I'm not sure if it's really luck, if the story that displaces you on the news turns out to be World War III. I sense the hand of Welch. If that story floats any longer, the mobs will be gone from your house, and over at the Chinese Embassy. And MJ will be the biggest hero of the new century."

"Hero?" I asked. "He was a real nice guy and a great athlete, but other than that he was just standing in the way when a bomb went off."

"Trust me," she said. "If the media confirm that the story is true, then in their version of things, it will be the same thing as MJ having personally died to save America. There'll be pressure on DoD to give him a posthumous Medal of Honor. There'll probably be pressure on the Pope to make him a saint. Betcha three weeks' groceries at the cabin next summer, if we have time to go."

"As long as we go together," I said.

There was an extremely awkward pause at that, and then we both found that the house needed vast amounts of cleaning up. But she didn't seem angry at me for having said it—she just suggested that in that case, we needed to put twin beds in there. "You still snore," she said, "and I'd rather have it across the room than in my ear."

WHEN AMOS GOT home, the bodyguard company decided to have me do a "back door switch," which is a pretty silly routine that Bobbi, a big strong woman who was captain of the detail, described as "an old trick that usually works as long as there's not too much light."

Dave, a bodyguard who looked something like me, would put on a sweatshirt and hat of mine, plus a big pair of black shades that covered most of his face. Then the company driver would drive us up to my house, we'd dash in with my "double" getting between me and the crowd like the bodyguard he was. Inside, I'd put on the sweatshirt, cap, and shades, and run back out as if I were the bodyguard. Amos thought it was pretty funny watching me and Dave, my double, practice the clothing exchange until we could do it in less than thirty seconds.

It went smoothly enough. As the car turned onto the street, people were running at it and yelling, and some of the more exuberant types were beating on the roof and yelling "MJ! MJ!" Dave looked pretty tense, and Bobbi, riding in the passenger seat, kept touching her shoulder holster.

We pulled up the driveway, and suddenly we were out of the crowd as two of the guards from the house blocked the crowd from following us. As close as possible to the door, we stopped, and Dave said, "Ready, go."

I dashed out the door, heading for my porch steps. The noise from the crowd was unbelievably loud; they sounded more excited than angry, as if this were some kind of carnival. A bottle smashed against the garage door beside me. Dave was standing tall and keeping himself between me and the mob as I sprinted up the steps and into the house.

The moment we were inside, we did the clothing exchange, and then I raced back out the door, down the steps, and into the car. As I closed the door, the driver backed up, just slowly enough so he could stop quickly and just fast enough so that people would get out of the way. We got down the driveway with no more than some hands and feet thumping the car. As I watched, the guards inside turned on a couple of lights upstairs in my house, and a brick bounced off just below the roof, inches from a window.

"Looks like we convinced them," I said.

Bobby grunted. "The old tricks are sometimes the best ones," she said. "We do this all the time for musicians. We'll be going to the company garage, if you don't mind, to do a switch of cars, too, before someone gets too clever about Thalia Blackstone's house. Anyway, we think we've guaranteed you a reasonably peaceful night."

"Thanks."

"That's what we're paid to do." She hesitated, and then said, "Can I ask you something? Don't answer if it's classified."

"All right."

"Is it really true that this is all some kind of Chinese attack on our space program, and MJ was just kind of caught in the crossfire? That you, personally, didn't have anything to do with it, really?"

"Um. I don't know if that's classified or not. And I've been kept pretty far out of the loop. But that's what many people who are in a position to know seem to think."

"I'm glad," she said. "I'm sorry for Mrs. James losing her lawsuit and all, but I'm glad that it wasn't you or any American company that caused it."

There was something about her tone that made me ask, "Do you know AnnaBeth James?"

"I was guarding her last week. She's a nice lady, and she's hurting bad."

We drove on in silence until we pulled in through the doors of the company garage. There, the driver and I moved over to a nondescript little minivan, the kind of thing that suburbs everywhere are crawling with, and he drove me back to my ex's house. He didn't say much on the way, but as we neared the house, he said, "I wanted to wish you good luck and a quiet night, sir."

"Thank you. I can use both."

"M J really was something, wasn't he? You knew him pretty well, I guess."

"I did know him. He was one of the best men I ever met. It was a terrible loss."

"Well, then, if it was the Chinese, I sure hope someone finds a way to pay those bastards back. Even if the public never gets to hear about it."

"Me too."

By the time he dropped me off at the house, Amos had finished his homework, it was fully dark, and Thalia had ordered a pizza and a couple of movies. "I thought about getting *Moonraker* and ordering Chinese," she said, "but I wasn't sure we could take the irony. So it's a great big veggie pizza, the first *Star*

Wars flick to get us to bedtime, and then *When Harry Met Sally* afterwards, till grownup bedtime."

I might have been able to see irony in those choices, myself, but I thought it wiser not to point it out. We were all tired, and stressed out, so mostly we just ate and watched the movies. Amos asked to stay up after *Star Wars*, and we said he could, but half an hour of a romantic movie was about as much as he could take before drifting off to bed. After that, we sat and watched the movie; it wasn't as much fun as the first time we'd seen it, when we'd been dating.

THE GUNSHOT, JUST outside the front window, woke me up. I was off the couch and groping for the bat in an instant. A moment later I saw the flickering light of a fire through the front window. One of the bodyguards rushed past me, hissing, "Stay down."

I did. I could hear the bodyguards waking up Thalia and Amos, telling them to come downstairs, not to turn on any lights, and to keep quiet. There were voices out on the lawn, and after a while the wail of a police siren, and then the honk-wheez of an ambulance. I ventured to whisper, "What's going on?" to the bodyguard watching the three of us, but he only shrugged; he didn't know, and his job was to watch us, not to give us the news.

After a couple of minutes, I heard water running, and realized that they'd hooked up the garden hose for something; the flames flickered out. More noise outside as an ambulance arrived, and then what sounded like cops arguing with several other people, went on for about half an hour by the wall clock. Just about three A.M., almost everyone seemed to leave all at once, in a great cloud of car noises: engines skittering and thumping awake, tires crunching on the drive, headlight beams sweeping across the windows for brief instants.

At last the chief, or captain, or whatever you call the bodyguard in charge, came in and said, "None of ours down, one of theirs. And it turns out it's a national security affair. There's someone here to talk to you all—he'll be inside in a couple of minutes."

We all sat up on the couch, and on an impulse, I went into the kitchen and turned on the coffeemaker, since it was already set up for the morning. The familiar smell and noise seemed to stir me out of this bizarre dream. Something big had happened out on the front lawn that I had mowed, right where I'd taught Amos how to throw a football. I didn't know exactly what, yet, but they'd said there was "one of theirs down," and the presence of fire and ambulance crews sounded like violence.

While I was in the kitchen, I heard the front door open and close a couple of times, and soft conversation.

I came out of the kitchen with a tray of eight cups of coffee, figuring everyone could use some, and discovered that Clifford Welch was sitting in the armchair across from the couch, looking a little weary himself. I set the tray of coffee down on the table and took a cup myself; Thalia grabbed another, and Welch and the lead bodyguard also picked up cups. "You might want to take a cup to each of the other guards, and to my man out by the garage," Welch said, dropping an obvious hint.

The lead bodyguard nodded and went out with the tray; I figured he wouldn't be back until somebody told him to.

"It sounds like Amos should maybe go back to his room for a bit," Thalia said.

Welch nodded. "If you're still upset, and would rather be out here with your folks, Amos, maybe you could just put on headphones and listen to some music, or watch something on TV?"

Without saying anything, Amos sat down and hooked himself up to the television with headphones; I was about to tell him not to tune in anything violent, or where they talked dirty, but he was way ahead of me—he found some fifty-year-old cartoon with singing flowers and bees, and seemed to zone right into it. When I saw that he was settled for the moment, I asked, "What's going on?"

Welch grunted. "Well. Things very nearly got out of hand, and it was lucky that they didn't go any worse. I came out here with one man, to keep an eye on your house, and found your security detail was pretty alert, so it took some time to work our way through them and sit down to keep our watch in the shadows in front of the garage. Then a man ran across your yard with something on fire—which turned out to be a Molotov cocktail. I didn't have any other way to stop him quickly, so I shot him. He fell over and landed on the Molotov cocktail, which went off before we could get to him, and it set his clothes and hair on fire."

"He's dead?" Thalia asked.

"Not yet, but if he's conscious, he must wish he were dead. God, what a way to go. He was burned all over, and it looks like my shot smashed one thighbone. If they can save his life, he won't thank them for it." He sighed. "But the paramedics still had a heartbeat when they left, and I've known of cases that looked just as bad and survived."

"Why did you come here tonight?" I asked.

Welch made a tight little smile. "I was here as a

backup, in case Andrew Riscaveau came here; we thought he'd be either running for the Chinese Embassy or more likely just trying to leave the country. It was just a gut instinct or something, a feeling I had that he might try something before running out on us. And I *think* it was Riscaveau. I didn't get a good look at him before, so it could conceivably be someone else, but it was about the right height and weight, and I don't know anyone else who would have had any reason to do this kind of thing."

It was finally beginning to sink into me; I said, "But—uh, Andrew Riscaveau is, or he was, the security guy at Republic Wright—"

"Yep. And also a defector—or at least he was planning to defect. For cash, we think. Heavy alimony, gambling habit, daughter at Smith, a bunch of cash withdrawals from most of his investments, over the last three years, that don't coordinate with his gambling binges, but I'd bet will turn out to trace to a drug habit or maybe a relationship with a high-priced prostitute. Andrew Riscaveau was yet another one of those strung-out cases, a guy in over his head who never really had any loyalty to anything except his career." Welch sighed. "No matter how many times the intelligence agencies get caught by these clowns, we always get surprised when another one comes along. And it's always the same guy with hardly any difference except details: it's your basic jerk under pressure, who realizes that he could solve his financial problems by selling a few pieces of information. And he says to himself, heck, the other side probably has all that information, already, anyway, so where's the harm? Besides, nobody appreciates how hard he works. And besides all that, as a political realist, he knows that the two sides are really the same anyway.

They all tell that same story to themselves.

"Anyway, we'd tied Riscaveau to the fire that destroyed your car, Thalia—nothing a regular cop would go to a grand jury with, but he was in town, he was unaccounted for at the right times, and it turned out he'd had a petty arson conviction as a teenager. Then he turned up again as probably the guy who dropped StarBird onto Nick; at least, between the lists of suspects, he was the only overlap. So we started checking, and sure enough, when you looked at his debts and expenses, he looked like a guy who, about three years ago, really needed a spare quarter of a million tax free—and found it. Shortly after a vacation in Thailand, which no accountant would have thought he could afford, there were some interesting deposits into his bank accounts, mostly transfers from offshore sources.

"So we went to have a nice chat with Mr. Riscaveau, at the DC office for Republic Wright Security, and . . . he took off. Saw us drive into the parking lot and just went straight out the back, jumped on the Metro, got a car on a fake ID and credit card, and was moving fast. We thought he'd just run to his Chinese bosses, but we couldn't be sure."

"Why did he come here to bomb this house?" Thalia asked.

"There might be several reasons. You can take your pick, and chances are we'll never know for sure. Could be personal—your family had gotten in his way one time too many, and he was mad at you. Or he was hoping, maybe, that you would all run outside, the bodyguards would be confused, and he could take one of you as a hostage.

"But the most likely thing, to me, is that he was being twisted into one last action. The Chinese work their agents hard and always treat them as expendable. I think probably they told him that he'd have to do one more thing before they'd take him out of the country. Even if he'd survived, I doubt he had any information that would have been any use to us—so from their standpoint, it was better, because it was cheaper, to try to get one more bit of action out of him, especially if we killed or captured him and spared them the nuisance of maintaining him. They didn't stand to lose anything except an unreliable employee who no longer had anything to offer."

I shuddered. "How can anyone work for people like that?"

Welch spread his hands and smiled slightly. "They're very nice while you still have anything they want. And if it's disgrace next week, or maybe getting caught two years from now, well, some people will pick the latter. Anyway, we don't know for sure, yet, that it's Riscaveau, but it fits the pattern. And we've already started to move on some interesting characters at Curtiss, as well—though that's a much tougher job. Unfortunately, dragging your feet because you take orders from Beijing happens to look very much like dragging your feet because you're stupid, or because your company is fat, dumb, and happy and doesn't like change.

"But we'll have the whole nasty lot of them, I think; the Chinese couldn't have made this work without confederates in our government, Curtiss, and RW, and they moved so fast and hard, and overplayed their hand so much, that most of their agents in place will have had to scramble around to keep up with it. We just look for who's been scrambling lately, and why.

"All this is just a reminder that you're never secure

against anything that the other side wants to do badly enough. Any agency out there can do almost anything, if they don't mind getting caught big time; during the whole Cold War, the KGB could always have shot the President, if they'd been willing to take the outrage, and luckily for us, there was never a situation where it was worth it. Our clever friends in Beijing—or more likely, just at Hainan—thought they might be able to gain so much that it would be worth the price. At this point, they're not going to get much . . . and the bill is coming due." He stood up. "I strongly suggest that you all go back to bed and sleep in. Scott, you'll be needed at a meeting tomorrow at three P.M., and you might want to dress up for it."

I was almost past the point of worrying about how much I got pushed from place to place, but when it looked like Welch was leaving, I asked, "Uh, where is this meeting?"

He smiled. "At the White House. I'll be there, and your brother Nick, and some other people you know. We have a job for you."

CHAPTER THIRTEEN

NICK:

The phone rang at six o'clock in the morning, just as I was getting out of the shower. It was Jagavitz. "Nick, I need to meet with you and Robertson in your office, seven o'clock. I've ordered breakfast. You'll need to be in a decent suit because we're off to talk to some bigwigs this afternoon. The good news is, this is my last day in your office."

It had been typical of Jagavitz that after I was injured, he temporarily took over Scorpion Shack himself, and saw them through that first, flawless StarCore I launch, and the by-the-book re-entry and safe landings of both StarBoosters. He claimed, anyway, that he hadn't had so much fun in years—not since his days with a small start-up company. Whatever the truth was, the day before, when I had at last gotten into my office to see how things were going, he'd had the whole place up to date and ready; there was no backlog of work for me to worry about.

"I'll be there," I said. "When and where's the meeting?"

"2:30, in DC. After we meet and discuss, we'll get right on the plane. So bring your bag. Can you get all that in an hour?"

"I live packed," I said. "See you at seven."

A few minutes later I was rolling down the white-painted asphalt path in the back of one of the company "golf carts," bag and briefcase beside me. The driver wasn't talkative—hardly surprising at the hour—and the sun was just up, barely clearing the horizon, a warm presence that would turn the humid air hot by eleven.

I figured this was going to be about a twenty-thousand-mile month; I have those. Maybe I could squeeze in time for a dinner with Thalia and Scott, before flying back here.

Jagavitz and Robertson were already there; it was too early in the morning for many pleasantries, so we just grabbed the bagels, cereal, and coffee and got our blood sugar up to where we could all be coherent. By 7:15 we were sitting down with a large stack of paper, each.

"After your accident," Jagavitz began, "when I came in here to take over, I found Ned's short report on the dual-StarBooster/StarCore I/StarRescue system. I discovered I agreed with both of you—that Ned was right, that there would be a better than fifty-fifty chance of success, and that you were right, that it was still far too much of a gamble as long as we had any other way to do it. But after the situation developed with the solid rocket boosters on *Atlantis*, I asked Ned to prepare a somewhat lengthier document."

Ned plunked a big pile of paper in front of me and

grinned in a way that made me even more nervous than I was already from seeing him in a non-rumpled suit without any pens in his pocket. "You don't have to read any of this," he said, "at the moment. You can spend the whole plane flight going over it with me. Just turn to the first page."

I did. It was a picture of a StarCore I, with a StarRescue and service module sitting on top of it. A cage that looked like a heavy-duty playpen wrapped the Centaur stage.

"Oh, man," I said. "You have to be kidding."

"No joke," Robertson said, and leaned back, putting his hands over his head. "The StarRescue was undamaged in the sabotage, and it's already built, and has had a number of flight tests of one kind or another. The dual StarBooster/StarCore I has just had a successful test shot all the way to orbit. The airframe checkout on the StarBoosters, after the test shot, two days ago, showed that there wasn't a thing about them that needed fixing. And that service module is just an aluminum wrapper around a couple of the same big thrusters we've been making for decades. So the only really untested technology is the I-bar cage around the Centaur, and that's already built, Nick. We have enough old-fashioned shop floor engineers around, and enough good machinists, so that they all worked through the night. The whole thing is being assembled out on our Pad Two, right here at Scorpion Shack."

"It's the only hope we've got for getting them off ISS in time," Jagavitz said. "Would you rather we didn't try?"

I stared at it. In my mind's eye, almost against my will, I could see it working, and in addition, a good engineer and my boss agreed that it would. "I think

I can accept it, mentally," I said, "but it may take a few hours. Emotionally, maybe a few days. We're going over all the specs, I assume, on the plane."

"Yep." Robertson reached out and flipped two pages.

The page now in front of me was a crude drawing of six astronauts, inside the crew compartment of the StarRescue, all being eaten by a giant amoeba. I stared at it for a long moment until I finally saw that the label below said ENCLOSING WATER RADIATION SHIELDING.

"You're going to put . . ."

"Water beds, basically," Ned said. "Big flat heavy vinyl bags of water. Also mostly built, now. They cover every inside surface. You're taking a ton of water along as radiation shielding. The pilot flies it from a keyboard/simulator with a cable that runs into the regular control panel, since that has to be covered up. The bag over the window is transparent, and we have a little pump for moving water in and out of it so that the pilot can go visual when he needs to. And since that's a lot of extra mass, we've got a neat little gadget that lets you dump it just before you start the aerobrake part of re-entry—a centrifugal pump from an old liquid-fueled rocket project that got canceled. Pressure tests are going on right now on the sections they've finished."

I sighed. "I guess it's better than not trying."

"There is that," Robertson said.

"Also," Jagavitz added, "it pains me to say it, because I'd like this to be totally an RW operation, but our counterparts over at Ghost Town, as the prime contractor on ISS, know the station much better than we do. They were able to work up a gadget that will let you stabilize the station when you get there, since none of the crew aboard are in any shape to cross over via EVA. So the job is for you to get up there with the pilot and the guy from Curtiss, make the jump to ISS, install the stabilizer, stabilize the station, push the Soyuz out of the dock, dock the StarRescue, load in the ISS crew, and come back home. About fifteen dental X-rays' worth of exposure, which will make your blood chemistry funny for a while but shouldn't have too many other consequences. Simple list of tasks, eh?" There was a strange twinkle in his eye.

"You are talking," I said, "very much as if you expected me to go, personally. And now that I think of it, Ned's been talking that way, too."

Jagavitz shrugged. "We've been working out who to send. The list is pretty short, to tell you the truth. Curtiss has just one guy that they think understands their miracle-stabilizer gadget as a whole—the supervising engineer from that one—so he goes. We were able to find just one qualified pilot who is already aware of the political situation. That was important because they don't want to brief another one. This mission will be flown, very much against my better judgment, as a covert mission after the old Soviet style. That is, if it works, they will announce it, and if it doesn't work, they never heard of us. I think it's a stupid way to do things, but that's why I'm a businessman and not a politician.

"Now, just for the sake of safety, we think we should send along someone who does know the total system architecture and could take action in an emergency—an engineer who's really familiar with the whole system, StarBoosters, StarCore, StarRescue, and all. You probably see the problem that we ran up against?"

I did. "Hardly anyone has an overview. Practically all our engineers specialize in just one aspect or another. The total system view is in the hands of, oh, I don't know, maybe seven or eight people. The four engineers in the master design review team, Ned, and my two deputy managers. Seven, I guess."

"Eight," Jagavitz said. "There's you. *And* you're the only one that's also a pilot with any significant time in jets. *And* three of your senior engineers and one manager are past sixty with heart problems—that's what a desk job with generous quantities of stress will do for you, it can cost you the chance to be blown up later in life, eh?" His chuckle was not reassuring. "Nick, you know we can't order you to do it, but of all the engineers who could go on this flight, you're the only one with no dependents, a broad knowledge of the total system—and no body of specialized knowledge that would be hard to replace. That doesn't mean you're not valuable—"

"But it does mean I'm the best candidate," I said. "No offense taken. So what it boils down to is, I go along as general repairman and Mr. Fixit?"

"The official title will probably be flight engineer."

I thought for all of one second. "When do I start?" I asked.

"Today. You spend three days studying and we let you play on the flight simulator. Then you go. The crew up there doesn't have much time."

Robertson added, "Just so you know, I volunteered to go and they pointed out that I have high blood pressure and I'm forty pounds overweight and I have two kids in junior high. But I'll be rooting for you anyway, you lucky bastard. Especially because if we ever get the big tourist ships flying, I'm buying a ticket on the first one."

"Hell, I'll buy you one," I said.

"I regret to say you'll also need to spend an hour or two being briefed by Caitlin Delamartin and Barbara Quentin about how to present yourself at the press conference afterwards."

I shrugged. "Oh, well, it's all showbiz nowadays." Then a thought struck me. "I don't know who the pilot is."

Robertson grinned. "Well, remember, this whole thing is being run as SCI, everything on a need-to-know basis, only people who already know being included in things. Now, the controls of the StarRescue were deliberately copied from the shuttle, so that a pilot who can handle one can handle the other, though the StarRescue will probably handle even more like a concrete block than the shuttle. As it happens, there is one shuttle-qualified pilot who has been in on most of this affair right from the beginning, and who knows about all the national security issues connected with it. Admittedly, he's on the reserve list, because he's gone civilian . . ."

I suddenly realized. "Oh my god. You mean Scott."

"Unh-hunh," Robertson said. "While he wasn't visiting you in the hospital, we even had him play on the StarRescue simulator. Great hands, quick thinker, super intuition, all that stuff you want a test pilot to be. When you all get back, we're going to offer him a job, and I hope he takes it."

I shook my head a few times, to clear it. "Oh, he's qualified enough. I'll feel perfectly safe, with Scott flying us, I'm sure. But . . . uh, did the poor idiot child ever mention being stuck in a swamp in the backwoods of Bangladesh for most of a day?"

CHAPTER FOURTEEN

SCOTT:

Nick enjoyed the heck out of watching my jaw drop when the President of the United States explained to me that I would be flying the StarRescue, but Nick's own jaw dropped pretty far when Eddie Killeret came in and was introduced as the third crew member. It made as much sense as anything else, though; the President wanted a small operation, kept as close as possible, because he was determined that if it failed, no one was to know anything. I thought about mentioning to him that for thirty years Presidents had been getting into more trouble for the coverup than for the offense, but that seemed like borrowing trouble.

He did have a point; he didn't want his hands tied in space, the way that Reagan's had been after *Challenger* blew up. "Mr. Reagan just had a couple years of trouble doing maintenance, and had to cancel some missions. If Congress went nuts on me and shut down or slowed down launches, we might never be able to regain our position in space at all," he said. "The crew dying on ISS would be bad—but having the public see the rescue attempt crashing would be worse."

Less than seventy-two hours later, I had landed StarRescue correctly eighteen times—on a simulator—and made sixteen correct rendezvous. Both of those were out of twenty tries, so I was giving my last day over to getting the rendezvous up to snuff. In this practice session, I was four for four, and was going for number five, when the simulation run was interrupted, as they often were, for another briefing.

Killeret's "tarantula" had finally arrived from Ghost Town, and he and Nick were practicing with it. Supposedly after making it over to the truss of the ISS, they would attach the first thruster next to the solar cells; then climb "up" the truss (since centrifugal force would be against them, it would feel like up) to a pre-selected strut where they would attach the first digital camera; from there to the center modules, where they would tie on another camera and another thruster, and add the CPU; then "down" the other side truss to put one more camera in the middle and one more thruster on the end. After some discussion, it had been decided that rather than try to re-rendezvous with StarRescue, they'd just climb into ISS and ride things out. In computer simulations, anyway, the tarantula had only taken about fifteen minutes to end the tumble.

It was called the tarantula because the cameras and thrusters all came off from the CPU on long coaxial cables, like the arms of a tarantula. Using a celestial navigation program, the CPU was supposed to be able to figure out the spin of the station, and then use the thrusters to damp it out in the most efficient possible way. I was nervous about letting a computer program do that job, but its record in simulations was much better than mine. Besides, if they had to, Nick and Eddie could hand-fire the thrusters, and probably get a good enough solution for me to be able to bring StarRescue in to dock.

Nick's engineers had built a full scale model of the ninety-foot-long truss in the hangar, and put it on a motorized turntable. What Nick and Eddie were doing was practicing going up and down it, counting struts, memorizing where the tarantula's units had to be connected. The major thing I was realizing was that, with two guys who had never gone EVA before, this would be the hard part. They seemed to be having fun, but I couldn't help thinking how much I'd rather have two experienced astronauts on the job, and let these guys phone in the fixes from the ground.

Finally they let me go back to flying simulations. I did three more correct rendezvous in a row, and told the engineer team that I felt about as ready as I was ever going to feel. They said that Nick and Eddie were going to do one more run in the buoyancy tank, practicing the attaching maneuvers, and then declare themselves ready. The next window to intercept ISS would be early the next morning, so their strong suggestion was that I have a good dinner and get to bed early.

I was just about to turn in when on an impulse I grabbed the phone and called Thalia. She and Amos knew what was up, and Welch had assured me that that line had been secured, so we could talk freely. I talked with Thalia for a while, and she said that, from a PR standpoint, if the mission came off, she thought my name would be about as clear as it was going to get. I talked with Amos for a minute or so—it was very awkward—and then he blurted out, "Dad, if you don't come back, I'm going to miss you a lot."

"I know," I said. "But, you know, for what it's worth, everyone has to worry about that. Sooner or later you don't see somebody again, because they die. And you miss them. But if you didn't love them in the first place, you'd have missed out on *everything*. I'll do my best to come back, but aren't you glad we got to have our time together, anyway?"

He sniffled. "I guess I'm greedy. I want more."

"Then I'm greedy too." It seemed like a good note to say "See you later" on, so I did. I stretched out on the bed in the Scorpion Shack visitor dorm, and noticed I had tears running down my face. Well, it was natural enough. A few minutes later I was sound asleep.

WE WERE IN StarRescue's cabin, which at the moment was like being inside a rolled-up water bed. "You know, they could have put a few goldfish in there to keep us entertained," Eddie said.

"Bad human engineering," Nick said. "We'd get attached to them and wouldn't want to pull the plug when the time came."

"Well, damn this working with humans thing, anyway," Killeret said. "Next lifetime, I'm working with well-trained monkeys."

I was busy with my checkouts, supposedly checking everything for the second time, actually for about the fifth—the level of paranoia I was reaching was pretty amazing. The first generation of astronauts had been nearly all test pilots, and they had been *used* to the idea of climbing into a tremendously complex ma-

chine that no one had flown before, and taking it up
to see what it did. This was my first real experience
of the kind.

Well, if I only did this once in my life, that would
be plenty for me. And at least I'd have talking rights
in the world's most exclusive locker room.

Nick and Eddie were doing their checkouts too,
when the voice crackled and said, "T minus forty
minutes and counting. All systems are nominal."

"Strange that they only need to tell us every ten
minutes," I said, "this late in the count."

"Simple system," Nick said. "That's what we built
it to be. The countdown time is just for us to do
multiple checks; everything was nominal by seven
this morning. If we didn't have to wait for the 8:43
launch window, we'd have been able to go an hour
ago." Something caught his attention on the screen in
front of him, but whatever it was didn't merit more
than a moment's frown and a couple of touches of
his keypad. After a minute he said, "You suppose that
we'll ever get to where we don't do a countdown?
Where all Mission Control says is 'Now departing
from gate two, concourse six?'"

"Never," Killeret said. "Airliners never have to hit
a moving target; spacecraft always do. If it moves, it's
got a window, and you have to make your time for
the window."

"Besides, there's the romance and tradition," I said.

"Pilots," Nick muttered, under his breath.

The countdown worked its way down and everything stayed absolutely fine as far as any instrument
could tell. Occasionally we'd get a "best wishes" or
"good luck" from one department or another, which
I always acknowledged with a short "Thank you." A
long time after, when I was reviewing the tape, I dis-

covered that I had thanked the President of the United States and my brother's secretary in exactly the same way. I don't think either of them was offended.

If everything went well, the checkout was the last time before orbit that I would be really doing a pilot's job. For the ascent, I was just a passenger; my piloting would come later. On a hurry-up mission like this, without much time for training, and over American territory where we had plenty of radar and transmitter stations available (our path would take us almost parallel to the Gulf Coast, almost directly over Memphis Columbus, and Montreal), it made sense to launch and fly completely under ground control. They'd get us all the way to orbit before it would be time to throw off the Centaur, power up the service module, and do any real flying.

The StarBooster engines thundered alive under us—two Atlas first stages pushing us upward, the effect rising to a roar. The takeoff was smoother than on the shuttle; for the first two and a half minutes, we were in pretty high acceleration, held down to our couches as if we were under a heap of sandbags. The sky swiftly darkened toward violet. The voice in my earpiece read off a litany of things that were going fine.

Booster separation felt as if someone had thrown a switch and turned off the gravity. The twin Star-Boosters shut down and released the StarCore simultaneously, and though I couldn't see them, I knew that they were flipping over away from us, turning over to get their bellies back toward the Earth, and beginning their glide back to Scorpion Shack. We were about twenty-five miles above the ground, moving upward at Mach 5.

For five seconds, to give the boosters time to get away, we moved upward on pure inertia, in free fall and therefore weightless. It seemed much longer.

Then the Castor 120 engine in the first stage of StarCore cut in. Weight returned and we were again roaring upward, gaining velocity rapidly. A minute and a half later, with a brief shudder, the first Castor 120 dropped off and the next one in line ignited; we had another ninety seconds of boost, and by now the sky was black as night. We were just under sixty miles up in the sky and at almost Mach 20; nearly the whole of the Earth's atmosphere was behind us.

The gravity "switched off" again, as the second Castor motor fell away and took the interstage adaptor with it. We hung weightless for most of half a minute, coasting upward, while the Centaur engine under us went through chilldown. Mission control read off a long list of things that were working right and told us we were "go for insertion"—that is, we would fire the Centaur stage and climb to orbit, rather than jettisoning it and trying to fly back down. They had barely finished confirming the go when the Centaur fired, and for the last time we were shoved back into the seats. The Centaur is a high-performance rocket, originally developed to be an Atlas upper stage, and it packs a mighty kick. Four minutes of the Centaur, and it cut out. We were weightless and in orbit.

"Scorpion Peripheral," a voice said in my ear, "this is Scorpion Central. You are on course for your rendezvous. Jettison extra equipment in three minutes. Are you prepared to take over manually?"

"Yes, Central, I am."

Clifford Welch and his boys had worried about somebody with a scanner picking us up, so we were using misleading code names. As far as I was concerned, Scorpion Central would still be "Mission Control"; I was just hoping I wouldn't forget and call them "Houston." And I hated having my craft called "Peripheral"—it made it sound like I was flying a floppy drive.

Everything looked green on my board, and the time counted down slowly. "How are you guys doing?" I asked.

"Just fine," Eddie Killeret said, "except that I don't quite believe I'm here."

"We're doing fine," Nick said, "and radiation counts are lower than we were afraid they might be."

I waited out the time, and then the voice in my ear said, "All right, over to you, Peripheral."

I checked out the service module. Everything was fine. I reached forward, threw the first switch to arm the jettison system, saw the green light, and said, "Jettisoning the Centaur." I flipped the second switch.

There was a thud that you could feel all through the StarRescue, and the Centaur in its I-beam cage separated and tumbled backward away from us. In our low orbit, its perigee would be low enough to deorbit it within a few days. I got busy with Scorpion Central, getting the figures for our first burn, to take us into the higher orbit that would eventually bring us up to ISS. "Stay belted in," I told the other two, unnecessarily. "You'll get to play in weightlessness once I put us on our way."

A BIT OVER two complete orbits, three hours later, we were closing in on ISS. Less than 500 meters away, huge in the window, it was weirdly distorted by the bag of water I was looking through. The central core was a giant set of cylinders, each the size of a double-wide trailer, forming a rough T-shape. The truss extended from it on both sides, triangular in cross section, three feet on a side, ninety feet long; at each end of the truss, the solar panels, dwarfing the station itself, spread out like rigid rectangular wings.

I had been watching the crippled station while depressurizing StarRescue. Rotation was slow, thank heavens, but still, swooping in between the panels to match velocity with part of the truss for a split second—and then getting back out without hitting anything—was going to be an interesting little problem. "Open the door now," I said, shutting off cabin pressure. "I don't want to get kicked sideways when I'm trying to do something precise."

Killeret did, and the three of us, in our pressure suits, were committed to the vacuum of space.

"Let's go for it," Nick said.

"I'm up for it too," Killeret agreed. "We can be ready in a couple minutes."

"Take your time," I said, "I just want to study this thing."

Behind me, they were setting up the bag with the tarantula in it, clipped to Nick's belt; Nick roped himself to Killeret with a three-meter cable; and Killeret, as the guy who had been better with the grapple in practice, was by the door. "How close can we get, Scott?"

"Close," I said. "No long throw. Wait for me to tell you when we're coming up on closest."

ISS was tumbling and precessing; what I was looking for was any place where I could be reasonably sure of getting in close enough to the solar panels that swung past like immense tennis rackets, with us as the potential ball. I approached, using little squirts of thrust to get closer, then killing the resulting relative velocity. Finally I was co-orbiting just about five meters from the edge of an imaginary sphere that roughly marked the outer path of the great whirling wings. I continued to watch, began to catch the rhythm, and finally said, "I can probably go right through, once, to let you guys try for an overhead grab. Riskier till you get there but easier once you do. All right, here we go . . . starting . . . NOW."

I canted the small craft, waited for a solar panel to move to the place I judged right, and gave us a quick forward thrust. We shot in, crossing the space in less than half a minute.

I had us positioned so that Killeret would have the truss passing just over the top of the door opening. Killeret was back to back with Nick, and Nick held the tarantula on his chest; they didn't want to get caught or tangled going out the door.

"Okay, Eddie," I said, "coming up on your throw, five, four, and-three, two, and . . . one, and—go!" My cadence was irregular because I was still adjusting to the tumbling station and the way we were passing through its terrifying whirling arms.

At my "go," Eddie tossed his grapple in an underhand throw; it snagged in the truss, and the moment Killeret saw it catch, he said "Good."

Nick kicked gently backwards with both legs, throwing himself and Killeret out the door. Star-Rescue lurched in reaction. The wing slid by beneath them silently, and they were clear of the ship. I let momentum take me back out of reach of the whirling ISS, then nulled relative velocity with a couple shots of the thrusters, and slowly yawed the co-orbiting StarRescue 180 degrees, so that I could keep ISS in the window continuously. I had coasted about twenty meters beyond the farthest reach of the solar panels.

I was plenty close enough to see what was happening to Eddie and Nick; they were still swinging on the cable attached to the truss, most of the way out toward the solar panel on the "short side" of the hub. Eddie was climbing steadily hand over hand, and as I watched, he caught the truss in his outstretched hand, pulled himself to it, clipped on, and hauled Nick and the tarantula in to him.

"Scorpion Central, the team is on the truss and looks fine," I said, into the radio. "Guys, can you hear me?"

"Right here, Peripheral," Nick's voice said. "Everything is looking pretty good. Got to work now. More when we know more."

Though it was nothing like the rapid death it would have been to be EVA up here a few weeks ago, the radiation was still much more than anyone wanted to take for long. For the moment, I had the safest seat up here, and all I could do was wait and watch.

NICK:

Every one of the hundreds of pilots and engineers I'd ever worked with, sooner or later, had always told me that drill is different from real, theory from practice, drawing from product, and I'd have sworn I knew it as well as any of them, but I don't think I grasped it until the moment when Killeret and I started to install the tarantula. I knew, in principle, that we needed to climb the truss more or less like a ladder, but nothing had mentally prepared me for the problem we were in with the slight centrifugal-force gravity where he had connected. That meant there was relatively little force between boot and truss, and we slipped and skidded constantly as we struggled downwards. You'd plant your feet a step below, and suddenly they'd fly outwards, waving around, as your mass tried to tug your grip loose from the truss, and the sky and Earth whirled slowly, inexorably around you, until your feet drifted back to the truss again and you began the whole process again. For safety, we worked on a short tether line the whole time, and it was astonishing how much harder it was to move the clip than it had been back in the Scorpion Shack hangar.

Nonetheless, we made our way all the way down there, and I gingerly opened the bag. Killeret reached in, grasped the thruster and camera units on the top—everything had been packed carefully so that things would come out in the right order, and not tangled, we hoped. The cable came smoothly. So far, so good.

I closed the bag, belayed it to the truss, carefully counted struts twice until I was sure I had the right one, and then wrapped my feet around one side of the truss and got to work clamping the thruster to the strut. Despite the Clancy clamps, which are designed to spin closed and thus not require any direct twisting force, I still managed to put considerable torque against my body, and nearly lost my foot-grip. It took twice as long as it ever had on the ground, and I was sweating and sore in unfamiliar places before I was done.

I felt a little twinge of competitive pleasure when I saw that Eddie didn't quite have the camera unit on yet; as I watched, grunting and swearing, he finally got it dogged down. "Okay, let's climb," he said, and we made our way up the truss to install the next camera and thruster.

There was only one twist in the whole bag, right after the tarantula's controlling computer, and it only took us about seven or eight minutes to straighten that out. The hub was a weird place to do it; gravity was almost zero, but changed very rapidly as you reached away, so that it was noticeably different between your feet and your head. That was disorienting, and of course there was the sensation of endless tumbling as the sun, Earth, and moon, all cavorted about us. After that, perhaps because we were going from a new task to a less-new one, climbing down the other side of the truss went much more smoothly, and the remaining cameras and thrusters went on without trouble.

"Okay, Scott," I said in the headphones. "Let us get up and inside, and then you can turn on the tarantula—and hopefully tame this rotating beast."

"Roger."

We scrambled up the truss to get to the airlock hatch; it was designed to be operated manually from either side. Stephen Tebworthy had gone out into the exposed part of the station, briefly, a few hours before and made sure the inner door was closed. We pushed into the airlock—in pressure suits, nearly weightless, it was like packing a phone booth while scuba diving—closed the outer door, and cycled the lock; pressure rose quickly to standard, and we opened the inner door and climbed the dizzying tunnel in front of us.

It was slightly worse in here, where you couldn't see the spinning, and the only light came from the improvised headlamps on our pressure suits, but we had practiced this many times, and to my great relief, we proceeded directly to where the Soyuz was docked, without getting lost or disoriented. We had thought it best to be here, for the next step, before trying to stabilize the station, because if anything went wrong we might get disoriented or thrown around, and we didn't want to lose any more time than we had to.

"Got a handhold, Eddie?"

"Yep."

I made sure my own grip on a railing was secure, and then said, "All right, Peripheral, we're go for the tarantula."

Scott's voice crackled in my earpiece. "Tarantula is powering up . . . checking out . . . ready to go in five, four, three, two, one . . . go."

There were a series of weird lurches and yanks as the thrusters gradually brought ISS under control and eventually into its prescribed alignment with the sun. The jolting, yanking, and swerving lasted about five minutes, as the controlling computer fired first one thruster and then another, trying to line up the cameras first with the horizon and then with the sun. We could feel it succeeding—each time the world shifted, it shifted less violently, and the pseudogravity caused by centrifugal force was less. At the end of it, we were weightless, though still in the dark.

"Got it, Scott," I said. "We're good in here."

"Good out here too," he said. "Let's proceed to our next step; we have just about one orbit till we have a descent window, and I'm sure we'd all like to get out of here."

The next part of the plan was simple; first we had to get that dead Soyuz out of the dock. We hoped that we would be able to work the manual eject system, which was basically a device for turning the couplings loose from each other. Since we had no way to reliably power the dead capsule up, after that, Scott would come up close, open the door of StarRescue, "lasso" the Soyuz solar panel with a big loop in a stiffened cable, and, using the thrusters, gently tug the Soyuz away from the station, putting it into motion so that it would drift out of our way.

The couplings separated at once, and we radioed the good news to Scott. About a minute later, we heard a whispering scrape as the dead capsule slid away from the station.

"I got the Soyuz moving," Scott said, over the radio, "and boy do I feel like a cowboy. I'm about fifty meters beyond the station and I'm going to jettison the tow cable, now; the Soyuz is definitely leaving for good. Then it's going to be some minutes more to repressurize and get ready to come in for a docking. Also, guys, I did start a very slight tumble in the station again, so hang on ... tarantula fires again in five, four, three, two, one ... there."

There was a faint rumble, and then we were stable and weightless again.

Less than five minutes later, with a thud, the hatch of StarRescue mated with ISS. "Okay, open up," Scott's voice said in my ears.

We did, and he swam in, dragging the medical kit and the three special pressure suits, folded into their bags, with him. He checked the air sampler and said, "All right, the air's okay in here," and we lifted visors for the first time.

The stench was terrible. Radiation poisoning slowly destroys the skin, sets the bowels going, leads to fluid loss through every available route; and the crew had been getting weaker and weaker, less able to care for and clean each other, eventually barely able to haul buckets of waste out into the other parts of the ISS. We all gagged, and Killeret retched.

To minimize exposure, the ISS crew had been told to stay in the storm cellar until we came for them. They had little or no cumulative dosage left to mess around with.

We zigzagged through the maze of improvised walls they had made from anything easy to shift; since radiation travels in straight lines, they had laid their improvised barriers out so that there were no straight paths to the storm cellar.

In preparing the rescue mission for what we might find up here, they had shown us photos of the *Lucky Dragon* crew, of some workers from the Chernobyl plant, and of the messy death of Louis Slotkin—all the cases of genuinely massive radiation poisoning that might be comparable with what we would find here. The ISS crew looked worse than some of the pictures, and better than others, but still, nothing can prepare you to encounter the real thing: the feel of the raised lumps of flesh through the thin working gloves of our suits; the stench of blood and shit and sickness; the scattering of teeth by each bed; the little floating blobs of fluid horror, and the smears on the walls; the clumps of hair sticking to our gloved hands with static and bodily fluids; worst of all, the twitches and winces of misery on the human faces.

Carl Tanaka was by far the sickest of the three. He had insisted on his right as commander to make more excursions into the outer, dangerous area than the other two did. He was puffy and red, as if he'd been stung by a swarm of bees; hundreds of little open sores on him leaked blood, and his hair drifted away in clumps when we went to move him. As gently as we could, we cleaned him with antibacterial wipes, trying to remove some of the feces, blood, and mucus without breaking or crumbling his ravaged skin, and gently powdered him so that we could slip him into his suit without doing more damage. He passed out as Killeret and I worked on him, which was probably for the best.

Doris McIntyre and Stephen Tebworthy were mostly able to clean and powder themselves, though they too were losing hair, leaking blood, and had patches of raw skin that looked like the worst case of poison ivy you could imagine. Scott helped them through that process, and had them in the pressure suits by the time we got the unconscious Carl Tanaka into his. "Vital signs *not* good," Killeret said, looking at the monitor. "Can we still make that first descent window to Edwards, Scott?"

"Yeah, if we hurry," he said. "If he's zipped in, let's go. You guys move him along. I'll help Doris and Stephen."

I don't exactly know how much trouble Scott had getting his two charges down the corridor to the dock; comparatively not much, I think, since he got them belted in and came back to help Killeret and me with the unconscious commander. Carl Tanaka's body had gone limp, except when it was racked by spasms that threatened to slam his head or his over-worked kidneys against the metal walls around him. "Probably nervous-system damage," Eddie muttered, as we guided him around yet another bend, Eddie leading, Scott and I keeping arms and legs from jamming or catching.

Taking things as carefully as we had to, it took five minutes to move him twenty meters, but Scott said we still had time "—if we move fast—" as we strapped the unconscious Tanaka to the seat. We pulled down our visors and strapped in ourselves. "Ready," I said, just as Eddie Killeret said it.

"Scorpion Central, this is Scorpion Peripheral. Can we still hit the window?"

"Transferring data. Answer is yes. Details are being loaded to ship's computer . . . all right, Scott, our screen says you've got all the data."

"Transfer was successful," he agreed. "All right, we're coming home."

SCOTT:

Heading into a window that's closing isn't intrinsically harder than any other re-entry, except that you have narrower error bars on everything; but any good pilot plans to hit right on the money. So what does it matter where all the wrong places are? You aren't going there anyway.

I used the service module thrusters to push us back from the dock. The attitude jets swung us around until we were orbiting tail first, the service module preceding us. Then I turned control over to the computer; I wanted this burn to be timed more precisely than my own hands and brain could do unaided.

Scorpion Central counted down for me, but the computer was doing all the work; at precisely zero, the big thrusters thundered, shaking the StarRescue for a ten full minutes, pushing against the direction of our orbit, and nearly exhausting their tanks. It was only about a one-percent drop in velocity, but that was enough to start us dropping toward the Earth.

ISS orbits, very roughly, a million feet above the ground; our loss of momentum from firing the thrusters caused us to begin a long fall into a much more eccentric lower orbit, one that would swing so low as to pass inside the atmosphere, where we could use the air's drag to slow us down and bring us in. Gingerly, I rotated us 90 degrees in two different axes, until we were pointed straight down at the Earth, looking at the wide blue South Pacific. Samoa flashed by the window like white dots on the interstate.

Half an hour later, the jagged curve of Baja sprawled out across the horizon to my right, and I was watching for the California coast dead ahead. StarRescue was more than halfway down—we were at about seventy-five miles above the Earth, still in space but coming down fast; the horizon of the Earth was still curved below us and the sky was jet black in broad daylight. Firing the service-module thrusters for the last time, I tilted StarRescue's nose up forty degrees to get it into re-entry attitude, with the heat shield pointed directly forward.

When I was sure that was satisfactory, I said, "Jettison coming up . . ." and hit the button. With a brief, mild lurch, the service module slid back and away behind us; unshielded from the heat of re-entry, and with less wind resistance than we had, it would tumble on ahead and burn up.

Twenty minutes later, we were down to 250,000 feet—about the altitude where you start feeling the air. There was thunder under the wings and fuselage. Weight returned and built up as the acceleration crept up toward three g's. StarRescue was re-entering.

"Time to see how good your plumbers are," I remarked to Nick. In space, it hadn't mattered that we had tons of water aboard as radiation shielding, but in the atmosphere, the increase in StarRescue's density would make it impossible to maintain an appropriate rate of descent—a fancy way of saying we were too heavy and we'd go in too steep. So Nick's team had come up with a set of pumps and tubes to empty the "water beds." I tripped the switch, and the shaking and rattling of StarRescue became more violent, but the bags all around us shrank steadily into the walls as we sprayed the water into the atmosphere. It was gone in three minutes—spread across hundreds of miles of sky, much higher than any cloud ever forms. At the time, I was too busy to realize that we were smearing the biggest contrail anyone ever saw across the clear blue Pacific sky, pointing northeast up to Los Angeles—a thousand-mile-long streak that drifted eastward for days before dissipating.

At 180,000 feet, with the sky still black and the curve of the Earth much farther away, streams of white-hot air flowed past the front window; we were entering the high-heat regime, and as we descended ten more miles toward the Earth, we were cut off from contact by that white plasma that blocked all radio.

As if a switch had been thrown, at 130,000 feet, the window cleared, and I looked at a dark blue sky. We were still screaming along at four times the speed of the fastest jet fighters, higher than the Blackbird reconnaissance planes flew, but we were flying, not orbiting, and that was a long step closer to home. "Hello, Scorpion Central," I said. "Looks like we're coming back fine."

"Glad to hear it, Peripheral. You're go for Edwards. Very little wind today, so if you want to aim for the shuttle runway per original plan, go for it."

"Roger."

StarRescue was never intended to be flown like the shuttle; it was a lifeboat, and its job was to get passengers to where they could be rescued. We had no landing gear and our rate of descent would have made a landing dangerous.

Instead, the idea was to get close enough to the ground, and then deploy a parawing, essentially a big, steerable rectangular parachute, to get us the rest of the way down. With no wind, and nothing in the way, it made sense to steer for the shuttle runway—it was a huge target, easy to hit, flat ground on which a landing would be safer, and most of all, equipped to get emergency vehicles out to an arriving aircraft.

The rest of the flight on wings was not much different from landing an extremely-high-performance jet or a super-fast glider; I pointed us in the right direction, kept us on the beam, and waited until it was time to do something else. The curving Earth became flat, the sky lightened, and after a while Catalina and San Clemente rushed by below us, and then the great brown smear of Los Angeles itself.

When the shuttle runway was looming huge in the windshield, and we were just a few thousand feet up, I pulled the lever, and the parawing popped out. With a hard shake, as if a giant dog had just caught us like a Frisbee, we dropped speed quickly down to only around 150 miles per hour. Working the less-familiar rudder and line control system, I brought us down to a final, grinding, bumpy touchdown on the tarmac. I released the parawing, which fell over in front of us like a giant jellyfish. By the time we got the door open, the ambulance crews were already there, waiting to rush in and grab the ISS crew the moment we got out of their way. Nick, Eddie, and I piled out of StarRescue, removing our helmets, into the hot California desert sunlight, blinking at the harsh light, noticing, for just a moment until it became normal again, how much gravity they have down here.

CHAPTER FIFTEEN

THALIA:

Scott and Nick hadn't really been able to tell Amos and me anything at all about where they were going or what they were doing. All we got was that it was an emergency, and it was important, and that they'd both be back in a few days. Then over the weekend, I got a call from Clifford Welch, who said he'd had a thought that Amos and I might like to see something at Edwards Air Force Base. That put four good clues together for me: that was where the shuttle often lands, Nick was involved with a project to build a new spacecraft, the shuttle couldn't do the ISS rescue in time, and Scott was a qualified pilot who had just spent time at Scorpion Shack. I agreed that we would like to see that, and we flew out with Welch.

When we got there, the combination of secrecy and VIP treatment was more than enough to give the rest of the story away. They set up raw feed in our guest quarters, so we were able to look over Scott's shoulder for much of the flight.

When Scott fired the rocket motors and started the return to Earth, there was a knock at our door, and when I opened it, Welch was standing there, saying, "We thought you'd like to go out to the runway, where he'll be bringing it in."

The van made a number of stops at other guest rooms. We picked up Eddie Killeret's father, and then a larger group that was the families of the ISS crew.

As we rode in the big van out to the runway, we listened to the communications between the ground and StarRescue. The blackout during the high-temperature part of the descent was maddening, of course, but it wasn't much different from what I'd been through during three shuttle landings. By the time that we were parked, and had stepped outside the van to watch, the StarRescue crew were back on the air and coming in, with everything fine.

For a while all there was to look at was the great white streak, high up in the southern sky, that was the weird contrail you make by dumping a ton of water in a straight line through the thermosphere. "I'd bet it's visible from Baja to Vancouver," Welch guessed.

Amos spotted the little dot of gleaming metal first, and stood up and yelled. I stood next to him, and then everybody saw it. It was coming in pretty fast and was quite high up; as we watched, it descended until we could just make out that it had wings and a fuselage. Lower and closer, we could see the shape of the stubby wings, the rounded nose, and the windshield. Then something that looked—just for a second—like orange smoke billowed out behind it. The parawing deployed fully, and StarRescue slowed and began its gentle descent to the tarmac.

"As long as we don't get in the way of the ambulances, I would imagine we can drive on over there," Welch said to the driver.

We parked in a row of a dozen other vans. Welch, sitting next to the driver, turned around and said, "Now, folks, we're eager to see them, but it's going to be a few minutes. Just in case something goes really wrong at the last minute, we want you all to stay here in the van—there's enough window space, you should all be able to see them come in. Once they're down, they'll dump the parawing, and a crew will run out to get that under control so it doesn't blow around and cause accidents. At the same time, the ambulances will go get the ISS crew—I'm afraid they all have to go direct to the hospital, but this van will take their families to the hospital to meet with the doctors who will be treating them. You'll be able to talk to your loved ones just as soon as the doctors say it's okay.

"For those of you with friends and family in the StarRescue crew, after the ambulances go, there's going to be one van that goes up and greets the crew before we do. That should only take about five minutes. Then this van will go up there so you can greet the crew. It will drop you off, and take the ISS crew's relatives to the hospital. You'll have about five minutes to say hello, and then your friends and relatives in the crew will have to do about half an hour of shaking hands and talking to press people, and then finally you'll all ride in the bus with them back to the main base. Everyone clear on how it's going to go?"

Any agreement was drowned out by our rush to

the windows, to watch StarRescue make its final descent to the runway. It came down at a steep, almost vertical angle, seemingly slowly as an elevator, hanging beneath the huge canopy. It touched down without a bounce, and the canopy released and fell over to one side. Out of the corner of my eye, I could see ground crew running toward the collapsing parawing, but I was watching the hatch on the side of the nose. It swung inward, leaving a round hole about the size of a small kitchen table, about three feet above the pavement, and ground crew people ran out to put a set of steps underneath it.

Scott, still in his pressure suit but with the helmet off, climbed out, followed by two other crew people—whom I suddenly recognized as Eddie Killeret and Nick. "Wow," Amos breathed, beside me, and I had to agree: "You're right, kid, wow."

The ambulance crews went in with a stretcher, and came back out carrying Major Tanaka. They went in again, and a few minutes later, Doris McIntyre emerged, supported on either arm by the paramedics. Stephen Tebworthy followed, also supported between medics, and managed a feeble wave. Each time, as soon as the patient was loaded in, the ambulance shot off, hurrying to get them to the hospital.

About the time that the ambulance with Tebworthy in it was just a dot down at the end of the road, a van swung out of the line and pulled up by where the crew was still standing.

"Mom, why do the people in that van get to see Dad before we do?" Amos asked. "I know they had to get the sick people to the ambulance, but why does—"

Then we saw who was getting out of the van to shake hands with the crew, and Amos fell silent.

"Well," I said, "he *is* the President, and it is a pretty big day."

The radio crackled on, and we got to hear the last of what the President was saying: "—who have not only accomplished so much for a grateful nation, but whom we also honor because of the further trails we expect them to blaze in our advance into this new frontier. Thank you all, God bless you all, and welcome home." The entourage applauded, the President stepped back, and they pulled out.

It was our turn next, and it was only as the door was opening that I realized I had no idea of what I was going to say to Scott. Amos shot out ahead of me, anyway, and by the time I got there he was hanging on to his father very, very tightly. So I thought about it for an instant, and decided that if Scott didn't like this, I could always claim it was old habit. I walked up and gave him a good long kiss. After a moment's surprise, he kissed back. When we stopped kissing, I was reasonably sure that he had liked it. "Now what?" he said.

"That was it," I said. "I don't intend it to lead anywhere. I just thought on a day like this you deserved more than a handshake."

THE DAY AFTER Thanksgiving—which was at our house, cooked by Nick, and attended by Eddie Killeret, and thus was the first real "Mars Four Reunion"—AnnaBeth James finally took Jasper Haverford's advice, and made the case go away.

By then, the cry of "Justice for MJ!" was fading, slowly worn away by bad weather, the coming of the holidays, and most of all the tendency of the press to lose a story when a bigger one turns up. The ISS rescue dwarfed the old news, and MJ was beginning to fade into the sort of permanent, less-active story that Princess Di had become—still brought up, instantly recognizable, but only occasionally covered.

That was just what I had been aiming for.

The day after Thanksgiving is normally a slow news day; the typical story is about how big the crowds are at the malls and the downtown department stores, and what the hottest-selling toys are. But late that afternoon, at the Algonquin Hotel in New York, Jasper Haverford brought AnnaBeth James out in front of a hastily assembled pack of press and media, and she sat down to talk to them.

She was in a plain, almost severe, black silk dress, with her hair pulled back, and though her face was dry today, she looked as if she had been crying for a century. She nodded at the press, clear-eyed and calm, and said, "When I first launched this lawsuit, there was so much we didn't know. We didn't know if Michael had been killed by negligence, or if someone had lied to him. We didn't know that it had been a terrorist attack, or that it had been intended to destroy the whole shuttle and leave no trace. Sometimes somebody starts a lawsuit just because they want to know why, why, why such a terrible thing could happen. And now, it seems to me, I know.

"And then there was anger; anger that no one had said that this would happen, anger at ourselves that we hadn't tried to keep him on the ground, anger at our loss . . . and that can keep something going for a while, too, you know.

"After that it can get to be so that you just feel like you'd be betraying him, like it would finish him off and make him completely dead, if you didn't carry through with this, even if maybe there wasn't much to the case anymore. Oh, God, he was a hard one to let go.

"These past few weeks, the family has been searching our hearts, looking for the right thing to do, because Michael James was always a one to do that, to know he was right before he made a move. And we've prayed, and talked, and watched so many of our old tapes of him . . . I want to thank you folks at the networks, for letting us have copies of so much, it's been such a comfort to us . . . and finally we had to say, what would he like? What would Michael have felt good about?

"And I think I know now. I do. I think his eyes were always upward, he was always wanting people to reach and to do and to try, himself most of all, but everyone. And if I were to press this suit . . . well, there's people out there that murdered Michael, and we all know that there are. But they aren't the people that built the shuttle, or flew it, or even the ones that sold him a ticket.

"And there are people out there that would be pretty happy if the whole human race just stayed home forever, and people that will do anything to hurt America, and probably people that thought a black man, or a civilian, or any number of other things that Michael was, has no business going to the stars. But they aren't the ones who are reaching for the stars. And it's the ones who *are* reaching that MJ wanted to be around, wanted to work with and spend time with.

"And if I press this suit, I'm very afraid that I would be hurting his friends, and helping the people he would have wanted us to fight." She looked around the room. "And I would say *that*, I like to think, even if I hadn't been allowed to look at some secret information from our government. And I trust and believe the men who told me what they had found out, though I can't discuss it here. It was a matter for national security, and it was a good thing to drop the case. But most of all, as I've learned more of what really happened and how it happened, I've come to conclude that there's no justice in this suit. I'm not ashamed or sorry to have started it, back when we knew nothing—but I'd be ashamed and sorry to continue it now.

"Like I said, it wouldn't be any kind of memorial for Michael.

"And that's why I didn't put up a fight when the case was dismissed. And that's why I'm asking all the people who have been so generous with their support, and their desire to see justice done . . . my friends, your hearts are good, and I am oh, so grateful for your willingness to stand up for MJ, but we honor him more, now, by letting this drop. It's over. Please, no more protests, no more marches, just accept what's happened; a terrible thing, but sometimes, when you reach for the stars, you don't live to get there. That's part of the cost, and MJ knew he might pay it, and as it happened, he did. Honor him by carrying on his dreams. Thank you."

There were a few, generally polite questions from the reporters, about her future plans (she had very few; he had provided generously for his family in his will, and probably none of his relatives would ever need to work again). She made a couple more brief statements, thanking Haverford, expressing her relief that the ISS crew had been rescued, and reminding people to pray for Carl Tanaka, who was to have a marrow transplant the next day.

When Nick finally clicked the set off, we all sat

silently for a while. "You know," he said, "no matter how well someone handles a tragedy, I always think how much better it would have been to see them at an occasion of joy."

Scott nodded. "I think maybe we just got a look at how MJ got to be MJ. Oh, we'll go on and we'll manage to make a better world out of this, but I think we'll always wonder how much better it might have been to have all our new successes and challenges in space—*and* Michael James."

EPILOG

THALIA:

"Did he say who he was bringing?" Scott asked.

"No," I said, and glanced over to where Nick was turning over an array of steaks and chicken legs on the grill we had set up on the deck. "Should you have started those before they get here?"

Nick smiled. "If Killeret is late, it will be the first time, ever. And this stuff takes a while to cook." He checked his watch. "He'll be here within eight minutes. Guaranteed. Bet me if you like."

"No bet," Scott said. "I saw enough of him when we flew. You can set your watch by the man. I wonder who he's bringing, though."

"It's going to be fun to have a Mars Four reunion here," I said, "in the summer, and at the cabin." We'd all gotten together about once a month since Christmas, but generally just at a restaurant in whatever place happened to be mutually convenient, for a shared meal and some conversation. "Eddie said after he drives his guest back, he'll be able to come down and stay a couple of cabins over, for the whole week."

Late June on the Virginia coast is great if you like temperature contrast; the sunny beach is hot, but the Atlantic is still chilly enough so that only tourists and kids are really anxious to go in. I watched Amos splash around in the shallow water, playing some complicated game with a group of kids he'd taken up with. It was good to see him having a social life again, and not clinging to Scott or me. As I watched, the kids, all shivering from the cold sea, rushed up and threw themselves onto the towels in the sun; I could hear them yelling and calling things to each other, but couldn't make out what.

"So if we were the Mars Four, what will those five be?" Scott asked, casually.

Nick flipped over two huge steaks and smeared sauce on the exposed tops. "Probably the Mars Five. Even with all the breakthroughs we're getting, it's still going to take twenty more years before people can go there. Once we've learned to handle interplanetary distances and expeditions of several years, then, maybe, the rest of the solar system will gradually open up . . . but Mars will be the frontier for another generation, I should guess, and maybe even longer. That's okay. A frontier nourishes a civilization; we don't have to have a new one until the old one closes."

There was a crunch of tires on the gravel out front, and Nick, looking at his watch, said, "Two minutes early." Scott and I sprang up and went through the house to meet Eddie Killeret and his guest. Eddie was already coming up the steps to the screen door, and directly behind him was Clifford Welch, in a suit and tie that looked particularly peculiar considering that all of us, including Eddie, were in gym shorts and T-shirt. "Unfortunately, I have a meeting in Washington late this afternoon," he said. "But Mr. Killeret has kindly offered me a spare bed in his cabin for the next few days, and I've just about decided to take him up on it."

I played hostess for a minute, making sure everyone had a cold drink, and then we went out to sit and watch Nick cook. He'd begun to throw heaps of sliced vegetables onto the grill, and was sprinkling some special sauce or other over that. "Dinner in twenty, or so," he said.

Welch nodded, sipped his iced tea, and said, "Actually I came here because yesterday, when I bumped into Ed, he told me that you'd all be here, and it seemed like a great opportunity to fill you all in, at once, on some things that I'm now at liberty to talk about. And if it's twenty minutes, that's plenty of time to cover it, before Amos gets back up here."

Nick nodded. "I can cook while I listen. What's up?"

"First, a small and perfectly public piece of news. The Federal order for StarBoosters will be stepped up to twelve. The four they have flying right now, with StarCore I's, are doing a great job, and NASA and the Air Force are realizing that this is saving their bacon—so they've decided to make sure it *stays* saved. Four more StarBoosters for NASA, four more for the Air Force—and maybe some up-front money toward getting StarBooster 350 into development, too. Also approval is going to come down—at least if everyone in Congress stays on the side they say they're on—for getting StarCore II and StarBird moving, as well, on a hurry-up schedule. So I think that at least two of you here have secure jobs.

"Second piece of news, also interesting, probably won't be reported in the media. Two nights ago, on Hainan, where they're developing the Long March II, the Chinese suffered a tragic accident. For some inexplicable reason they're blaming it on sabotage or a commando raid by Taiwan, Vietnam, the Philippines, and sometimes us. They seem to have a hard time sorting out their villains, and exactly what happened.

"That may be because there's not much left on the ground. The Long March II booster, which was supposed to be the first test flight later this week, blew up while a group of dignitaries and specialists was taking a tour. Among those killed were three men who I have very good reason to believe created and ordered the plan that killed MJ, and two physicists just back from a tour of duty as advisors to Pakistan. The Chinese government has made a number of ugly accusations without proof, which I doubt that our press will even bother to report. At least, they won't, if they want any more news leaks in the next twenty years.

"That brings me to some highly confidential stuff. We've finally closed the investigation into the late and unlamented Mr. Riscaveau and his friends at the Chinese Embassy. It would appear that Mr. Riscaveau was probably a talented petty liar all his life; he forged some of the credentials that got him each job, until eventually he made it to chief of security for RW. A couple of RW managers seem to have failed to notice several good reasons for not allowing him to be promoted, and we're looking to see whether that was a matter of incompetence, successful deception by Mr. Riscaveau, blackmail of some kind . . . or perhaps something more sinister.

"But before his incompetence was detected, he found a golden friendship, during his little trip to Thailand. The Chinese, you see, weren't just a source of income. Intelligence services tend to know a lot about other kinds of spies—and always have a few spies and snitches of their own that they are eager to get rid of. Riscaveau was getting a list every few weeks, from the Chinese, of people he could 'catch,' to make his reputation grow."

"And it did," Nick said. "Everyone in the company always said that he seemed not very smart, and he was very annoying, but you couldn't argue with his results—he caught spies like nobody else."

"Same gimmick that Aldrich Ames used," Welch said, nodding. "Along with a dozen other double agents throughout history. It works as long as your bosses have enough small fry to sacrifice. Perhaps they were running out of petty traitors and rival spies to turn in, and decided to end the charade. More likely Riscaveau was at the end of his usefulness, and they decided to expend him in one big operation.

"At any rate, it would appear that when *Columbia* made it back down to the ground with much of the evidence intact and some of the crew still alive, the plot began to unravel, and all sorts of things, including the Pakistani proton bomb, were moved up in the schedule. That also meant that enormous pressure was put on Mr. Riscaveau to keep the lid on and prevent anyone's taking effective action for a few weeks. A cleverer man might have found ways, but Andrew Riscaveau prided himself on his mastery of standard procedure and his ability to treat things as routine, no matter how extraordinary they were. I think it was Isaac Asimov who said that 'Violence is the last resort of the incompetent,' but he was wrong;

real incompetence gets violent before it needs to, or when it doesn't need to. There were hundreds of subtler and trickier ways he could have helped the James lawsuit along, and stymied the Starcraft project, but when a man spends his life thinking like a thug, the thoughts that come naturally to mind are threats, arson, and sabotage. I suspect that if Riscaveau had made it to China, after a couple of years, they'd have shot him themselves, just as a matter of convenience.

"As far as we can tell he acted with Chinese help, but not on their orders, and he acted alone. There's no larger conspiracy or ring out there waiting to get either Thalia or Scott. You can safely pull the bodyguards whenever you like."

"Actually," Nick said, "since there had been no incidents since Riscaveau's death, we pulled them a month ago."

Welch shrugged amiably. "You're all a bunch of amateurs. And it's probably a good thing that we live in a world where you can safely *be* amateurs. But no hurt, no foul, as M J might have said, and I wish he'd had the chance to say it.

"All right, now here's one more piece of news, and I've saved the best for last. After that, I have a trivial question for you all. The news is this: the President will be giving a space policy speech in July or early August, and he's going to be announcing a whole series of commitments to space. He'll talk about streamlining and simplifying the laws so that launch services are easy to buy, and about a federal anchor tenancy so that there's a guaranteed market for space—and about committing to buying the whole Starcraft series, right up through StarBird IIs and StarCore IIIs, from Republic Wright.

"American companies will be launching hotels in

space, and hundred-passenger ships will be carrying
people up to them, and by the end of the decade we'll
probably have increased the number of Americans
who have flown into space tenfold. And by 2015,
we'll have a vast experience with long-term habitats
and all the other expertise needed to get the process
going, and mount a serious Mars expedition of fifty
or a hundred people, most of them scientists, that will
be able to stay over for a couple of years on the Mar-
tian surface and do real exploration.

"If all goes well, they might even arrive there in
2019, for the fiftieth anniversary of the first lunar
landing. The frontier is open again."

Nick sighed. "Well," he said, "there go a few more
vacations, I bet."

"On the other hand, there's only one member of
the Mars Four that hasn't been to space now," I
pointed out, "and all this talk of commercial passengers and space hotels sounds like there might very
well be a chance."

"Funny you should mention that," Welch said,
leaning back and looking about as relaxed as he was
ever going to. "Because one thing we discovered,
when we broke into Riscaveau's encrypted files and
obtained some decrypts of various messages to and
from the Chinese, was that for the last few months
that he was working for them, right up to his death,
he was absolutely certain that there was a secret project going on, some big leap in American technology
or some secret military operation, called Mars Four.
He and his Chinese bosses expended hours and hours
trying to find out what it was and who was involved
and so forth. They thought that either Nick or Ed
must be the leader or head of it, and that all of you
were in on it, and they had a long, long list of things

it might be and how it might be carried out, and I would guess that one out of every ten Chinese agents in the USA was working on the problem.

"Now, I happen to know that there is no project anywhere in our government called Mars Four, but then I have some advantages over the Chinese in finding that out. It's worked out pretty well for us, these past few months, because anyone who seems to be trying to find out what Mars Four is, and where it's located, turns out to be a Chinese agent. So we're poised to roll up some of their intelligence network, and to feed the rest all kinds of disinformation for decades. Call it just another little payback for their recent bad behavior."

I was trying very hard not to laugh, and I noticed that Scott was choking and turning a deep red. Ed Killeret and Nick Blackstone weren't doing any better job of controlling it. Welch looked around, smiled broadly, and went on, "It would appear that the Chinese are convinced that Mars Four is going to be some kind of super-secret ultrahigh technology which is going to catapult us ahead of everyone in space for generations to come, something more like magic than technology, if you see what I mean. Probably they arrived at this opinion because Mr. Riscaveau had a knack for exaggerating his importance and stretching the truth, in the first place, and secondly because of the tendency of intelligence agencies to think that anything you haven't penetrated yet must be very big.

"Rather in a spirit of fun, we've begun to include the words 'Mars Four' in some of the gibberish that we send out routinely as filler in our coded transmissions, and we've done a few little things to make it look like some very unimportant weather stations in remote locations, and some basic research at the national laboratories, has something to do with Mars Four.

"But we'd really like to know what it really is, and the four of you turned up frequently in Andrew Riscaveau's original notes on the subject. Now, from the way you're all laughing, I think you probably can tell me what it is."

So we did tell him, in bits and pieces, then, and over lunch, as we would remember one incident or another. Amos and a couple of his friends were there, whispering to each other; I wondered if maybe Scott had been right, and we were seeing the start of another secret society.

Lunch ended with everyone having over-eaten—a hard thing to avoid when Nick was cooking. The adults went out to sit on the deck and watch the afternoon waves roll in from the blue-green Atlantic, and sit and talk for an hour or so until Eddie would have to drive Welch back up to DC. Welch went so far as to take off his coat and vest and put his necktie in his pocket. "You'll see," he said, grinning. "When I come down here to stay with Ed, I'll bring along boat shoes and maybe even a pair of shorts and a ball cap."

For a while we just watched the kids running back and forth and yelling to each other, and let our eyes drift off to the far horizon. I wasn't sure there would be any more conversation.

"Funny," Welch said, after a while. "The Chinese thought we must be planning to leap to the stars—that somewhere there had to be the superproject that would do everything. And yet the whole point is, we're not leaping. We're taking one careful step at a time, better booster, better upper stage, better orbiter, each one just enough better to make it worth the cost and risk of developing, each one working a small improvement. We've learned not to be Superman—we don't leap a tall building at a single bound—we climb it, one foot and handhold at a time, staying on belay the whole way. We always knew that was the right way, and now we're doing it."

"The reason they looked so hard for Mars Four was because they thought there had to be one," Nick mused. He leaned forward and pointed to the gathered circle of kids, who had surrounded something or other that had washed in from the tide, and appeared to be deep in argument over it. "And yet that's all it was." He gestured at the intent ring, the boys and girls packed in close as they examined whatever they had found.

Welch sat forward and said, "Maybe they weren't so very wrong, in that regard. Take a human child, give it lots of time and attention, a secure place to come home to but plenty of things to explore. Let it find all kinds of challenges and let it stumble and make mistakes and learn to get back on its feet. Eventually you get something that can go to the stars. Sure, you also get armies of kids who use their time and freedom to watch television, and their security and support to get complacent and smug. But if you just leave the door open to the big world . . . some of them go through it. Like your Mars Four. They find out about small steps and big failures and how to *use* their confidence and *use* their doubt. . . . And finally there's nothing that they can't do or find out about. Maybe my opposite numbers, over on the other side of the world, *did* find out the name—or one of the names, anyway—of our secret. They just didn't know what *kind* of a secret it was."

Amos came running up the beach then, followed

by his four friends. "Hey, Dad, can you look at something with us, and tell us what it is?"

"I can look," Scott said, easing out of his chair, slipping into his sandals, and walking down the wooden steps onto the beach, where the gaggle of children surrounded him. "That's always the first step. After that, who knows?"

TOR

Award-winning authors
Compelling stories

Please join us at the website
below for more information
about this author and other great
Tor selections, and to sign up for
our monthly newsletter!

TOR